"I loved *The Kosambi Intrigue*. I was captivated by the story and characters, created with beguiling yet compelling simplicity....The characters are distinctive and alive, the dramatic narrative unfolds at a steady, engaging pace and the world of the Buddha's time is sketched with great vividness, attention to detail and conviction. Although the situation described occurred more than two thousand years ago, it is just as true of idiosyncratic humanity now as it was then. The book draws out what is timeless and universal in what is otherwise a remote and unfamiliar place and time. The way the intrigue unfolds from a single silly incident and then envelops the life of the entire city and ultimately proves resistant even to the Buddha's entreaties is brilliantly done."

Stephen Batchelor
author of best-selling *Buddhism Without Beliefs*

"I really enjoyed reading this book. It transports one back 2,500 years to another time and another place - a setting that students of Buddhism will recognize but find so much richer than they ever encountered before. But even if one isn't interested in ancient Buddhism, or any form of Buddhism, it's a very well crafted, unique story that any reader will enjoy."

Leigh Brasington
author, *Practical Jhanas*, forthcoming

"A page-turner. It has both drama and Dharma."

Kathleen Kistler, Ph.D.
former Manager, Patient Care Volunteer Services, Eureka/
Arcata (CA) Hospice

"A compellingly human tale of conflict, compassion, ambition and the divergent visions of two strong personalities on a collision course."

Bruce Toien
database designer, citizen journalist

"Buddhist practitioners, historians, lay people, all will find valuable teachings in Stone's wise text."
    Judith Toy
    Zen teacher, author, *Murder as a Call to Love*

"A true delight. It adds a rich dimension to my practice... the teachings become even more accessible as the lived experience of real human beings. Like me."
    Sharon Beckman-Brindley, Ph.D.
    Guiding teacher, Insight Meditation Community of
    Charlottesville; Senior Teacher of Insight Dialogue,
    Metta Programs

"You don't have to know anything about Buddhism to love this book."
    Wendy Eisner
    Professor of Geography, University of Cincinnati

"Fascinating, daring and intriguing...It is giving me so much pleasure, new information and inspiration."
    Asha Greer, Murshida
    Sufi Ruhaniat International

"Tender, piercing, instructive, and heartwarming. I was drawn in immediately... Many of the [Buddha's] teachings I have long been familiar with, but now that I have read her book, they are alive inside me. A deep bow to her."
    Toinette Lippe
    East Asian brush artist and author, *Caught in the Act*

THE
KOSAMBI
INTRIGUE

A TALE IN THE TIME OF THE BUDDHA

BY
SUSAN CAROL STONE

THIS
BREATH
PRESS

THIS
BREATH
PRESS

susancarolstone.com
P.O. Box 4871
Charlottesville, Virginia 22905
U.S.A.

Cover and interior design by Denise Gibson, Design Den

ISBN 978-1479363049

> "Always exercise your heart's knowing.
> You might as well attempt something real
> Along the path."
>   Hafiz

CONTENTS

Preface...7
   1. The Waterjar Incident...9
   2. Royal Resentment...21
   3. Schism in the Monastic Order...41
   4. Candana's Depression...55
   5. The Buddha's Arrival in Kosambi...65
   6. A Killing in the Monastery and Other Violence...79
   7. Sagata's Execution...97
   8. Samavati in a Royal Prison...111
   9. Monastic Intrigue and Palace Rivalry...133
10. Samavati's Secret...145
11. Sati in Love...159
12. Growing Up, Marital Harmony...169
13. Arittha's Adventures in Bhagguland...183
14. Facing the Consequences...195
15. The Deepening Schism...209
16. Intransigence...223
17. The Buddha's Abrupt Departure; Harika's Loss...229
18. Peace in a New Key...241
19. The Turning Wheel of Samsara...259
About Gratitude—Those Who Have Helped...269
About Time—Notes on Fictionalizing Buddhist History...271
About Terms...279
About the Author...288

PREFACE

A work of fiction about the Buddha is rare. One focusing, as this one does, on a drama in his monastic order and on the politics of the time is practically its own genre. Though the story is based on historical events, you can read it as you would any other novel—just pick it up and begin. You needn't consult another note. If, however, you are curious to distinguish fact from imagination or to gain an understanding of the historical context, "About Time—Notes on Fictionalizing Buddhist History" at the end of the story will be helpful. If you find the names and Pali-language terms in the story confusing or hard to remember, you may want to consult "About Terms," the glossary at the end of the book. In "About Gratitude—Those Who Have Helped," also at the end of the book, I am very happy to acknowledge the many fine people who supported me as I wrote.

And now, I bow to you, the reader. May this story touch and nourish your mind and heart.

CHAPTER 1

THE WATERJAR INCIDENT

T he leaves dance in the light breeze, casting a fluttering shadow around his feet in the little grove of rosewood trees known as *simsapa*. Although it is only February 23rd, the weather in Kosambi is turning hot early this year, 446 BCE. Already everything is going dry and brown. Some of the leaves, delicately heart-shaped, have begun to fall; others will live on for another season but have lost the brightness of youth. Sati isn't noticing color however; he is entranced by the shadowy movement. It occurs to him that the leaves are bearing quivering witness to their common fate.

Sati's large eyes, which are usually bright with intelligence, take on a remote cast. At 17, he is slightly taller than average, with a strong body and a broad sensitive face, a fair complexion and regular features. If he had hair, it would swirl in a small cowlick atop his forehead, but his head is shaven, for he is a novice in the Buddha's order.

Sati is escaping boredom. He is supposed to be meditating. That's what monks do at this time of day. After the noonday meal, after a nap if they are inclined, now—now is time for a long afternoon of meditation. Sati envisions the good monks of the monastery sitting cross-legged on meditation mats on their small porches—it's too hot to sit inside—all deeply immersed in mindfulness or bliss or other some other heavenly state. Not him! Sati's thoughts simply will not cooperate with his intentions. Ignoring his repeated admonitions, they run every which way like panicky ants whose hill has been leveled. It has been going on like this all afternoon and Sati is worn out. He's tired of futile efforts. Why did he ever think of becoming a monk?

So it was a relief to notice the need for a little trip to the latrine. Ah, a break! Sati happily takes his time now, dawdling in his favorite part of the monastery, the simsapa grove, watching the dancing leaves and their shadows flitting over the forest floor, which is covered with generations of the leathery fallen ones and their remains, parched and brown. And all around, a host of downy simsapa shoots, heads still bowed as though praying for light and space to grow. How many will make it to maturity he wonders. Then his attention is caught by a small dark beetle, and he watches closely as she makes her way among the downed leaves. She seems to know exactly where she is going. Slowly, carefully, nothing to do but walk up and over or under each leafy obstacle, one tiny step at a time. Sati doesn't realize that his thoughts have dropped into a natural accord with the woody environment, becoming quieter than they were when he tried to still them in meditation this afternoon.

Now, as if from a distance, a growing inner pressure nudges him out of his reverie and brings him back to the matter at hand. I could do it here, he thinks, right here in the grove, nobody would know. His hand on the gray-brown trunk of a mature tree, its bark peeling in narrow strips, he envisions squatting and peeing. But Sati is aware that if peeing everywhere were common practice, the smell in the monastic park during the dry season would be overpowering. There's even a rule against it. He shakes his head ruefully. Rules, always rules.

Sati acknowledges the need for them if you are going to live in community; however, the profusion of restrictions governing all aspects of monastic life, major and minor, is a continual aggravation. The no-peeing-in-the-park rule makes sense, but a lot of them don't, not as far as he can see, anyway. Well, there's no rule against complaining to myself. Or is there? he smiles wryly at that one and continues on his way to the latrine.

In Ghositarama or Ghosita's Park, a refuge dedicated to the use of the Buddha's order, the lavatory is situated for hygiene purposes at a distance from the monks' huts. You need to walk through the small stand of simsapas back toward the city ramparts, which form part of the monastery wall, a short distance from the northern bank of the Yamuna River. Sati resumes his modest mission. How long has he been standing here? Glancing up through the leafy canopy, he marks that the sun has traveled significantly on its westward journey through the afternoon sky.

Urgency makes him pick up his pace now, though he still walks with mindful restraint—as befits a monk, a *bhikkhu*. Another rule: A bhikkhu should walk with dignity. Well, he thinks, not exactly a rule, but certainly it's a strict standard, a protocol—we do it like this, *not* like that—it's one of those. Will I ever remember them all? The Venerable Migajala flashes into his mind. *He* seems to observe the nuances of the Discipline naturally, even though he has only been ordained eight months. Like a fish in water, Sati grumbles. How does the man manage it? He throws a quick prayer to the Buddha for help with his own sad case, but he's doubtful. Rules don't suit him.

It's not as though his childhood were spent without rules. It's just that his family really didn't fit anywhere; they seemed to be an exception to all the social rules. Born of the noble class, Sati has spent over half his life among fisherfolk, who are outcastes, beyond the pale of the four classes in the hierarchy that has already begun to define the social order in the Indian subcontinent. Sati's father was a government official in Kosambi, the capital of Vamsa, until he lost his post. There had been political intrigue— his parents didn't talk much about it—and, when Sati was eight, their small family moved away from government circles in the capital and downward, down into the suburbs and into the anonymity of the classless. They were nobles living as outcastes and not accepted by either.

They were happy though. Unlike most in their society, Sati's family lived in a nuclear group because their relatives found their social disgrace hard to accept. Ostracization made relations among the three of them closer. They were each other's world. As far as is possible for family members to live together in harmony, respect and love—nothing is ever perfect—Sati's family did.

A movement ahead makes Sati stop on the path. The Venerables Migajala and Harika are standing in the covered entranceway to the latrine. I was just thinking about you, Sati observes silently, look-ing at Migajala. The pair is whispering, their heads together like conspirators.

It is clear who is dominant. At twenty-six, small and thin, Migajala is looking at the ground and listening intently, while the Venerable Harika gesticulates and speaks vigorously, though softly. Harika is thirty-one, and having been ordained for five years, he is one of the more senior bhikkhus in the young order where monastic rank depends on the date of ordination. All in all, his body is unremarkable, you hardly notice it. That's because Harika hardly notices it himself. Of medium height and build, he is round-shouldered, as though hunched under the weight of a great hoard of thoughts. Indeed, Harika views his body as a mere conveyance for his intellect, which, if questioned, he would assert is located in his heart, because everybody knows that the brain is simply the marrow of the skull. No matter, wherever it resides, Harika's intellect is his master, and right now, from Sati's perspective, it seems to be communicating important information to the younger monk.

The two men are so engrossed they don't notice Sati. After a moment, the novice instinctively ducks behind the trunk of an old simsapa that stands just before the clearing. What are they about? Something's wrong—it's more than unseemly for monks to conspire, but for all the world that's what they seem to be doing. Then a brief inner caution, uh oh, judgment, Sati, you're making a judgment. And look who's being conspiratorial—me, hiding behind trees. Talk about unseemly! But he stands there anyway, his eyes riveted on the pair. Sati trusts his intuition.

He watches Harika reach over to the low shelf in the entranceway and pick up one of four gourds that are used as waterjars. Harika turns to the cistern nearby, takes off the lid and tips it to allow a small stream of water to flow into the vessel. In silence, too, Harika holds the gourd aloft, showing it to Migajala as though it were a trophy; his usually grim features break into a smile. It isn't a friendly smile. A slight nod of understanding passes between them, then the younger monk turns and leaves. Sati stiffens and takes a small step further behind the tree's hospitable trunk, hoping Migajala won't notice him. He can't move further around because he'd be in Harika's line of vision.

Walking quickly and full of purpose, Migajala doesn't notice. The young man exhales in relief. But Harika is still to come, and he's more observant. Sati watches, holding his breath again while Harika waits a few moments, then follows. Sati inches back around the tree as Harika comes on, careful not to trip over a young sucker growing from the tree's root. He dearly hopes the crunch of leaves underfoot as he moves out of sight won't draw the venerable's attention. Harika walks slowly in an upright, monkly manner, and he carries the half-full gourd with him. He doesn't notice Sati.

Once Harika disappears around the turn in the path, Sati emerges from his hiding place. Not a moment too soon! A good deal of time has passed since he left his hut on this mission and his kidneys are now signaling an all-out emergency. He dashes into the latrine, grinning at his unseemly pace. But his heart is beating rapidly—something important is about to happen. He can't imagine what, but he senses it won't be for the better. He'll follow and find out; first, however, bodily need.

Despite his haste, Sati doesn't forget to wash after urinating, as monastic protocol and his own natural sense of cleanliness require. Returning to the entranceway and filling one of the gourds—quickly but carefully so there won't be a large excess of water—Sati washes as he stands there, his back to the path. Then he turns and tips the gourd so that the remainder trickles onto a thirsty plant near the building.

Good man, he thinks, congratulating himself on his conscientiousness. Sati is glad to water the little plant, which is struggling in this dry season. Like other monks in the order, he is careful to protect life whenever possible. This is another monastic restriction, one Sati takes to naturally. It's an expression of the Buddha's teaching of non-harming—all living beings are to be honored and treated with kindness.

Concluding latrine business, Sati hurries off, readily overlooking his reversal of prescribed latrine activities: He should have filled the vessel first and taken it into the latrine in order to wash in privacy, then brought the jar out and emptied what was left onto the earth. Well, too bad, no time for that.

As Sati walks into the central common area, he hears a commotion. An area where silence customarily prevails, even when all twenty-four monks are in residence, is now clamorous with voices.

"What do you mean you emptied the waterjar?" The Venerable Harika is almost shouting, "You deny it? Here it is, right here, half-full," shaking the gourd in the face of a somewhat older monk. He turns to the circle of monks that has formed around them and, holding the jar aloft, slowly passes it before the gaze of the bhikkhus; then, certain he has their attention, he pours the water onto the ground. "You weren't mindful, friend. It's plain and simple. It's a breach of the Discipline! A serious breach!"

As though on cue, Migajala begins to gesticulate. His voice soaring to a high register, he interjects, "Venerable sir! I didn't pass you on the path and I was at the lavatory too and the Venerable Harika was there and he found the waterjar, just as you left it shortly before—it was still half full—and..." He pauses for a much-needed breath. The gathered bhikkhus are wide-eyed. What in the world is going on? Harika, even in his presumed rage, notes that Migajala is blundering into the histrionic. No subtlety there at all! Harika doesn't give thought to his own histrionics. Migajala resumes his rehearsed script, still waving his hands, fingers apart, palms up, to underscore the outrage, "and we all know the cleanliness rule, the one that states..."

"Yes, yes, friend, we do know that protocol," interrupts the Venerable Candana, quietly, but careful not to call it a rule. "Which is why of course I emptied the remaining water on a plant at the edge of the path. As always," he adds for good measure. Candana stands still and upright as he speaks. "I did *not* forget," he concludes with soft finality.

The Venerable Candana is a tall, well built man, in his mid-forties, his complexion light, his features regular, animated by both strength and kindliness. He has a natural dignity that some attribute to his *brahmanic* birth and to the privileges of upbringing in a wealthy family. But his training in the Buddha's *Dhamma* or Teaching, runs deep and Candana has dropped identification with his past. He is a noble one in the true sense, an *ariya*, in the order where nobility refers to spiritual attainment, not birth. Learned in the Dhamma as well as in the rules and protocols of the Discipline, he has the flexible mind of one who has learned to see things as they are and who possesses the common sense to act on them wisely. His inner ease translates into an ease in relationships with others.

Which is why the Buddha, in an unusual move, sent Candana to Ghosita's Park thirteen months earlier. Ghosita's Park is one of the first monastic centers in the Buddha's order to house full-time resident monks. At a much later date, Candana would be called an abbot, but in these days, when bhikkhus in the order are largely itinerant and organization into residential communities is new, Candana is simply the most senior and most respected monk in the community. So now the bhikkhus who have gathered around, listen in disbelief to the two seniors engaged in an unseemly argument.

"Are you calling me a liar, friend?" Harika hurls back in rage. His eyes, which are his most outstanding physical feature, are copper; sometimes they appear the color of his robes; now they glint like metal.

"No, friend, I'm not calling you a liar," Candana responds softly, drawing out the word "friend" for emphasis. The irony, though ignored, is not lost on Harika nor on the clutch of observers. "I'm not calling you a liar, but clearly there has been a mistake."

"Words!" Harika shoots back. "'Mistake,' 'lie,' what's the difference? This vessel says you forgot and you're denying it because you don't want to admit that you lapsed in the Discipline. A monk who doesn't honor the Discipline…"

Candana holds his head askance and looks hard at Harika as he runs on. What is this man about? His speech itself is a lapse of monastic decorum, not to mention a lapse in simple truth and kindness. Angry words are unwise speech, and the tongue that speaks them is an ax in the mouth. The Buddha teaches that. If Harika thinks I forgot to empty the gourd and feels it even worthy of comment—such a ridiculous, such a trivial, event!—he should talk to me privately, not in front of our brothers. Though Candana doesn't put it past Harika to be angered by any disciplinary breach, even a trivial one, his words are wildly disproportionate to the occasion. A waterjar! Candana senses that not anger, but design drives the monk. Harika is deliberately creating a scene. Who knows what's going on in that devious mind!

Candana needs time to think, to consider the implications. So, he interrupts Harika's invective and addresses Migajala. "Friend, you didn't pass me on the path because I didn't go that way when I returned. I walked through the grove. I wanted to take a few moments to enjoy the trees—uh, to *mindfully* appreciate them." Candana warily amends his statement, lest Harika assert that "enjoyment" reflects laxity in practice and is inappropriate for a bhikkhu. He wouldn't put it past Harika.

Sati is startled. He didn't see Candana and the grove isn't so big that you could easily miss him. Then he remembers—ah, yes, the leaves and shadows. And the beetle.

Candana notices Sati standing silently on the outskirts of the group. Their eyes meet for an instant. Then very deliberately, Candana looks back at Harika, his mind made up. He says, "Maybe you're right. Maybe I *did* forget. But if I did," he adds quickly, "it isn't an offense."

"So now you admit it!" crows Harika triumphantly, aglow with victory, looking around at the monks to make sure they are marking the outcome of this matter. And in victory, a little magnanimity. He says in a decidedly quieter tone though still with an edge, "Be warned, friend Candana." But he is not so magnanimous as to trouble himself with the honorific "Venerable." "Be warned, friend, this *is* an offense, and this one won't be forgotten—I'll tell you that!" as though Candana has committed a string of others that haven't been addressed. He turns abruptly and leaves—without saluting Candana as monastic rules require. Migajala hesitates a moment, glances indecisively at both men, then with eyes downcast hurriedly follows Harika.

The other monks look at Candana, in wonderment. Can he explain to them what's going on? Candana, however, is silent and without looking at them, walks away. Shaking their heads and talking softly among themselves, they too disperse. They just witnessed an extraordinary spectacle: a senior shouting, threatening the most senior monk in the monastery, a man sent by the Blessed One himself. Over an issue so tiny that it borders on the comic, except that the passions it aroused in the Venerable Harika seem truly ominous.

Tensions have been rising in the monastery for several months. Little violations of monastic rules and protocols, little differences among them have been disrupting the harmony of the community. Not that anyone is purposely trying to create dissension—none of them believe there is an agenda here, no, not for a minute—but it seems to be happening anyway. The monks feel helpless, as though they were being sucked into one of the whirlpools that sometimes punctuate the long, slow flow of the Yamuna River. And now this.

Sati catches up with his mentor. He watched the exchange in silence. He dearly wanted to speak up—his mouth was open, words ready to pour forth—but he's just a novice. He has no business intruding in an argument between seniors. His words would have been brushed aside anyway, though Harika would have remembered and would have made an unpleasant point over it later—Sati has no doubt of that. Anyway, Candana was moving too fast. His admission about the jar is bewildering. Why did he say that? It's weird!

Now, with his heart beating hard, Sati confides in Candana. He deeply respects this man and, when he allows himself to acknowledge it, yes, he is growing to love him. Sati's father died last year, and, without trying to do so, Candana is beginning to assume that role. Sati's husky voice is usually soft, but now, as he tries to keep outrage from showing, his voice cracks with the effort, "Sir, I was there! I saw it! I saw the Venerable Harika fill the gourd!"

Candana stops and silently regards the young man.

Sati rushes on, "I was going to the latrine and saw the Venerables Harika and Migajala talking in the entranceway. Looked like they were doing more than talking. Something wasn't right. So I hid behind a tree and watched." Sati makes the admission a bit sheepishly and glances away. Candana still says nothing, giving Sati chance to finish.

"I don't understand. Why did Venerable Harika say those things?" Sati doesn't bother to wonder about Migajala. "What's he trying to do? It's a lie. It's wrong speech. Really, really wrong," he concludes lamely, his voice going small with anxiety and confusion.

Candana looks closely at Sati, whose usually open sunny demeanor is contracted into a troubled frown. "I know it, son," Candana says kindly. "I know it. And now I need to figure out how to respond and do as little damage as possible."

"But I don't understand. It's not right, it's—"

"Yes, all right, Sati," Candana holds up a hand in stop position. "I'm going to explain some things to you. I think you can help. Not now, though, we can't talk here—too many people around. Come to my hut in a little while, after sunset. We'll talk then."

The youth nods unhappily and watches as his mentor turns and leaves. Despite the accusations that assaulted him, Candana walks with the same lovely dignity that caught Sati's attention when he first saw him over a year ago.

Over a year ago. Sati can hardly bear to think of it. His mother was already dead. He and his father were on their way to market with their morning's catch. His father saw him first, carrying his alms bowl through the street—it was one of the poorer quarters—walking on almsround with two other monks. "Look, son, look at that bhikkhu, the one in the center. I haven't seen him before. Have you? There's something unusual about him, something really compelling." His father used the word "compelling," for he was an educated man. He was literate at a time when few possessed such knowledge. Both Sati and his father were silent as they watched the monks make their way through the street. And now his father was dead. Sati's mind refuses to think on these things. They are too painful.

"Come in, Sati," the Venerable Candana says when the young man appears on the porch of his tiny hut and taps at the open door. "And close the door behind you." Sati enters with his palms joined in anjali, a sign of respect. Candana points to one of the two sitting mats, now moved from the porch. Sati sits facing him.

"I saw you standing in the grove this afternoon on my way back from the lavatory, but you didn't see me." Candana smiles slightly as he says it.

"Yes sir." Sati doesn't feel like explaining about the beetle.

Candana nods, then says, "Sati, I'm going to tell you some things that will be hard to hear. It's not why you've gone forth, you didn't ordain for this, and you shouldn't have to be pulled into it." He shakes his head as he speaks. "But what you witnessed today can't be explained in any other way except by the truth. You're young in age and in training, but I think you can handle it." His voice, already grave, grows softer as he leans his head toward Sati and adds, "And the stakes are high."

With a sigh, Candana explains what he knows and what he half-knows. "If I continued to deny the accusation, it would have been my word against his. The bhikkhus would have to take sides, and that could have meant schism. It would weaken our community and the whole order."

Although Candana doesn't say so, the Buddha sent him to Kosambi to promote harmony. Itinerant monks had passed on rumors about rising tensions at Ghosita's Park and the Buddha witnessed them himself when he visited a year and a half earlier. There were just little things, more like the first hint of a restless breeze that presages a storm. But the Buddha knew. And he felt that if anybody could maintain harmony there, it was Candana.

"By agreeing to Harika's accusation," Candana explains, "I was hoping he'd be satisfied with a little victory, adding another small sour incident to our daily lives and letting it go at that. I was hoping we could cover it with grass," referring to a common way people in the region move past disagreement when there is no consensus, like farmers spreading straw over animal manure so animals and humans can walk there without treading in the muck.

"But it looks like he isn't going to do that. I should have known. In fact I did know; I heard it in his voice. But there wasn't time to think..." Candana lapses into silence. Sati waits.

Sati scrutinizes the frayed edge of the orange cotton sitting mat where a few threads are escaping from the rigor of the rectangle. Two of them, at right angles to the mat, are positioned like slender legs delicately crossed at the ankles. Appreciating the grace of the pattern, Sati allows his mind to rest there momentarily. It's a more inviting place than this new world that Candana's words are depicting. Out there people are deceitful, Sati knows that, but it's supposed to be different here. Here, it's not supposed to be like this!

Reluctantly, like a child parting with a treasured stick or bit of string, he thinks, Okay, Sati, my man, this is what's going on—no point pretending otherwise. And his heart tells him that whatever is happening, in the midst of it all, he trusts Candana, he has trusted him ever since he and his father saw him that first morning near the fish market. And the Buddha, too, of course, I trust him, Sati adds quickly in a dutiful after-thought and passes on. Who knows where this is heading! He looks up at the Venerable Candana with his heart's trust in his eyes.

CHAPTER 2

ROYAL RESENTMENT

February 25. "Where's the wine!" Udena bellows.

A female servant stands ready, always, to offer the king his wine, whether he is dining or, as now, conferring mid-morning with his ministers in the council pavilion. The pavilion is a free-standing building on the west side of the palace grounds where the king's council meets during the hot months. Its open structure, a roof and wooden pillars set in a stone floor, takes advantage of the slightest breeze. Although it isn't summer yet, the day is unusually warm, and Udena, who gets overheated easily, decided to hold the meeting here for the first time this season.

Servants cleaned the area of the winter's debris, and early this morning they laid antelope skins and patterned rugs and arranged a multitude of colorful cushions where the ministers now recline. Small cloth-covered tables are scattered about, holding wine bowls. Not all of the ministers partake, but Udena is doing so heartily. When, a moment ago, his extended right hand lifted his bowl and found it too light by half, he abruptly turned from the discussion with his royal treasurer to stare incredulously at the offending bowl.

"Where's the wine!" was a statement of outrage, not a question. Udena, who is twenty-eight, is just short of middling height and has a fair complexion and undistinguished features. His indulgent habits are creating a middle-aged paunch and fleshy jowls before his time. In this he resembles his father, King Parantapa. Like his father, Udena too expects his wishes to be immediately gratified—a justifiable kingly trait perhaps, but Udena doesn't hesitate to severely punish those who fail in their duty, nor does he restrain himself from grabbing what he wants when others don't provide.

The servant now rushes to fill his bowl and prays there will be no repercussions. She wonders if he's going to humiliate her by seizing the carafe from her hands, which have begun to shake.

Grabbing characterized Parantapa's life, as well. He conquered and created a kingdom out of a congeries of tribes and villages in the southern Ganges basin and assumed the title of Great King or Maharaja of Vamsa. And he declared the ancient city of Kosambi his capital. Work to transform the bustling commercial center into the kingdom's capital city continued throughout Parantapa's life. He had the ramparts expanded and reinforced, a moat dug around the city and public facilities upgraded. In accord with the kingly ideal of ancient Vedic tradition, Parantapa styled himself a "world-turning monarch."

As a child, Udena longed to prove himself to his father, but he never succeeded. Eventually, the boy's desire hardened into a determination to become an even greater ruler than Parantapa, though he didn't know how he could top a world-turning monarch. And even if he did succeed, Parantapa would have to be dead; so he'd never know. The king gave Udena his chance when, at age thirty-seven, he died of liver problems. The prince was nineteen. Officials attending the extravagant coronation celebrations shook their heads bleakly. "Two of a kind," they observed, anticipating more of the tensions that had characterized royal government service under Parantapa.

Udena feels that his inheritance is blighted by the fact that Vamsa can never become a predominant power. Though it is one of four larger kingdoms in the Middle Land and is stronger than Avanti to its south, Vamsa is greatly overshadowed by two eastern kingdoms, Kosala and Magadha. Moreover, it is locked in a triangle of land, a doab, between the Ganges and Yamuna Rivers, which, at their confluence, define his eastern border. It is true that his capital, Kosambi on the Yamuna is a busy port and a jewel of a commercial center, but greatness means land, and the only realistic way to acquire more is to march westward. Attacking the northern kingdoms would be folly, and southern expansion is unthinkable because Udena is married to the daughter of Avanti's king. No, Udena's army would need to march from Kosambi in the east through subjugated territories, territories that offer an ongoing challenge to his diplomatic skills as it is; then, his men would have to venture into fierce tribal lands that even his father failed to annex. Udena despairs of ever achieving his dream of greatness.

The king's wine bowl is now filled to the brim, and the servant has stepped back, still shaking. Udena swallows a long draft, ahhhhs appreciatively and turns back to his royal treasurer. The servant relaxes, sensing he isn't going to make an issue of her oversight.

"So when's the recluse arriving—have you had word?" Udena growls at Anupama Ghosita, who is reclining on cushions to his left. The question has been gnawing at the king ever since his spies informed him months ago that the ascetic Gotama, whom many call "the Buddha," the awakened one, would be spending the rainy season at the park owned by Ghosita here in Kosambi. Three whole months! Udena fumes to himself.

The monsoon rains last from mid-June to mid-September, and each year, the Buddha, like all other religious wanderers in the Middle Land, settles down for the season. It is simply too muddy to travel; indeed the land is often flooded. Unlike other wanderers, however, the Buddha realizes that the rainy season is an opportunity for his peripatetic monks to gather in communities to deepen their understanding of his teachings as well as strengthen their connection with the brotherhood of monks. They spend the three months in a retreat called *Vassa*. In many locations, senior bhikkhus in the Buddha's order share the teachings with their fellow monks, and each year some accompany the Buddha to his chosen retreat location and learn directly from him. It is a great honor to spend Vassa with the Buddha.

This year the Buddha will be coming to the park that Ghosita donated to him and his disciples. Most of the parks being given to the Buddha for the use of his monks, his monastic *sangha*, are located close to urban areas but outside town; Ghosita's Park, however, is within the city of Kosambi. Ghosita's father acquired the large tract of prime land just inside the southeastern ramparts of the ancient city. The tract was well-forested then, as was much of the surrounding area, and Ghosita has maintained it in its pristine condition. Later he had monastic facilities built and added flowering trees and shrubs for the monks' enjoyment. It is a jewel.

"I don't know for certain, Great King," Ghosita replies care-fully, maintaining a neutral tone. "But he usually arrives several days before the rains start. That's what he did in Magadha in the past and among the Bhaggu too," referring to the clan whose territory was an-nexed by Parantapa and where the Buddha spent vassa last year. "I assume he'll get here about the same time this year."

The tension underlying their conversation is palpable. King Udena suspects conspiracy everywhere, and he is convinced that the recluse's arrival in the heart of his kingdom is part of one. He believes that the kings of Kosala and Magadha are trying to undermine his power and are using the recluse as part of their strategy. Is Ghosita involved in the conspiracy, too, or is he just a fool? Udena wonders. It's a question he has asked himself often. The latter, he assumes, for he knows the family. The man's father, from the business class, was a merchant who amassed great wealth in banking even as his own father was creating the kingdom. The two men rose together so to speak, each supporting the other. Ghosita's family is deeply rooted in Kosambi; he has nothing to gain by looking elsewhere. Still Udena is suspicious.

The Buddha has had stunning success in Magadha when, early in his mission, the idealistic young king, Seniya Bimbisara, whole-heartedly converted to the Buddha's teaching or Dhamma. That con-version opened the most powerful kingdom in the Ganges basin to him and produced many hundreds of followers. Almost as stunning is the strong relationship that is developing between King Agnidatta Pasenadi of Kosala and the Buddha. Although Pasenadi has limited interest in spiritual matters, he holds a sturdy respect for the Buddha's growing influence. He too has proclaimed himself a follower. These two facts alone are enough to ensure Udena's opposition.

Udena hasn't tried to analyze how the Buddha's presence in his kingdom could undermine him; he simply reacts instinctively: The friend of my enemies is my enemy. That universal political dynamic is abundantly manifesting in this age when the region's political config-uration is undergoing radical change. Who needs to think? Thinking isn't Udena's strong point. Besides, he can't abide the many religious charlatans who are traipsing around the region in various guises, pretending to offer wisdom and salvation while they're really mooching off of hard-working folk. Earn their food? No, they just beg from others—no pride at all.

That is Udena's view. This shaveling ascetic is no different. Except he's alarmingly successful. Adherents are flocking to him left and right—and no doubt he's spreading favorable propaganda about Bimbisara and Pasenadi as he travels. Maybe collecting information for them, too. Well, he'll be damned if he'll let Gotama the Sakiyan make inroads here in Kosambi. Then his thoughts fly in frustration to the many Kosambians who are welcoming him when he visits, inviting him and his shaven-headed beggars to meals and listening oh so devotedly to his teachings. How do you control them? Oooofff! Well, he sure as hell won't become a follower like this fool next to him. Udena almost hoots his derision at the thought. The sooner the ascetic and his monastic brood are out of Vamsa, the happier he'll be.

Ghosita studies the king's clouded face. The sour expression sits naturally on him. Ghosita's mind flashes a vision of what the man will look like ten years from now; the result is so distasteful that he immediately comes back to the conversation. And he chides himself, I'm an idiot to let my attention wander even a hair's breadth in this bastard's presence. Unless I want to end up in prison or dead. And where's the merit in that?

Anupama Ghosita, at forty-two years old, is of medium height, three finger-widths taller than Udena, and he is of athletic build. A sweetness of temper usually graces his features, though it is absent at the moment. He is the richest man in Kosambi, president of the bankers' guild as well as royal treasurer. By his thirties however, Ghosita realized that these acquisitions weren't enough; something was missing from his life. A few years ago, when he and two associates were in Savatthi, the capital of Kosala, on business matters, they attended a talk given by the Buddha. They'd heard stories of the recluse's sublime attainment, his magnetic presence, and his impact on those who listen to him teach.

"Don't believe what I say," the Buddha asserted. "Come find it true for yourself." That night, Ghosita and his friends found it—

they found what was missing. For the first time Ghosita understood that worldly life is transient, it can never make one really happy. The Blessed One taught that everything people value and love is lost sooner or later, and when that happens, they suffer. True happiness only comes when one lets go and lives in the present moment mindfully and with kindness.

That night the Buddha also explained how bhikkhus and laypeople support each other, one offering the Dhamma, the Teaching, and the other gaining merit by providing the material essentials the bhikkhus needed. I can provide a lot of essentials, Ghosita thought excitedly, and gain merit while I'm at it—yes, I need that! He not only proclaimed himself a follower for life, he offered his beautiful park in Kosambi to the Buddha. His two associates, both of whom owned smaller parks just outside of town, did the same.

Now in the council pavilion, Udena asks a few more questions about the Buddha's arrival, once again making clear more by his tone than his words, how deeply opposed he is to the whole endeavor. Ghosita didn't consider the king's opposition when he first offered his pleasure park. He was so inspired by the teachings and so joyful when the Buddha accepted—it was a high point in his life—that political repercussions weren't a consideration. Since then though, he has occasionally wondered if he would have made the offer had he realized how deeply opposed Udena would be. He knows the answer. It is yes. No matter what the risk to his mundane existence, practicing the Dhamma is more important. It is what this life and all his future lives are about. Of course he supports the Blessed One!

So when several months ago the Venerable Candana suggested that Ghosita invite the Buddha to stay in his monastic center for this year's rains retreat, he didn't hesitate. The presence of the monks who are living in Ghosita's Park is a source of great merit. But this, this is a dream he hardly dared hope would be realized so soon! What incalculable merit will flow to him! Ghosita could not appreciate the trouble that would flow to him, too.

Udena now turns to Unnabha Bharadvaja, his royal chaplain, a brahmin of the great Bharadvaja clan, who is reclining stiffly on cushions opposite him. Bharadvaja would be more comfortable in a chair. He assumed his post as chaplain only three years ago, after his uncle, Nadi Bharadvaja, died when bitten by a deadly krait while stargazing in his garden. Nadi had been Udena's childhood tutor, and in accord with the custom of the day, he became first among the great men surrounding the king, assuming the position of royal chaplain when Udena ascended the throne. A man of piety and wisdom, he had been a voice of restraint in the life of the wayward young prince, and once Udena became king, Nadi played a similar role in the royal council, offering sound advice on matters both spiritual and worldly. The king was bound to listen to him with a humility he accorded no one else. But Udena never liked him—restraint is against his principles—and when Nadi died, he was relieved to be rid of him. His royal ministers were concerned though. Who would temper the king's impulsiveness now?

Because Nadi had no sons, the position of royal chaplain passed to his nephew, Unnabha Bharadvaja, whom Udena doesn't like either. The two men are temperamentally incompatible. Bharadvaja is a small, ascetic man, with a narrow face and not an extra bit of flesh on him. He has a subtle turn of mind, and when he speaks, his voice is shrill, precise, sharp as a knife. His eyes are the same way: They drill ruthlessly into whomever he is looking at, especially someone from the lower classes—and all other classes are lower as far as he is concerned.

Bharadvaja's mission in life is to ensure the preeminence of the brahmin class, especially his own great clan, and to gain wider reverence for, or more precisely, fear of the Vedic rituals that brahmin priests perform. He believes that brahmins are divinely blessed by the gods; they are pure while all others, not being so blessed, are irredeemably polluted. He has scriptural references to back up his claims and cites them often. The king who is of the noble class, scoffs at such claims, but he scoffs silently because just maybe Bharadvaja is right. This possibility causes Udena no end of anxiety, and he is careful to consult his royal chaplain often on all matters concerning ritual and sacrifice.

Bharadvaja is as firmly entrenched in his beliefs as Udena is in his, but neither notices the similarity. They tolerate one another because each finds the other useful. Anything can be expected in politics, one of the other ministers thinks as he observes them now.

Looking at his chaplain Udena is asking, "How is your son, Bharadvaja?" He regularly asks after the sons of his ministers and high officials since in all likelihood they will succeed their fathers in their posts.

"He is well, great king," the chaplain replies proudly, referring to eleven-year old Pindola. Like all high officials, he takes advantage of the question to praise his son. He adds, "He's a very bright boy, he excels at his studies." No one begrudges Bharadvaja his comment, though they've heard it many times. They similarly praise their own sons. But it does get boring. What Bharadvaja doesn't say is that Pindola asks too many questions. There are some things you just need to accept. It's one of the lessons his son hasn't learned yet.

The king smiles indulgently, then changes the subject. "And your religious duties?"

"Very well," replies the brahmin, gazing at him meaningfully.

The other officials exchange covert glances. Here they go again. The others know this isn't casual conversation; it's not about Bharadvaja's priestly functions nor the state of religious affairs. For the past several months the king and his chaplain have been exchanging such remarks from time to time. Obviously they're referring to matters the others aren't privy to.

Udena and Bharadvaja have a mutual interest that they don't acknowledge publicly: Gotama of the Sakiyas. Bharadvaja considers the recluse Gotama an upstart, a scheming wanderer who has appropriated parts of Vedic wisdom for his own purposes while denying other parts. Especially serious are the recluse's criticism of brahmanic sacrifices and his insistence that people of all classes are equal in their ability to awaken spiritually. The assertions scandalize him. If these beliefs became popular, the ancient orthodoxy and brahmanic claims to social and spiritual preeminence would be dangerously undermined. They are not to be tolerated.

The king replies genially, "Stay after the meeting, Bharadvaja, and tell me about it." The brahmin assents in silence, wagging his head from side to side in the lateral figure eight that signifies yes, no matter what class you belong to.

February 26. "There are two kinds of searches, friends. The common search is where someone—himself subject to birth, aging, sickness and death—attaches to other beings, who are subject to the same processes. Wives, parents, children, slaves, livestock, even gold and silver ingots—all are subject to birth in their own ways. Anyone who is tied to, lost in, a commitment to these things experiences sorrow; there's no way he can be free from sorrow or escape it. On the other hand, the noble search is where someone, though himself subject to birth, aging, sickness and death, sees the danger in what is subject to birth. This person seeks instead the unborn supreme security from bondage; he seeks Nibbana."

The Venerable Musila is speaking in the lecture hall this evening, reciting the Buddha's teaching. The hall is a pavilion and the bamboo partitions are raised because it has been warm. Resident bhikkhus, townspeople and a few religious wanderers are assembled, inside and out, as they are every evening when a Dhamma talk is given and the partitions raised. Like all bhikkhus of his day, Musila articulates the Buddha's teaching almost exactly as the Buddha spoke it. In this oral culture, where Dhamma wisdom has not yet been preserved in writing, verbal accuracy and a good memory are essential. Each teaching bhikkhu is a guardian who strives to maintain the purity of the Dhamma. So there is no pull for bhikkhus to find their own individual voice or to express the teachings in new ways.

Still, Musila speaks to his audience with the immediacy of one who has made the teaching his own. "Which is your search, friends? Common or noble? It makes no difference whether you're a bhikkhu or householder, rich or poor. A bhikkhu who, though he has ordained, may still be attached to things that pass away; he won't find an end to suffering; he can't find freedom. On the other hand, a householder who carries out the responsibilities of worldly life, if he has relinquished attachment, can make an end to suffering; he can find freedom."

Sitting toward the back of the group of monks as his novice status requires, though in front of the laypeople, Sati listens closely. During the lost months after his father had died, Sati often visited Ghosita's Park to hear to talks given by senior bhikkhus. Sati felt the authenticity of the Venerable Musila's presence when he spoke; it was almost as strong as the Venerable Candana's, which seemed the very essence of the Dhamma. Sati felt then he had come home. These talks led him into the inner sanctuary he longed for, even though he'd not been aware of it. They resonated as if his own heart had uttered them. A few months later the young man shaved his head and went forth into the holy life, becoming a novice in the Buddha's sangha.

Tonight however, as he listens to Musila, Sati is distraught. His shoulders droop and his head hangs lower with each word. There is no use pretending: He *is* attached. Attachment is as thick as the mud that gums up roads during the rains. He misses his parents. He misses the warmth of their life together, each dear little familiar thing about it. For all its hardship, his family life was sunshine. Now it's gone, and sitting in this hall this evening, Sati feels unprepared to carry on without them, unfit for the noble search. He is a fraud. Tears well up uncontrollably. Ashamed, Sati hunches over further hoping no one will see them roll down his cheeks and, falling, make dark spots on his saffron robe. Yielding to his need, he lets them fall freely. His shoulders shake. And if someone does notice? Well, certainly it wouldn't be the first time they've seen a novice cry.

The image of his father's body lying on the riverbank with his little skiff overturned in the mud flashes into mind. Losing his mother and the baby, a boy whom she'd been unable to bring into life, had been devastating. His father's death from the accident a year later was unbearable. No one needs to explain to him the first Noble Truth, the truth of suffering. Sati knows that one like an old sandal. Could things get worse? he wonders. Of course they could! Coming back to the present, he observes that they look poised to do just that. But for the moment, even that mess is usurped by the pain of losing his parents. And by the fact that he lives in limbo: neither there with his parents, nor fully here in the monastery—that's the worst part of it.

After the talk is over, monks and laypeople alike proclaim the obligatory "excellent, excellent, excellent," and most really mean it, but Sati is silent. He walks glumly to his little wooden hut, glad to be alone. No one can fill the void he feels. Candana noticed Sati crying, and now he watches the young novice depart. This isn't the time to intervene. I'll speak with the boy tomorrow, he promises himself.

February 27. The next morning before the monks set off to town on their almsround, Candana pulls Sati aside as he stands near the monastery gate waiting for the Venerable Arittha, his almsround partner. The young man's face is drawn as though he hasn't slept.

"How are you, friend Sati?" Candana asks casually.

Sati's throat constricts. He grips his begging bowl tighter against his belly, and although it is made of heavy clay and not easily shattered, his strong arms seem intent on accomplishing the feat. The simple question disarms him and he has to brace against tears, which threaten to surge past his throat into his eyes. Someone actually cares! Exerting all his determination to keep from crying, Sati finds a response beyond him. Instead he looks down at the cracked earth. It is as barren as he feels.

Candana continues as if he didn't notice. "What did you think of the Venerable Musila's talk?" he asks. Again, no answer.

"Son," Candana says gently, guessing the heart of the matter, "you've recently lost both parents. It's natural to grieve. To cry. That's what human beings do when they care for someone."

It is too much. Tears win and his shoulders shake in silent sobs. He continues to focus on the dry stubble at his feet. Even as he cries though, Sati notes that Candana knows what he's thinking. Can he read my thoughts? That's alarming. But words, the ones that had kept him awake all night, tumble out on their own, preempting other concerns. "It's no use, no good at all. I don't belong here, I can't do it. I'll never be nonattached. And it's a stupid idea anyway!" He looks up at Candana with defiance. "It's not real, it's not life, not..."

"Don't worry about nonattachment," the older man interrupts. "It will happen when it happens."

"But I don't want it to happen!" Sati almost shouts. There! He said it. He looks to see if his mentor is shocked. "I don't want it to happen. I loved my parents, I love them still. Not even the Buddha can make me stop loving them!" Now he is sure he's done it. His feet plant themselves in fighting stance, a bit further than hip-distance apart; his body braces for what will come next. He is sure his entire existence rests on this moment. He foresees a future as a householder.

The Venerable Candana smiles kindly. "The Buddha isn't going to try to make you stop loving your parents. Neither am I. You're young, Sati. Some day you'll see that loving doesn't stop because you're training in the Dhamma. You just love from a different place."

These words make no sense to Sati. But no matter—his mind locks onto "someday you'll see." I will? Does he mean there's hope for me? Is that what he's saying? I'm not hopeless? Relief at that stunning prospect washes over him. He feels like one of the quivering fish he used to throw back into the river because it was too small; he sometimes wondered what their rediscovery of water was like. It must have been like this.

Despite the tension, Sati notices humor in the lurching of his thoughts and emotions: Last night he was sure the bhikkhu's life wasn't for him, and now he is relieved to think it might be. He questions himself, Do you mean you really want to be here? In this crazy place, trying to live this crazy life? Because he not only convinced himself that he isn't cut out to be a monk but that he doesn't want to—it was all so very clear last night: He, Sati, doesn't belong anywhere, he is a misfit. It is as simple as that. The only place I've ever belonged, he told himself mournfully, was with Poppa and Momma and they're gone. Emotion threatens to overwhelm him again—except he is aware of Candana's voice. What's he saying? He breathes deeply and refocuses.

"...only after years of practice. You can't force it. If you try to be nonattached too soon, you bury the truth of your feelings. That never works. Our reactions don't go away because they're buried, they just fester inside and become cankerous. Bhikkhus can easily make that mistake, then they become hard, rigid, afraid of what's inside. That's not what our practice is about. Don't let it happen to you, son. Come and talk with me whenever you need to."

Sati mutely nods a lateral figure eight, assenting, grateful.

Candana pauses, assessing whether to say more or not and, thinking, It's probably too much but as long as he's here, well, why not? He says, "You need to live into the teachings, friend—our practice is about becoming the teachings, making them your own. That's what the Blessed One means when he says "penetrate the Dhamma well by view." He means find out how they express in your own life. Find out their reality for yourself. Does this make sense?"

Another silent figure eight.

Candana thinks, He doesn't get it. And he says, "You're doing fine, Sati. Just keep practicing sincerely. Things will take care of themselves, you'll see. Come and talk with me when you need to."

As he moves away, Candana regrets having confided in the boy yesterday. He's not ready for it; he's got too much to deal with. All because of my craving. Because I wanted support, a friend, maybe a son... Delusion, delusion! He berates himself, even though he knows he had to give some explanation; Sati had seen too much. But he continues to criticize himself: It was mistake number two. And as he thinks this, mistake number one tightens its grip in his chest where it has lodged since he'd reversed himself on the waterjar issue yesterday. Ummmhh! A good intention gone wrong—a mistake on top of a lie. What a mess!

Candana knows there isn't any way to get things right all the time: Sometimes one is skillful, sometimes not—even when you're trying hard. And he *has* been trying hard. As the senior monk at

Ghosita's Park he is often called on to make decisions. He has made many sound ones, but at this moment, the two unsound ones swamp his vision and he loses perspective. Have I made any progress at all in this training? He doubts it. The Venerable Candana shakes his head and suddenly feels lonely. Very lonely.

February 27. "This is beyond revolting!" Arittha exclaims, his dark, craggy features wrinkle in disgust. "Everyone is so worried about dis-cipline these days, why don't they remind our reverend brothers to use some of it here!" Arittha and Sati are standing in the lavatory build-ing with cleaning materials in hand. "Forgetting to empty the water-jar, my eye! What about that!" pointing to a deposit of vomit on the floor. The clay brick has absorbed a good part of the liquid but chunks of semi-digested food remain, surrounded by flies and stinking. "Who did that?" he asks, though he has a pretty good idea. "Couldn't he take a few more steps?" pointing to the privy. "No, instead they assign us lowly ones, to clean it up."

Sati winces. Not again! He knows Arittha isn't referring to their monastic status. Both of them reside at the very bottom in that respect. As a novice, one who hasn't yet received full ordination, Sati hardly counts, while Arittha who ordained eleven months earlier is still a junior in the small community at Ghosita's Park.

But something else galls Arittha: social status. Cleaning priv-ies is a job for slaves and outcastes, and that is just what he is by birth—an outcaste. He is convinced that his job assignment is meant to remind him of the fact. The tall angular man was born to the hawker's trade, catching and training raptors for small game hunt-ing, an activity that would become a popular sport among the ruling classes in another fifteen hundred years, but now is a reviled occupa-tion. Arittha also hunted bigger game, deer and the like, but in ac-cord with custom, he is known by his inherited occupation, which is commonly called "bird-catching," or, more contemptuously, "vulture tormenting" and "vulture killing," epithets that ignore the fact that vultures aren't actually in the picture because they're scavengers, not hunting birds.

Trades involving killing are relegated to outcaste status by a society that officially abhors killing even though brahmin priests, at the other end of the social spectrum, ritually kill animals by the thousands and call it holy. Hawkers or falconers are a hardy folk who live much of their lives deep in the forests, using hawks that dive into cover for prey, or in open marshy areas, using falcons. They are generally happy enough in their independence, but the social price of their inheritance is high.

The price didn't matter much to Arittha. He lived alone in the forest with his hawks and a dog that he used when hunting. At twenty, he wanted to marry, but, when another marriage was arranged for the girl, he didn't try again. After that, he left the village where he had lived with his father and brother as a youngster to follow his heart in another way: He moved deeper into the forest and began hunting with hawks. His contact with people was limited mainly to occasional visits to a woman in one of the villages. He was a natural recluse.

He loved his birds though. There was mutual trust between him and the creatures, fierce and wild, and Arittha grew to resemble them. They taught him much about freedom, for a hunting hawk that isn't handled with respect will fly off. They always have that choice. Eventually, however, Arittha realized that even the hawk's freedom wasn't enough; there was still something more—he was sure of it— and he longed to discover what it was. Which is how he came to the Buddha's path.

Wandering bhikkhus in the Buddha's order occasionally found their way to the remote area where Arittha lived. The first time he saw one, the monk was sitting under an old banyan tree, its wide canopy sheltering him from the scorch of the sun. Arittha had encountered wandering ascetics from time to time with their long, matted locks and rags and bodies smeared with ashes to protect them from heat. They looked dirty. Being fastidious about personal cleanliness—he cleaned up whenever possible though sometimes it might be weeks—Arittha was repelled by them. He stared at this monk, though. His orange robes weren't exactly clean, but they were simple and his head shaven, covered right now by a mere fuzz of hair. No tangled masses. Something about him was clean.

The monk was still, like a tiger when it spots prey and is immobile, completely focused, waiting for the right moment to spring. Except this man sat that way, next to the tree's main trunk, all afternoon. Arittha stationed himself by one of the tree's many outlying trunks, actually prop roots that had grown down from the far-flung branches, stalactites forming a great roomy cave. He watched, intrigued. When the monk finally stirred, Arittha approached uncertainly. After a brief courteous greeting, he offered the monk food, and he received his introduction to monastic habits in the Buddha's order—monks don't eat after noon. Arittha respected that.

The Venerable Lakkhana stayed for two months, living at the foot of the banyan tree while Arittha supplied almsfood. In the evenings, they sat together under the tree and the venerable spoke quietly about the Buddha's Dhamma. Arittha wasn't much of a talker, but he asked good questions and he knew how to listen. And he was impressed by how this man could leave at any time. If he, Arittha, hadn't been offering food, the venerable would have picked up his bowl and moved on. So simple, so free. So like a hawk.

Arittha processed things slowly—there was no rush. Two years later, at the age of twenty-six, he went forth. He traveled to Kosambi, the nearest town and went to Ghosita's Park where he met the Venerable Candana and asked to be ordained. Then everything changed. Since formally becoming a recluse, Arittha has been with people continually. His dream of wandering freely has been thwarted because his mentor requires him to spend these initial months in residence, training with him.

What a paradox! It's hard enough to be with people he likes, like Sati; to be with those he dislikes—there are several in the monastery—is excruciating. Even in the Buddha's order, where social prejudice is officially nonexistent, Arittha is doubly disadvantaged, by his outcaste status and by his dark skin. He often feels its stab. Innuendo, which some monks excel at, is especially hard to bear. Go ahead and say it outright, man! he fumes. He is growing bitter and longs for the solitude of his forest.

As Arittha rants now, Sati sighs. He and Arittha are regularly assigned the lavatory work detail and it usually goes like this: First, Arittha sounds off, then eventually his sense of duty prevails and he gets down to work.

I may as well start with the vomit and get it over with, Sati thinks. From a clay pot he set on the floor, he picks out a rag, squats and begins scooping up the mess and shakes it into the pot. His stomach turns as the odor assails him.

For a quiet man, Arittha sure talks a lot, Sati reflects, and he turns away from the stream of bitter words to his own musings. Arittha doesn't seem to like anyone except me and Nakula. Such strange choices, he muses. Nakula and I aren't anything alike, and we're not like Arittha either. Why us? For his part, Sati isn't sure he cares for Arittha all that much. He's hard to listen to; he's as trapped in social judgment as everybody he criticizes, except he's coming from the other end. It's no good telling him that of course—he'd only get madder. Sati sighs quietly and, nauseated, he scrubs the floor, waiting for Arittha's voice to exhaust itself so that he can pitch in. So far it shows no sign of winding down.

Sati has tried both reason and anger with Arittha, without effect. The man doesn't mean ill but he seems incapable of change, and since they are regularly assigned here, Sati has accepted that this is how it's going to be. For his part, Sati is sure there is nothing personal in the assignment. Or maybe there is, but not for the reason Arittha suspects. Maybe the Venerable Udayi, who makes the work assignments, does do it purposely, but as a teaching—a way to bring Arittha face to face with his anger, and to test Sati's reactivity too, because he is of quasi-outcaste status. Sati has seen enough of monastic life to understand that monastic training isn't only about meditating, almsrounds, and listening to Dhamma talks; it includes every aspect of life. Well, whatever the point, Sati concludes, it's not working with Arittha.

Despite his irritation, Sati feels protective of the man. Though ten years younger, he often feels senior. For all his independent-mindedness, Arittha seems so raw and vulnerable, so young. Sati has experienced the pain of prejudice too, but things are different for him—he's been cherished, he knows his worth and no one can make him doubt it, at least not completely. His father crosses his mind and his chest hurts. Sitting back on his haunches, forearm resting on his knee and the rag held loosely in his right hand, Sati looks out the open door into the sky.

Perhaps Arittha notices, or maybe he just has had his say; in any case, he picks up a broom, made of slender twigs tied to a straight branch, and begins to sweep. As he does, he issues a final declaration, "Whoever did it—the ass!—he'd better be careful or he'll be expelled, too! It's a breach of the discipline. Absolutely unsanitary!"

Arittha hasn't gotten around to gentle speech yet. Whenever he considers it, which isn't often, he concludes it is something he can deal with later, after he reaches higher attainment—if that ever happens.

"What do you mean 'too'?" Sati asks, his attention jerking back to Arittha as he catches the implication. His husky voice has dropped so low it is almost inaudible. He already knows.

"Haven't you heard? Well, I guess not—being just a novice and all, you're not included in these matters. My eleven months as a fully ordained bhikkhu gives me the honor to hear all the news. I wish I didn't."

"So?" Sati says impatiently.

"So, here it is: The Venerable Harika is trying to get everybody to agree to expel the Venerable Candana. I'm sorry to tell you, Sati. Candana's my mentor too, but I know how much you…"

Sati interrupts, "Expel him! On what grounds? He didn't even do it. It's a setup!" Sati has already confided the story to Arittha, at least the part he had witnessed. He needed to tell someone. "It's ridiculous!" he objects, but he knows that the real issue is anything but ridiculous.

"The problem is, friend,"—and Arittha means it when he calls Sati "friend"—"that first he said no, then he admitted it, but denies it's an offense. The waterjar business is a tiny matter, emptying it is just one of those little things we do, but why the quick turnaround? Did he forget and then remember? Or was it a lie to begin with? Personally I think the whole thing should be covered with grass—it's such a little matter, but Harika is blowing it up, like forgetting to empty a waterjar is the biggest offense a monk can commit. It's crazy. But he's saying Candana is denying the Discipline, which *does* make it a big deal, if you see what I mean."

Sati sees perfectly.

Arittha continues, "You know letter-of-the-law Harika." "Letter of the law" is a phrase Arittha has learned at the monastery. He is getting a peculiar kind of education. "Harika could confuse the Blessed One himself with his legalities. He is saying that morale around here is sinking daily. Well, of course it is! Look who's making it sink!" Arittha editorializes. "And he's warning us that we can't be too careful. We need to enforce every lapse. Uttara is going along with him, of course. What else would you expect?"

The Venerable Uttara was the most senior monk in the monastery until Candana arrived. And he knew, as everybody else did, that Candana had been sent by the Blessed One. Uttara was stung by the Buddha's decision; he takes Candana's arrival as condemnation of his own leadership. The more he ruminates on it—and he hasn't stopped doing so since the day Candana arrived—the more Uttara finds fault with him.

Most monks have a natural preference either for the Teaching, the Dhamma, or for the body of regulations known as the Discipline, the *Vinaya*. Some of them, however, especially those favoring the Discipline, have recently gotten righteous about their preference and assert that it is the central feature of the Buddha's teaching. Uttara is one of them. He has decided that the Venerable Candana wrongfully gives precedence to the Teaching. He recognizes that Candana is erudite—he is well-versed in both Vinaya and Dhamma—but clearly his real interest lies with the Dhamma, and that's his mistake. The abysmal decline in monastic discipline is proof of just how wrong Candana it is. Uttara is convinced that they would not be in this predicament if he himself were still in charge. Still, he defers, as required by the Vinaya, to Candana's senior status. Deference doesn't mean though that he likes the man or approves of his views.

"Sati, I'm afraid if the Venerable Candana continues to deny that it's an offense, he's cooked. They're going to get him."

Here it is again. First his father and now his mentor—victims of intrigue. Will this evil never end? Sati's disturbed stomach turns over again and for a moment he is afraid he's going to add a fresh mess on the floor. He was too young to help his father, but he remembers well the tension of those days. It is stored in his body like fire in a clay oven the next morning: It seems to be dead but only needs a bit of tinder to set it ablaze. Now though, he is a man, and he doesn't have to be a passive witness. He can take action. Right there in the latrine, Sati vows that this time he is going to do something. He'll do whatever is necessary to support Candana.

CHAPTER 3.
SCHISM IN THE MONASTIC ORDER

Arittha is right. They *are* out to get Candana. The target date is March 1st, which is *Uposatha*. Uposatha is the observance where monks at Ghosita's Park gather to reaffirm their adherence to the Dhamma and confess any violations of the Vinaya.

Near the beginning of his teaching mission nine years earlier, the Buddha declared that his bhikkhus, who were all itinerants, should gather every six years to affirm their steadfastness in the Dhamma. The first such meeting was held three years ago, and Harika, then a young monk, attended. By then Ghosita's Park was already established and a handful of bhikkhus were living there much of the year.

When Harika returned, he was on fire. The new, full, and half moon days were traditional days of fasting among the pious in the Middle Land regardless of religious persuasion, and the Buddha continued the observance in his growing order. Harika went a step further, recognizing that the bi-monthly Uposatha was a perfect occasion to promote the Discipline. In addition to fasting, Harika proposed that bhikkhus at Ghosita's Park recite their vows at each Uposatha and thus affirm the Dhamma. Moreover, he brilliantly advocated that each Uposatha should include a recitation of the major rules governing the order, followed by confessions. Each monk would be called on to confess any transgressions, and a senior would levy penalties. Well-disciplined monks made good monks. The more disciplined, the better. Harika readily convinced the Venerable Uttara, then the presiding senior, but, in accord with custom, all resident bhikkhus present at the time had to agree.

They did agree, but they altered Harika's focus a bit, to his chagrin. The bhikkhus recognized that confession needn't be viewed as punitive. The Venerable Musila pointed out that confession could promote progress on the path to liberation: By telling the truth and receiving an appropriate penalty, the monk in violation would have acknowledged his unwholesome actions and be washed clean the evil consequences of his actions; thus he would be free to move on toward awakening.

As a result of Harika's initiative, Uposatha took on wider significance at Ghosita's Park. Eventually, the practice would be adopted throughout the Buddha's order and become part of Harika's contribution to the monastic sangha.

But at this point Harika doesn't have an eye on the future. In recent months, his focus has become narrower and meaner. With prompting from outside sources, he has come to argue that disciplinary lapses, even trivial ones, are endangering the very existence of the monastic community in Kosambi. He has been insinuating, and sometimes making outright claims, that Candana's preference for the Dhamma over the Discipline is a threat to the community.

And now the so-called waterjar incident. It furthers Harika's purpose beautifully. He is calling for Candana's expulsion. Harika is seen about the monastery grounds garnering support for his strategy, talking in earnest hushed tones, huddling with monks individually and in small groups. He argues for expulsion, but in fact he knows he can't get the unanimity that the penalty requires, and this is all right with him. Because expulsion isn't his real aim. What he really wants, but doesn't say so, is to weaken those who don't properly value the Discipline. By attacking the top man, even if he's not expelled, the others of his ilk will be undermined. And if that leads to schism, well, so be it. Harika is convinced that in the long run the community at Ghosita's Park will benefit. Not to mention the fact that he himself will emerge in a stronger position.

Another issue lurks on the periphery of Harika's plans. He is bothered by the fact that the Buddha sent Candana to Ghosita's Park. Does it signify the Buddha's long-range intention to exert control over local communities? Does it mean that he's going to appoint his own man to head each center? Harika wants to make sure this doesn't happen. A successful case against Candana would strengthen the authority of their community with respect to the Buddha, and it would set an important precedent for relations between the Teacher and all settled monastic communities, which, though still few, are growing in number.

Harika is a legal genius. He can no more refrain from focusing on the law than he can from eating; both functions are vital to his life. He believes that promoting the Discipline is a high cause and that he himself is its servant. The only effective response to legal violations, he is convinced, is rigorous enforcement of the Discipline and stronger penalties for transgressions. Anyone who believes otherwise is wrong.

Though Candana isn't aware of all the implications of the issue, he recognizes that ensuring support among the bhikkhus is urgently important. He has been talking with monks whom he counts as supporters, meeting with them in his hut or theirs. His friends are puzzled. They trust him completely but can't get past the sense that something is amiss. Why did he deny the accusation, then admit it afterwards? And why has such a trivial matter assumed such importance—why is Harika calling for expulsion? Why is he so vindictive?

For many monks—those in both camps—the body of monastic rules is too confusing to think about. The rules are not yet fully codified; indeed they are still being formulated. To date, the Buddha has stipulated forty-two major rules or precepts that bhikkhus are bound to observe. Emptying a waterjar after urinating and washing is not one of them. Penalties for violating the forty-two aren't clearly stipulated. Nor is there agreement about how to respond to infractions of the many protocols springing up in at Ghosita's Park and elsewhere. The Buddha has not yet commented on these. As far as Candana's supporters are concerned, emptying a waterjar is just another protocol, one of the many little things they do to enable community life to function smoothly. What do rules and protocols have to do with spiritual progress anyway? They ordained to become liberated, not to become lawyers.

Candana can't tell his friends the real story. Not even Musila, the brother he feels closest to. He can only point to the insubstantial nature of the case. Musila looks at him with a question in his big dark eyes, and Candana simply says, "Trust me now, friend. Bhagava will be here soon." He is referring to the Buddha, using the title of reverence by which religious leaders are commonly addressed. "Then we'll put it to him." Candana is deeply distressed that he has to lie.

Musila does trust him, as do fourteen others, including Sati. Candana has warned Sati to say nothing about what he witnessed. "Speaking up would do a lot of damage and it wouldn't serve any good purpose. At present this matter seems to be about a moot disciplinary infraction. If I told the full story, part of which I'm only guessing at, our brothers would be even more demoralized. I'd have to implicate government officials, and that would hardly be wise."

Candana also knows that even if he limited his comments to Harika and the waterjar, they would just end up hurling charges at each other—his word against Harika's. So he says merely, "This matter didn't start here at Ghosita's Park and we can't resolve it here, at least not right now."

Sati listens anxiously, and he feels guilty because he has already told Arittha. Maybe Candana had cautioned him that first night, he can't remember—there was so much to take in. Feeling like a naughty child, he chastises himself, Why didn't I have sense enough to be quiet? He confesses to Candana, but then adds in his defense, "I only told him what I saw, not the other things."

"Ummmm. You need to make it clear to him that he mustn't tell others, not even Nakula," Candana comments, but he isn't too worried. Arittha isn't the talking type; he stores things up and vents with his few friends. "And you, too, Sati, you must promise me that no matter what is said at Uposatha, you won't say what you know." He looks into Sati's eyes.

"But…" Sati objects. Would he have to be useless again? A child forever?

"No, friend, it *must* be like this."

March 1. Uposatha. On the new-moon day at the beginning of March, they gather in the lecture hall, the designated Uposatha meeting place. Candana sits at front of the group as usual. The Venerable Udayi, also up front, opens the observance by reciting the disciplinary code: "Supreme is Nibbana, so say the Buddhas. Not to do any evil, but cultivate the good, to purify one's mind, this is the Buddhas' teaching. Not insulting, not harming, restraint according to rule, moderation in food, seclusion of dwelling, devotion to high thinking, this is the Buddhas' teaching."

Every monk present, including the Venerable Harika, thrills to hear the words. This is what animates their lives. It's their highest aspiration—even Harika's, though he has an extra aspiration or two.

Udayi continues with their community's innovation, reciting the forty-two primary rules or precepts for monastic living. The Buddha formulated these in response to excesses that have occasionally arisen in the order, and all bhikkhus are required to learn them. Shortly after he had arrived at Ghosita's Park, the Venerable Candana coined the term "*patimokkha*," to refer to these rules. It expresses precisely what the more liberal bhikkhus had in mind when they agreed to Harika's suggestion to hold periodic confession, because "patimokkha" means "unburdening" or "freeing" oneself. And it tipped off the bhikkhus as to where Candana stood on the Dhamma-Discipline issue.

Assessing another's position on this issue is about as automatic as determining one's social class; monks do it without thinking: Are the teachings primary? Are the rules? Some combination of both? Monks are primed to pick up subtle cues. Candana's suggestion clearly shows that he sides with the teaching. He is saying that confession isn't simply about censure for wrong-doing but is an aid on the path to liberation. He is a Dhamma man.

Udayi, his eyes closed, begins the Patimokkha, saying, "Today is the sacred day of the new moon. Let the community hold Uposatha, let it repeat the Patimokkha. Whosoever has incurred a fault, let him declare it. If no fault has been incurred, it is appropriate to keep silent."

As Udayi recites, Candana laments what is about to happen. "Patimokkha" means to get free but today it's being used to divide the sangha. What a terrible irony! An ideal twisted into a nightmare. He looks at each of the bhikkhus, the people he's been living with for over a year, and feels many of them to be strangers. In fact, at this moment he feels a stranger to himself. How did this all happen? He shivers and listens helplessly.

After Udayi recites the precepts—a process that takes thirteen minutes—he asked three times, "Are you pure in these matters?" A few monks speak up, confessing minor offences, and penalties are assigned. Candana is silent.

In line with the custom at Ghosita's Park, a bhikkhu must acknowledge that an action is an offense before he can be penalized. While Candana has confessed to the action (much to his regret), he doesn't intend to admit that it is an offense. It's a fine line to be sure, but Candana is betting that Harika, whose life is about fine lines, won't be able to cross it.

When first instituting the new aspects of Uposatha, Harika argued that seniors should have authority to penalize any member of the community who committed an infraction, whether he acknowledged it as such or not. But more moderate monks prevailed. The point of confession they insisted is for a monk to recognize his offense and thus willingly submit to penalty; a penalty imposed without acknowledgment of offense would be coercive. Harika had no choice but to concede. He has regretted it ever since.

Candana's stomach churns, his body braces. Here we go. The Venerable Harika speaks up. He is going to ignore fine lines and take another approach.

"Venerable sirs," he begins, "the Venerable Candana is the senior bhikkhu in this center. He of all the bhikkhus needs to be absolutely pure in matters of the Discipline. His actions need to be beyond any shadow of question. Yet…" and he repeats the sequence of events concerning the waterjar and launches into his litany about how the only hope of safeguarding the community in these evil times lies in strengthening observance of the Vinaya.

Everybody is heartily sick of this argument, even his supporters. Moreover his supporters are uneasy about the effort to expel Candana; they're not sure they have the authority, seeing as the Buddha appointed him. But Harika has assured them, and now the repetition of his litany confers credibility on his position. The tendency to believe an oft-repeated lie is a response politicians have exploited throughout time.

"Our very existence is in jeopardy!" His body has become rigid, his eyes blaze with righteousness. "The bhikkhu who leads us must have an impeccable reputation. That has always been the intention of the Blessed One. To fulfill this intention, for the sake of our community and to preserve the precious Dhamma, which we all honor, the Venerable Candana must be expelled!"

Sati wants to vomit. That urge seems to be arising frequently these days. He has seen brutality and mean-spiritedness before, but he has never witnessed such bald malice.

Candana remains silent and immobile. There is nothing more he can do. Musila, who had been gritting his teeth since the start of the proceedings, protests angrily. He feels he is all that stands between unity and schism. It's up to him. Anticipating the thrust of Harika's argument wasn't hard, and the points he needed to make in response were obvious enough—he has rehearsed them well. But self-control and sweet reason are crucial, and he doesn't feel the least bit reasonable.

Struggling to moderate his tone, Musila says, "Venerable sirs! We're all aware of the importance of the Vinaya. No one disputes it. Every one of us wants to protect our community. But we need to look very closely at the implications of what the Venerable Harika is proposing. The Venerable Candana is silent—he doesn't admit that this is an offense, so we aren't in a position to levy a penalty. We'd be committing an offense ourselves if we did. Moreover, we're not of one mind..."

Faltering, he breathes deeply, then continues, "Sirs, since we're not united on this, any action now—even further discussion—wouldn't safeguard the community, it would weaken it. We'd be creating further dissension, setting brother against brother. That's schism. It would harm us and harm the order as a whole. Think carefully about this, friends, think about it."

Some of the monks shift uncomfortably.

"I propose..." he concludes quickly, "I propose that we wait until Bhagava arrives. We can discuss it further and set the matter before him," and he looks around, hoping.

Ah! Just what I've been waiting for! Harika gloats silently. Good job, Musila, perfect timing. He rejoins unctuously, "The Blessed One, the King of Truth, is all wise. We know this. But he is not here. He's at Rajagaha. And in these troubled times, we can't wait for him. We need to, we *must*, take responsibility for our own issues! Now before matters get further out of hand. We can't wait." If he'd been sitting in a chair, Harika would have leaned back contentedly. Almost smiling, he thinks smugly, let them deal with that one!

Harika's comment is shocking. Like all religious teachers of his time, the Buddha is the final arbiter of issues concerning his followers. The budding growth of settled communities of bhikkhus in the Buddha's order is adding new complexity to the relationship, but no one except Harika has thought much about it yet. In effect, Harika is challenging the authority of the Buddha and the very structure on which the order is based! For the moment the bhikkhus are speechless.

Harika pauses, but only for an instant, just enough time throw them off balance but not enough to give them time to think. Now he moves in swiftly for the final thrust. This is war. "Who stands with me on the importance of protecting our community and laying a strong penalty on the Venerable Candana? Show your support with a nod!"

He looks at each of his supporters waiting for assent. Some glance around nervously—they are out of their depth. In the end, they all nod agreement—eight bhikkhus, including the Venerables Uttara and Migajala.

Harika looks at Candana triumphantly and proclaims, "We declare ourselves a separate communion! We dwell in the same residence as you and live within the same boundary, but henceforth we are our own community!"

Things have happened too quickly. Everyone except Harika is stunned. Some of the dissenters look down, unable to meet their brothers' gazes. They thought the issue was expulsion, but—how's this?—they've been sucked into schism. Capitalizing on their confusion, Harika stands and announces sententiously that it is imperative that they leave the hall at once. Obediently, the others scramble to their feet, and he begins shepherding them out like a goose with her goslings.

Too surprised and dismayed to speak, the remaining monks look at each other. Candana feared this might happen but he doesn't want to believe it. He is close to tears. *If only I'd stuck to the truth! If I'd denied the charge, well, maybe it would have ended the same way—my word against his—but at least it would have been true! I've been here too long.* His fourteen months at Ghosita's Park feel like fourteen years. Too many clever solutions, too many times trying to stay a step ahead of Harika, trying to dodge the king's snares.

Finding his voice at last, Candana says, "This is a sad, sad day, friends. Our community is divided. We're the first community in the order to fall into schism. A sad day..." his voice trails off.

"It won't be long now, Bhagava will be here soon. Then things will be set right," Musila offers too brightly.

Candana nods but says nothing.

May 1. It is the beginning of May and another new-moon Uposatha is at hand. The bhikkhus are now divided into two communities, and this means that they need to meet in separate places for Uposatha. The main body of monks continues to meet in the lecture hall, while the dissenters, those favoring expulsion, meet in the dining hall, the only other space large enough to accommodate them.

It isn't only at Uposatha either. The two groups keep themselves apart as much as possible—when meditating, eating, walking on almsrounds, and on more informal occasions. They come together only at the public Dhamma talks. Deciding who would speak on which evening has been a bitter affair, and some of Harika's group are now skipping the talks because they are usually given by Candana or one of the seniors in his group. When the Venerable Harika talks, he invariably expounds on the Vinaya, which puts most people to sleep regardless of faction. Occasionally the Venerable Uttara recites the Dhamma, but several bhikkhus, from both factions, absent themselves and have been doing so for years; Uttara has only superficial understanding and usually sticks to a simple recitation of the Four Noble Truths, the most basic teaching. Every monk in the center can do that, even Sati who has only been there a few months.

Although the split represents the pattern of social interaction that already existed between the more rule-oriented monks and those favoring the Dhamma, the degree of non-communication and the intensity of the acrimony are unprecedented. Torrid heat makes matters worse. In these stifling weeks before the rains when nothing seems to move and it is hard to breathe, everybody is edgy. The generosity of spirit that enabled many bhikkhus to accept friction among them without becoming reactive wears thin. Quarrels and even physical violence arise.

One noontime the Venerables Kottitha and Vappa, from Candana's and Harika's factions respectively, reach the door of the dining hall at the same time and neither will give way. The building is a pavilion like the lecture hall and the bamboo screens are raised, so either one could step sideways and enter at the opening next to the door, but being young monks in their early twenties, they vie for precedence. With their clay alms bowls in their arms, they shout and push. Vappa drops his bowl, and it shatters on a rock at the doorstep, splattering its contents on the ground and on his and Kottitha's robes. They're about to exchange blows when other bhikkhus separate them. If the Buddha hadn't been scheduled to arrive soon, several bhikkhus would have disrobed right there and then. After this, many drift into their own worlds, like grains of sand on the same beach but with little connection.

May 6. A pied-crested cuckoo perches on the branch of a bush near Candana's hut and peers steadily at Candana, who is sitting on the porch in meditation posture. Candana opens one eye and looks up. "You know, don't you?" He asks aloud, opening the other eye. He can't fool the bird. Or himself. This is a charade.

It is too hot to sit inside, and he can't bring himself to sit in the lecture hall where a few monks of his faction still doggedly gather for afternoon meditation. So he opted to sit in the portico, but it hardly makes a difference. Candana feels like a fraud. Did he ever know how to meditate?

Gazing at the slender bird, starkly black and white against the green leaves, Candana gives up all pretense and allows his mind ramble room. The arrival of this bird in the spring is widely regarded as harbinger of the coming monsoon or, rather, it is emblematic of the heart's yearning of a people for the life-giving relief that the rains bring. Will you bring rain? he wonders. Frankly he can't see much prospect for relief either way. Rain or no rain, life looks bleak.

Lately Candana is spending more time alone, avoiding others, performing only necessary duties. He's going to have to explain this to Bhagava. This year, the cuckoo is a harbinger of that too. He'll have to explain his dismal failure, this monastery that's falling to pieces. He wishes the bird hadn't come, and he shuts his eyes to block it out.

He doesn't hear him arrive. "Friend Candana," a voice says softly. Candana opens his eyes again. For a moment, he can't believe it. Is this a hallucination? But no. "Candana," the voice repeats.

Candana sees before him a bhikkhu in his mid-thirties, tall and well-built and smiling warmly. The Venerable Ananda. Although he hasn't yet become the Buddha's attendant—that won't happen for another sixteen years—Ananda is one of the Buddha's closest advisors and his cousin.

Candana's face breaks into a smile too. "Ananda, my friend! You're here?" This is the best thing to have happened in many weeks. Candana stands up and would have hugged the man except physical contact is forbidden. That restriction makes their meeting more poignant; the joy of seeing each other has to be held in the heart, and both are full with it.

"Welcome, welcome, Ananda! Come sit—or do you need to rest and refresh yourself?" When Ananda shakes his head, Candana motions to the two mats on the porch and they sit together, friend by friend. Candana glances up at the shrub. The bird, the harbinger, has flown, having accomplished its mission for the day.

"I can't tell you what a joy it is to see you! I was hoping you'd be coming with Bhagava for Vassa. But so soon! Why so early?"

Now it is Ananda's turn to be surprised. "Why? Because you sent for me, of course!" He looks at Candana and sees that he doesn't understand. "You sent for me and others, but I wanted to get here as soon as possible, so I took a boat at Pataliputta."

Boats regularly ply the waterways between Pataliputta, modern day Patna, on the Ganges, and Kosambi, which is near the confluence of the Ganges and Yamuna. The voyage reduces travel time by days, but monks usually walk because boat travel means that the boat's captain either has to be persuaded to ferry them free since monks don't handle money or that a lay supporter must pay the passage.

Ananda feels his friend's continued befuddlement and adds, smiling, "This is important; so special arrangements were made. The captain will be paid later."

"But I didn't send for you!" Candana exclaims. "I mean I couldn't be happier that you're here, but I didn't send for you."

"Oh?" It's Ananda's turn again. "The Venerable Cunda—he said you want us to come. He arrived in Rajagaha two weeks ago and said the community has fallen into schism—his story doesn't hang together frankly—anyway, he said you're asking for support. Not many of us can come. They'll be elsewhere for Vassa, but four others will be arriving with Bhagava, and I'm here now."

Candana looks at him with conflicting emotions—great gratitude for his friendship and deepening recognition that there has been another sickening turn of events. This was getting worse every day! He puts his hand to his forehead and shakes his head. "No, I didn't send Cunda," he says helplessly. "I knew he was gone of course. He's been gone for a few weeks, but he's part of Harika's faction and, well, I no longer know what's going on with those bhikkhus."

Candana tells him the story, all the details, his assumptions, his mistakes. And he concludes, "I wanted to keep this quiet, contained. I wanted to handle it here. Or mishandle it here," he adds with a tight little laugh. "Spreading the news was the last thing on my mind! It's bad enough that our community is split, that we're in schism. I absolutely didn't, don't, want others to feel they need to take sides—on my behalf." He groans.

Ananda nods and says gently, "I hear, I hear, friend."

"I'm tired, Ananda."

There is no word for depression, but that doesn't stop people from experiencing it. Candana is doubting everything. How could he have let this happen? What could he have done to prevent it? And why, why did he agree to the Buddha's request in the first place? He didn't question his ability to take the senior position at Ghosita's Park—what silly, ill-founded pride! Doubts and questions have been dogging him for weeks, and though his meditation sometimes provides respite, that is happening less frequently these days. And in any case, dismal reality is all too sickeningly present once his meditation is over.

This isn't why he became a monk. He thinks of the Buddha's comment that a householder's life is dusty and filled with suffering. In fact, his life as a householder was a lot less anguished than this miserable situation. Being a wealthy brahmin, Candana held a respected position in Savatthi's society. His wife, to whom he was devoted, had died several years earlier; he has two fine daughters, both of whom are well married and have families of their own. His worldly position was as secure as any could be. He could have peacefully continued his spiritual pursuits as a layperson. But this…this is hell! And now the larger sangha knows all about it. He sighs again.

Candana wonders fleetingly where Cunda is. He hasn't returned to Ghosita's Park yet. Maybe from Rajagaha he's going to Savatthi—

Candana's chest tightens at that thought—oh, no! He sees the scenario: Cunda will tell the bhikkhus who gather for the rains retreat; he'll probably stay there for Vassa, and of course laypeople in town will hear about it. Everybody in his hometown will know about his disgrace! Candana feels he is drowning.

Again, he says, "I'm so tired."

They sit silently for a few moments. The man that Ananda sees before him bears little resemblance to the friend he had said goodbye to fifteen months earlier in Savatthi. Candana's robust physique is now noticeably thinner, his fine face is gaunt, and dark smudges appear under his eyes. Most of all, it's his attitude, the attitude of a defeated man. A tide of compassion washes through Ananda's chest. "You couldn't have done anything else, Candana," he says gently. "This isn't your fault."

Candana looks down.

"Bhagava asked me to tell you that he trusts you completely. And he supports you."

Tears come to Candana's eyes, and he lets them flow without shame. He's been doing a lot of crying lately. "I'm grateful," he says, expressing in words the bow he would have performed had he been in the Buddha's presence. But it doesn't diminish his pain.

He looks up at Ananda and says, "I'm going to disrobe, Ananda. I'm going to leave the order. I'll wait until Bhagava arrives—I won't just walk out, though it probably wouldn't matter if I did. I could leave tomorrow and hardly anybody would notice, except maybe one or two," thinking of Sati. "I can't provide guidance or leadership, and I'm not helping myself by being here. There's no point staying."

CHAPTER 4.

CANDANA'S DEPRESSION

*B*hikkhus in Harika's faction regard Ananda uncomfortably, and Ananda wonders whether they're uncomfortable with him or whether they expect the converse to be true. Probably both, he concludes. Harika is openly antagonistic. His world is divided into for and against these days; nonalignment isn't an option, and there is no question in his mind where Ananda stands. He's right.

Ananda was concerned before he arrived and now, having spoken with Candana, he is deeply troubled. The situation at the monastery is grave for sure, but most of all Ananda is worried about his friend. To see this wise man so ensnared in suffering makes Ananda want to weep. Chords of compassion and caring, always strong in him, now resound around one theme in his heart and mind: Help Candana. It is an assignment from life. And Ananda is certain that this is what Bhagava had in mind when he urged him leave Rajagaha immediately and go to Kosambi. Bhagava knew, Bhagava always knows. Now Ananda commits to the task with all the energy and sensitivity that he would, many years later, devote to service as the Buddha's attendant. Monastery business can wait—rather, helping Candana *is* monastery business; it's the first priority.

There's a time limit, if he's to believe Candana's declaration that he'll disrobe when the Buddha arrives. One month, or a little more. Is it possible to recover in such a short time? Why not? Ananda asks himself. He has faith in the power of the Dhamma, which is the only way he knows to help. Ananda, being modest, doesn't reckon on the power of his caring heart.

He spends a lot of time with Candana, meditating, sitting silently on his porch, walking almsrounds with him. Ananda has to coax him to eat regularly, for the man has gotten out of the habit. When they talk, which is only occasionally, it's mainly about trivial matters and even that is an effort for Candana. Ananda knows intuitively that he mustn't rush things.

He also makes a point of talking with the other bhikkhus, on both sides, ignoring the looks he gets from those in Harika's faction. But none except Harika avoid him completely because they know he's the Buddha's cousin and confidante, and they're afraid to alienate him. Believing that the Buddha has supernatural powers, though they're not sure exactly what they are, they assume some of those powers must have rubbed off on Ananda, like the pollen that bedecks bees on their flowery rounds. It's not smart to oppose the Buddha's power. Ananda doesn't have to follow this line of thinking to know there are a lot of confused people in the monastery.

May 11. One afternoon five days after his arrival when they are sitting on Candana's porch, Ananda says, "You're wrong, you know."

"What?"

"You're wrong that few people will miss you when you leave."

Candana looks at him without interest.

"I've been talking to the bhikkhus and a lot of them will miss you—and not only ones in your faction, by the way."

"You told them I'm disrobing?" Candana asks alarmed. He feels a rising sense of betrayal.

"No. I asked them who is the most important bhikkhu in their lives, whom they respect most. You'd be surprised how many mentioned you. Aside from young Sati who thinks his world would fall apart if you're not in it, there are many, even those on the other side, for whom you're an example. For them you're what a bhikkhu should be, what they're striving to become. They count on you, even in the current mess, maybe *especially* in the current mess."

Candana sighs, that's just the problem—people counting on him and he's let them down. He drops his eyes and gazes at his sitting mat.

"Several in Harika's faction are uncomfortable with the way things are now. They don't like it, but they don't know how to dig out."

There is a pause, then Ananda says, "This isn't about you, Candana. You're taking this personally, but it isn't about you."

"Listen," Candana jerks his head up and snaps at Ananda, "Bhagava sent me here to do a job—to maintain harmony in this center and I've failed. I've failed him utterly. I've failed everybody, and I don't know what to do. Don't say it's not about me. I can't accept that!"

Ananda doesn't respond. They sit in silence for a few moments, then begin meditating.

May 27. Royal Treasurer Ghosita is excited. He has news. Anxious to speak with Candana, he goes at the monastery in the late afternoon, before the public arrives. As the monastery's patron, Ghosita is welcome at any time. He goes straight to Candana's hut, where the two meet frequently. He is a devoted follower and in the Blessed One's absence, Candana is his spiritual guide. In addition to spiritual matters, maintenance is a frequent topic between them: A hole in the guesthouse roof, a shelf in the dining hall needing fixing—nothing is too small. Ghosita takes pride in keeping the matters of his life in good order, and the park is his special treasure. All must be perfect there, especially now, when the Teacher is about to arrive.

Candana is not on his porch. The door is open though, and Ghosita accepts his absence as an invitation to step onto the porch and peek inside. Candana is asleep on his cot, a thin cloth mattress resting on split bamboo lathes supported by wooden legs. Like most monks, Candana naps after the noonday meal when heat and digestion make for drowsiness. However, he usually spends the rest of the afternoon meditating, and that is how Ghosita expected to find him today. But Candana has not been sleeping well at night, and today his efforts at meditation weren't successful; so he did the next best thing and napped again.

Ghosita hesitates just a moment, then knocks on the open door. His news is important. In a well-trained monastic response, Candana sits up instantly as though ready for any contingency. Wearing only his under-robe, he adjusts the belt at his waist and, blinking, says, "Yes, Mr. Minister, how can I help you?"

Standing respectfully on the doorstep, Ghosita performs *anjali*, palm against palm, and apologizes for waking him, "But," he says in a rush, "I have news you need to hear. I'll wait on the porch," tipping his head sideways in the direction of the two mats. Their position inside or out signals the talking place.

Ghosita seats himself in the portico under the small overhang of thatch and waits. After he'd heard a rumor in town about the schism, Ghosita rushed to Candana's hut, angry that he had to learn by hearsay. Candana had planned to send word, but the heavy blanket of depression was settling over him, and he hadn't gotten around to it. At that meeting, Candana apologized to the minister, and the trust that lived between them plus Ghosita's own good nature allayed the anger. On that occasion, as Candana recounted the events at Uposatha, he tried to appear equanimous rather than numb, and the other man, deeply distressed, didn't notice anything unusual. The meeting was short and once Ghosita left, Candana slipped back under the blanket of listlessness.

Since then, Ghosita has been traveling on business and otherwise occupied with business and state matters. An assistant has been acting as liaison with the monastery in his stead. This is his second meeting with Candana since the schism, and now nothing can disguise the change in Candana's appearance. As he emerges into the daylight, Ghosita squints up at his gaunt face, startled. He asks quickly, "Are you well, Venerable?"

Candana replies curtly, "Yes, yes, I'm fine, Ghosita."

Ghosita knows that bhikkhus don't readily discuss personal problems with laypeople, but he's not ready to let this one go. Candana clearly isn't well. Ghosita is prepared to ask three times if necessary, in line with the custom of obtaining a concession (in this case, accurate information about Candana's health) only after a request is made thrice. "I have a very fine physician—a fine medical man. I'd be happy to send him to you if you need treatment," trying a different tack.

In fact, Sirivaddha frequently treats monks at the center at Ghosita's expense, and Candana knows him well.

"You are very kind, Mr. Minister, but it's *not* necessary."

Recognizing there's no getting around the "Mr. Minister," Ghosita bows his head in acknowledgment and refrains from a third try. But he's doubtful. He believes the welfare of the monastery rests on Candana's shoulders and right now they don't look up to the job.

He moves on. "There's news. In counsel yesterday, the king and Bharadvaja talked about the schism. It's the first time I've heard them speak so openly about the monastery—quite a change from their usual code words and sly smiles. And they were laughing—if you can imagine Bharadvaja laughing!"

Candana can't, but he's silent. Frequently enough, his discussions with Ghosita move into politics. Ghosita regularly recounts Udena's latest comments, which typically contain little content but much attitude; and he also discusses his suspicions about Bharadvaja. Vague as the information is, Candana considers it crucial to his mission. Strictly, however, he shouldn't be discussing politics with anyone, much less with a layperson. The Buddha teaches that politics and a host of other subjects distract bhikkhus' attention from spiritual training; the mind, fascinated with ever-changing events, gets caught in reacting in favor or against, and simple awareness of the present moment is forgotten. For these reasons, the Buddha regards talking about politics as unwise speech and an unwise use of attention.

Cananda thinks fleetingly of Harika. He should hear what we're talking about now! If he's counting the waterjar as an offense, what would he say about this? Allowing himself a small flash of dark humor, he envisions Harika's outrage and smirks. Candana is sure of his ground here.

When the Buddha, who is ever practical in outlook, sent him to Kosambi with the mandate to maintain harmony, he warned, "You're going to have to get involved in politics, internally and externally." Candana didn't know what "internally and externally" meant, but he has found out.

Ghosita continues, "I'd say they were taking personal pride in the schism, like they'd created it. The king gloated and said he'd be surprised if the center lasts another year." He grimaces. "I'm sure they were speaking for my benefit—and yours too, Venerable. I've said before that Bharadvaja is the king's man, that he's working to destroy the monastery. This confirms it."

"And there's more," he runs on a little breathlessly. "Today I talked with Bhadda Kukkuta." Candana is well acquainted with the man. Also a wealthy banker, Kukkuta is Ghosita's friend, and he donated his park outside of Kosambi to the Buddha at the same time Ghosita did. It is smaller than Ghosita's, but Kukkuta is as devout as Ghosita.

"His wife Vijaya—you know her, don't you?" Candana nods. "Well, she told Kukkuta that she's seen the Venerable Harika entering Gopaka Phagguna's house on almsrounds two times in the past ten days. We live in the same quarter, you know." Candana nods again. Ghosita's house on Commerce Street faces Phagguna's in the wealthiest section of town, the quarter where Kosambi's millionaire merchants reside.

"She called him 'the bhikkhu with the orange eyes.'" Kukkuta and Vijaya frequently attend public talks at Ghosita's Park. They heard Harika speak once or twice, enough to notice his unusual eyes and to know that they weren't interested in attending any more of his talks.

"She said he arrives at Phagguna's alone, goes inside, and stays a while. Of course, maybe the venerable been invited in to give teaching to the household, but we all know that Phagguna and his family are hardly the Blessed One's followers. Last year he funded one of the biggest sacrifices in town—thousands of animals were slaughtered. You remember?"

Another nod and an imperceptible shudder.

"Bharadvaja officiated. I know for a fact that Phagguna compensated him very handsomely for his ministrations."

Now Ghosita's voice rises as he announces portentously, "And here's the last link." He pauses, relishing the moment. "Vijaya says that each time the venerable was there so was Bharadvaja! They arrived at about the same time and left at the same time. Vijaya is *quite* observant. The last time was three days ago."

Both men envision her standing behind the latticework of an upper story balcony avidly watching the comings and goings below. Whatever their views about the ways that wealthy, underemployed women spend their time, they're grateful to Vijaya.

"So the question is what's Harika doing in that house?" Ghosita's anger gets the better of his deference; he drops the "venerable," and his hands, palms upward with fingers spread, shake as they underscore the pertinence of the point. Ghosita stops and waits for Candana's response to this cartload.

At last! Out of the shadows at last. Candana feels a dark weight lifting. The schism *isn't* entirely due to his ineptness. He says, "We've *finally* got something concrete to work with! Bless Vijaya and her observant eyes; they've gained great merit on this one!" He smiles; it's his first smile in over a month, not counting his welcome to Ananda.

It's clear to them now that being a fine role model, reassuring bhikkhus and townspeople, and giving inspiring Dhamma talks—all of which Candana has been doing admirably—aren't enough. This is about Udena, and they are all too aware they don't have his support. Which is why the Buddha is coming to Kosambi for Vassa. That's been the plan all along: The three-month retreat should give him ample time to connect with the king. Now however they appreciate just how tough the project is going to be. The Buddha has gained the adherence of Kings Bimbisara and Pasenadi, who rule the largest kingdoms in the region, but gaining Udena's, well, that's another story.

Having been mired in darkness for so long, Candana's mind now switches energetically into action mode, and he says confidently, "Bhagava needs to talk with the king—soon. Meanwhile, Ghosita, it would help to get at the roots of his opposition. Why is he so opposed? That's a critical piece of information. Do you think you can find out?" He doesn't need to say more. Both men are so in accord on this matter they practically read each other's minds.

In a far different mood from the outset of their meeting, Candana asks, "You're going to the talk tonight? The Venerable Ananda will be speaking. There should be quite a crowd."

Ghosita nods, and smiling, he takes this as an appropriate moment to leave. It's been quite a day. He is anxious to walk and relax in the peacefulness of the grounds. As he rises, Ghosita salutes Candana and, departing, says, "Please let me know if I can send my physician, Venerable. Any time." The third try.

Candana offers a head bobble and a slight smile.

May 28. As soon as he can, Candana tells Ananda. Restraint is built right into the fabric of the monastic routine. He couldn't speak that evening because Ananda was giving the public talk and afterwards was too late. So the next morning, before they set off on almsround together, Candana mentions that he has news, he'll share it after lunch. His voice hints at his excitement. Talking is frowned on during almsrounds and, though it's permitted over lunch, both prefer eating in silence. Finally, after lunch, which they eat on Candana's porch because it's too hot to be indoors, they talk. Neither is in the mood for a nap.

Important as the news is, Ananda is more interested in his friend. He feels the shift and is immensely relieved. The old Candana isn't lost; he's not all back yet, but he's on his way.

"Friend," he says gently after they discuss the news, "you've been stuck. You got caught in aversion to very unpleasant, deeply distressing events. You identified with them, assumed responsibility for them, and so you were pulled into the whole morass. In effect, you allowed yourself to be born into a sense of failure, and you ended up suffering terribly."

This is the Buddha's teaching on dependent origination, how living from the illusion of a separate self triggers an experiential process, which he analyzes into twelve sequential steps. The process invariably lead to misery. To help listeners remember, the Buddha has devised standard formulations for key teachings, including dependent origination, and he repeats the same words each time he teaches.

Ananda and other bhikkhus use the same formulas when giving formal talks, but now, because Ananda is speaking informally to his friend, he uses his own words.

"Over and over during these past couple of months, you created suffering for yourself, you've unleashed it by letting yourself be sucked into a sense of responsibility and failure."

Candana is finally ready to hear. Every word Ananda says resonates. He knows these truths too, but he forgot them under the pressure of events. Like a ferry that has taken on too many passengers, he has been sinking.

Ananda continues, "Bhagava sent you here with a mission, yes, but you have a bigger mission—to wake up. You've been letting your worldly mission overwhelm the spiritual one. All the schisms in the world, all the political intrigues, don't outweigh a single person's waking up. They're of two totally different orders."

Candana is silent and, looking at him hard, says, "You're ruthless, Ananda." Then he smiles, big and open. The old Candana smile is back. "And you're right."

Ananda replies seriously, "No, it's not me. It's the medicine of the Dhamma."

Candana remembers Ghosita offering his physician's aid, and he reflects, That was the wrong kind of medicine. This is the medicine I need.

"It's not about you, you know," Ananda observes, repeating what he said a couple of weeks ago, words Candana rejected. "There's nothing personal in it, just an impersonal process unfolding."

"Moreover I'll say *ruthlessly*"—emphasizing the word Candana just used; he smiles—"you're *still* stuck. You still think it's about you. Events have turned; the political developments are bad news, but in terms of you personally, they're favorable: Once the facts are known, nobody will be able to blame you. You can't even reasonably blame yourself. Right? So now you're relieved and can hold things more lightly."

He doesn't give Candana a chance to respond. "Even that is the notion of a self—a "you" who's investing in conditions as though they're ultimately significant. More illusion. The whole point—you know it as well as I do—is to not invest in *any* conditions, favorable, unfavorable, whatever; to live them as needed, with all compassion and clarity, and not to get stuck in them. You forgot that, Candana. So I'm reminding you." Then he adds, "And I expect you to do the same for me someday."

And he means it about doing the same for him. Neither man is fully enlightened yet. Both experience times of forgetting, when the grip of events is so convincing, when it so obstructs their view, that what they deeply know becomes as distant as the Himalayas. Then they tumble into misery. Those are times when reminding each other is a profound act of friendship.

Candana is abashed. Has he been so obvious? Has he been so deluded? He knows the answer—the uncomfortable answer—and he is aware of a rising sense of disappointment. He expects more of himself! He should do better than this. Then—an instant—he sees: Here it is again! A self is happening, a prideful self that thinks it should be better, that thinks it shouldn't fall flat on its face. But regardless of the position his self thinks it should maintain, he *has* been flat on his face—and now, sliding beyond the conventional perspective, Candana knows it doesn't matter. The switch happens. He laughs. It's a laugh that embraces the whole impossible paradox of being human.

Ananda looks at him questioningly, and Candana explains. And they both laugh, Candana uproariously.

CHAPTER 5

THE BUDDHA'S ARRIVAL IN KOSAMBI

June 10. She stands with her hands to her mouth, open-mouthed and wide-eyed with uncertainty. The scrawny six-year old, her hair a stranger to a comb, is dressed in a red cotton lower garment tied at the waist. It is tattered but as clean as a skirt can be when it is worn by an active child on the streets in the dust and swelter of high summer. She observes the man on the ground, while her brother and his friend, both a couple of years older than she, dart forward and back, poking him, squealing with delight, then retreating. She is sure this isn't a good idea but looks on silently. Each step kicks up dust from the parched ground, which hangs in the air momentarily, then settles on the prone form, covering him with fine gray powder. The children have seen men drunk before and once in a while even a woman, but they've never seen a monk in orange robes laid out flat like this.

"We should tell Mama!" she urges. But the boys ignore her.

She is afraid. Her family puts food into the bowls of the orange-robed ones when they sometimes come by in the mornings on alms-rounds; she knows it's a blessing to give. The people in her quarter are poor and have little to spare, but they do it gladly. The girl and her siblings have been taught to respect the bhikkhus, but she wonders how they can be a blessing when this man is no better than her father. Worse even, because she's never seen her father dead drunk like this. She doesn't know what to make of it.

The bhikkhu Sagata didn't notice anything strange on his alms-round today when people at several houses were liberal with wine offerings but niggardly with food. He likes his wine and happily accepted, and since he knew he couldn't hold the wine without food in his belly, he ate on the sly, gobbling the scant bits in his bowl, his gaze darting from side to side to make sure no one was noticing. His judgment fuzzed anyway, and as he stumbled down the street from one

grand house to the next, people laughed, or were saddened, depending on their connection with the Buddha's order.

Now the children stand nervously outside Kosambi's east gate
at noon on this the tenth day of June, the cusp of the monsoon season. The sky has been ominously empty for days and people are edgy:
Will the rains come at all this year? Right now, though, the children's
attention is fixed fully on the hippopotamus of a man who lies before them, unlovely in the glare. He is insensible of them. Flies zigzag
around the regurgitated liquid and food on his robe, and he stinks.

The girl notices that her brother and his friend have stopped
their game and are staring over her shoulder. She turns to look.
Approaching is another orange-robed one, a shaven-headed man
and, behind him in the flat distance and walking in their direction, is
a small group of them, four in all. They look like a formidable group
and they are coming straight at them. Will they be angry? Maybe they
saw the boys kicking the drunk one. If monks bless, can they curse
too? Frightened, the children scamper off.

A little behind schedule, the Buddha is arriving in Kosambi.
He and four senior monks have walked five weeks from Rajagaha
where he's been teaching. Though he has visited Kosambi several
times, he hasn't spent Vassa here. He wanted to be sure the time was
right before he did. He knows that King Udena is hostile. Which is
partly why last year he spent Vassa with the Bhaggu people on tribal
land some forty miles northwest of Kosambi. Bhaggu territory was
an ideal spot to gain second-hand information, close enough to learn
much about the irascible king's rule, without having to commit to a
three-month stay in town before he was ready.

He's not ready now either, but this visit, long planned, has
become urgent. Candana's few messages, carried verbally by trusted
itinerant bhikkhus, have indicated that morale in the community
and the king's hostility are rapidly moving in opposite directions.
And the Venerable Cunda's recent appearance in Rajagaha with his
story about schism was deeply alarming. The Buddha hopes he can
restore harmony and gain the king's adherence, or at least reduce
his opposition.

These are the Buddha's hopes and plans as he draws near Kosambi. He is not prepared for the sight that greets him now. He sends the Venerable Kamabhu on ahead of the group, for in this level landscape significantly denuded of trees, the figure lying outside the city gate is visible from afar, and the color of his garments leaves no doubt about who is on the ground. "Hurry, Kamabhu, see if you can help the bhikkhu."

As Kamabhu approaches the body the problem is evident. He thinks, In some places, the whole town turns out to greet us, but here, what do we get? A drunk monk. Welcome to Kosambi!

By the time the Buddha and his group reach the gate, several people from the suburbs have gathered. Kamabhu turns to the Buddha and quietly states the obvious. "Drunk, sir. He's drunk." The Venerable Upavana, the Buddha's attendant, who is standing behind his master, notices that his shoulders stiffen slightly.

The Buddha is a strikingly handsome man, in his early forties, tall, lean, with skin of a golden hue; his features are regular and his presence, both serene and commanding. "Does anybody know who this bhikkhu is?" he asks quietly. No one does.

The Buddha looks at Sagata's inert body and says softly, "We need to carry him to the monastery." The Venerables Kamabhu and Narada, both strong men, lift the body and groan under the weight. They try not to show revulsion, for in the stifling heat, the odor is almost overpowering. Sagata's fleshiness is a mystery and a joke among the residents of Ghosita's Park. How does he do it living on almsfood? For the two bhikkhus carrying him now though, it is no joke; they continue to grunt with exertion.

The bhikkhus make their way through the gate carrying their inert brother and head toward the monastery. The monastery entrance is only a few blocks from the east gate, but it seems miles. Though the monks are silent as they travel through the streets, the townspeople aren't. Muffled guffaws and whispered comments follow the procession, while a few devotees stand by dispirited. Disappointment overwhelms their awe at the Buddha's presence; they've seen him before, but they've never observed such a miserable showing on the part of any of his bhikkhus.

The resident monks at Ghosita's Park have returned from the almsrounds and are on hand to greet the sweaty, dusty travelers as they enter the gate with their unexpected burden. All are dismayed, except Harika who is silent and unnoticed. Two immediately step forward to relieve the travelers of their burden.

The Venerable Candana salutes the Buddha with a bow, palms joined in anjali; his face is illuminated with a joyous smile that neither the sorry issue at hand nor his personal troubles, now much transformed, can dim. "Bhagava," he says simply and his tone conveys the wordless depths of his love. The two exchange a few comments. Candana turns to the other newcomers, bhikkhus he has trained with, and he briefly welcomes them. He has missed these brothers. As prearranged, the Venerable Uttara steps forth and greets the Buddha, effusively. A welcome from each faction.

Standing among the gathering of bhikkhus, Sati watches the proceedings. He's not surprised to see Sagata in this condition. It's not the first time. He looks curiously at the Buddha, excited to see him in person finally. But mostly he watches Candana, and he is happy. Overjoyed really. Candana is back. Simply to see his gladness as he greets the Buddha makes Sati smile.

During the dismal weeks of Candana's depression, Sati was frantic. He felt like an abandoned child plunked down in a forest and unable to find his way home. He tried to talk with Candana twice during those weeks, going to his hut early in the evening with meditation questions. It was a ruse. He wanted connect any way possible. He couldn't plead "don't leave me"—for Sati sensed Candana's intention, and even though his mentor was bodily present at the moment, he seemed to have already left. Asking questions about meditation was the most creditable way Sati knew of to reach his beloved mentor. He wouldn't have cared if Candana had addressed him with his chilliest "friend." He would have settled for that. But Candana hardly addressed him at all. He just said, "I can't talk now" and turned away. It was unbearable.

Nor could Sati confide in anyone, not even Musila. Each of the residents was dealing with his own version of misery. So when

Ananda came to him several weeks ago asking him which bhikkhu he respected most, he poured out his fears. During that conversation, Sati conceived a trust and respect for Ananda that would last a lifetime, and in later years it would bloom into friendship.

Now, as Candana and Uttara exchange welcomes with their teacher, the two resident volunteers strain visibly under their load and try to retain the contents of their stomachs. They anxiously wait for the formalities to end. The Venerable Musila, who holds Sagata's shoulders, thinks, If this lasts much longer, I'm going to puke right here. He's assessing the direction of a tentative breeze that has just sprung up to determine the upwind position. Maybe the wind will provide relief from the smell. Relief comes instead when Candana, sensible of their predicament, instructs the bearers to carry Sagata to his hut. "Clean him up and get him into a fresh robe." They need no encouragement.

Musila is a tall man in his late thirties, and, being from a military family, he has trained in warfare, though he did more farming than fighting. Now though, he has to will his muscles to rise to this challenge, for in the past six years he has carried little more than an alms bowl. As they head off toward their destination, Musila notices gratefully that by being at Sagata's head, he is upwind. Yes! Poor Kottitha. He casts a compassionate thought toward his young companion, but doesn't want to change places. He wonders how the two venerables managed to carry Sagata all the way from the city gate.

Other bhikkhus show the newcomers to their quarters, the modest guesthouse where the Venerable Ananda is already lodged. Two of them have stayed here before. Although the center is small in comparison to the Bamboo Grove in Rajagaha from which they have just come, Ghosita has been generous with accommodations. Visiting bhikkhus don't have to bivouac in makeshift shelters of leaves and branches as in some centers in these early days in the Buddha's career. The guesthouse is a wooden building, five adjoined rooms side by side, each with its own door and a window in the opposite wall. Hot enough inside, but well-protected from sun and rain. The modular structure would become the prototype a few centuries later for residents' cells built from stone.

Now the newcomers are grateful to settle in and count their accommodations comfortable. The Venerables Candana and Uttara accompany the Blessed One to his hut, a structure slightly larger than those of the residents. It is specially built and is reserved for him any time he visits.

As they walk, the Buddha comments, "We've certainly had a memorable welcome to Kosambi."

Candana smiles wryly, "Kosambi is an exceptional place, sir."

"I believe that."

Nothing stirs in the white heat of the afternoon, not a bird or an insect or a frog on the riverbank, nothing except Candana's fingers. They're busy mending the hem of his outer robe. He noticed the rip this morning on almsround and, in keeping with the practice of not letting the sun set on a torn garment, he's sewing, using the needle and thread that are standard items in the scant inventory of a monk's possessions. He's glad for the task. Later, one of the newly arrived monks will summon him for a talk with his teacher, and he's nervous. He wants to keep himself occupied. He has waited so long, for months really, and now on the verge of the moment, he's dreading the possibility that the Buddha will criticize him for his failure, projecting onto his teacher the self-judgment that has so debilitated him recently.

An angry voice interrupts the silence. He sighs, What now? No monk shouts like this—with one exception—and no layperson comes at this unseemly time when the heat is scorching, unless there's an emergency.

"No, I would *not* like to come back later! I'm going to talk about this now!" Even before he reaches the porch where Candana is seated, the newcomer has transferred his indignation from the young monk who escorted him and has been trying to calm him to the older one. The man, stout and red-faced with his effort, is shaking his fist and shouting from the path as he approaches Candana.

"What kind of ascetics are you? Getting drunk, assaulting people! This isn't the holy life—or does the recluse Gotama have some new idea about what's holy? It's outrageous!" Ignoring protocol, he now stands before Candana, his face contorted in righteous anger, his right fist getting a workout. Bows and courteous preliminaries aren't going to be part of this encounter.

Candana doesn't recognize the man, but his dress indicates wealth and his belligerence, a sense of high self-importance. "Why don't you sit down," Candana suggests mildly, pointing to the other sitting mat, "and tell me what the problem is?" He carefully secures the needle in the cloth and sets the robe beside him on the rush mat that forms the porch flooring.

"The problem, recluse," the man says, still standing, "is that one of your group attacked my servant this morning. He punched him in the face, gave him a black eye. Is that how you behave around here?"

Now he sits, and hurries on. "He came to my house, begging of course. I'm no follower of your ascetic Gotama, but I'm a learned man, a good man, and an important member of the community, and we gave him food and drink—very generously I'll tell you that. I'm generous at my house. But was he content? No! He wanted more. He shouted at my servant, pushed and then hit him, demanding more wine. It's disgraceful!"

Candana, wishing he were any place but here, says, "I'm sorry, very, very sorry to hear this, Mister...?"

"Bhadrakka. Bhadrakka the banker—you've probably heard of me."

He has. It's Candana's business to be informed about influential people in town, and Ghosita is a superb source of information. Candana knows, too, that Bhadrakka has a reputation for being unscrupulous. "I'm sorry Mr. Bhadrakka."

"Sorry doesn't help my servant. It doesn't help me. I want that pathetic excuse of a monk punished! I want him handed over to the authorities. Let them deal with him, the criminal! We're a law-abiding town; we don't tolerate criminals here."

Candana is alarmed. "Mr. Bhadrakka, the monk…"

"What's his name anyway?"

"Bhikkhu Sagata." The familiar blanket of depression threatens to rise up again—Candana feels its seduction, inviting him to slip under and away. It would be so easy… If only he could go and meditate at the foot of a tree like a simple monk. But he breathes deeply and steps into his responsibilities, as he has been doing lately.

He explains, "Bhikkhu Sagata will be punished according to his actions, but I think you know that religious orders aren't subject to worldly jurisdiction. If a bhikkhu violates a worldly law, we deal with him, not the civil authorities—you do understand that, don't you?"

Bhadrakka nods grudgingly.

"I can assure you that this kind of thing has not happened before, and it's important to us that it not happen again. This bhikkhu will be dealt with by us, quite appropriately, you can be sure of it."

This seems to mollify Bhadrakka who says more quietly, "I want the recluse Gotama to hear about this. I want him to know just what his so-called religious people are up to."

"Oh, he'll know, all right. If he hasn't heard it from you already," referring to Bhadrakka's clamor, "he'll hear it from me soon. He arrived at mid-day today." He's sure Bhadrakka already knows this. "And I'll be telling him myself."

Then trying to end the conversation, he says soothingly, "If there's anything we can do for your servant, send a physician to him, send him blessings…"

"My servant doesn't need your physicians or your blessings!" Bhadrakka erupts again. "I take care of my servants very well without your blessings! There's nothing you can do for me or my household, monk. Just take care of your own—they need it. And he'd better not come back to my house!" With that conclusion, Bhadrakka rises heavily and stalks away.

Candana, glad to be rid of him, watches his departing back thoughtfully. He is concerned of course, but why is he also puzzled? Something doesn't fit. He knows Sagata can be violent when drunk— it has happened at the monastery—and he was certainly drunk this morning. But a feeling, one that's been gnawing at him all afternoon, is stronger now: The whole situation is so neat—or so messy. It doesn't feel entirely true.

The summons has come. So, with his outer robe only partly mended but suitably arranged over his left shoulder, Candana approaches the porch of the Buddha's hut, bows and takes the seat offered. Dispensing with pleasantries, the Buddha asks, "How are you, Candana?"

Candana nods, more to indicate that he has heard the question than to supply an answer.

The Buddha doesn't ask details. In fact, he already knows because Ananda has briefed him. He looks into Candana's eyes with deep concern and says, "Ananda told me about the waterjar incident and how it arose. You've been doing a fine job, under very difficult circumstances—very difficult. I want you to know that I appreciate your hard choices and your efforts, Candana."

He pauses, giving Candana time to receive the support. "I want you to remain in charge of Vassa arrangements. In fact I want you to remain in charge of the monastery, as you've been doing. Tomorrow I'll announce this to the community—or the communities, as the case may be. I want everyone to be very clear about your role."

The Buddha doesn't often use the first person singular, because he doesn't identify with an "I"; he's devoid of a sense of self, but now he intentionally repeats the word. It's a personal touch and he wants to reassure Candana.

"To remain in charge even though I'm creating schism?" Candana asks doubtfully.

"Even though you're *the occasion* for schism," the Buddha repeats with a slight adjustment. "It's an exceptional situation. You said so yourself, Kosambi is an exceptional place."

He isn't blaming me and he cares! For a moment Candana feels utterly disarmed, and—a shooting star—intense relief blazes in his chest. When he thought about it clearly, Candana couldn't imagine the Buddha holding him responsible, but the emotional chaos that engulfed him made the notion convincing. But now he *is* all right!

"Well, no doubt the bhikkhus will accept your directive, Bhagava," there's a slight lilt to his voice, "but some will do it very grudgingly! And of course that won't solve the schism issue; in fact it will make it worse."

"Probably," he nods. "But their acceptance is the important part; we'll work on begrudgment and schism later." Then with a small smile he says, "So now, Candana, tell me what's going on."

Ah! Candana draws a long breath, exhales, and begins. He spoke with Sagata after Bhadrakka had left—there was just enough time to talk with him before Upavana summoned him to this meeting. Though badly hung over, Sagata was coherent enough to relate his story, the gist of which Candana now tells the Buddha: how Sagata was given palm wine at several houses consecutively, how he passed out at one of them—he thinks it was Bhadrakka's and doesn't remember anything until he woke up on his cot. He denies hitting Bhadrakka's servant. Candana also relates his own later encounter with the banker. "There's more to this than a drunk and foolish monk, Bhagava. Too many coincidences—it's got to be part of the king's plan."

Candana tries to gauge the Buddha's response but sees only transparency and attentiveness. He doesn't seem to be analyzing the situation or thinking about how to respond; he's just listening. Candana has observed this many times in the Blessed One, and always it's a teaching. Even now, in the midst of this crisis, he's empty, allowing thoughts to flow from stillness.

Receiving the Buddha's silence as an invitation, he continues with his speculation. "What are the chances that he'd stumble at the city gate in his stupor—*outside* the gate, mind you, which wasn't on his route—and pass out next to the road just in time for your arrival? No, someone with a very precise sense of timing managed this. I've got some ideas about who and how, but in any case, I think Sagata was your welcome message from the king."

"And why did he walk alone in the first place?" Candana continues, speculatively. "He usually walks with a brother. I asked him. He says the Venerable Harika suggested that they walk together, which is interesting because Sagata isn't in Harika's faction. Anyway, he waited for Harika this morning, but he came late and said he was ill and told Sagata to go on without him. Everyone else had left, so he walked alone. And—more interesting—Harika told him to visit those houses, said the residents were expecting them and had special almsfood and drink." Then Candana adds archly, "Sagata has never been one to refuse drink," and, imagining him noisily draining a bowl, wine dribbling from his chins, Candana grimaces.

The Buddha raises his eyebrows, and Candana remembers, Oh right! I forget he gets into people's minds. There's not much loving-kindness in mine right now. And he sends a thought-apology to his teacher: I'm sorry. I'll try to do better. The Buddha smiles slightly.

He continues from another angle, "The Venerable Harika seems to be present whenever things go awry. You know about the waterjar, and now Ghosita told me something that puts an end to guessing." And he relates the big one—Ghosita's news.

"And there's something else, sir: I didn't ask the Venerable Cunda to go to Rajagaha or any place else to tell the brothers about the schism. When Ananda told me he'd been there, I was surprised—dismayed, in fact. If I'd wanted to create schism, that's what I would have done, I'd have pulled other parts of the order into our community's troubles, obliged bhikkhus to take sides. Uuumph!" he grunts.

The Buddha nods. "I wondered about that."

Did he? Candana questions. If he followed my thoughts about Sagata, why not on this matter too? How much of this conversation is necessary? Or any conversation? But he decides not to get tripped up in that impossible conundrum.

The Buddha interrupts his thoughts and asks about Sagata.

"Well, sir, Bhikkhu Sagata had a problem with drink before he went forth and not much has changed since. He can't drink here like he used to, but when he does, he has no restraint. He's been drunk in the monastery, but I think it's the first time he's been drunk in town.

Someone knew exactly who they were targeting with their alms wine. When sober, he's kind enough, though he's undisciplined. He told me that his family was relieved when he went forth—I can understand that. He's the younger son of a wealthy merchant family, indulged all his life and was frequently into trouble. He said ordaining was his only hope; otherwise, he'd end up a wreck. So he's using monastic life to shape up."

"Isn't everybody here doing the same thing one way or another? Isn't that what the holy life is about—shaping up, getting rid of hindrances, eliminating suffering?" the Buddha asked.

Candana grins, appreciating how the Teacher can see spiritual principle at the heart of even unsavory matters.

He goes on, "Unfortunately, Sagata has a bad temper. When he's drunk, he can be violent. Maybe he did strike the servant. Or maybe not. Very possibly, it's a fabrication, part of the bigger plot.

"Yes, maybe," the Buddha sighs, "but, either way, it's clear that a new training rule is needed." The rules guiding the holy life in the order are established incrementally, in response to situations as they arise, and the Buddha is the sole legislator. No one questions this, except Harika.

"From now on bhikkhus are not to drink fermented beverages. As long as they drank in moderation, it could be allowed, even though liquor impairs mindfulness. But if we don't address this monk's lack of restraint now, we'd have to do it later. If it's not him, it would be someone else."

Candana is definitely sorry to hear it but not surprised. It's a pity how one immature bhikkhu can spoil it for the rest of us, he thinks. But Bhagava is right: There would be others. And he nods.

"Candana, I want you to meet with this bhikkhu tomorrow. He's jeopardizing our position in this town, and it's already precarious enough. This can't be allowed to continue. By tomorrow, he'll have had time to think about what happened. Find out all you can. And I'll have the Venerable Upavana announce the training rule tomorrow evening before my talk; everyone will know the reason for it of course. Tell Bhikkhu Sagata to be present. He needs to bear the consequences of his actions. The new rule will be hard on him—maybe not doable—but the shame will be harder."

The Buddha goes on, "Have someone work with him on the drinking problem—or you can do it yourself. Let's see if we can help him overcome it. If not—we'll go slowly—but if he continues, he'll have to be expelled. You can warn him tomorrow."

Candana nods but knows this isn't going to be easy. Sagata doesn't have much of a monastic future, Candana is pretty sure of that, though he can't know just how short it's going to be.

Then the Buddha adds, "Oh, and make sure someone accompanies him on his almsrounds from now on. No more solo rounds. And never again to banker Bhadrakka's house."

Candana smiles; the Blessed One is thorough. He thinks of Sati—that's who he'll ask. The two get along well when Sagata is sober. When drunk, Sagata doesn't get along with anybody. Sati has a pleasing manner with people, and Sagata takes an avuncular interest in him. Hopefully Sati will be able to keep him away from wine if it's offered and remind him to avoid the banker's house. If anybody can manage it, Sati will, and he'll do it in ways that Sagata might accept without resentment.

The Buddha sighs and raises a hand. "Now, Candana," the Buddha says, "enough. It's been a long day."

It has indeed. Candana realizes he's exhausted—he hasn't noticed before. And he can imagine how the Blessed One must be feeling, having traveled for weeks. Or maybe I can't imagine, he second-guesses himself. With his spiritual powers, who's to say whether he's exhausted or not?

"I'm exhausted," the Buddha comments, and he laughs. It is a jovial laugh from the depths of his chest, and his shoulders shake. It is the most welcome sound Candana has heard on this landmark day.

Candana smiles. How do you explain the adventure of conversing with someone who seems to read your mind? With his step lighter than on the way over, Candana returns to his hut to finish his mending while there's still daylight.

CHAPTER 6.

A KILLING IN THE MONASTERY AND OTHER VIOLENCE

June 11. Sati is late getting to the lecture hall. It isn't because he has so much to do but because clouds glow pink in the long, low rays of the setting sun, and the simsapa grove is quiet and inviting. The air remains stifling, and growing humidity adds to his discomfort, but at least the air is clean. And the gathering clouds promise that relief is on its way—the monsoon is coming—though not tonight. Despite the fact that the lecture hall is a pavilion, when it is filled, as it soon will be—sweaty itchy bodies bearing every kind of rash imaginable— the air inside becomes acrid with perspiration. No, Sati is not in a hurry.

Once Sati learned the word, not too long ago, he decided that one of his *sankharas*, karmic knots, is arriving on time. He knows that community life depends on bhikkhus showing up when expected, but it's hard—so many things invite his attention along the way. Especially this evening. By the time he arrives at the hall, townsfolk are already seated on the mud-brick floor in the back two-thirds and along the perimeter, and they block the way to the circle of monks at the front, who are waiting quietly on their meditation rugs around the Buddha's still empty seat.

News spread quickly in town yesterday that the Blessed One had arrived and would speak on this, his second night; he was too weary to talk the night of his arrival. No one expected him to, but when King Udena heard the news, he smirked. "I'll bet he's weary! May his rest be long!"

Everyone knows about Sagata's drama too, which is another reason, truth be told, why some are present. In lives devoid of much diversion, a drunk monk is a juicy topic, and tonight's event is filled with promise. How will the recluse Gotama respond?

The colorful crowd looks like an extravagant blossom—townsmen in white, women in colors, bright petals encircling the orange-clad monks. The latter include not only those of Ghosita's Park but also monks from the two smaller monasteries nearby. They are prepared to wade through monsoon floods if necessary to be with their teacher. Scattered among the crowd are wandering ascetics who have settled in Kosambi for the coming rains. They wear rags and their hair is matted; their faces and bodies are embellished with *kol* and fragrant sandalwood pastes, reds and yellows, whites and blacks to protect them from the heat. People who can't find space inside the wooden structure sit, fallen petals, on the ground outside, separated from the rest only by the low brick ledge that runs around the bottom perimeter to keep ground water out when it rains.

A raised dais is centered at the end of the hall opposite the doors. These serve little purpose when the partitions are raised as they are now, because people don't hesitate to step over the ledge to enter. The Buddha's meditation mat is on the dais so that his head is elevated above the rest—it's disrespectful for your head to be higher than the Teacher's.

His attendant, the Venerable Upavana, also sits up front on a mat on the left side of the Buddha. Candana, as the senior in the monastery, ordinarily would sit on the Buddha's right, but because of the legal controversy, he sits up front but at a distance from the Buddha; that way, his position isn't quite definable.

As promised, the Buddha announced his support for Candana today. He called the monks together for a special meeting after the noon meal and, while gracefully acknowledging the existence of differences in the community—he refrained from using the word "schism"—and without taking sides, he stated that the Venerable Candana would continue to serve as the senior bhikkhu on matters relating to the monastery as a whole and would oversee arrangements for Vassa. He noted that Candana had managed rains retreats at the Bamboo Grove when he, the Buddha, was in residence; no other bhikkhu at Ghosita's Park has such experience. Harika acknowledges the truth of this grudgingly. The Venerable Uttara on the other hand is jealous; he hoped the controversy would mean that he'd be reinstated as the senior-most monk and would be in charge of Vassa. He desperately wants the Buddha's attention and approval.

Sati arrives and hesitates on the outskirts of the crowd. A layman kindly offers to clear the way so he can join the other monks, but just then the Buddha enters, and Sati declines. Right away Sati is sure it's a mistake and begins to redden. A monk shouldn't be sitting among laypeople. He argues the alternative to himself: It would be worse to create disruption while the Buddha is coming in and everybody is looking. So here it is, he thinks—the consequence of my karmic knot; it sure didn't waste any time happening.

The Buddha's entry brings the townspeople to silence. The bhikkhus are already silent. Many of them are trying to meditate, though in this hot, fidgety crowd, achieving meditation practically requires the concentrative powers of an arahant, the highest level of spiritual attainment, and few of those assembled yet qualify. So they just sit silently.

Upavana clears his throat; then he makes the announcement. "Bhagava is issuing a new training rule." Disciplinary rules are usually private monastic matters, but there are obvious advantages to letting townspeople know about this one. "Bhikkhus may not drink intoxicating beverages. And they may not accept them if offered as alms. All fermented drinks are prohibited."

Muffled groans. Several lay devotees spontaneously voice dismay. Their concern is not so much for the bhikkhus as for themselves. They are disciples too, and where feasible, they try to observe the disciplinary rules—but this one? Some move around, shifting their sitting position, and their murmurs are audible as they whisper to each other. They'll need to do some inner work to reconcile themselves to this one. Many won't try.

Good, thinks Candana. That will be around town by morning. There's one response for Udena. Then his thoughts shift to Sagata whom he is glad to see has showed up. Earlier in the day during their meeting, Candana told him about the new rule, explaining it would be announced in the evening and that they expected him to be present. Sagata was profoundly uncomfortable, and Candana wondered if he'd come. He is impressed that he did. He's accepting responsibility—that's promising, Candana thinks.

At the announcement, the bhikkhus, observing monastic restraint, barely move. In fact they're rigid with distress. Those in a position to do it stare daggers at Sagata. There is still enough daylight to see him in the hall, which is lit only at the front by lamps burning ghee, clarified butter. Others turn their heads ever so slightly and hurl daggers from the corner of their eyes. Sagata, now recovered from yesterday's immoderation, finds a sudden absorbing interest in his meditation rug. Those close to him, however, see the redness rising from his thick neck and suffusing his face.

Though Sati can see only the back of Sagata's shaven head, it takes no great insight to know what the man is experiencing and, from the precincts of his own present embarrassment, he feels sympathy. He glances at the Blessed One, who is impassive, and then at Candana. His mentor is taking in the whole predictable scene. Is there a slight smile on his lips?

In fact, like Sati, Candana is sympathizing with Sagata. His own recent agony, though triggered by very different circumstances, has made him acutely sensitive. He sends blessings of lovingkindness to Sagata. Then his thoughts shift, and he considers the Buddha's teaching that says a supremely enlightened being doesn't tremble before any man. Sagata, who clearly would like to disappear right now, isn't anywhere in the vicinity of enlightenment, but what about me? Candana wonders. He trembled before Bhagava yesterday when he feared his censure, and when the opposite happened, he was delighted. That's a form of trembling too, isn't it, he asks himself, since my delight was contingent on circumstances. Candana knows that the teaching points beyond the circumstantial. So how am I different from Sagata? Candana is an honest man.

Now the Buddha begins to speak and all are hushed. "Bhikkhus, householders of Kosambi, we are glad to be here for the rains retreat.

We hope you are all faring well, that you're healthy and content." After continuing in this vein for a few minutes, he makes an oblique reference to difficulties in the monastic sangha and then says, "There are two things that cause a bhikkhu to live in discomfort here and now, bringing upon himself trouble and distress, and when the body perishes causing a bad rebirth. What are they? Not guarding the sense doors and being immoderate in eating and drinking." The sense doors are the eye, ear, nose, tongue, body and mind. The Buddha includes the mind in the list of sense organs. He continues, "A bhikkhu who leaves them unguarded, who is uncontrolled and immoderate in eating and drinking, experiences bodily and mental suffering. He lives in discomfort day and night and is tormented by the body and mind." Sagata squirms on his mat.

Then the Buddha articulates the opposite case, saying "A bhikkhu who is moderate in eating and drinking and who controls his senses experiences bodily and mental happiness and lives in comfort both day and night." To illustrate, he continues with a long narrative about the moderation of an ancient king, the kind of tale his listeners delight in.

This was the first time Sati has heard the Buddha teach, but although he tries, he can't stay with the talk. His thoughts jump around wildly—back to Sagata and his misery, and then to himself. He has certainly been trying to restrain his senses but is he comfortable? Far from it! In fact, every good monk in this monastery is on edge one way or another. He's sure guarding the senses isn't the whole story. He sighs.

Finally managing to bring his attention back to the Buddha, Sati finds that, despite his unruly mind, he is moved. He is touched not so much by the words, most of which he hasn't heard, but by the Buddha's presence. He is glad the Blessed One will be at the monastery for the rains and he vows to listen better next time.

When the talk ends, the crowd is silent. Although the Buddha addressed bhikkhus specifically, townspeople readily apply his words to themselves, and they are stunned. Religious sermons in the Middle Land usually deal with Vedic ceremonies and sacrifices; they underscore the role of brahmin priests as holy mediators between the gods and humans and the need to properly recompense the priests to ensure security, prosperity and happiness. The Buddha however is saying that one's own behavior, not rituals or priests, make a person happy. This is radical! Even those who have heard him speak before and regularly attend talks here when he's not in residence find the words liberating.

After a moment, cries of "excellent, excellent, excellent" burst forth from the assembly, and a number of townspeople who came out of curiosity, proclaim themselves adherents. Even some of yesterday's jeerers convert. "From this day forth, let Master Gotama accept me as a lay follower who has gone to him for refuge for life." This is a regular occurrence at the Buddha's talks.

Sagata has sat through the evening in a daze, and in the same state he returns to his hut now.

As Sati walks back to his own hut, several paces behind Sagata, the Venerable Migajala stops him and advises that it's unseemly for a bhikkhu, even a novice, to sit among laypeople. "You really need to remember monastic decorum, Sati."

June 12. They are getting a late start. Most of the other monks have already left on almsround, but Sagata still hasn't arrived. He and Sati agreed to meet at the monastery gate, a pair of wide wooden doors that are now unbolted to allow the monks to exit. He's worse than I am, thinks Sati, grumbling at Sagata's lateness. But this isn't just about karmic knots. Sagata's got another problem—unless alcohol is a karmic knot too, Sati muses, uncertain.

Sati shifts from foot to foot in growing impatience. Where is he? If we don't leave soon we won't have time to get back and eat before noon. The practice of not eating after noon not only fosters restraint, it keeps bhikkhus from begging at all times of day, which would try the patience of even devoted followers. The Buddha teaches that one meal a day is a healthful dietary regimen, and many of the bhikkhus, mainly the young men, take pride in the austerity.

When Sagata finally appears, his breath is sour. Sati recoils. This is bad news! Liquor was banned yesterday but today he's drunk! He sure didn't waste any time. What does he have—a stash in his hut?

Then kinder thoughts arise: Today of all days, he needs it of course, an alcoholic stupor, to be out of his mind. He was shamed in front of everybody and now he has to walk into town—I guess I'd need it too.

And as if to prove the point about being out of his mind, Sagata stumbles around, uttering unmonkly language. Oh heavens! What to do now? Sati wonders. I'm supposed to make sure he doesn't drink, but it's too late already. Quickly assessing the options, he knows that walking into town isn't one of them. Sagata mustn't go. I've got to stop him.

Sati is strong, the result of years of catching and hauling fish, but he's no match for Sagata's bulk. He wouldn't be able to restrain the man if it came to that, and he's afraid it will. He looks around for help, and not seeing anyone, Sati desperately backtracks into the monastery grounds. Sagata doesn't notice he's gone. Then in the common area, relief!—Arittha and Nakula are still here, also getting a late start. Sati runs to them, hastily explains, and the three dash toward Sagata. They slow down to a seemly walk, just before Sagata lifts his head to notice. Struggling to sound both calm and authoritative, Sati, as designated watchmonk, declares, "Sagata! We need to talk to you!"

"Ya need what? Whaddaya need to talk to me for?" Sagata slurs his words and looks around in a haze.

"Oh, shit!" mutters Arittha.

Casting around for what to say next, Sati repeats, "We need to talk to you. We think you should stay here today. Don't go to town. We'll bring almsfood back for you. You can rest."

"Rest!" Sagata shouts. "Why the hell should I rest? Whaddaya want me to rest for? Noneaya know what I need. Noneaya! Ye're all against me. I'm goin' and I don't give one fat damn if ya come along or not!"

Sati puts a hand on the man's shoulder in a gesture of restraint. It's a mistake. Sagata looks down at his hand as though it were a fly and growls, "Take yer hands offa me, ya sonofafisherman. If ya touch me, anyofya, even one finger, ye'll be sorry!"

The other two look at each other, then move in together. Nakula throws a feeble punch at Sagata's belly. It is an act of bravery, not to say foolishness, because the Venerable Nakula is a small, frail man; a potter in lay life, and he is utterly inadequate to this task. Arittha, who is taller than Sagata but half his girth, jumps on him from behind. He looks like a giant spider with his long arms and legs clinging to the man's back as he tries to wrench his head and throw him off balance. Sagata ignores him and grabs Nakula by the throat, shouting "I toldja to lay off! Now ye'll see I mean what I say!" and he starts to throttle him.

Sati shouts and pulls at Nakula's waist to extract him, while Nakula's hands fly to his throat, trying to pry Sagata's fingers loose. It is no use: Nakula is a child in a bear's grasp. Sati tries a different tactic. He lets go of Nakula and starts kicking Sagata, looking to land a punch in his groin, but he can't get between the two men. Sagata is beyond feeling any of the blows; he continues to strangle the man with all the one-pointed concentration he lacks in meditation. Then, suddenly, he seems to realize what he is doing, and abruptly he thrusts Nakula from him, as though he were holding a poisonous snake and has just noticed. Later Sati thinks that if he had been quicker, he could have broken Nakula's fall; but then, thinking again, he would have had to be very fast indeed because Nakula's body hurtled past with the speed of a star falling from the night sky.

Nakula's head hits a stone and he is still. All three monks stand stunned for a moment. Sagata looks down at his hands and then at the inert body, registering what has just happened. And then he runs.

He runs and stumbles, but with flailing arms and legs, he regains his balance, and wildly he propels his big body out the gate and into the city. Sati and Arittha don't move to stop him. They bend down to Nakula and try to revive him, but they have no success.

Right after the noon meal the monks, both residents and those who have arrived with the Buddha, gather in the lecture hall to discuss details of Nakula's cremation, for he will be cremated in keeping with burial practices of the times. In deep shock, they feel unprepared to grapple with the practicalities before them. The breathless air under a cloud-darkened sky doesn't help clear their minds.

The Venerable Harika though, is eager to make a proposal. As soon as the Buddha opens the meeting, Harika speaks up and urges that the cremation be held on the Ganges, the Holy Mother Ganga. Harika is a brahmin who was raised in the sacred city of Varanasi on the banks of the Ganges, and even though he's now a bhikkhu, the Vedic rituals and beliefs he grew up with are locked within, as though in a precious trunk, which he opens occasionally in order to view and venerate its contents. This is one of those occasions. The idea is so obviously unfeasible that the Venerable Sariputta, who arrived with the Buddha, observes simply that the Ganges is some thirty-five miles away, referring to the confluence of the Ganges and Yamuna. He doesn't need to point out that in the heat and with the rains almost upon them, a three-and-a-half-day trip on foot carrying the fast-decaying body isn't feasible.

Harika counters zealously, "Well, we can cremate him here then, and afterward take his ashes to the Ganges to be scattered." There is testy discussion of this proposal. The Venerable Candana is silent, knowing his words, whatever their content or merit, would raise dissension.

The Buddha ends it by observing, "The only water that's holy is the water of a purified mind and that can be found wherever there's a bhikkhu who has reached the higher training." These words, gently spoken, strike at the very heart of Vedic belief. Harika hears them but doesn't let the truth they point to find its way into his well-guarded trunk. If he is ever going to awaken to this truth, it's not going to be today.

The Buddha adds, "We will perform the cremation here this evening within the privacy of the compound." Most of those assembled appreciate the fact that it isn't seemly to publicly cremate the body of a brother who was killed by another of their number. "Then clansman Nakula's ashes will be scattered on the Yamuna tomorrow, and since it joins the Ganges, they will be carried out to sea all the same—or not."

So it is agreed.

With that matter settled, the Venerable Arittha speaks; his voice is shaking. "Venerable sirs," he begins, using the formal salutation bhikkhus employ in community meetings. The formality alone is enough to undo him, for Arittha isn't accustomed to speaking in public. Raptors and a feral pariah dog were his main companions for years; monastic counsels with their agenda of administrative and legal matters reduce him to silence. But there is something he must say. His numbness eases the process; the shock of the morning's events makes the meeting unreal, as though it were happening at a distance, to someone else.

"Nakula's family needs to be told. I'm prepared to do that. I could leave tomorrow and even with the rains I should be able to get there in six, maybe seven, days."

Everyone turns to look at him and Arittha shifts nervously on his mat, but he is determined to make his case. He needs to do something for his friend, to make some effort since he failed so horribly this morning. Arittha has re-fought that struggle several times, and he's convinced if he had done it differently he could have saved Nakula. He blames himself for the tragedy.

"His family should be told soon. To wait three months until after the rains would surely be lacking in compassion."

Well said, thinks Sati, whose own innards feel like stone while his mind floats in some strange zone. Who can argue against compassion? Arittha came to Sati's hut after lunch and confided his proposal; they rehearsed responses to the likely objections. Sati appreciates that his friend has carefully thought about his presentation.

"But you can't travel during the rains. It's a breach of Discipline," asserts the Venerable Migajala.

The comment surprises no one. And it makes sense. Travel is extremely difficult during the rains. Dirt roads become quagmires, and on the flat Ganges plain, flooding rivers bloat, swallowing up landscape for miles around. In the earliest days of the Buddha's ministry, hardy bhikkhus did travel during the monsoon season, avoiding roads and cutting through rice fields, but complaints from farmers whose tender rice seedlings were damaged by the traffic put an end to it. Now monastic rules confine them to designated areas during Vassa; boundaries are specially set in each retreat location. In Kosambi, the Vassa boundary includes Ghosita's Park, the other two nearby monasteries outside the city as well as the city itself and its suburbs. This means monks can go on almsrounds as usual but are forbidden to travel beyond. To do that they need special permission.

Arittha is prepared. "Bhagava," he says, turning and appealing to the Buddha, "this situation is special, and I can do this. I've lived in the forest most of my life—during winter, summer—*and the rains*," he adds for emphasis, referring to the three seasons in the Middle Land. "I've traveled most of the way to Bhaggu territory before. I can walk through the forest; I don't need to travel on roads or through fields."

Listening to Arittha, the Buddha can easily envision his long lean body moving through the forest like a deer. But having stayed in Bhaggu territory last year, he appreciates, too, the difficulties of the journey, even when it isn't raining. The Bhaggus live well off the trade routes, in a remote, heavily forested area northwest of Kosambi. After the initial stretch, there are few inhabitants to turn to for food or assistance if trouble arises. No major north-south waterways connect the Yamuna and Ganges between here and there, it's true, so there shouldn't be a problem with flooding, but you never know in the monsoon season. Still, he trusts Arittha's experience.

"And what about food," asks the Venerable Harika. "Or do you plan to kill game with hunting birds?"

Both Arittha and Sati recoil. So do others; tension becomes palpable. There goes Harika, wielding the ax in his mouth, thinks Candana. Even Harika feels the group stiffen and drops his gaze.

He didn't mean to cut—well, didn't *entirely* mean to. My tongue just does that, he thinks. Especially when it hits the mark, as this one does. Harika understands behavior in terms of the law; it's how he makes sense of the world. His mind quickly ran through the legal implications of Arittha's proposal, the negative ones. How would he get food without killing for it? Certainly there aren't many dwellings along the way, much less villages. Besides, Arittha is an outcaste, and killing game is how he procured food, so wouldn't he be tempted to do it again?

Numb as he is, Arittha feels the sting of the jibe, but he ignores it. "I can carry some food with me. The trip to Bhaggu country ordinarily takes five days by the road, but assuming the rains have come and I'll be walking through the forest, I should be able to do it in six or seven. I don't need much food and there are some villages and a few isolated houses along the way. I know them." Arittha doesn't mention that although he knows most of the area, he has never traveled in this direction during the rains.

Harika stops listening. Arittha's comments, whatever they are, aren't important. From his point of view, it's better to wait anyway. What's the hurry? he wonders. The family could have three more months of peace. Wouldn't that be more compassionate? But not being a legal observation, he doesn't voice it. He is bored.

Harika has made his proposal and registered his objection, and the decision won't be in his hands. So, for the fun of it, while the discussion continues, he plays with the case in favor of travel: Under exceptional conditions, which these certainly are, allowance is made for travel during Vassa. And this case is uniquely exceptional, it's precedent-setting; it's the first time a bhikkhu has been killed by a brother. How do we notify the family? With special permission a bhikkhu can travel during Vassa for up to seven days, but the need for a longer period can be reasonably argued here. And about food— bhikkhus have been known to take food when traveling through the desert; this isn't a desert but the principle is the same. And what about sickness? Harika is getting carried away. When a bhikkhu is sick, it's permissible to keep medicines for up to seven days, and this case is analogous to sickness, isn't it? Both are extraordinary circumstances. Yes, he concludes, traveling can be justified. Still, he's not comfortable with the irregularity of it all. He speaks none of this.

The Buddha is assessing the matter too. He remembers Nakula's family, especially his gentle father and mother, whom he considers the most trusting of his lay followers. The Venerable Nakula inherited their beautiful characteristics. Such a loss! The Buddha also remembers Nakula's outspoken wife, who so strongly opposed his ordination. Arittha wouldn't face an easy reception.

Everyone waits for his decision. Finally he says, "All right, all right, friend Arittha. The purpose is important. You may go and take the time you need. Just travel safely."

Arittha's heart flares with gladness, and Sati is happy for him, all the more so because he knows there's another reason for his proposal: In his grief, Arittha naturally wants to return to the forest; it's his home, his refuge, his place of healing.

The Buddha continues to gaze at him, and Arittha senses that nothing is hidden from him. "Safe journey, friend," the Buddha says, smiling kindly. Arittha's solemn face breaks into a rare grin. Bhagava knows and he approves! he thinks with relief and great gratitude. He bows to his teacher in anjali.

The Buddha adds, "Stay after we adjourn, Arittha. I want to tell you some things about the Bhaggus. And Upavana can give you a few pointers for your journey," referring to the fact that his attendant accompanied him to Bhaggu territory last year. "The rest will be up to you." Again Arittha nods.

The monks build the funeral pyre in the middle of the courtyard. More than two feet high and six feet long, the pyre is constructed from the monastery's store of firewood, limbs from the simsapa and from other trees fallen on the monastery grounds as well donations from townspeople who have cut trees in the area surrounding the city. Ghee is poured on the branches to help them burn. Just before the ceremony, the body, sewn into one of Nakula's orange cotton robes so that it's completely covered, is carried from his hut and laid next to the pyre atop a length of natural cotton, which is folded twice for strength.

They gather early in the evening and sit on their mats around the pyre. The Blessed One speaks a few words. He ordained Nakula at the end of last year's rains retreat on Crocodile Mountain. He recalls the gentle, quiet man and commends his virtues to the assembly, and he speaks briefly about impermanence and the importance of training now with great ardency, as Nakula was doing.

Then the Blessed One and four other monks rise to carry the body to the pyre. These include Arittha and Sati, who were the last to see him alive, and two others, monks Nakula frequently walked with on almsrounds. The men stand side by side next to the body, with the Blessed One at the head and Sati, the youngest in training, at the feet; they bend, take hold of the blanket, and using it as a sling, lift and carry the body to the pyre where they set it down; then they stand back and Candana lights the pyre. That night the monks sit in meditation until the body and wood are thoroughly burned.

June 12. Udena gets both pieces of news at the same time: A large number of townsfolk attended the recluse Gotama's talk last evening and many converted; and a monk was killed in the monastery this morning. Harika keeps Bharadvaja well informed.

Ah yes, thinks the king, Bharadvaja's favorite, Sagata, the monk who did so well by us the other day. This couldn't be better if we'd planned it ourselves. Let's see what their great enlightened recluse does now. The whole town will be watching. Udena savors the possibilities. His thoughts are interrupted by a tap on the door of his chamber. "Come in!" he commands.

"Great King," a servant in his sixties announces, "the monk Gotama requests an interview with you; his monastic messenger is in the anteroom awaiting your reply." Tuttha knows better than to refer to Master Gotama as "the Buddha," although he is a follower.

The timing is terrible. The Buddha knows it, but what else can he do? He has no alternative but to try to speak with the king. He doesn't hold much hope for success.

Udena doesn't need to think; his voice takes a vindictive tone. "Tell the messenger he can go and—" he pauses and, noticing the shocked expression on his servant's face, changes his mind and says, "No, no, Tuttha. Tell him I'm indisposed; I can't see him."

"Yes, Great King." Tuttha bows and turns to leave, earnestly wishing he weren't involved in this.

"Wait!" Udena stops him. The servant's heart drops.

"Tell the messenger we know the murderer is loose in town and our people are terrorized. This is a criminal act. Be very clear about that part. It's a criminal act of great concern to our people and the civil authorities. We don't tolerate murderers in our kingdom. That's all."

Tuttha offers a perfunctory nod. Though he's one of the people who are theoretically terrorized, he doesn't know what the king is talking about. Still, his job is merely to deliver the king's messages. He hurries out before his master can say more.

June 12. That night, a man stumbles into a tiny room in the basket-makers' quarter in the suburbs. Two little girls are asleep in one corner; their mother, in another, wakes up at the sound of his entry.

"Shhhhh!" she says sharply. "You'll wake the children!"

"Whoya tellinta b'quiet?"

"Shhhhhh!"

He strides over to the frayed cotton sheet thrown over straw where she's been sleeping, where they've often slept together, and lifts her up like a toy so her eyes are even with his. "I said who'dja think y'are!"

This time he says it loudly, waking the children, and they begin to cry. Smelling the liquor on his breath, she knows it's dangerous to resist, but her babies' cries made her angry. "Look what you've done, you big oaf! Put me down!"

"I'll putcha down all right!" he shouts. He slaps her and throws her onto the mat. All the terrible emotions of the past few days, which he lacks any ability to deal with, explode, and he leans over and blindly punches her in the face.

She writhes like a little worm, covering her face with her hands and moaning; blood begins to ooze from under her fingers. Now the terrified children are shrieking. There's a commotion in the adjoining house and sounds of running feet. Sagata heaves himself through the door out into the night.

June 13. The next morning, several monks rise early for the ceremonial scattering of the ashes. Although participation is optional, those who carried the body last night, except for the Blessed One, participate. In addition, the Venerables Sariputta, Ananda, and Candana as well as a few others take part.

The ceremony is held before almsrounds to enable Arittha to get an early start on his journey. The morning is windy, and on the western horizon a line of dark clouds is rolling in like an advancing army, hurling lightning and thunder in its path. Today is the day. Flocks of crows and falcons fly before the oncoming storm. The small party of monks walks from the monastery out of the city's east gate through the suburbs to the river. People are hurrying through the lanes, looking at the sky in joyous anticipation, ready to celebrate the arrival. On the river fishermen are busily bringing in their catch before the storm breaks.

The Venerable Sariputta, who is the Buddha's foremost disciple and acting in his stead at this ceremony, chooses a small promontory on the riverbank where shrubbery allows for some seclusion. Sati is glad they stop here because his parents' home, his home, is a bit farther down river and he doesn't want to see it. A few laughing children join them. They are welcome. For the children, this is a party. They know it's a scattering of ashes—they've seen it many times before—but it's one that bhikkhus are performing, and that makes it special. It makes it part of the celebration of the coming of the blessed monsoon.

A dark shadow slides over the landscape, and a rising wind begins to whip the monks' robes about them. Sariputta and Candana say prayers, but their words blow past the group. Then they dip their hands into the earthenware jar containing Nakula's ashes and scatter them over the water. The wind, however, carries the fine dust back onto the bank, and the bhikkhus and children step aside so as not to be covered. Candana observes silently that Sariputta should have chosen the east side of the little spit for this ceremony, not the west. He also notes there is no need to mention the wind-born ashes to Harika. It simply is as it is: Nakula's ashes may eventually be carried by the Yamuna to the Ganges and then to the sea, but probably not right away. Some will be lifted by the coming floodwater, and no doubt some will remain and nourish the soil here.

When all the ashes are dispersed and the ceremony completed, the others leave, but Sati and Arittha remain on the bank, side by side. They look at the river, now roughed with white-capped wavelets, and at the dried leaves and other bits of flora blowing around them, and they feel as turbulent as the weather. It's hard to believe that only yesterday Nakula was alive. What a brave man he was!

A great flash of lightning and thunder so loud they feel the vibrations in their bodies, and the clouds burst right over their heads. Sati and Arittha are pelted by fat drops, falling harder and faster, quickly becoming an unbroken sheet of heavy water. They stand, looking at each other and, in a gesture every human being understands, they embrace. It is as if the tumult around them is giving them permission to express their emotion openly. Their tears mix with the deluge, and they have no need for words, and later neither feels compelled to confess as an offense this violation of the rule prohibiting physical contact. Then Sati turns to go back to the monastery, and Arittha heads west on his journey.

CHAPTER 7.
SAGATA'S EXECUTION

June 14. The next day, in an afternoon downpour, a householder and a young woman appear at Ghosita's Park. The man, in his thirties, and his sister stand drenched, dripping little pools of water on the floor of Candana's hut where they have been ushered. Their simple clothes and deferential bearing show they are from the lower trades. She keeps her head down, as women do in the presence of men, but there is more than modesty in her demeanor: Her face is battered—her left eye is swollen shut and a gash infects the left side of her mouth, which is unnaturally arranged on her face; her jaw looks broken. The man is agitated. The welter of anger, shame, and awkwardness in the unfamiliar setting is so powerful he's hardly aware of what he is saying.

"One of your people did this! This!" he blurts out, pointing to his sister.

With his heart pumping so hard Candana can barely articulate, he mumbles and points to one of the mats, now located inside, then seats himself on the other. He needs to collect himself. The man sits while the woman squats beside him on her haunches in the posture of humility. It's only after they've arranged themselves that it occurs to Candana to get another mat for the poor woman, but that would mean going to another hut, and the man is already launched into his story. Besides, he knows that she is accustomed to the posture and sees nothing amiss.

Sagata has been sleeping with the man's sister. "She's a widow." He spits out the word as if it didn't deserve a place on his tongue. "She lives with her two daughters in her husband's hut, next to her husband's family." While in a later era widows will be exhorted to express devotion by joining their husband's corpse on his funeral pyre and sharing the cremation, as yet they are still permitted to live, but rather as pariahs, robbed of status, bringers of ill fortune, servants in their husband's family, especially if they haven't borne sons.

"We're good people, sir, our family. We're hard-working, independent folk, basket-makers. But she—she was a good enough wife while her husband was alive, but she's gone bad—you can't trust a woman to live alone. She's brought shame to our family... shame!..." and, unable to continue, he looks down at her with disgust and nearly breaks into tears. She keeps her gaze—her half-gaze—averted. She doesn't need to look at him to feel the depth of his revulsion. She wishes she were dead, but, no, for her babies' sake she must live, whatever that means.

Candana's chest aches for them both. Such suffering! Right before his eyes is the truth of suffering, the first Noble Truth as the Buddha teaches it—in all its anguish.

The details spill out. The man's family lives in a village close to Kosambi and his sister moved to the suburbs when she married into her husband's family, also basket-makers, six years ago. Now the family is refusing to keep her, quite rightly, and she and her children will have to move back with his own family—along with his wife, three children, his elderly mother and both of his wife's parents, and what good will she be with a face like that, she hasn't been able to eat since he hit her and she's already skinny as a stick, so who knows how she'll manage or who will take care of her daughters if she can't, since his wife is too busy with their own children and aged parents on both sides. "No good can come of this," he laments.

Then he adds, "Her husband's family has complained to the guild headman and he's reporting it to town authorities. They'll know of it; they'll take action. That man is a criminal!"

This is a disaster, every aspect of it! When banker Bhadrakka made the same assertion a few days earlier, Candana doubted. But now, a killing later and with this battered woman before him, he has no doubts. Whether they'll ever see Sagata again is uncertain—he might disappear into the countryside—but now, how to deal with this?

He is visited with an idea, there *is* something he can do: He can make sure the woman gets medical treatment; he'll speak with Sirivaddha, the doctor who attends sick monks, Ghosita's physician, and request another act of generosity. And another idea, just a possibility, begins to take shape. Candana asks the man's family name and village. "Take her home now," he says kindly, "and we'll send a doctor to treat her, be sure of that." The woman lifts her head and with her good eye looks at him in speechless gratitude, and Candana smiles.

After they leave, Candana goes to the Buddha's hut and interrupts his meditation.

June 16. Sagata returns to the monastery the next night while everyone is asleep. They find out early the next morning when one of the monks sees him walking toward the latrine. Within minutes, the entire monastery knows.

Forty-five minutes later Candana reluctantly makes his way to Sagata's hut. He's just had an urgent meeting with the Buddha, Sariputta and Ananda, and they've devised a plan. Now he's taking the next step. With equanimity? No, though he often gives talks on the virtue of equanimity and has long cultivated it. At this moment, however, early in the day as it is, he's too spent to be equanimous. He taps on the door.

Sagata opens it, wearing only his under-robe. His belly hangs over the cotton belt that secures the garment; both the cloth and his legs from mid-calf downwards are muddy. His chin and head are fuzzed with a dark stubble, and he is haggard despite his excessive flesh. He is however completely sober.

Sagata looks down, unable to meet Candana's gaze. There are no preliminary niceties. Candana steps in, closes the door behind him and sits on the sitting-cloth, while Sagata drops heavily onto his cot. They are beyond observing protocol here—whose head is higher than whose is the last thing on their minds. Hunching over, his elbows on his thighs and head in his hands, Sagata breaks into sobs of increasing volume. Between the sobs and hiccups of air, he blubbers, "I said I'd end up like this if I kept on drinking and now it's happened…It's my fault, all my fault. I'm no damned good. My parents warned me and they were right. No damned good." Completely undone, his voice ascends to a wail; once or twice he pauses to wipe the snot dripping from his nose with the back of his hand.

Candana is repulsed. At the same time, hating seeing anyone in torment, as this man so dramatically is, he wants to comfort him; equally he wants to scream in outrage. Instead, he's impassive. He waits for Sagata's histrionics to subside to a snivel. The man needs to be able to hear what he's about to say. Finally, Candana determines the moment has come and declares, "You're right, Sagata, it *is* your fault. You've blighted your life and others with heinous deeds and callousness. You've created tremendous suffering—you've killed a man, assaulted a woman, and…" Sagata looks up in surprise. How does he know that?

"Yes, we know. She came here with her brother; I spoke to them. She's in serious condition. You broke her jaw and she may lose sight in one eye. She'll never be pain-free again." Sagata puts his head back in his hands and groans.

"In your selfishness, you've created serious trouble for the whole monastery, but I won't talk about that—that's our problem; we'll have to deal with it. And within less than a week, you've caused the Blessed One to issue a new disciplinary rule and you've violated one of the basic rules of the order, non-harming. Quite a legacy!" He shakes his head.

Political fallout and monastic rules are hardly Sagata's main concerns, but he groans again, for he has betrayed the brothers with whom he has trained, however inadequately, for the past three years.

Candana pauses, then in an even graver tone, he says, "You know the penalty for killing, Sagata. You are expelled, you're no longer a bhikkhu. And you are no longer under our protection. You need to know that the town authorities, the king himself, demands that you be handed over for punishment. You are subject to the state's laws now, and that means…" he doesn't finish the sentence. He doesn't need to.

"But," he adds more gently, "you have a choice. We can turn you over to the civil authorities today or you can stay here and be turned over tomorrow. Which do you choose?"

Sagata doesn't have to think about it. "Good," replies Candana. "Stay here and get cleaned up. Householder garments will be brought to you; put them on. And get something to eat"—then he quickly clarifies, "no, not almsround—we'll bring food to you. Quiet yourself and prepare. I hope you'll spend this day wisely, Sagata. Is there anything special you want to ask for?"

Sagata is silent for a few moments, then says, "Yes, I'd like to talk to Sati."

Candana starts in surprise. The man didn't say he wants to speak with Bhagava or me or any of the other seniors now in residence. He wants to talk with Sati. Well, he's facing his death and this is his choice, so be it. "I think that can be arranged," he responds. "Stay here and rest. Sati will come after almsround, and you can talk then." Although he doesn't say it, Candana respects Sagata's courage for returning. He has some character after all.

Candana was taking a gamble when he told Sagata he could stay the day in the monastery, but he was pretty sure it was safe one. He shudders at the stakes. Even as they were speaking, the Buddha was sending Ananda to the king, to arrive as early as seemly in order to preempt Harika's message, which surely will be transmitted to the king as quickly as a cobra's strike. Ananda is to inform Udena that Sagata has returned and plead that he be allowed to remain in the monastery for the day and handed over to authorities tomorrow. He is to point out that this would give Udena time to prepare for the execution—there is no arguing the nature of the punishment—without having to bother about housing the prisoner.

The Buddha knows that the offer to relieve Udena of the burden of imprisoning Sagata for the day won't carry much weight. One more person incarcerated in the well-populated royal prison would hardly make a difference. But that is just the advantage: It wouldn't make a difference; so Udena won't care much one way or the other. To clinch the proposal, Ananda is to add incentive that Udena won't want to refuse, namely, the entire monastery.

"You'll be able to prepare for the event and then take the prisoner into custody and punish him the same day, if that's your wish," explains Ananda as he faces the king. What is understood is that the offer is contingent on their actually being able to deliver Sagata. Between now and tomorrow, he mustn't be allowed to escape—that's the only word for it. Sagata is a prisoner in the monastery.

It is a private meeting in a small room on the second floor of the south building of the palace. Udena chose the venue because he doesn't want the conversation to become the subject of court gossip, but that was probably an unnecessary precaution: Few courtiers would have troubled to be present at a meeting even in the usual audience chamber. What could a monk possibly say that's of interest so soon after sunrise?

The king decided he doesn't require the services of his female attendants either. These women usually see to his comfort by fanning him and whisking away flies, but it is early enough that no flies are yet about and the temperature is still moderate. So the only one in attendance is the royal barber, who is appraising the shave job on Ananda's head. The man, who is entrusted with shaving the royal face, cutting and dressing the royal hair and tweezing the king's body hair, is Udena's confidante. He often takes part in meetings to which even the highest ministers aren't privy.

On this occasion Udena appreciates that the man's low-class origin will make a favorable impression on Ananda, since Gotama's Dhamma officially disregards class distinctions—not that Udena cares about making an impression on Ananda! Barbers belong to the *sudda* class, the lowest of the four classes, and the man doesn't need to identify his status for Ananda to know. Indians are as practiced at detecting the subtle and not-so subtle signs of class as they are at breathing. Everybody might as well walk around with a badge on his or her forehead saying, "Hello, I'm a sudda" and so forth.

The king sits cross-legged on a large, finely carved wooden chair, made comfortable with cushions and set on a raised dais. The barber stands nearby, and Ananda has been bidden to sit on a modest cane-bottomed chair at floor level in front of the king. Ananda sits upright but not rigid, conveying an apparent sense of ease, which belies the fact that his belly is actually in a knot.

Udena listens as Ananda presents his proposal. The king already knows about the assault on the woman and intends to widely publicize the execution, including in the suburbs. While the basketmakers guild isn't powerful, by immediately responding to their grievance, Udena can demonstrate his concern for the lower classes and show himself to be a just monarch of all his people. It's quite perfect.

"And if we fail to hand the prisoner over tomorrow," Ananda adds, preempting Udena's inevitable question, "we would understand that we have betrayed the king's trust, in which case we would no longer deserve a place of refuge in Kosambi."

Udena smiles in disbelief. This is too good to pass up—he can't lose either way!

Ananda hopes the king will appreciate the Buddha's openness—he isn't trying to hide Sagata—and in this way maybe reassure the king about his general trustworthiness. But more likely Udena will think the Buddha a fool for proposing such terms. Well, maybe that impression will be reassuring, too, Ananda speculates wryly. He doesn't try to explain that from the Buddha's point of view, giving one person, even a criminal, a single day in which to move closer to awakening is worth the risk.

Sati taps on the door. "Come in," Sagata says from his bed, where he is sprawling after washing and changing into layman's clothing.

Sati steps into the hut. "Hello, Sagata."

"'Lo, Sati," Sagata mumbles. "Thanks for coming."

Sati says nothing. He sits on the mat on the floor, waiting.

"You're the only one who ever understood me."

Sati is startled. That's not what you said the other day, he retorts silently. He listens.

Sagata sits up and says in a dull voice, "I've really fucked things up. Really, really fucked up." Big tears roll down his face.

This is undeniable, and Sati remains silent.

"Poor Nakula. Poor little man. He never hurt anyone. Never. I'm so, so sorry. I didn't know what I was doing."

More tears. "Sati, will you promise me something? Promise me that you'll tell his people how sorry I am? That I didn't mean to do it, that I wish I hadn't?"

Sati doesn't want to explain that Arittha has already left to talk with the family, and Sagata, preoccupied with his thoughts, doesn't wait for a response. He continues with another item on his agenda. "And also tell my parents how sorry I am. I've been such a bad son. I wish I could change it."

Now Sagata looks at him sharply and pleads, "Please! Please do these things for me! You *will*, won't you?" Sati nods because he can't refuse, but he doesn't know how he'll manage.

They lapse again into silence. Eventually Sati speaks.

"Tell me, Sagata, you were here this morning when we got up. You must have arrived in the middle of the night but the gates were locked from the inside, so how did you get in?"

A little smile crosses Sagata's thick lips and he says, "A secret, my boy." He didn't tell Candana when he had asked the same question earlier. He lied, saying that he had arrived before the gates had closed yesterday evening, that no one had seen him and he had spent the night in the monastery. Now though he sighs, Oh hell, what's the point of secrets? And he confesses, "There's hidden entrance, a break in the ramparts where they join the monastery wall in the back. Actually, I had a little hand in creating it, and I did a good job too. Shrubs on both sides hide it nicely," he says, pride creeping into his voice.

"But why?" asks Sati. "Why bother? We're not prisoners. You can go out the gate anytime."

Sagata gives a little laugh "Ah, young tiger cub, it was for a woman, of course. You can't get out in the middle of the night, and that's the important time when it comes to women. You know that, don't you?" and he looks at Sati questioningly.

Sati reddens as he thinks of his sexual longings, which are considerable, and his experience, which is not. Comparing himself with Sagata, he comes out much on the short end. Involuntarily, he remembers the daughter of one of the fisherfolk families. They were so young, but no longer children...and it wasn't at night! But this isn't the time to exchange confidences.

"And is that where you went when you ran out of the monastery the other day, to your woman?" asks Sati, moving on.

The older man nods. "She lives in the suburbs, not far from my special door. I thought she'd take me in. But when I told her what happened, she threw me out, said she never wanted to see me again." He concocts a prettier story than the real one, and Sati, who doesn't know the difference, accepts it.

"So what did you do for the past four days?" Sati is trying hard to keep judgment at bay, but Sagata has killed a man and has regularly violated his monastic vows. It's a hard not to be judgmental.

"What did I do? I went to my parents' house. Oh, they didn't know," he adds quickly, "but one of the servants, someone I know well, hid me. She brought me food, even found me a change of clothes and washed my robes." He pauses. "But I had to come back. I can't keep hiding. I can't hide from myself. There's no place else to go, this is it..."

Sagata lets that thought hang a moment and then approaches the next one gravely. "And then there's tomorrow." They both know what awaits him. They've witnessed it before. Neither is aware that the Venerable Ananda has just spoken with the king and, among other things pleaded for a quick execution, but the king would have none of it. He wants to make the most of the spectacle. Sagata will have his arms bound behind him and will be taken to a public square where red brick dust will be poured on his head and red flowers placed around his neck as signs of humiliation. Then he'll be scourged with whips in every square in town and finally led to a place of execution, to the sound of drums signaling his end.

"What am I going to do, Sati? How am I going to handle this?"

Sati replies almost immediately with a certainty that surprises him. He doesn't know where it came from because he has never heard any of the seniors say it quite like this. "You have a short time left. You'll live it as a Noble One. Whatever happens to you tomorrow, nothing can rob you of this. Because it's beyond anybody's power to give it or take it away. Despite everything, Sagata, deep inside you *are* a Noble One. Know that."

Sagata looks at him doubtfully. Then he asks, "Will you shave my head tomorrow morning? Beforehand... I can meet you at the bathhouse. I know I'm not a bhikkhu any more but, well, I want to have a shaved head." And Sati agrees.

Sati intends to report the conversation to Candana, but not just yet. He needs time by himself, because he is overwhelmed by the crowd of horrors that clogs his mind like the demons in ghost stories he heard as a child. He heads back past the monks' huts toward the grove that has become ever more a place of refuge. It will be hot, steamy and buggy there but better than his hut; at least he can walk around because he surely can't sit still. The growth of jasmine edging the path to the grove is alit with starry blossoms that have burst into bloom with the rain. He yields to their commanding scent and breathes deeply, struggling to evade the jumble of images that vie for his attention. Suddenly though, as he enters the grove, one image wins: the hole in the wall! What if Sagata changes his mind about facing tomorrow? What if he escapes through his secret exit and the monastery can't deliver him to the authorities? Sati knows enough about the political situation to know that would mean trouble. Jasmine and all else forgotten, he turns and runs to Candana.

Straightaway, two bhikkhus are at the ramparts bricking up the hole. But because the mud won't dry in this humidity, two sturdy bhikkhus are stationed there, whether it's raining or not, to be relieved successively by others throughout the night and into the morning until the city officials arrive. Already a pair is doing similar sentry duty at the monastery gate.

That evening, the Buddha sends for him. Sagata is escorted to the hut in a state of high anxiety, wishing mightily he didn't have to face this. It's the first time Sagata has been alone in the Teacher's presence, because during the Buddha's past visits Sagata avoided him, and he certainly wasn't in a state to see him when he arrived this time.

Now here he is, standing quietly in his room as Sagata is shown in. Sagata keeps his eyes down—he's trembling violently. He kneels to touch the Buddha's feet with his forehead, feeling faint. "Venerable sir," he croaks.

"Get up, Sagata." The Buddha doesn't call him "friend" or "bhikkhu." Sagata rises shakily and the Buddha points to one of the two mats in the hut. He sits and then the Buddha does the same. Unable to keep silent, Sagata starts to mumble something, anything, unaware of what he's saying. The Buddha interrupts him.

"You are a misguided, confused man."

Sagata wags his head miserably. Too true.

"You've had a precious human life. Do you know how rare that is? Take a look at the creatures—have you ever really noticed? Have you ever really seen the poignancy of their lives?" He looks Sagata in the eye.

Whatever Bhagava is referring to, Sagata is sure he hasn't. He shakes his head.

The Buddha continues. "None of them has choice; they eat and are eaten by others. Striving to survive, they live and die with no complaint, with dignity, but limited means. But you're a human being; you've had the means to make different choices, and you've wasted it. Wasted it on bodily cravings and violence—with much complaint and no dignity, blundering from one immoderation to another, one rage to another, mired in hell realms. You've tossed away your life like a discarded mango skin, so little have you valued it or the lives of others. Harming just for the sake of harming—no animal does that. You're leaving a trail of misery behind you, Sagata, and you've deprived the Venerable Nakula of a chance to awaken in this lifetime."

Sagata's head is bobbling in a non-stop nod. This is worse than his execution tomorrow.

The Buddha pauses. "Tomorrow you come to the end of this life, and it's the lawful consequence of your actions, Sagata. You're the heir to your karma. You created it and you must bear the consequences."

His tone deepens. "The wheel of life rolls on and on; the round of birth continues. Until the senses are restrained and anger rightly understood and abandoned, there is only wandering in the cycle of existence. But I know that within you, deeply buried, there's a sincere desire for liberation. I know it better than you do yourself. So now I send with you a blessing: In future lives, may heavy karma be swiftly worked through so that the time will arrive, not too many lifetimes hence, when liberation is attained."

Sagata's mumbling has stopped. He is speechless. Then the Buddha says, "You may go now."

Rising numbly, Sagata leaves the Buddha's presence without ceremony and without noticing his oversight. He is exhausted and despite the traumas of the past several days and the finality of tomorrow, he sleeps soundly this night.

June 17. The next morning, the town's chief law officer stands at the monastery gate with a small group of guards behind him, waiting to take Sagata into custody. It is still early, before almsrounds, and all the long-term residents of Ghosita's Park line the path leading to the

gate. Several are sleepy because of sentry duty. Candana stands with Sagata at the door of the lecture hall and then together they move down the path. Sagata's shiny bald head looks shockingly vulnerable in the early morning light. Wearing white householder's garments, he walks with an unaccustomed dignity. As he passes them, each monk, one by one, says a silent prayer for their brother, for divided as they are among themselves, in their hearts they still feel him to be a brother. Even Harika, who rejoices in this victory for the Discipline, this cleansing of an unworthy one from the sangha, is touched for a moment. As Sagata moves past Sati, their eyes meet; it is a look Sati never forgets. At the end of the path, Candana unlocks the gate, hands Sagata to the town authority and turns back, shutting the gate behind him.

CHAPTER 8

SAMAVATI IN A ROYAL PRISON

June 17. Udena is standing in the reception hall talking with one of his counselors. Other officials are arriving this evening, and the hall, spacious as it is, is becoming crowded. The king is dressed in the finest white muslin from Varanasi. His undergarment falls to mid-calf and a toga-like outer garment drapes over his shoulder. A colorful garland encircles his neck, and his signature red, yellow and black turban, some thirteen feet of cloth arranged by a professional, adorns his head. The turban is artfully punctuated with a cluster of diamonds affixed on the left side above his brow. On the index finger of his right hand is a ring set with a significant emerald, which he enjoys wearing on special occasions. Like this one. In fact this is a celebration: A monk was executed in town today, and the prestige of the recluse Gotama has been seriously compromised. What a victory! Udena gloats, while Royal Chaplain Bharadvaja stands by quietly with a smug expression.

The king appears to be in an ebullient mood, but in fact, at this moment, his mind isn't really on celebration or conversation. He is thinking, once again, about a central tragedy in his life: his height. The official he is talking to is an impressively tall man, while he, Udena, is many finger-widths shorter. He is just under of average height, and the soles of his white leather slippers, though of great thickness, bring him nowhere near the vicinity of his aspiration. Nothing allays his sense of inadequacy when it comes to altitude. Udena's unimposing stature was an endless disappointment to his father, for even as a boy, he was small. Parantapa, who himself was only of average height, blamed the boy's hapless mother for not having adequately rewarded the brahmin priest she consulted assiduously while carrying the baby.

King Parantapa expected his heir to possess all the desirable characteristics of a great ruler. An imposing stature was one of them. When young, the boy tried mightily to please his father, copying his every mannerism and hoping for a spurt of growth, but nothing worked. He never fully gained his father's affection, and he knew why. So now, as Udena stands next to his tall royal counselor, the old pain arises. He shoves it away of course, and he laughs raucously.

Samavati walks into the room at this moment, announced by the servant at the door and accompanied by a maidservant. Women don't usually attend social gatherings—attending such functions is men's prerogative, and it is one that Samavati is happy not to share. But Udena wants her to be present on this occasion. He wants his wife to experience his victory and to relish her discomfort, for she is a follower of the recluse Gotama.

She's stunning, like a jewel, Udena thinks appreciatively, gazing past his own concerns for a moment and seeing the beautiful woman, his queen—his third queen, that is—who walks with quiet assurance. She is wearing crimson garments of silk, a material that is just now becoming known in the Middle Land. Introduced by merchants traveling from China, silk is yet a rare commodity—few except the wealthiest are wearing it. Samavati's lower garment is elaborately pleated in front and falls to her ankles; it is fastened at her waist by a girdle of linked gold adorned with hanging ropes of pearls, while her silken upper garment gracefully drapes her torso. Her long, dark hair is arranged in a bun at the nape of her neck according to the style of the day, and it is entwined with pearls and gold ropes, one of which reaches to the center of her forehead and dangles a rare ruby. Clusters of gems hang from her ears, and bracelets of gold set with gems encircle her arms and ankles. Her lips and the tips of her fingers and toes are dyed red with lac, as are her palms and the soles of her feet. The men steal appreciative glances at this ravishing vision. It is unseemly to look too obviously at another man's wife, and the king enjoys their little dilemma. As maharaja, he can openly admire any woman he wishes, and he does.

Achieving such visual perfection required two and a half hours of labor on the part of Samavati's body servants this evening. Even had the reason for the evening's event been to her liking, she would be out of sorts. Like all the women in the king's harem, an elaborate toilette occupies the major portion of her mornings, and today she has had to endure the routine twice, subjecting her body to the washings and tweezings and powderings and paintings that aesthetic standards for high feminine beauty require. Samavati has learned to submit to the beautifications, but they are hard to endure. She is impatient partly because her own natural beauty requires no adornment, but also because commonsense as well as her spiritual practice tell her that the elaborate beauty rituals are a colossal waste of time.

Finance Minister Ghosita's heart leaps when he sees his step-daughter. Like everybody else, he is present by royal command, and he is especially uncomfortable. He wonders if his monastic park and the monastic community here will ever recover from today's shame. The prospect of enduring the evening was dismal, until Samavati entered. Her presence is an unanticipated gift, a brightness amid the gloom.

As the company begins to move into the formal dining hall, Ghosita steps next to her and asks quietly, "How are you, my dear?" She looks at him with deep love and smiles. Ghosita knows it's impossible for her to be happy in this palace, and he grieves for her plight, but her love soothes his heart, making this miserable occasion bearable.

The dining hall is a large square room, its stone floor partly covered with a scatter of rich carpets. In the center is a circle of divans, heads facing toward the middle. Each is spread with cotton coverlets designed with animal figures and flowers and laden with an abundance of cushions. The king's divan, the highest and most ornate, is made of sandalwood inlaid with gold and spread with antelope skins. Each official knows his place in the circle, which is based on rank within the council of ministers and other complex considerations. They've done this often. Nonetheless servants instructed in the nuances of the night's seating—it varies slightly depending on the status of the guests attending—stand ready to show those who don't carry the calculus in their minds to their proper place.

Samavati is placed on the divan next to her husband, and she notes with dismay that Bharadvaja, who usually occupies this divan, is on her other side. She sighs. It wouldn't have been hard to place her stepfather next to her, but even had someone suggested it, she's sure Udena would have objected. Ghosita is reclining on a divan on the other side of the king between the prime minister and another official.

Servants enter with wet towels so that the king, queen and his guests can clean their hands. Others bear a profusion of well-spiced dishes—mutton, fish, deer and gazelle meat, rice and corn, an array of vegetables, curries, fruits and sweets. The king wants to celebrate lavishly tonight.

The dishes are offered first to the king and then to Samavati; then servants walk among the divans offering to the guests. Selecting foods of their choice, they take portions with their hands from the serving dishes and place them on their plates, gold and silver, which are set on small tables next to each divan. The prohibition against sharing meals with persons of different social classes, commensality, hasn't developed yet, and they eat and drink without a sense of class restraint.

Samavati looks up at her husband and sighs. He's been drinking too much as usual. The meal has hardly begun and already he's drunk. She is past being concerned about Udena's excesses. This marriage wasn't her wish, nor that of her stepfather. Knowing well the kind of man the king is, Ghosita initially refused the king's demand. Udena had seen her with Ghosita at a public gathering and decided on the spot that he had to have her.

The prospect of such a match appalled Ghosita and he objected. Like a thwarted and dangerous child, Udena threw a tantrum. He banished his un-obliging finance minister and seized his property. It was too much; Samavati yielded. But first, she obtained the king's promise to reinstate her stepfather if she came to him of her own accord. Thus he relented; Ghosita regained his property and position, and Samavati became the third consort to King Udena.

Samavati knows of course why the king's spirits are high to-night, and she regards him with loathing. He is gesticulating and laughing loudly—over some crude joke she thinks, though she's not really listening. Then she remembers the Blessed One's teaching. This is her heart's refuge. Samavati begins to silently repeat the Buddha's words: "As a mother would risk her own life to protect her only child, so, too, towards all living beings one should cultivate a boundless heart." It isn't easy to cultivate a boundless heart toward this barbarian, but she is trying. Oh, how she's trying!

She sits silently and without expression. Her eyes, which are lined with kol, a black cosmetic believed to protect from ill-fortune, are cast down. Outwardly she is immobile, but inwardly, in her heart, she is diligently trying to arouse lovingkindness, *metta*, for the crude man who neither exhibits nor appreciates it. Ghosita looks at her, past the prime minister and king. She lifts her eyes and their gazes meet momentarily. Each knows what the other is thinking.

The same evening, the mood at Ghosita's Park is somber. The bhikkhus are mostly silent, too shocked and grieved to converse. The Buddha would likewise prefer silence, but he knows that tonight especially he must speak. The monks need support individually; they also critically need it as a community because, badly divided as they are, they *are* a community. How many blows can any community sustain before it falls apart?

The Buddha has no guidelines. No other tradition in the Middle Land maintains centers for long-term residents, and there are as yet only a few in his. The Buddha foresees, however, that decades hence his bhikkhus will settle, at least part of the time, in centers like this one. This means Ghosita's Park is a place of the future, a model where rules for living together are being tested in all their rawness. It *must* succeed.

He also wants to support his lay followers, who are badly shaken by the execution. Some are likely to turn away from the Dhamma as a result. He needs to reassure them, provide the Dhammic context in which they can hold their doubts and distress. It's a tall order. As for attracting others who are not yet converts, well, this isn't the time to think about that.

Tonight, the bamboo partitions have been dropped from beams around the perimeter of the lecture pavilion and pegged into the ground against the rain, which is falling steadily. It cascades down the bamboo and seeps into the pavilion, making dark spreading blotches on the floor. That the partitions do an imperfect job doesn't faze those assembled. Getting wet is a small price to pay for the life-giving benefits of the monsoon. There's little else to celebrate this evening though. It is a subdued crowd—with a few exceptions. Bharadvaja's agents have given handsome incentive to some individuals to heckle the Buddha.

As the Buddha enters the hall, a few of the jeerers begin, but several in the audience growl at them and their numbers are persuasive. Besides, although they willingly entered into this task, the jeerers know that such behavior at a religious gathering is outrageous, and they are embarrassed. The Buddha sits quietly looking at the audience. He is in no hurry to speak. Gradually everyone, including the fractious ones, grows silent and watch him. They wait.

Finally he speaks—loudly so he can be heard over the din of the rain. He wants everyone to hear this, especially the king. He knows Udena follows events at Ghosita's Park with resentful interest, and the Buddha wants his message tonight to be conveyed accurately. "Bhikkhus, householders, today Sagata, the merchant's son, has been executed. Like all men, Sagata created his misfortune. Like all men, he was the owner of his karma, heir to his karma, and born of his karma. Whatever karma each one of us does, whether good or evil, we are heir to it. These truths must always be reflected on. If Sagata had adequately reflected on them, he wouldn't have acted as he did, he wouldn't have committed harmful acts and created great suffering for others. He would have honored his monastic vows and lived a life of a worthy one. But he didn't reflect on them, and he has met an evil end.

"We offer compassion to those who have been harmed by Sagata's misdeeds, wherever they may be, whether they are present tonight or not—to the family of the bhikkhu Nakula, who was a fine bhikkhu and whom Sagata killed, to the widow of Jotika the basket-maker whom Sagata assaulted and seriously injured, to her two daughters and her family in the basket-makers' quarter in town and in Mau village, and to any others whom he harmed, including members of his own family. To them all we offer compassion." The Buddha wants to publicly acknowledge Sagata's deeds; nothing can be gained by hiding them. And he wants to remind people that Sagata's family is among those who are suffering, and thus urge townsfolk not to turn away or revile them.

News of the beating has been all over town almost from the moment it happened. On almsrounds, bhikkhus have been barraged by comments from householders, some of them sorrowful, many indignant. But somehow Sati hasn't heard. He has been too numb and withdrawn since Nakula's death, moving as in a dream. He skipped the meal one day—he had no appetite—and on another, one of the bhikkhus brought almsfood to him; otherwise he has slipped in and out of town quickly, silent and unapproachable. Though he was galvanized momentarily when he realized the implications of Sagata's hole in the wall, once that information was delivered, paralysis returned. But now the Buddha's announcement jolts him, and fury erupts. Sagata didn't mention beating the woman! Outrage surges past his numbness and inundates what the Buddha is saying. Sati knows the teaching that "even if bandits were severing you savagely limb from limb, he who gives rise to a mind of hate would not be carrying out my teaching," but he plunges into rage anyway—no effort to stem it, no inner apology. With all the energy of his youth, Sati allows the mind of hate to engulf him. Sagata was a despicable, violent liar right up to the end! Even this very morning when Sati was shaving his head and he was pretending to be so remorseful, he was lying! What kind of man was he?

The Buddha continues, "Tomorrow evening I'll speak about the heavenly mind-state of compassion. When practicing this

Dhamma, you must cultivate lovingkindness for those who are suffering; this is compassion. And if you yourself are included among the suffering, then you are one who is most worthy of receiving your own compassion.

"Tomorrow we will speak on that. Now though, I urge each of you to remember Sagata's example and learn from it. This life passes quickly and before you know it, it comes to an end. So think deeply about this: You are of the nature to decay; you have not gone beyond decay. You are of the nature to be diseased; you have not gone beyond disease. You are of the nature to die; you have not gone beyond death. All that is yours, dear and delightful, will change and vanish. This is the law, ancient and inexhaustible. Let Sagata's example remind you, my friends, of these truths so that you may live a life that is blameless."

Now he turns to the division within the monastic community. "And for those who have left the householders' life and have gone forth into homelessness under me, those who now dwell in community in this park, so generously donated by Minister Ghosita, do not waste time! Practice diligently. Live in accord with one another, with mutual appreciation, blending like milk and water. View each other with kindly eyes and live with lovingkindness for each other and compassion for the world. Live for the good, the welfare and happiness of all beings."

Then the Buddha closes his eyes and moves into meditation, his legs crossed, hands resting in his lap and his attention turning wordlessly within. There will be no stories or questions and responses tonight. A few members of the audience get up to leave, but most stay—even some of the would-be hecklers—and they meditate as well. Sati, however, feels ready to burst with anger. He looks around for an exit, but there is none: There is no way to move past the seated bhikkhus and townspeople unobtrusively; so he sits and fidgets. At last, the Buddha ends his meditation, and the gathering disperses. With his meditation mat under his arm, Sati practically races away.

But there's no getting away from what's inside. Back in his hut, Sati paces. Sleep isn't going to happen and meditation isn't possible.

He looks at his roommates, the geckos, which are scuttling around the rafters, their little bellies already plump with insects that have proliferated in the rains. He looks at the narrow bed with its laths of split bamboo, comfortable enough when you're in the mood to sleep. He looks at his meditation mat, which is as wet as he is from the drenching rain; at the small shelf, a board resting on two mud bricks, that holds his neatly folded outer robe, alms bowl and a few other monastic items. All form the familiar texture of his life, and there is no help in any of it, nothing to distract him. I could recite some of the teachings, he thinks. Ah, no—I'm not in the mood. What about Papa's poetry? His father wrote verses, etching them on strips of birch bark. Sati no longer has the poems, but it doesn't matter because he knows the verses by memory. He periodically recites them for comfort. But not tonight. Tonight there is no comfort, anywhere.

June 18. The next morning in the midst of a downpour, the Buddha visits the nobles' quarter on almsround. It is important that he appear in the influential heart of town today, the day after the execution. He hopes townspeople will take the message that the holy life flows on despite worldly changes—fame or shame, praise or blame, rain or sunshine. Accompanying him are two of the recently arrived senior bhikkhus, the Venerables Upavana and Sariputta.

Queen Samavati stands at the window in the sitting room of her suite, watching for the bhikkhus, especially the Blessed One. The palace is located in town on extensive grounds in the center of the nobles' quarter. Three city blocks dead-end at the east and west perimeters of the royal grounds, while the north and south perimeters face streets fronted by nobles' houses. Samavati's large suite on the roof of the women's wing of the palace offers a fine view of the street to the north.

When Udena was planning to marry her, he had the suite specially built because the other apartments, which are on the second floor, were already occupied by his other wives, Vasuladatta and Magandiya, and his nine concubines. The new rooftop suite is a quarter as large as the entire third floor. It is the biggest of the queens' apartments, and it has the best view. Udena first offered it to each of his other two consorts, with the plan that Samavati could move into one of their apartments, but they refused. They were already lavishly lodged in their corner suites on the second floor and were greatly insulted by the proposal that they climb up, past the maidservants' quarters on the third floor, to the roof. Moreover, the stairs to the roof are external to the building; no queen should have to climb them. Udena plans to have a covered stairway built but hasn't done it yet.

Samavati doesn't mind however. She is young, and she loves the privacy of her beautiful quarters with its views front and back. Her only complaint is that she can't sit on the rooftop at dusk to look at the sky, so soft and lovely. She hopes to persuade Udena to have potted trees brought up so that she can sit outside among them without being observed from the nobles' houses or elsewhere in the palace.

Like most women of the upper classes, Samavati's activities are severely restricted. She can't leave the palace without her husband's permission and then only with a male escort. Going to Ghosita's Park to hear the Buddha or other seniors speak isn't possible since Udena isn't about to consent. She can however watch for them from her suite as they walk on almsrounds. It is her joy. And so she stands at the window now. Next to her is her attendant, Khujjuttara, who is also a follower of the Blessed One. On this, the morning after the execution and the unhappy dinner party, Samavati feels desolate. She longs to see the Buddha today—it would be a special blessing.

She's in luck. There he is, begging for almsfood at the mansion across the street, almost as though he knew how desperately she wanted to catch sight of him. She and Khujjuttara smile at each other.

As they stand at the window, there is a knock on the door. Khujjuttara tends to it and, returning, says in a tight voice, "Mistress, it's masons, two of them. And a guard."

"Masons?" Samavati asks, puzzled.

"Yes, mistress. They say they've been sent by the king. They say they're to brick up the windows." Tears have formed in Khujjuttara's eyes.

"Brick up the windows? Which windows? Why?"

"They don't know why. I asked. They say they're following the king's orders. They're bricking this window," pointing with her chin to the window they are standing at, "and the bed chamber window that looks onto the street."

Samavati whispers something under her breath and puts her hand to her forehead. She knows: To stop her from watching the Blessed One on his rounds—it's just the vile sort of thing Udena would do. He didn't even give her notice, and now strange men are in her quarters. She feels violated.

"Tell the men to wait a few minutes," she says slowly, her voice shaking. She tries to arrange her thoughts. She mustn't leave them here alone, but it is unthinkable that she stay with them. Deciding, she directs Khujjuttara to summon two maids who attend her—they are due to arrive shortly for her morning toilette—they can remain in the apartment while the men work. "Once they've arrived, please come down and join me in the courtyard." It is not an order. "Please," she begs.

The palace consists of five multi-storied wooden buildings configured in the shape of a squared-off figure eight, enclosing two courtyards. The lower building on the south side contains the public areas—the audience chamber, the reception hall, the dining hall and meeting rooms, large and small. It is in a meeting room on the second floor of this building that Udena's council of ministers gathers during cold weather and the rains. He also receives his spies in this room; and here it was that he met Ananda the day before yesterday. Public access to the building is from the street on the south side, but there are also doorways on the north side to the lower courtyard. This courtyard serves as a utility area for the many services needed to support the functioning of the palace.

Udena's spacious quarters occupy the entire first floor of the central building. They include an elaborate bathroom with tiled walls and floor, painted pillars and a sunken tank where he sits daily while his manservants and female attendants bathe him with scented water. Several of his key servants have apartments on the smaller second floor, but most male servants live in the two-storied building on the west side of the complex. The east building houses the kitchens, pantries and multiple storage rooms on the first floor and in the cellars, while the cooks and married servants live on the second floor.

The women's building, the tallest of the structures on the palace grounds, is at the top of the figure eight, toward the back or north part of the complex. The inner side of the building gives onto the upper courtyard; its outer facade, onto the street. While the women's quarters can be accessed internally from either of the side buildings, east and west, the only external entrance is from the courtyard. There is no street entrance. The architecture alone tells the story of the women's confinement.

The upper courtyard is a beautifully tended garden, planted with ornamental shrubs and trees and an abundance of flowers. It contains a small lotus pond where brightly colored fish dart about, and throughout the courtyard, winding pathways and scattered benches offer lovely views. Swings hang by brass chains from limbs of two of the trees and provide a favorite pastime for the bored, well-bred ladies of the palace and their children. Samavati doesn't enjoy swinging, and some of the women whisper among themselves that unless she changes her ways, she won't be fertile, that after all, she's already been queen for these many months without result. In a life where bearing children is of consummate importance, the custom connecting swings with fruitfulness is taken seriously. Some of the women swing daily. Though Samavati is not one of them, she does love the flowers and trees and often walks among them. At one end of the garden, a portico, an area sheltered by the overhanging roof of the building and fronted by shrubbery, offers quick and private refuge from the sun or rain or prying eyes.

No one is in the courtyard when Samavati enters. The rain has just stopped, and the sun has escaped the cloud cover to shine for the first time this morning. Despite her agitation, her eyes take refuge for a moment in the sparkling droplets that tip the leaves and blossoms of the jasmine shrubs growing by the door of the woman's building. She knows if she looks closely she'll see the blossoms reflected right there in each droplet, a magic mirror to the flowery world. But she has no heart for magic today. She passes into the garden and soon enough Udena joins her. He's been watching for her, knowing she would come here while the masons are working. He doesn't want to miss the chance to make his point at the moment when she is most distressed.

Walking over to her, he says malevolently, "I trust you find the new arrangement in your apartment to your liking."

She doesn't respond.

"It will keep you, madam, from standing at your window and watching that ascetic with cow eyes when he comes by on almsrounds."

Samavati is flabbergasted. She stares at the man, unable to believe what she is hearing. Cow eyes!

"You heard me. I won't have you longing after that man. From now on, you won't be able to see him—or any of his handsome friends." And he adds viciously, "Who you drool after!"

Udena is thinking especially of Ananda, whose extraordinary good looks attract the attention of both men and women. Even without hair! the king seethes. Udena has resented Ananda since he first set eyes on him last year. At the time, the Buddha was staying for a few weeks in Kosambi, and Udena, wanting to please Samavati whom he had newly married, acquiesced to her request to invite the Buddha to instruct the women at the royal pleasure park outside of town. The palace would have been a more convenient location; however, no men except the king and an elderly watchman are allowed in the women's quarters. Not even a monk. (The two workmen who are currently altering Samavati's suite are an exception—but no matter.) Nor would Udena allow his women to meet in one of the public rooms in the south building, where there is plenty of space. So the pleasure park it was. But the Buddha did not go. He sent Ananda instead. What an insult! Udena still bears a grudge.

Naturally the women flocked to hear the pretty boy! I'll bet they wanted instruction! Udena sneered at the time. His own growing paunch, his skin which no longer glowed with good health, and his less than middling height bore unfavorable comparison to the Buddha and Ananda. By all the gods, it was unfair! He was younger than both, but already he was losing his looks. None of those bastards will ever meet with his women again! he vowed after Ananda's success. Udena can't acknowledge that he is jealous, because kings aren't jealous. It's a rule. But the heat of his emotion, whatever its name, was aroused again when he met with Ananda two days ago and he remembered just how good-looking the man is.

"But..." Samavati starts to protest, then stops. She knows it is useless. Her husband has never had a single spiritual aspiration, and when it comes to relations between men and women, he understands only one thing. Why try to explain?

"Let's see how you much you enjoy their almsrounds now!" Udena crows and struts away. This tops his victory dinner last night—it's a masterful move. He's shown her just how far she can get with her fantasies about handsome monks!

Khujjuttara joins her mistress a few minutes later. Still standing in the spot where Udena left her, Samavati is shaking. "Come, mistress, come. Let's sit in the portico," Khujjuttara urges gently and guides her to a bench. In the privacy of the enclosed area, Samavati begins to weep. Khujjuttara puts her arms around her, cradling her like a child, and Samavati leans against her breast and sobs out the story.

Neither of them considers the social prohibition that prevents a slave from touching anyone from an upper class, much less a queen. Khujjuttara is a slave, one beyond the pale of the class structure, lower even than outcastes. Palace slaves are treated with greater liberality than those in society at large; otherwise they would have to be shunned and would be useless to their royal masters. Nonetheless, embracing a slave is officially an act of pollution that can be cleansed only when the upper-class person has undergone an elaborate purification ritual. But purification is not on the minds of either woman.

Rain starts to fall again, and they huddle together in the portico like two orphaned sparrows weathering a storm.

After the mid-day meal, which she was unable to eat, Samavati returns to her apartment with Khujjuttara. The gloom, heat and stickiness of the rooms enfold her like a shroud. Where her windows were there are now clay bricks, sloppily mortared together. The smell of fresh mud still hangs heavily in the humid air. True, the masons left openings near the top, interlaying bricks to allow for cross-ventilation, and the opposite windows are still brilliant with light and offer a view of the garden courtyard. The change however is dramatic: It has cut the light by half and has obliterated Samavati's view of the world beyond this hateful palace. It has also destroyed her ability to see her teacher. Samavati breaks down and cries again.

"It's not a palace, it's a prison," she wails. "I can't bear this life. What did I do to deserve this?" She puts her head on Khujjuttara's breast for the second time today.

"Ah, mistress, mistress," Khujjuttara murmurs soothingly as she strokes Samavati's hair, "none of us can know that. Only the Blessed One knows."

Khujjuttara has much reason to ponder the same question. Born of a slave in the palace, Khujjuttara has a plain face, and one leg that is shorter than the other. At seven, she suffered a badly broken leg when she was kicked by the state horse. Always curious, the young Khujjuttara often watched the king, then Parantapa, on his daily visits to his royal mount. Knowing when he and his royal equerry would cross the compound from the palace to the stable grounds, she would hide behind the large earthenware feed containers and peek out to watch. One afternoon, after they had finished their inspection and all the stable attendants were elsewhere, she saw her chance to take a closer look at the animal that the king spent so much time fussing over. She silently slipped the latch, crept into the stall, and started talking as she had heard the king do. The splendid chestnut stallion was looking out a window facing the opposite direction and was startled. He kicked with both hind legs, and one hoof landed on her left thigh, breaking the bone. The horse's personal attendant was fired for inattentiveness and insufficient virtue. (Virtue is considered a key qualification of anyone charged with tending the august beast, and the accident was evidence of the man's inadequate supply.) Khujjuttara's bone wasn't properly set, and the growth of her leg was permanently stunted. She has walked with a painful limp ever since. Fifteen years older than Samavati, Khujjuttara hasn't married because no one wants a cripple. Who can tell the reasons for one's misfortune? Now though, Khujjuttara speaks to her mistress not with bitterness, but with love and deep compassion. "Hush, hush, now, my dear, hush."

The two women are more than mistress and servant. Breaking all convention, they are friends. It started a year ago, soon after Samavati was married and arrived at the palace and Khujjuttara assigned as her personal attendant. At the time, the Buddha was visiting Kosambi for a few weeks on his way to Bhaggu territory for the rains retreat. A local garland-maker invited Khujjuttara to participate in a meal he was offering the Blessed One and to stay and listen to his talk afterwards. It was a life-changing event. That evening Khujjuttara deeply heard the truth of the Dhamma; her understanding split wide open and she experienced an awakening.

Samavati knew something had changed as soon as her attendant walked into her suite the next morning. She carried herself differently, behaved differently. Samavati had looked at her and asked simply, "Khujjuttara?"

Brimming with the great news, the woman could hardly contain herself. "I've heard the Blessed One teach, my mistress, and... and well, everything is different now! It's hard to explain. I don't have the words but, oh, you must hear for yourself, you must!"

Khujjuttara didn't give Samavati time to respond because she had something else to say and it was urgent. She stood more upright, took a deep breath, then in a shaky voice confessed, "My mistress, I've been stealing from you. Yes, I have. You give me eight coins every day to buy flowers and I spend only four; I've been keeping the other four."

Khujjuttara had been awake all night, for already the new reality was leading her. Whatever the consequences, she had to confess.

She had no choice. Now she paused expectantly, maybe she'd get a tongue-lashing—maybe worse; maybe she'd be whipped and dismissed. But Samavati was silent, and Khujjuttara continued. "I can't go on doing what I've been doing. I'm no longer who I was. I have to say this." She concluded quietly and looked down at the floor, waiting.

Samavati's body stiffened with anger. At the same time however, something resonated. When the maid's story finished, the two women sat in silence while Samavati struggled to make sense of the forces contending within her. Slowly, clarity cut through the tension: A woman who could tell the truth at the risk of her future was a woman to be trusted. Samavati relaxed and smiled.

The two talked long about Khujjuttara's experience and about the Buddha. Samavati was drawn in a way she'd never experienced before; she had to know more.

Since Samavati couldn't leave the palace to hear the Blessed One, she asked Khujjuttara to listen and bring his teaching back and share it. The woman readily agreed. She went to Ghosita's Park every evening that the Buddha spoke, and after he left town, she attended talks given by other bhikkhus at the monastery. Gifted with a prodigious memory, she was able to repeat accurately what she had heard.

Over time Samavati and Khujjuttara invited the other women in the harem to join their sessions. Though neither of the other queens chose to attend—Samavati would have been surprised if they had—a few of the concubines did. The sessions were held in the mornings after the women's toilettes were accomplished. They met in a large sitting room on the first floor of their building; the floor was sunken and cool to the feet, and the perimeter was lined with three steps on which, at one end, the women gathered. With Samavati sitting next to her, Khujjuttara sat on the highest step and recited what she had heard, while the others gathered around.

For those who didn't attend the sessions, the Buddha's teachings were a matter of indifference, but the seating arrangement was not. It scandalized them. "A slave sitting higher than palace women! It's outrageous! Not to be allowed! I must speak with Udena," ranted Magandiya. Many agreed with her.

June 19. On the second day after the execution, Candana looks for Sati in the dining hall at lunch and, not finding him, goes to his door. Sati greets him listlessly. Except for passing comments, Candana hasn't spoken with him recently, and Sati hasn't made much effort to seek him out. Now, refusing Sati's invitation to step inside, Candana stands on the doorstep and says, "Friend Sati, you are to go to speak with Sagata's family this afternoon."

Sati protests, "Sir, I can't do it!"

"No? Why not?" And without waiting for an answer, Candana states, "You promised, and they're expecting you. You need to think of their ordeal, too, Sati."

Sati would like to think of their ordeal but his own keeps claiming his attention. He can't help that. He could explain that since Nakula was killed, he has barely eaten or slept and is hardly in condition to walk to the latrine much less into town (though somehow his legs have managed to convey him there on almsrounds). He could say that he hates Sagata like he's never hated anybody—even worse than Harika; or that he's not qualified to comfort the parents when in fact he can't comfort himself, he'd be a hypocrite to try. He could say that he's scared. But no, he won't say any of it. Instead lifting his shoulders and turning palms upwards, he says plaintively, "Can't somebody else go?"

Candana looks at him.

There is no point arguing. "Yes, Venerable sir," he mutters in resignation.

The rain stopped mid-morning, but as Sati starts out, a fierce deluge soaks him, and his robes slap angrily against his body, sticking to his legs. Even the weather and his clothing are against him.

Barefoot, he trudges to the wealthy merchants' quarter. He carries no umbrella because it would be useless against the slantwise onslaught.

Outside the three-storied mansion that is Sagata's family home he stops. As is customary, he washes the mud off his feet and ankles, using the cloth and waterjar stationed near the door. There is nothing he can do about his dripping robes though. These cling to him uncomfortably. Sati tries to adjust them discreetly but it's no use; they stick to him anew. A servant shows him into a parlor. It is a jungle of a room, overrun by expensive objects—chairs, tables, stands, couches, divans, cushions, canopies, animal skins—all held within plastered walls painted with twining creepers. Sati has hazy memories of opulence from his early childhood, but this display holds no interest for him.

Camped in the center is a man a few years older than Sagata, his brother Sati guesses. The man rises from one of the chairs and greets Sati tersely, "Venerable." He is unaware that Sati is a novice who hasn't yet achieved that honorific, and Sati blushes. Bowing slightly, the man indicates a chair, one that has been covered with an extra cloth to protect the expensive fabric underneath from the dampness. Sati sits at the edge uncomfortably. It's been a long time since he sat in a chair. Across from him huddled on one of the couches are Sagata's elderly parents, both dressed in white, signaling mourning. In contrast to the brother, who maintains a stony demeanor, their faces are naked with grief.

The brother dispenses with the formalities that usually preface social interchange among strangers and says curtly, "We've been told you have a message from my brother."

"Yes, I do." Sati is sure he's more anxious to get this over with than the brother is. "I saw him that last day in the monastery. He asked to see me. He asked me to tell you," and he turns to the parents, "he asked me to say that he was sorry he was a bad son; he wished he could change that." Sagata's mother breaks into sobs, her shoulders shake; his father looks away and tears course down his cheeks.

They sit in silence, and Sati is drawn into their grief, inundated by it like the earth is being inundated with rain. The realness of their anguish is so big, so powerful that Sati's own suddenly feels puny, even petty, a little boy's tantrum. Immense tenderness bursts in his chest and possesses him. He wants to do whatever he can to comfort these people; he'd turn himself inside out if he could.

Speaking from the bloom of this feeling, Sati adds in a voice grown soft as a rose petal, "And he said he loves you and is sorry he never told you so himself; no son could have better parents and he wants you to know it."

It's not a lie, not false speech, Sati rationalizes. It's compassion, they need to hear it. Besides, I know it's what Sagata *really* meant.

The father manages to whisper, "We're grateful to you, son, Venerable, we're grateful."

Again silence emerges as each sits cloistered in his and her own grief. The mother sobs uncontrollably; the father, quietly. Then with another effort the father clears his throat, the back of his hand brushing at his tears, and says, "Would you kindly take a message to the Venerable Candana?" Sati is astonished to hear the name spoken in this room. How does he know?

"Please tell him that we've thought about it, and we're prepared to help the family," he lowers his voice, "the family of the woman our son, ummmm, battered. We know they're not his children, but we want to provide a dowry for the two girls so that when they come of age they'll be able to marry suitably."

Sati's eyes open wide. The shift in frame of reference is too fast, what he is hearing too heart-wrenching. "Excuse me—what did you say?" He needs to hear it again.

The man thinks Sati hasn't heard, for he naively assumes that his meeting with the Venerable Candana yesterday is common knowledge at Ghosita's Park, that behind the mysterious monastery walls all monks know each other's business. But in fact no one but the Buddha knows about the meeting. The two had consulted privately and decided that Candana should visit the family and give them an account of their son in his last days. Which he did, though he omitted reference to the three days Sagata had hidden in their house; there was no need to implicate the servant or to add to their burden by letting them know he had been so close. Importantly, he explained the plight of the impoverished family who fared so badly at Sagata's hands; this they needed to know.

The father repeats his message and adds, "Our son's memory can bring happiness in this one way at least. I'm instructing our guild to attend to the matter. I'll be opening a special account, and when the girls are ready to marry, the funds will be there for them. Please tell him that."

"I will," Sati promises feebly. He can't keep up with what this piece of news is unleashing in him. He needs time; he needs to leave.

As courtesy requires, the brother offers Sati juice as a refreshment, but Sati declines. It's over! Sati stands up, maybe a little too quickly. With equal alacrity, the brother does the same. He accompanies Sati to the door, then without making further comment, he stiffly nods farewell.

Back on the streets, Sati is limp. He feels like one of the fishing nets he used to cast into the river, all drape and compliance. The size of these people's grief; their unbounded gratitude for their son's words; their stunning generosity to the widow's family, which isn't calculated to gain merit but is for love's sake alone, for the sake of their beloved errant son; and the paradox of the lie that he himself has just told them (aren't there such things as good lies? he wonders. Was Sagata's last lie to him that last morning really so terrible?)—these things flood him as he makes his way back to the monastery. It's too much to think about now, so he doesn't try. Slowly Sati becomes aware that the rain has become soft and soothing on his skin. Un-hunching his shoulders and taking a deep breath, he gazes at the clouds. They're beginning to break. Sati realizes he's hungry and very tired. It's too late to eat today; so he speaks kindly to his young stomach: I'm sorry, friend, you'll have to wait until tomorrow. You can do it.

Once he's back, Sati goes straight to his hut. There will be time to deliver his message later. Now he needs to sleep.

CHAPTER 9

MONASTIC INTRIGUE
AND PALACE
RIVALRY

June 21. "We need to give more public Dhamma talks," the Buddha declares to the small group of seniors. He is walking in the rosewood grove this late afternoon with the Venerables Sariputta, Ananda, Upavana and Candana. The leaf-strewn ground, damp and cool, feels pleasant under their bare feet.

It is about the only thing that is pleasant though. The Buddha is concerned. There is much grumbling and dissatisfaction in town regarding the monastic community. Sagata's misdeeds have done great damage to their reputation, which was already shaky enough due to the schism. But the Buddha is not ready to give up.

Following Candana's suggestion, Ghosita managed to extract from the king the reason why he opposes the Buddha. It wasn't hard to do actually, because Udena was drunk and talkative. Udena is convinced the Buddha is a spy for his rivals, the kings of Kosala and Magadha, and that the ascetic is working to weaken him so that the others can seize control and split his kingdom between them. Ghosita reported this bit of insanity to Candana. The Buddha doesn't know yet how he'll respond; he is willing to bide his time so that an appropriate response can show itself.

He can, however, do something now about the townspeople. The teaching of "clear comprehension"—the ability to see clearly what needs to be done in each circumstance and do it unhindered by habitual reactions—the Buddha is a master at it.

"We'll increase the talks to twice weekly," he says, referring to the Dhamma talks, which have been offered once a week during Vassa. "I'll give one talk and one of you will give the other," he says, looking at Sariputta and Ananda. The Venerable Upavana isn't included because he isn't a teaching monk. The Buddha turns to Candana and says, "I'm sorry Candana, but it wouldn't be wise for you to do it now. I know you understand." And Candana does.

"And we'll have an ordination ceremony." This was Candana's suggestion. Ordinations aren't usually performed during Vassa because it's a time for those already ordained to train more deeply, not to bring in new men. But ordinations at this point will have the advantages of affirming the robustness of the community. The monks nod their agreement.

"So what about young Sati?" the Buddha asks, picking up on the conversation he had earlier with Candana. "How old is he?"

"He's 17, sir. He'll be 18 in a few months. And he's an orphan," referring to the fact that no family needs to be consulted.

"Hmmm." The Buddha prefers not to give full ordination to men younger than 20. Later on this would become a fixed rule, but now it's only a guideline, and it's one that the Buddha decides to ignore in this case. The reasons for ordaining Sati now are compelling; moreover, in his short career as a novice Sati has faced more challenges than many fully ordained bhikkhus face in a decade. "He's remarkably mature for his age."

Candana nods.

"Tell me about the others," the Buddha prompts. Candana mentions a novice who lives at Kukkuta's Park, which is one of the nearby monastic centers, and two laymen who've long been expressing a wish to go forth. About the latter he says, "I don't know if they still want to though; we need to check. I'll ask the Venerable Musila to speak with them. Also the wanderer Sivaka—he had been a member of Ajita's sect but had become a lay follower of the Buddha two years ago; he was in the audience the night of your first talk, maybe on the second night, too, but I didn't notice. I'll ask Musila to check with him too."

"Good. The more the better. What do you know about Sivaka?" the Buddha asks Candana.

"Not much, except that he's sincere in his practice."

"Bring him to me then, before the ordination. I want to talk with him." The Buddha wants to determine whether Sivaka should enter on probation, which is the order's practice for members of other sects, or whether he should enter as a novice, as do lay candidates. Probation gives the individual and the sangha opportunity to see if taking robes is the best course for both.

"Let's set a date—say, a week from today." The Buddha knows that Sati and the other novice need almost no notice, and the wanderer shouldn't need much. If the two laymen can't make arrangements in time, well, they'll have another chance later. He wants the ceremony to happen soon. "Let's hope there won't be any more unpleasant surprises between now and then," he adds with a hint of black humor.

Candana nods, fervently hoping the same.

"Now, about housing," the Buddha looks at Candana again. "It can be simple enough for the present; they can sleep in the dining hall or lecture hall or maybe there's room at Kukkuta's Park or Pavarikambavanna," referring to the third center in the Kosambi area, "but it would be better if they stayed here while I'm in residence. Have someone look into it, will you, Candana? Long-term arrangements can be thought about later."

Candana nods assent again but grumbles to himself, I'm the one who'll be looking into it of course—as if there weren't enough to do already! And it *isn't* so simple. He's says nothing, though. The Buddha's gaze remains on him for a long moment.

From the outside, it looks like one community. The buildings, the saffron-robed bhikkhus, the Buddha's presence create the illusion of a single community. But in fact the schism continues unabated. Members of both factions still refuse to sit with each other in the dining hall or walk together on almsrounds, and they are holding Uposatha in separate locations. Most of all, they still carry a hardness in their hearts that splits their monastic world in two.

The fact that the Venerable Candana is in the Buddha's confidence makes matters worse. Harika's forehead and jaw are continually tensed these days. He points out that Candana's central role at a time when his actions have created deep division is an insult to all the bhikkhus. That Candana's continued prominence also undermines Harika's opposition weighs heavily on his mind, but he doesn't mention it.

Harika slyly uses the Buddha's presence to intensify discontent. To his followers he remarks that the Blessed One at a distance is one thing, but here at Ghosita's Park—well, great and wise teacher that he is, he's an outsider. "He comes here decreeing how things should be; he works with his minion, Candana, to manage events and enforce rules; he even creates new ones. A new training rule within a day of his arrival—it gives our community a bad name! Think of the unfavorable attention! No wonder we're losing ground among townspeople!" he exclaims indignantly.

"If Bhagava hadn't arrived the day Sagata passed out, there would no rule prohibiting drinking. We could have dealt with Sagata ourselves. We could have expelled him immediately." It is a questionable assertion, but nobody challenges it. Nor do any of Harika's followers suspect he had a hand in the incident.

He continues, "And Nakula wouldn't have been killed, he would still be with us, good bhikkhu that he was." Harika actually disdained Nakula, considering him low-born and boringly commonplace. "And there wouldn't have been a public execution of a bhikkhu—a *former* bhikkhu," he says, correcting the apparent inadvertence, "and all the shame that has meant for us. Discipline has been lax; so now we're saddled with a reputation for bloodshed and drunkenness. Aren't these things obvious?" he asks.

Yes, they do seem obvious to impressionable bhikkhus who can't be bothered to think about these confusing matters. It's easier to agree. Talking among themselves, they take comfort in their shared beliefs and, in the process, they become more entrenched in them.

Harika and the Venerable Uttara often commiserate with each other, for the latter is almost as aggrieved as Harika. They rally

around the fiction that they are beleaguered Kosambians, though neither is actually native to the town, but they've been here longer than
Candana, and that's what counts.

June 23. Harika has a more important connection than Uttara and
the other bhikkhus in his faction. This morning on almsround he is
headed again for the home of the merchant Gopaka Phagguna. With
a respectful bow, a servant opens the door, and Harika steps into the
cool, stone-floored foyer. An observer might assume the Venerable
Harika has been invited to offer teachings, but the vigilant Vijaya,
who is watching from behind a lattice in her house across the street,
knows better. Tightly gripping the fretwork with a jeweled hand, her
heartbeat quickens, and she waits for Bharadvaja's arrival. Here's another event to report to her husband!

Since the only time Harika can reasonably meet is during almsrounds, they can't use the cover of night for secrecy. So Bharadvaja
and Harika have periodically switched meeting places in order not to
attract attention. Phagguna's is their latest venue, and the merchant
is deeply honored. Shortly after Harika's arrival, Phagguna personally
greets the minister at the door and obsequiously shows him into the
parlor where Harika is waiting; then he carefully closes the doors
and ascends to the third floor to talk with his wife. He longs to be
privy to the meeting, but he is flattered at least to be trusted to provide a venue for the high brahmin minister and the grim, orange-
eyed ascetic.

Bharadvaja listens and mirrors Harika's satisfaction as the bhikkhu describes events in the monastery just before and after Sagata's
execution. From Bharadvaja's viewpoint, the event has created gratifying controversy. He senses a shift in the people's favor away from
the Buddha and his order, and he wants to take advantage of it.

Bharadvaja always frames his comments to Harika carefully.
He appreciates Harika's subtle, legalistic mind—the man is no fool.

And Harika's brahmanic origin goes a long way toward commending him to the minister. But his main asset as far as Bharadvaja is concerned, the things that really make Harika a useful part of his plans, are his passion for disciplinary enforcement and his avowed opposition to the Venerable Candana.

Bharadvaja has readily perceived Harika's agenda: With Candana out of the way, Harika plans to temporarily work through Uttara, whom he patently regards as a dolt, and eventually to become the senior-most bhikkhu at Ghosita's Park. In that position he desires not only to formulate the disciplinary rules for the monastery, but to shape the Discipline of the whole order. It's quite apparent.

The two men have common ground, but Bharadvaja knows it has to be carefully cultivated. He cannot not let Harika suspect that his—and the king's—real purpose is to rid Kosambi of the recluse Gotama and all his bhikkhus. Harika would never accept that. Fortunately, there is not much danger of his guessing. For all his brilliance, Harika is too blinded by his own opinions and ambition to see the obvious.

The cagey minister patronizes Harika, making oblique and tantalizing references to possibilities supportive of the monk's goals, without getting too specific as to how they might be achieved. He points out that the king wants to maintain lawful order throughout his domain because a kingdom is only as strong as all its parts. Since there is separation between civil and religious authority and the Kosambi sangha is not subject to state jurisdiction, there needs to be informal cooperation between them. The great and mighty King Udena thinks the Venerable Harika is the right man to be the liaison.

Bharadvaja explains that Harika has the power of mind and proper respect for the law—unlike some outsiders—to do this important work. Of course the connection needs to be held confidentially since there are individuals in the sangha who wouldn't understand, their views being narrowly focused on religious affairs. But the king must take the broader view: He must consider the good of *both* civil and religious spheres, he must uphold civil and religious law. Having inherited the kingdom from his father—those were times of great turmoil indeed—he is now strengthening the realm by ensuring order so that peace can flourish for the good and happiness of all its inhabitants. This is to be the hallmark, the glory of his reign.

Ahhhh, yes! Harika swells with the knowledge of his place at the center of this great endeavor. The king is right. He *is* the man for this job. The king can rely on him. How perfectly things are transpiring! He can strengthen the order of bhikkhus (to which in his complicated way Harika is deeply devoted) while helping safeguard the whole kingdom. His father flashes to mind—a priest who didn't think beyond the next ritual. Harika always knew he was meant for something bigger, and here it is, his karmic inheritance coming to fruit!

Harika's voice resonates with the thrill of this realization as he confides the latest piece of monastic news: "The Blessed One will be performing ordinations in five days." Immediately though, tightness catches in his throat like a large glob of sticky rice because Harika considers the ordinations a personal defeat. Though he doesn't admit it to Bharadvaja, he's sure the Buddha will ordain men who side with Candana's faction. The novice from Kukkuta's Park already has. As for Sati, he's practically Candana's slave—the less he thinks about that one, the happier he is.

Bharadvaja, catching the shift in timbre and deducing its cause, refrains from comment. The numbers game between monastic factions is trivial as far as he is concerned. The pot is boiling—that's what's important—the king can take care of the rest.

Harika continues. "The novice Sati Abhaya will receive full *upasampada* ordination as will the novice, Kappa Ramaputta, from Kukkuta's Park. Two young townsmen will go forth as novices in *pabbaja* ordination, and a wanderer will be accepted on probation. In accord with our Rule, he'll be on probation four to six months to ensure that he's suitable." Despite his bitterness, Harika is getting carried away. He loves talking about the Discipline in any of its manifestations and he tends to run on. "We expect many townspeople to attend."

Bharadvaja has stopped listening to the tedious stuff. "Sati Abhaya?" he asks.

"Yes, the fisherman's son. Do you know him?" Harika peers at Bharadvaja, startled. Why would he be interested in Sati?

Bharadvaja doesn't respond. "And who are the two townsmen?"

The conversation flows on with Harika happily elaborating, but Bharadvaja stores the bit of information about Sati in the back of his mind. It is something to think about later, for he does indeed know Sati. More to the point, he knew Sati's father and opposed him years earlier when he was a government official. In fact, Bharadvadja constructed his downfall. He shares none of this with Harika.

June 25. "How do you suppose he knew? The king, I mean. How do you suppose he knew we watched the monks on their almsrounds?" Samavati muses, turning to Khujjuttara a few days after the windows were sealed. She says "we" not "I", for it was their shared activity.

They are sitting in her apartment this morning, and it is the time when bhikkhus are making their rounds. The brilliant light from the windows facing the inner courtyard do nothing to offset their feeling of gloom. Nor do the profusion of flowers that Khujjuttara buys daily and the many ghee lamps that she lights in the chamber. Looking at each other, they both know the answer: It was Jenti. One of Samavati's maids, Jenti watches her mistress closely, gathering information and relaying it to Queen Magandiya, from whom she receives handsome recompense. Neither Samavati nor Khujjuttara have any proof of their suspicion, but in the claustrophobic world of the harem, they all know each other very well. Every gesture and eye movement tells a story; words are hardly necessary. Everyone knows that Jenti is Magandiya's spy, and despite the fact that there seems to be no secrets among them to ferret out, Magandiya has a voracious appetite for the details of her rival's life.

Magandiya is the second consort. She is a woman of great beauty and of equally great spite. She has accepted Queen Vasuladatta, the first consort—that is as it should be. The young king had to marry someone, after all, and Vasuladatta is a princess, the daughter of the king of Avanti, and attractive enough in a waspish sort of way. Happily, Vasuladatta is a cold woman who hasn't been able to satisfy Udena. She, Magandiya, plans to do that. She will make him happy and will supply him with an heir. Vasuladatta has already borne a daughter, who doesn't count, and a son who is so sickly that no one seriously thinks he'll live to maturity—Magandiya has already dispensed with him in her fantasies. No, her own son will inherit the kingdom, and she'll have several after him, just in case. Those are her dreams, but it hasn't worked like that: In her four years of marriage, Magandiya hasn't borne a single child. As a result, she couldn't stand Samavati from the moment she heard that the king planned to marry again. In the flesh, Samavati is even worse. She is not only beautiful, she is sweet, intelligent, and loving. The king adored her, at least at the beginning. It's been nauseating. No one that sweet is real, Magandiya has concluded, unable to see past her own cramped heart.

Magandiya's hatred grew when Samavati became a follower of the recluse Gotama. Before Magandiya married Udena, her parents, who are wealthy brahmins, had offered their daughter to the Buddha in marriage. They were new to the Dhamma that year—it was six years ago, when the Teacher visited Kosambi for the first time. They were so impressed that they offered him their greatest treasure. The Buddha responded with a teaching on the repulsiveness of the body, which is aimed at lessening preoccupation with physical attraction. It was not perhaps the most skillful of responses under the circumstances, but the couple not only understood that their offer was rejected, but they also heard the deep truth in his words. They became followers. Magandiya on the other hand was insulted. Her beauty was her great vanity and anyone who rejected her with some long-winded blabber about repulsiveness of the body was her enemy. Her marriage to Udena shortly afterwards did nothing to alter her hatred for the Buddha.

It was Magandiya of course who told the king that Samavati watched the monks on almsrounds. Just as earlier she had told him about Khujjuttara sitting on the top step when reciting the Buddha's teachings. Magandiya gloated when she learned about Samavati's windows. It serves her right, miss-all-high-and-mighty up there in her roof-top domain. That honey-pot of a bitch!

June 27. Magandiya is at it again. Now that Udena has blocked Samavati's windows, it's the time to take advantage of the situation; her enemy is weak. And an auspicious occasion is at hand, because the king is visiting her this week.

On the third night, after the king has spent himself in love-making in her bed with its comfortable cotton-stuffed mattress, gorgeous canopy, and aromatic flower-strewn linens, Magandiya whispers sweetly, "Great King, greatest of men."

Udena hears the words with contentment, "Yes, Light of My Eyes?" he murmurs drowsily.

"Great King, my endless love for you makes me say something I wish I didn't have to say."

Udena becomes alert. Uh-oh, what's she up to? He knows Magandiya.

"My dearest master, I fear I must tell you that the recluse Gotama makes his way into the palace almost daily."

"What!" the king roars, the perfidy of this trespass propels him upright.

"Please, dearest, I don't mean to alarm you. The truth is that the crippled slave goes to hear the recluse every time he gives a talk, and she brings his words into the women's quarters. They sit around her like lambs suckling at their mothers' teats, listening to every word."

Oh—that old one! He lies back down again with a groan. Udena has already had the seating arrangement changed. Khujjuttara now sits on the floor, and the ladies sit on the steps as they listen. He thought that would satisfy Magandiya.

But she is still indignant. "Around her, a slave! And it's happening more often lately. Your high-class women are hanging onto her words—it's disgraceful!" There is genuine outrage in her voice. The teaching sessions offend Magandiya's finely honed sense of social propriety. Regardless of the seating arrangement, she won't be satisfied until the slave is silenced. Besides, it suits her other purpose to stir this pot.

Udena doesn't respond. Nor does he mention that he suspects that Khujjuttara is his half-sister. He doesn't know this for sure, but Khujjuttara's mother was a slave in the palace; she never married; and like most kings—in fact like Udena himself—Parantapa considered all women in the palace his personal property. Udena suspects that Khujjuttara was never openly acknowledged as one of the king's bastard daughters because she is ugly and deformed. They were embarrassed. But now, as Magandiya denigrates her, Udena bristles.

Recognizing that she isn't getting anywhere on the topic of social outrage, Magandiya switches back to her original line, "The recluse is as much in the women's quarters as if he were present in his actual own physical body, and Queen Samavati is foremost among those who are eager for his words. I think you should know this," she concludes sweetly.

Udena groans again. Magandiya is so tedious! So one-track minded. It's fine with him if Samavati and others are listening to the recluse's teachings. As long as Gotama and his cronies don't set foot in the palace, he doesn't mind. In fact, if the ascetic's words, even transmitted through a slave, help his women maintain a sweet, gentle disposition, he's glad for the sessions. It is most unpleasant to sleep with a bitter woman.

He lies back down, wishing the viper next to him would listen to the recluse's words once in a while; it might do her some good. But he isn't in the mood to argue. Turning from her, he says, "Don't worry about it, Magandiya. Go to sleep."

Udena won't be spending the night here—he never spends the night in his women's rooms—but he's not ready to return to his quarters yet. Still, if he can't get some peace and quiet, he'll do just that. And it wouldn't be hard either to drop his plans about sleeping with her the next few nights. There are others.

Magandiya knows this. She sighs and observes to herself philo-sophically, That was a flop. But there are other ways to work this, and she spends part of the night thinking about options.

CHAPTER 10.

SAMAVATI'S SECRET

*J*une 28. There *is* one secret in the women's quarters, surprising as it might seem. A very well guarded secret. Samavati has been driven to it by desolation. She has known hardship before, but she has always been surrounded by love and, until a year ago, she was relatively free in her movements judging by the standards of the day. Moreover, she was useful. Now, at eighteen, her world has constricted and she wonders why she is alive. She is married to a man she loathes and fears. For all practical purposes, she is locked into the women's quarters of the palace. Almost every movement is watched. An elderly eunuch makes nightly rounds to make sure the occupants are safe and, more to the point, that no one except the king is sharing their beds. By day, her life is afflicted by Magandiya's implacable hostility and by the triviality of her own routine. She has no useful work and, worst of all, her husband doesn't trust her. The bricked-up windows are a cruel reminder that he misunderstands her motives and that he is driven by a small-minded nastiness.

Her life feels to be a desert. A special hardship is the absence of her stepfather. Samavati has always confided in him. But now sharing her predicament would only cause him to worry, all the more so because he's powerless to change it. Nor is it a good idea to frequently ask permission to visit him. This would only remind her capricious husband of their closeness and likely arouse his jealousy, giving him pretext to retaliate again.

Among the palace women, Magandiya isn't Samavati's only problem. She has never gotten past Vasuladatta's cold exterior, and several of the concubines are distant as well, some openly resentful: Samavati is a queen after all. Her position secure, while they may be supplanted by a younger woman at any time, especially if they don't bear the king a son. Only one so far has been successful. Haunted by their fears, they make obsessive use of the garden swings and resort to esoteric fertility-inducing potions; they have little energy for real friendship. Even the few who attend the Dhamma sessions are constrained. No, there is only Khujjuttara.

Dear Khujjuttara—Samavati trusts her completely. She can share with her every fear, depression and unhappy thought, every dream and desire. Samavati is immensely grateful for their friendship. More than that, she has come to love Khujjuttara like a mother. Khujjuttara possesses wisdom that is ageless, and she has an apparently boundless capacity for caring, which she generously bestows on the motherless young woman. Still, Samavati doesn't want to harp on her own unhappiness. Why carry on day after day? Khujjuttara already knows anyway.

Khujjuttara is also her mentor. She has been encouraging Samavati to deepen her lovingkindness practice. Months ago, the Venerable Candana, speaking with Khujjuttara about Samavati's spiritual practice, advised lovingkindness, one of the Buddha's main teachings. He knew it was a balm that could ease her suffering. The practice feels more urgent than ever now. And Khujjuttara has been urging the younger woman not to neglect herself when practicing: Among all the people to whom Samavati sends thoughts of lovingkindness, she needs to be first on her own list.

This morning, other duties prevented Khujjuttara from going to market early; so they sit in Samavati's apartment surrounded by lit ghee lamps and seriously wilted flowers, as many of them were purchased yesterday or before. Now that the windows are bricked, they have been meditating in the mornings when the monks are on their almsrounds. It feels like a special time. Placing cushions in the center of the floor atop the thick-pile woolen carpets, they sit face to face and practice a mindfulness technique Khujjuttara learned at Ghosita's Park. They are starting with only brief periods of meditation, but they plan to gradually increase, inspired by the monks who meditate for long periods at a time. "Why not us?" they ask themselves, though they know their goals need to be tempered by the realities of the palace schedule.

Samavati has something very important to share. An idea arose, spontaneously it seemed, during yesterday morning's meditation. She's been thinking about it ever since, holding it up to the light of her attention as though it were one of her costly gems, examining every facet. Why not do it? she has been asking herself excitedly. Yes, they should!

Now, with their meditation finished, it is time to speak. "Khujjuttara, I've got an idea, something really wonderful!" she says breathlessly. "It's a secret. It's got to be a secret between us."

Khujjuttara listens. As far as she's concerned, everything that passes between them is held in confidence; she guards it with her life, and Samavati knows it.

Not waiting for Khujjuttara to indicate assent, she rushes on. "Every time you hear the Blessed One give a talk, you can recite it to me again, separately, after we've met with the other women, and I'll write it down! That way we'll have them. We can look at them whenever we want to, and study them!"

She stops and looks at Khujjuttara expectantly. The idea is radical. Nobody writes down the teachings. They never have. Script has been known in the Middle Land for a few hundred years now, but relatively few use it. There are no books. Writing is for business and legal documents, practical things of passing importance, not for what's sacred and eternal. Writing the sacred knowledge would put a lot of brahmin priests out of business. They are the only ones empowered to memorize and recite the Vedas; you can't have just anybody accessing these things. A general understanding has thus evolved that religious teachings of all kinds—including the Buddhadhamma—are too important to confine to birch bark, which is a pretty flimsy material in any case. No, the mind is the only worthy receptacle for holy matters. Many people would consider Samavati's idea blasphemous.

Khujjuttara's smile is twin to Samavati's. She is as excited as her mistress. She knows Samavati can read and write, though neither talks about it much. Samavati has had no opportunity to use her skill in the palace; indeed, it is dangerous to call Udena's attention to her ability. His interest in matters of the mind is nonexistent, and though he doubtlessly knows she is literate, it has pleased him to forget. Before she married, Ghosita warned her to be very private about the matter. "He's a jealous man and he's likely to feel threatened by a wife who can read and write. He can't, of course, or only barely."

Samavati learned early on just how wise this advice is. Not only would she expose herself to her husband's jealousy but also to that of other women in the palace, none of whom are literate. She doesn't need more of that.

In an era when few men can read and write, the idea of a woman knowing how to is unthinkable. Why would a woman need to be literate? Her job is to bear and raise children, keep the house and serve her husband. Literacy makes her independent. It gives her ideas that might contradict her husband's. It is a dangerous skill.

Samavati's father, a merchant in Bhaddavati in the kingdom of Avanti, doted on his daughter. She was an only child, bright and curious. When she was eight, he suggested to his wife that he teach Samavati to read and write. Her mother was appalled. "It will make her unmarriageable!" she exclaimed. "What man wants to marry a smart woman?"

"She's smart whether she knows how to read and write or not," he countered. "She may as well be smart and use her abilities rather than be smart and bored."

His wife was dubious. What's wrong with being bored? Besides, she could keep the girl busy with chores.

He added slyly, "I could use good, free help with the books. It would be a great financial advantage to us." Now this made more sense. Though not an avaricious woman, Samavati's mother *was* practical.

"With the way the business is expanding, when the time comes for her to marry, we will be able to make a good match for her. We'll supply her with a large dowry—her work with the books will help us do that. And we'll find her a man who won't mind that she's literate, someone who will appreciate her, someone who will make her happy."

Put that way, there was little to object to. His wife relented, and soon enough Samavati was learning. Even though young, she eventually became skilled in managing parts of their business, and as her father had predicted, it thrived.

When the plague struck seven years later, Samavati, who was fifteen, fled with her parents and many others to Kosambi. It was the city nearest Bhaddavati, and they had heard that King Udena had established a food and medical center for refugees. Within a couple of days of their arrival in town, however, her parents died of the plague, and Samavati was left alone and grieving. As a young, unprotected woman, a stranger in the community, she was in an extremely vulnerable position. At the time, Samavati was too shocked to reflect much—getting through each day was challenge enough—but now she has had many idle hours for pondering and has often wondered at the unfolding of events. Anything might have happened! She could never have anticipated the surprising ways her life was to open.

As a result of her business experience and her considerable store of commonsense, within the first few days of her arrival in Kosambi, Samavati noticed ways that the refugee center could operate more efficiently. She suggested them to the center's director; they were adopted with conspicuous success; and she soon attracted the attention of Finance Minister Ghosita, whose duties took him to the center. He was moved by her plight and intelligence, not to mention by her beauty and obvious good-breeding. He offered to adopt her, and she gratefully accepted.

Now Samavati elaborates on her idea to Khujjuttara, letting the thoughts that have thrilled her since yesterday and have kept her awake much of last night pour forth. "We'll make two copies of each talk, not one. I'll keep one here so we can study it. I'll hide it; no one must know—it's too dangerous. And even then, you never know what can happen; if there's only one copy any misfortune could destroy it. Baba can keep the second copy," she says, referring to her stepfather. "I'm sure he'll agree. He'll keep it safe so others can read it in the future."

Both women are silent before the immensity of the idea—preserving the Buddha's wisdom! This will be an offering to people through the ages, a gift to humankind. It is breathtaking! And it's also dangerous.

Samavati is prescient about the duplicates: Magandiya's treacherous inclinations were to culminate several years later in a nighttime fire in the women's wing of the palace. The entire building, which was constructed of wood, was destroyed. Asleep in the upper stories, all the women were trapped and burned to death, all except Magandiya, who was away at the time. The contents of the building were also destroyed, including Samavati's copy of the Buddha's words. Ghosita's copy, however, was preserved and eventually it became known as the *Itivuttaka*, a word that translates, "Thus it was said" because that was how Khujjuttara began all the passages when reciting them to Samavati and other palace women. The text became part of the collection of the Buddha's teachings known as the *Pali Canon*. Magandiya was later tricked into admitting her treachery, and Udena had her put to death in a particularly painful manner.

Thrilled by their project, Samavati and Khujjuttara start working immediately. They work mainly in the afternoons after napping, when the other women and their attendants repair to the garden courtyard to while away hours in pleasant pastimes, in the earnest business of swinging, and in stupefying boredom. Samavati and Khujjuttara finish by late afternoon so that Samavati can join the others at the bathing pool. Secluded on the grounds among ornamental trees and shrubs east of the women's building, the pool is a large manmade tank where the women enjoy cooling themselves after the heat of the day. It is beautified by pink lotuses floating atop the clear water and is bordered by a colorful multitude of flowers. Benches are set about the perimeter for the women's comfort, and they lay their clothing on them when entering the pool. Attendants stand by, guarding small chests in which their mistresses place their splendorous jewelry so that they may bathe unencumbered. The king often joins his women here, relaxing and frolicking according to his mood. Samavati knows she needs to be present.

The other women notice Samavati's afternoon absences from the courtyard, and many think her standoffish. Magandiya spreads the rumor that Samavati and Khujjuttara are engaged in what she calls "an unnatural dalliance," and points out that it is all the more deviant because Khujjuttara is a slave.

"It's twice an abomination!" proclaims Magandiya, and some of the concubines believe her. They coyly ask Samavati what keeps her so busy in the afternoons and they giggle. By the time the accusation reaches Udena—Magandiya makes sure it does—Samavati has prepared her response.

When questioned by him, she firmly denies the sexual allegation. "Oh, my lord, can you truly believe that? Surely, you know that you are the only one I desire. It has always been that way and always will be." Udena believes her right away. It is inconceivable that any woman could prefer someone else, male or female, to him. And the idea that his beautiful Samavati might prefer a misshapen female slave was ludicrous from the start. No, Magandiya is just up to her usual tricks.

Samavati adds, "It's true though that Khujjuttara is a treasure. She has spent her life here in the palace; she knows the ways of the palace and has helped me be a queen worthy of you. I hope I please you, my king and husband." She gazes up at him and deploys her most dazzling smile.

She's not ready to stop yet. To forestall his future questions, something needs to be said about her absences from courtyard in the afternoon. She hates lying, but the truth would be perilous; so she says, "I spend time in the courtyard in the mornings, when fewer people are about. It's quieter then; there's less chatter." This part is true enough, and it won't hurt for Udena, who has little patience with women's talk, to recognize that he and she are alike in this regard. Then the lie: "In the afternoons, I rest so that I can be fresh for the evenings when you are among us." She smiles again and hates herself. She feels as vile as Magandiya. And her lie makes her and Khujjuttara's work more dangerous. No one must ever find out what she really does in the afternoon!

In a small, neat hand, Samavati scratches the words onto the baby-soft inner skin of the birch-bark strips, using an iron stylus. It is the same process she learned from her father, though for an entirely new purpose. These are not business matters, but deep truths—simply transcribing them is exhilarating. At moments, Samavati feels she is in a heavenly realm consorting with divine beings; however, the challenges involved in transcription invariably bring her back to task. The talks include philosophical words that haven't been written before; Samavati is the first to do it. She and Khujjuttara discuss difficult points. The activity provides both of them with an education and increases the subtlety of their minds. She spells words phonetically, using consonants, and keeps a separate compendium for consistency, which is another first of its kind.

Samavati and Khujjuttara have to devise ruses to smuggle the birch bark sheets into the palace. There are many adventures and near discoveries, but they are successful. They also face the dilemma of where to hide the texts. No place is safe. For easy access, the transcripts need to be in her suite, but servants clean her rooms daily—the sitting room, the bedchamber, the dressing room and bath (both of which are attached to the bedchamber), even her storage closet and small pantry. Her personal servants, who oversee her toilette every morning, freely open her chests and pick through her shelves to select her clothing and jewelry. Washing her in the bathroom, they are into every nook and storage space.

Samavati decides that the only place that has a chance of escaping detection is in the two chests that are stored on a top shelf of the closet. Here she keeps possessions that belonged to her parents. These are items her mother and father brought when they fled Bhaddavati, things that have little monetary value—like garments and one of her father's accounting records and her mother's comb—but they are deeply meaningful to Samavati. She has Khujjuttara buy locks for each chest, and she carefully hides the flattened bark strips under the garments in one of them. To protect the inscriptions, she places fine pieces of muslin between the strips. Over time, as the number of strips grows, she begins to use the second chest as well.

After the Buddha's departure from Kosambi, Samavati and Khujjuttara make a decision that significantly adds to the volume of their work: They will transcribe highlights of talks given by some of the senior bhikkhus at Ghosita's Park, most notably the Venerable Candana. Because there are many such talks, they decide to make only one copy. As with those of the Buddha, Samavati reads aloud after she transcribes them, and Khujjuttara listens, though she doesn't really need to hear them because they are recorded in her memory. These talks, too, are prefaced with Khujjuttara's words, "Thus it was said." In this way, despite the poison around them, they are happily engaged for many years transcribing the Dhamma onto bark strips. Neither the transcripts nor the compendium survived the fire, though the copy given to Ghosita remained safe.

As Samavati and Khujjuttara work on their secret project, their love for the Dhamma deepens and, too, their practice. They continue to meditate each morning during the monks' almsrounds, even after the windows are unbricked. It doesn't occur to either that, despite the profligacy of palace existence, they are living a householder's version of the monastic life.

June 28. "Come, O bhikkhu, well taught is the doctrine. Lead a holy life for the sake of the complete extinction of suffering." These are the words the Buddha addresses to Sati as he confers full ordination on him. They are in the lecture hall in the presence of all the bhikkhus and a large gathering of townspeople. A novice no longer, Sati has entered the ranks of the bhikkhus, those of upright conduct, those who are practicing well. He has achieved the title "venerable."

Sati doesn't feel like a venerable though. He is keenly aware that encomiums must be earned by each venerable every day, and it's a hard road. He has seen too many fall short. What about me? he wonders as he kneels on his meditation rug before the Exalted One. He bows and briefly touches his head to the Buddha's feet. Contrary to a passage that the bhikkhus regularly recite, asserting that they are a field of merit for the world, Sati notes that he hasn't been transported to a field of merit, nor does one feel to be his eventual destination. He decides not to jump to conclusions, however. All he knows is that he'll do his best now.

Remaining in the suppliant's posture, he turns to listen while the Buddha moves on and addresses the same words to Kappa. The

man is six years older than Sati, but, because he became a novice shortly after Sati, Kappa is now his junior as a fully ordained
bhikkhu by three minutes. Sati assumes Kappa doesn't feel like a
venerable either.

After Kappa receives ordination, the Buddha moves to the two
others, one of the townsmen and the wanderer Sivaka. The second
townsman couldn't arrange his affairs on the short notice; so he'll
ordain later. Having talked with Sivaka, the Buddha decided that the
man could forego the probationary period after all: He has left behind
the materialistic views of his former sect and, having been practicing
the Buddha's Dhamma for the past two years, Sivaka is now ready to
enter as a novice.

Each man in turn receives the words of novice ordination,
then touches his head to the Buddha's feet. The two new novices
rise and stand next to their mats, and the Buddha and the Venerable
Sariputta begin to shave the men's heads. Silently reciting a short
verse of invocation, the Teacher and his foremost disciple shave several locks, carefully putting them in a bowl, which is placed on a low
table next to each, then turn and hand the razors to Candana and
Uttara to finish the job.

Even townspeople who aren't followers are moved by the so-
lemnity and symbolism of the ceremony. Harika however fumes, his
lips clamped in a tight line of resentment. A man who prides himself
on being guided by the logic of law, Harika doesn't notice how often
he's moved by other than logical considerations. He well knows that
it's appropriate for Candana and Uttara to finish the shaving since
they are senior to him; however in deference to his central role at the
monastery and to his important work with Baradvaja (of which most
others aren't aware), Harika believes he properly should be one of
the head shavers. All the more so because he disagrees with Sivaka's
novice ordination. Such is his angry logic.

Harika is convinced the wanderer should be on probation for
at least four months, in accord with the Discipline. Bhagava is wrong.
He has an infuriating way of treating the Discipline as if it were fluid,
making changes whenever he wishes. In fact, it should be hard and

fast—clear. That's the only way to protect it and those who follow it. In fact, Harika is centuries ahead of developments: The disciplinary rules are still evolving—they *are* fluid—but eventually, long after the Buddha's death, they will be held with a rigidity that even Harika would have approved of.

Now, however, the present fully claims Harika's attention. He feels that his participation as a head-shaver would signal also that they are one community, Uttara being just a figurehead. And isn't that the hypocritical message the Exalted One is trying to convey here—one community, he asks himself.

After the shaving, the new novices are each given three robes, a bowl and a water filter (to strain living creatures so they won't be unintentionally swallowed). The two leave the hall to put on their robes, casting aside forever their worldly garments, though Sivaka's garments were practically monastic already. When they return, the Buddha provides Dhamma instruction to all of the newly ordained and for the benefit of everyone gathered.

This ordination ceremony is different from others. It has the element of show about it, just as Harika grasped, and the Buddha doesn't like shows. He has never performed an ordination with such an eye to political impact or with such a sense of being at a disadvantage. He hopes these ordinations will demonstrate to Udena and others that the monastic community in Kosambi is a vibrant growing entity, despite the shame of the execution.

Political aims aside, the Buddha and Harika are in accord on one issue. They are the only ones who fully recognize another difference about this event: While for the most part, newly ordained bhikkhus become itinerants, here at Ghosita's Park most, maybe all, will reside in this community. They will travel, but probably less than other bhikkhus, and they will return home to Ghosita's Park and know each other as brothers. Not only proximity but also Uposatha has fostered this sense of community. Monks who confess together, abide together. Paradoxically, the king's opposition and even their schism have intensified community awareness. They have differences about who is in and who is out, but there is no doubt in anybody's mind that there is something here to be in or out of.

June 29. Sati's heart beats quickly, his belly is knotted. This is a moment he has been waiting for: He is about to receive his meditation topic from the Blessed One. Every monk attending the rains retreat has one. It's what they meditate with, usually for long periods at a time. And when they experience a problem or breakthrough, they consult the Buddha. For many, the topic is a *kasina*, a simple mental object like a disk that they focus on to train their mind in concentration. For others it is a perception, like impermanence or mindfulness of their breath or selflessness or danger. Sati hopes for a kasina.

A kasina—that's what Sati is convinced he needs to bring some order to the chaos in his mind. The Venerable Candana instructed him in mindfulness meditation, known as *Vipassana* even before he went forth: how to observe his breath and notice its subtle changes and thus cultivate mindfulness. The instructions were clear enough, but doing it is another matter. Sati thinks his mind is like a bunch of mosquitoes over a stagnant pond—up, down and sideways in endless frenzy. How can you watch your breath when all that's going on?

Looking for relief from his mosquito mind, Sati walks quickly to the Buddha's hut this afternoon, the day after his ordination. Each of the men who participated in yesterday's ceremony is having a private interview; Sati is first.

The Buddha is on his porch, and in the steamy humidity of the afternoon, he is perspiring freely. As is Sati. With palm facing palm in respect, Sati quickly sits on the mat across from him. The Buddha greets him, "Welcome, Bhikkhu Sati." It's strange to hear himself addressed as "bhikkhu," but no doubt he'll get used to it.

To put Sati at ease, the Buddha inquires about how he's faring, and they exchange a few pleasant comments. Then he says "Now for your meditation topic." Sati sits straighter and holds his breath: Here's my future.

"Meditate on lovingkindness, metta."

Sati stares at him. Metta! He doesn't have to meditate on metta; he's been practicing it since he was a child. It was either that or rage, and he learned early on that lovingkindness felt better inside when kids made fun of him. Surely Bhagava knows he's been doing it practically all his life! Why more of the same? Because you're a miserable failure, that's why, his mind retorts, flaying him. Bhagava is saying you can't handle a kasina and your metta practice stinks. You'll never be a successful bhikkhu. That's what he's telling you, stupid! Sati feels overwhelmingly depressed. He is sure disappointment shows all over his face.

The Buddha is continuing, "Cultivate it deeply, experience how it feels in your body and expand that feeling so that your whole body is suffused with it, every part of you should be drenched with lovingkindness—just like we're drenched with sweat now—but inside as well as out. If you learn to do this well, it will take you into deep states of absorption."

Sati's shoulders droop. Not good enough! I don't belong here, I knew it! The kids were right, I *am* a misfit. His mind has launched into its well-rehearsed litany. Outcaste—I'm beyond the bottom of the order, and I always will be. I'll never be enlightened. He ignores his father's counsel, which whispers to him at times like this when he gets stuck: "No one is an outcaste, no one is low class. All people are holy, son. Never forget it. Stay close to the Holy Inner One."

Sati notices that the Buddha has finished speaking, and he assents, "yes, Venerable sir," to whatever it was that the Teacher was saying. He wants to get out of here before he puddles into tears right here at the Exalted One's feet.

The Buddha raises a hand and says smiling, "Are you practicing metta now?"

Sati looks at him blankly.

"Metta for yourself. Are you being kind to yourself? You're not." And he explains, "I'm giving you metta, friend, because this sangha is in turmoil."

Lovingkindness isn't a topic the Buddha usually assigns, but these aren't ordinary circumstances. He will be giving metta as a meditation subject to Kappa, too.

He continues, "How can your mind be other than in turmoil amid so much divisiveness and ill-will? If I gave you a kasina, you wouldn't be able to stick with it. A kasina will come later. Metta is your refuge now, meditate with it, and for heaven's sake, practice it in daily life with your brothers. They need it! And so do you."

Oh! Suddenly Sati wants to cry again, but a different kind of crying. "Yes, Bhagava," he repeats. "I'll do it!"

CHAPTER 11.
SATI IN LOVE

July 1. Maybe I've been misjudging him, Sati thinks as he walks with the Venerable Migajala, who joined him on the way to the lecture hall this evening. Sati has never especially liked the rule-bound bhikkhu, but since the waterjar incident, he has actively avoided him whenever possible—the despicable, lying toad. And Migajala's attitude toward him has been reciprocal, colder than the Himalayan snows. So they are even.

Avoiding each other hasn't been a problem, what with the monastic split; nonetheless, Sati is well aware that Migajala continues to criticize the Venerable Candana's "disciplinary lapse." In his whiny way, he has been busily grousing about the stalled action over expulsion, making a significant contribution to the unpleasantness of everybody's days.

So why is it now that Migajala is so friendly? Sati puzzles about it as they walk to the hall together. Maybe because I'm ordained now and that's what happens when you become a real member of the community? No, not likely. Then remembering the Buddha's counsel last week, he thinks, maybe Migajala is practicing lovingkindness! Ooooff! Sati's stomach lurches as that astounding thought settles in, and his own abysmal lapse in this area sickens him.

In the past few days, Migajala has been falling into step with him as they walk to the lecture hall in the evenings. Their huts are close and both seem to be going in the same direction at the same time quite regularly. "Tomorrow I'm going to Commerce Street on almsround," Migajala comments, referring to the affluent area of lavish, multi-story homes. "Have you been there?" Sati hasn't.

"You should, you know," Migajala advises. "You should give those people a chance to gain merit too. They're just as deserving of merit as the poorer folk you like to visit."

Sati glances at him sidelong. Is this his son-of-the-fisherman sarcasm again or am I being too sensitive? It's so strange, he thinks.

Here I am, noble-born but ready to feel insulted because of a slur—a *possible* slur—from one born of the merchant class. Suffering! Just as Bhagava says, it's everywhere!

Oblivious to Sati's line of thought, Migajala continues, being very friendly indeed. "Why don't you come along with me, Sati? It would be a good experience for you."

I *have* been wrong, Sati concludes, abashed. He really means well. Happy to make amends, Sati agrees.

The following morning, Sati joins Migajala and another bhik-khu, also of Harika's faction. After exchanging greetings, which are amicable enough, they leave the monastery grounds, walking silently because chattering on almsrounds is unseemly. Sati doesn't have much to say to these two anyway. Clouds are building but it looks as if it won't rain for a while yet. Sati contemplates the possibility that Migajala's invitation may signal the start of the easing of factional animosity. A swell of pride runs through him: He is playing a part in bringing about harmony in the sangha. His posture straightens a bit.

When they reach Commerce Street, Sati glances up. He is impressed. The houses are even grander than Sagata's family home, which is a few blocks away. But quickly remembering monastic decorum, he looks down, regaining custody of his eyes. Sati knows it is inappropriate for bhikkhus to visually engage in urban bustle—it is so easy for one's attention to be caught up; by keeping the eyes downcast, they can more readily maintain a sweet mindfulness. Almsrounds then are more than the daily business of getting food. They are spiritual practice, training in cultivating wakefulness and equanimity in the midst of life's countless distractions.

The trio stands silently at the door of one of the great houses, eyes downcast, their robes arranged over their left shoulders, begging bowls in hand. When no one emerges, they move on to the next house. Here three servants come forth, each carrying a savory dish. After an initial bow, the servants begin making the rounds, offering the food to each monk. Sati glances up and notices that one of them is a beautiful young woman. She has large eyes, delicate features, and a slender body that her pale yellow garment reveals as much as conceals. She moves gracefully, spooning a rich curry into each bowl, keeping her eyes down as she does so. She is doing a far better job in that department than Sati is. She comes to him last, places food in his bowl, then steps back to join the other two who, having already completed their offerings, are waiting for her. The servants bow and the bhikkhus silently turn to leave.

Sati's thoughts don't leave though. Walking back to the monastery with fragrant aromas wafting around him, Sati is oblivious to all but the heavenly vision he has just encountered—her slender form, her gestures all grace, the caress of air between them when she offered him food, their bodies just inches apart. That evening he volunteers to walk with Migajala on almsround again the next day.

And the days after that. Each day the same young woman offers him food last and she seems to linger a bit longer on each occasion—or is it his imagination? And for Sati, each day becomes the story of his longing. He dwells on the brief moments near her, re-visualizing them in minute detail, and yearning for so much more.

On the fourth day, a slight breeze is blowing, and as she walks toward him, it momentarily flattens her garment against her chest, revealing the outline of her breasts, small, high and firm. Sati is already familiar with them and with other parts of her body, having fantasized about them daily, but now he audibly catches his breath. As she looks up and sees him staring, he glances away, embarrassed. Irresistibly however his gaze is pulled back and finds she is still looking at him. In other circumstances, he would have judged her stare an inexcusable lack of modesty, but now he looks into her eyes hungrily, with a directness and intensity that he hasn't experienced before. A crack fractures his world and he falls in. Sati is sure he'll never be the same again.

On the fifth day, her hand brushes his as she ladles food into his bowl. Involuntarily he leans toward her and reaches out, his hand drawn toward the soft skin he has come to know intimately in his imagination.

Sati doesn't know what might have happened next—afterwards he tells himself that nothing would have happened, he wouldn't have touched her—but in his preoccupation with the girl, Sati hasn't noticed that Migajala is watching closely. "This is inexcusable!" Migajala exclaims.

Sati's hand freezes in midair, his fingers a hair's breadth from her arm. Migajala shouts so loudly that the other servants gape, a passerby on the street stops to stare and the girl flees into the house. Migajala doesn't care about her. He says in outrage, "This is a serious breach of discipline. This is an offense!"

July 6. Lying on his cot, Sati hardly remembers the trip back. He left the house immediately in shame and confusion. He needed to get as far away from Migajala as possible.

Now in his hut, Sati is possessed by images of the shattered morning. The moment when they were so close…he can hardly bear to think about it. The horror of Migajala's voice cutting through— why did he shout like that? It was way out of line with what actually happened, though not out of proportion to the desire bursting within him. There can be only one reason: It was a setup from the start; Migajala has been trapping him. Of course! That means he's acting on Harika's instructions. Sati blames himself--not for his desire, but for his gullibility. How could he have been so deluded to think that Migajala was motivated by kindness? Rats don't change their nature. Sati knows the Buddha would differ on this point, but he doesn't care. Up until now, he has been naïve, incredibly naïve; he vows he'll never be duped again. Bitterness enters his heart, and he decides to hate Migajala—even if Bhagava doesn't approve! So that makes three— Migajala, Harika and Sagata, though he has moderated his attitude about Sagata lately. Did he have to become a monk to learn to hate? he asks himself.

His thoughts return to the girl, and he wonders if he'll see her again. Which raises the question that has been gnawing at the edge of his mind since he first saw her: Is he meant to be a bhikkhu? Maybe not. He doesn't want to marry her, no, not at all—well, not just yet anyway. But the fact that those few moments near her have thrown him into such chaos makes him wonder, it makes him doubt everything. What is he doing with his life?

Sati knows he has to tell Candana. His mentor won't be surprised of course because, as soon as he returns from almsround, Migajala will make sure the whole monastery knows. He'll paint the event in lurid colors.

Three anguished hours later, Sati wills himself to walk to Candana's hut. His mentor is sitting on his small porch, watching him approach. Candana doesn't smile or give a sign of greeting. Once Sati bows and seats himself, he says, "Yes, Sati?"

Sati briefly explains and Candana asks quietly, "Is that all?" He knows the story already.

"Yes, Venerable sir."

Candana sighs. "A bhikkhu's life is hard. You knew that when you joined the order and now you're finding out for yourself one way that's true. You've already encountered a few others. You're a young man, friend, and you need to honestly consider if you want to follow the monastic path. Maybe you acted too quickly in going forth. Maybe *we* made a mistake ordaining you so soon. Perhaps it would have been wiser to wait and give you more time."

Sati is desolate. His mentor doubts him! Never mind that he doubts himself, but Candana—he expected Candana, he counted on Candana—to support him, to understand and forgive. It isn't only his words but the tone of his voice, especially the way he says "friend," that opens an impersonal chasm between them that feels unbridgeable. Sati hates it. Maybe he *should* disrobe.

Unable to respond, Sati looks down. Candana waits. The silence between them lengthens. Gradually in the midst of his desolation, a different kind of silence stirs in Sati, a wordless knowing that is deeper than the cyclone engulfing him now. From some place beyond himself or deep, deep within, Sati knows that, regardless of who supports him and who doesn't, even if Candana never speaks to him again, he wants to be a bhikkhu.

Finally he looks up and says simply, "I want to be a bhikkhu."

Silence. "I made a mistake, or rather," he fumbles to express it, "my body wanted one thing but I want something else. I want to be a bhikkhu."

Candana looks at the young man and imperceptibly his shoulders relax. But he isn't ready to drop the matter. He speaks. "The holy life challenges men to their limits in all ways. And then beyond their limits. Eventually, it requires everything. It's not easy for anyone, but it can be a little easier for those of us who've been married." Sati knows that Candana had been married and has two daughters who are now also married and that his wife died several years ago.

"Those of us who've been married and have lived the worldly life know some things. As a result we may have fewer longings, and being more mature, we're less likely to be overwhelmed by them. But you, friend" (this time the word doesn't bite quite so much) "you're young, you don't know women and you don't know..."

"That's not exactly true, sir," Sati interrupts.

"Not *exactly* true?"

"Well, not true."

"I see," says the Venerable Candana. "And when did this happen?" he asks warily. "While you were here at the monastery?"

"No. No, sir, I was at home."

"I see," he repeats, relieved that this isn't going to be disciplinary problem— it would have been a major one. And secretly Candana is glad too that Sati has had some experience with women.

"And what about this young servant woman now? What do you plan to do about her?"

Sati shakes his head and says slowly, "Nothing. I don't plan to do anything," then adds with passion, "I wish her well!"

"I see," for a third time. Candana takes Sati at his word and is ready to move on, for no useful purpose would be served by further discussion now. Nothing will change Sati's natural longings, only time will do that, and in Sati's case it is going to be a long time. The young man will continue to be deeply challenged by the absence of a woman and worldly love in his life—as most monks are. The issue will certainly arise again and, when it does, it will need to be addressed.

In the meantime, there is this unpleasantness. "You acted in a manner most unseemly for a monk, Sati. You need to learn from it and not repeat it. And you need to confess at Uposatha, you know that." Sati nods.

"In itself this isn't a major offense; nothing much actually happened between you and the young woman, but in your thoughts and body a great deal happened, didn't it?" He holds Sati with a look that he can't evade. While outlining the situation, Sati has omitted mentioning his thoughts and physical responses.

"You'll need to confess these things." In the Buddha's teaching, intention is as important as action.

Sati nods miserably. He's been a bhikkhu for just a little more than a week and already he has committed an offense! Actually two— one, that he touched a woman, although inadvertently—she touched him first and he didn't quite touch her back, though he *wishes* he had, and in more satisfying ways. And the other, that he touched himself, quite deliberately. He squirms at the prospect of confessing. These things are so, well, personal, and the girl so dear—talking about her, putting her out into the counsel of monks, feels to be a brutality.

Candana continues as though he were responding to Sati's thoughts. "Almost every bhikkhu in this community has experienced such problems, longing for a woman or another man. You're hardly the first. And even if there's no offense in that area, every one of them has faced the ordeal of confessing something he would rather not talk about. I'd wonder about someone who has never confessed— that's not perfection, it's more likely rigidity and dishonesty. Someday, friend, you'll see that confession is just part of the process of letting go; it's an important part of training. In a way, it's not personal."

Sati doesn't understand, but Candana's comments make him feel better. Still he dreads Uposatha.

Then Candana's tone shifts, "Ordinarily once one confesses and penalty is determined, the matter is resolved, legally speaking. But these aren't ordinary times. This will increase divisiveness here in the sangha and I think that's the larger point. To be honest, Sati, you were used."

Doesn't he know it! Sati regrets the harm he has done to the community, but more than that, he's nauseated by his naiveté. He deluded himself by thinking he was contributing to healing differences when in fact the opposite was true. Even worse, his pride in his understanding of the world's duplicity based on his experience in the suburbs has come in for drastic revision. How could he have been so horribly wrong?

Candana is continuing. "Why did you decide to do almsrounds with Migajala?"

Sati explains and sheepishly admits, "I thought maybe he was trying to make it up, to create a little harmony. That maybe he was expressing lovingkindness."

Candana smiles wryly. "That's a beautiful thought, son. I hope you never lose your trusting nature."

Sati doesn't say that he has already lost it, that he'll never trust Migajala again.

"I wish things were so simple, but if someone wanted to increase disharmony"—Candana doesn't need to mention names—"and undermine me by discrediting those who support me, this would be an obvious way to do it. It doesn't take much insight to know you'd fall for a beautiful young woman."

A new thought crashes in on Sati: What if his beloved—that's how he thinks of her—what if she was used, too? What if she was instructed to do it? Maybe she didn't mean any of it! By the heavens, maybe she was forced against her will, in which case, his love has created more anguish for her! Of all the devastating insights of the day, these are the most unbearable. Too pained to think about them now, Sati turns his attention back to Candana.

"Which house was it?" he is asking.

Sati doesn't follow. "Which house? Oh, a big one. On Commerce Street."

"Yes, but which one? Describe it."

Sati does his best, but he didn't pay much attention at the time and he isn't doing so now. But he's trying. As he gropes to focus, something Sagata told him during their last meeting emerges from a corner of his mind. Up until now, he has shied from thinking about Sagata, but now there's this thought.

"Sir!" Sati declares excitedly, "Sagata told me he regularly visited houses on Commerce Street—it's close to his family's home—and that's where he was the day he passed out. Maybe there's a connection!"

Candana already knows this—Sagata told him after he had sobered up a bit. But Candana smiles to himself, the boy isn't so befuddled by the woman that his mind has stopped working.

"I think you may be right. Maybe there is a connection. We'll have to wait and see."

CHAPTER 12.

GROWING UP,
MARITAL
HARMONY

*J*uly 15. The only good thing about this Uposatha is that bhikkhus from Harika's faction aren't here. Sati doesn't have to confess that he touched a woman and touched himself before Migajala, Harika and other hostile ones; they are off observing their own Uposatha in the dining hall.

Still, it is hard enough, excruciating in fact. During the intervening days, Sati has interpreted disapproval in subtle gestures and expressions of even members of his own faction. He is so embarrassed that he can't make himself small enough. His posture has shriveled as he walks. He wishes he were invisible. Sati doesn't realize his outcaste script is running amok, that he is projecting his own judgments.

Now at the Uposatha meeting, in addition to members of his own faction, two of the visiting seniors, the Venerables Ananda and Kamabhu, are present. In view of the schism, the Buddha decided that the visiting seniors would split, three and two, and would alternate their attendance between the groups; in this way they won't take sides. The Buddha doesn't attend either observance.

The Venerable Udayi again takes the role of preceptor. A tall, shy man in his fifties, Udayi is older than most of the monks at Ghosita's Park. He is also a senior, having ordained at the same ceremony but a few minutes after Uttara. Udayi has a rich voice and a good memory, and he is often is called on to recite the Patimokkha at Uposatha.

The recitation now consists of forty-three precepts, the new one being Sagata's enduring legacy to the sangha. After the recitation, Udayi asks the assembly if they are pure in these matters and Sati mumbles his confession. It is news to no one. Udayi asks him how many times he masturbated. It's not a mean-spirited question; the severity of the penalty depends on the answer, but being unprepared for it, Sati responds, his husky voice a hoarse whisper, "I don't know."

Udayi, who is kind, doesn't press. Instead he says, "Since the Venerable Sati admits his offenses but is uncertain about the frequency of the second offence, it would be appropriate to lay three days of penance on him; after that he is rehabilitated." He repeats the judgment three times, each time asking those approving to remain silent, those disapproving to speak up. No one speaks up. Sati is too young in monastic training to realize that since most of the others have undergone penance for the same offense, they're sympathetic.

With his face going pomegranate red and eyes downcast in embarrassment, Sati moves to the front of the group next to Udayi, and, following prescribed behavior, he squats on his haunches in the humble posture, his palms outstretched, and states his offences. Then he declares his intention not to repeat them. This is the gesture he will repeat to the assembly of monks for the next three days. It is their custom—which again Harika inspired—to gather in the lecture hall immediately after the noonday meal to hear penance. But since most monks prefer to sleep after lunch, part of Udayi's job is to make sure at least a monk or two is present in the hall when one of the brothers does penance. It's all quite simple. Except there's no guaranteeing now that members of Harika's faction won't choose to be in the hall when Sati does his.

Migajala, leaving his Uposatha observance in the dining hall, passes Sati in the common area and leers at him. He didn't have to be in the lecture hall to know that the young monk was called to make confession and was penalized. Migajala relishes the knowledge. Sati ignores him, however. These past few days, Sati has been taking mean enjoyment in looking the other way when Migajala passes. But now Sati simply doesn't notice, for he is absorbed in the discovery that, despite his humiliation, his heart actually does feel lighter for confessing. How strange!

As he ponders this unexpected turn, Sati fails to see Harika who is standing at the entrance of the dining hall observing him, too.

Harika is conflicted, a state to which he is unaccustomed. Framing Candana was necessary, he reflects, because the goal was important. Harika isn't one to quibble over ends and means. But Sati is unimportant, just a gullible kid. Not that he likes Sati, mind you—hardly! Sati's devotion to Candana is enough to ensure his active dislike. But that's not the point. Bharadvaja is.

It bothers Harika that the minister targeted Sati. He complied with Bharadvaja's wish of course and instructed Migajala, but Harika reasons that since they've already achieved schism, their focus needs to be on generating dissatisfaction in town. The townspeople need to be angry enough about the sangha's laxity that they demand change and give the king reason to require it. This little business of Sati's won't hurt the cause, but still, the few townspeople who hear about it will likely wink and approve of this evidence that the young monk is a young man all the same. No points gained there.

No, the question is why did Bharadvaja target Sati? There's something that Harika doesn't understand, and it makes him uneasy. They've been allies, each working in his own sphere for a common goal, a lofty one at that, but now it looks as if Bharadvaja hasn't been entirely open. Harika has been so intent on his own goals, not all of which he has shared with the minister, that it hasn't occurred to him that Bharadvaja might be playing the same game. Now he is visited with the appalling possibility that he might be as gullible as Sati. He quickly closes the door on the thought.

July 18. On the afternoon that Sati completes his penance, the Venerable Ananda invites him to walk with him on almsround the next day. Sati is enormously flattered, especially because it comes so soon after his shame. He gloats, Here is one of the most senior, most respected bhikkhus in the order, a bhikkhu I really like, and he wants to walk with me! He nods his agreement with a gigantic smile.

As the day goes on, however, commonsense sets in. Come on, Sati, he's not asking because he likes you or because you're such a great monk or because of your good looks. He snickers at the thought. With his high cheekbones, well-proportioned features and eyes that are slightly slanted, the Venerable Ananda is one of the most handsome men Sati has ever seen. So why *is* he asking? By the time they are ready to leave on almsround the next morning, Sati is apprehensive.

When he nears the monastery gate where he's to meet Ananda, Sati's anxiety skyrockets: The Venerable Sariputta is standing with Ananda, holding his begging bowl! The venerable has remained aloof since he arrived at Ghosita's Park, and Sati is intimidated by his reputation. The prospect of walking on almsround with Sariputta as well as Ananda is completely unnerving.

They nod greetings to Sati in silence and start out. Ananda falls into step beside Sati, who keeps his eyes appropriately downcast, looking at the path ahead. At least I don't have to say anything, Sati counsels himself. All I have to do is walk and that's simple enough. But his legs feel remarkably liquid. Come on, Sati, steady up. You can walk, this is just in your mind. He focuses his attention on the sensations of each foot, moving through the air, meeting the ground, receiving the weight of his body. Stepping, stepping, stepping.

So far, so good, he thinks, allowing himself a little satisfaction. Then he notices the direction they are taking, and his tiny pleasure evaporates, his breath starts to come in hard little gasps: They are walking toward Commerce Street! Oh no—it's the last place he wants to be! How can he endure this? It's another setup! These venerables are cruel!

As they turn onto the street, Ananda whispers, "Show me the house." Sati's head bobbles weakly.

They stand silently outside the door but no one opens. Sati begins to feel hopeful. He sends urgent thought messages to the servants inside: "Don't come!" and to Ananda: "Let's go, let's go." Ananda, however, doesn't move. Finally, after quite a lengthy stand—Sati has begun shifting his weight from foot to foot, wishing he could dash away—the door opens. Two flustered, apologetic servants appear with food offerings. She is not one of them. Sati recognizes the elderly manservant; the other is a stranger. They distribute the food, then bow, and the bhikkhus move on.

By the time they return to the monastery, Sati is exhausted. Before they part, Ananda says, "We'll walk together again tomorrow." It's a command.

And so they walk on almsround for the next two days, once with another senior and once just the two of them. Why is the Venerable Ananda doing this to him? But he doesn't ask because something tells him that Ananda has a good reason and it will become clear in time. Sati is angry but he also trusts Ananda.

Each day, they return to the same house first, and Sati holds his breath at the door. Servants emerge bearing food, but she doesn't appear. As they leave the house on the third day, Sati can't contain himself any longer; he whispers the obvious to Ananda: "She isn't here."

Ananda nods, whispering back that very possibly she's been dismissed. Sati's heart sinks; he feared as much. "I don't know whether she has been or not," Ananda clarifies, still whispering, "but it was an unpleasantness, though a minor one, and it involved a bhikkhu. Whatever her role—whether she was instructed to behave as she did or not—she *was* part of it, and so she would be thought to bring ill fortune to the whole house."

Sati's shoulders droop. He is responsible, he brought harm to the very woman he so cares for. Oh, what a fool he's been! If he could only help her!

As though reading his thoughts, Ananda says kindly, "You can't help her, friend. She has to bear her karma." Then he says, "Come, let's go back to the monastery." And he signals to the Venerable Narada, who is walking with them, to continue without them. Since their bowls aren't full yet, Narada will bring back additional food to share.

Though almsrounds are usually conducted in silence, this exchange is important. It's a teaching Sati needs to hear. As they walk back, Ananda comments, "You can do one thing, though. You can send her lovingkindness. Doing that is no small thing, for what happens in your mind and heart has an impact in this world. Know that for sure, friend Sati, and make what happens in your mind beautiful.

You will help the world more than you can know; you may help her, too."

Sati nods wholehearted assent, and from that day on, for the rest of his life, he sends metta to Sumana, for he knows her name— he heard one of the servants address her—and she lives in his mind, forever young, forever desirable, even when he is past the age of desire, but he never sees her again.

July 22. That evening outside the lecture hall, the Venerable Ananda approaches Sati, and Sati is ashamed to notice that, while he likes the kindly monk immensely, he's dismayed to see him coming. What does he want now?

Ananda smiles at him in his stunning way. Sati is guarded. "Will you walk with me in the grove for a few minutes? There's something I want to say and we have time before the talk starts."

As they leave the small group that has already assembled, the Venerable Harika watches. He knows Sati has been walking with Ananda on almsrounds— Migajala, who is keeping an eye on Sati, informed him—and now here is another sign of their growing connection. Why is everyone so interested in this no-account kid? He assumes some political maneuver is afoot.

"Friend Sati," the Venerable Ananda begins once they enter the simsapa grove, "we talked about the possibility that the young woman was dismissed." Sati's jaw tenses. "It raises an even bigger issue, because her plight is one that most women face: They are used. They're valued by most men only if they are beautiful and because they bear children. Oh, and of course, for their family connections, if they have them. That's it. Beyond that, they're regarded as inferior in every way. In effect, they belong to a separate class: Regardless of the class they're born into, there's the class of women."

Sati is astounded. He's never heard such an idea! Why is the venerable telling him this? Ananda begins to warm up to the subject.

"It's an utterly distorted view. It's wrong. It creates suffering for half of the human race."

Sati listens in wonderment. Although his wise father taught him that all people are essentially equal and that class is merely an idea people impose on each other—a system that works to the advantage of some and to the disadvantage of most—he never talked about the worth of women. He lived it though. Sati's parents lived together as friends as well as husband and wife. His mother was an intelligent woman, with a sunny, kindly disposition—Sati inherited this from her. She didn't hesitate to express her views, and they invariably made good sense. She provided all the model Sati needed. But now here is the Venerable Ananda talking about the social position of women in general.

And he's right, thinks Sati. He's been agonizing over Sumana's fate, weighing the possibly drastic consequences she is facing, while he had a mere penance imposed on him. It is so unjust! He is ready to consider the plight of all women, and to consider it with deep sympathy.

"Women have always been subject to the whims of men. Why? Not because they're inferior but because they're not as strong physically, and because our society values what men know—aggression and so forth; it devalues women's traits, like receptivity, tenderness and patience. These are considered weaknesses. But the truth is that any society that values only one and dismisses the other is crippled. A healthy society, like a truly healthy person, needs to value both. Without both there's no balance. That's the Middle Way," Ananda declares passionately, referring to the term that the Buddha uses to describe his Dhamma.

Then he says something even more radical: "Women are as able to attain enlightenment as men are. They're not inferior in that regard. Which is why Bhagava allows a nuns' sangha." He stops, partly out of modesty, for Ananda had pivotal influence in the Buddha's decision six years earlier to permit the formation of an order of nuns. Partly, too, he stops because he knows he has given Sati enough to think about for now.

These ideas take Sati's breath away! He knows there is a bhik-khuni order, but they're not here, he hasn't seen a nun, and he's never thought much about them. He has enough on his mind as it is. Over time though Ananda's ideas will take root, and within a few years, Sati will grow to firmly support the sangha of nuns.

Ananda smiles and says, "So friend, when you think of the young woman"—Sati hasn't shared her name; that at least is his—"when you think of her, and perhaps grieve for her, I hope you'll be able to see hers as the plight of countless others. It's not about her alone. This is suffering. Regard it all with compassion, *karuna*. See it truly—and you'll experience greater peace."

Sati understands intuitively, and he says simply, "I'll try."

"Well now," Ananda's tone shifts, "shall we return?" As they walk back, the older monk comments, "I'll see you in the morning for almsround." Sati notices he doesn't feel aversion at the prospect.

July 23. Today they walk in a different quarter. Sati is relieved, but a little disappointed too. He wants—just for a moment—to walk on Commerce Street again to test his equanimity. Especially now, when he's pretty sure Sumana won't be there. He resolves to do it again soon, but he doesn't get around to it for several years. By that time Sati has realized how, by insisting that they walk there together, Ananda helped him face his inner turmoil, instead of burying it.

As they walk now in a new quarter, Sati is free enough from his concerns to notice closely how Ananda conducts himself. Ananda carefully maintains custody of his eyes, keeping them appropriately lowered even in the midst of the bustle of people scurrying to put food into his bowl. His equanimity is especially notable because the townspeople keep looking at him, and many stumble over themselves to offer him food. This isn't only because he is a high bhikkhu. His good looks are hard to ignore.

In fact, Ananda's good looks are a reason why the Blessed One frequently sends him to teach. Not only is his trusted disciple well-versed in the Dhamma—Ananda's remarkable memory enables him to recite the teachings accurately long after he has heard them, he understands them well and explains clearly—but additionally the Teacher, being eminently practical, uses to the advantage of his mission the human inclination to be drawn to physically attractive people. It is one of the many ways Ananda serves the Dhamma.

Beyond this, the Buddha sends Ananda into public out of concern for his spiritual progress: The man's extraordinary beauty, considered a blessing by most, is ultimately a bond that keeps him locked into a limited sense of self. It prevents him from experiencing the freedom of pure awareness. Ananda, being human, isn't oblivious to the many admiring glances. He is practicing hard to free himself from enjoying the attention, and sometimes his efforts are so intense that he experiences aversion when he's admired. But he is stuck, nonetheless, because, whether his reaction is pleasant or unpleasant, he is focused on his physical appearance, and that reinforces a notion of self. The Buddha knows that transcending this formidable obstacle may take years of spiritual practice, and he wants to give Ananda as many opportunities to do the work as possible.

As they walk together, Sati has no way of gauging the subtleties of Ananda's attachments; he only notices that the man seemed unaffected by the flurry of attention, and he contrasts Ananda's response with his own immersion in just one little glance. *I have a lot to learn,* he concludes accurately.

It's exactly the conclusion the Venerable Candana wants him to reach. He wants Sati to experience the deportment of a superlative senior monk on almsrounds, having so recently had such an unsatisfactory experience with a junior. Candana knows that Ananda, for the very reason of his beauty, is the perfect one to teach him, and that is why he asked Ananda to walk with Sati.

July 24. Udena looks down from a window in his quarters in the central building onto the garden courtyard where Samavati is sitting with Khujjuttara. He is relieved to see her; it's been a hard morning. He met with one of his spies and a councilor to discuss a problem that has been simmering for months. His spy, who managed to travel from afar despite the rains, reported a deteriorating situation in the Kora district. Now the meeting is over, and Udena feels battered. Gentle Samavati, yes, she is just the person I want to see. He goes down to her.

"My husband, Great King," Samavati rises from the bench in greeting, the corners of her lovely lips lifting slightly. Khujjuttara also rises and discretely backs away, retreating to another section of the yard so as to be on hand afterwards.

"Greetings, wife. I hope your day is going well."

"Well enough," she replies. "And I hope the same for you."

"No. It's been terrible," he declares bluntly. Udena doesn't usually discuss state matters with his wives but this morning he needs to talk. He sits on the bench and gestures for her to do the same.

Leaning back, he stretches his legs, locks his fingers behind his head and looks off into the sky. Samavati notices that the soft bulge of his belly under his garment has enlarged since they last slept together—which was a considerable while ago. Personally Samavati doesn't mind the hiatus—Udena isn't a sensitive lover—but she is concerned that she hasn't yet performed her queenly duty of bearing a son.

Udena continues, "There's a problem with Vasula Sutasoma— that young rogue, a disgrace to his family!"

She listens.

"He was my tax collector in Kora," naming a tribal village in the upper doab. "He raped a tribal girl. He was drunk—he admits it but blows it off as unimportant. Of course he's right," he adds hastily, "it *is* unimportant, but the reactions, *they* haven't been unimportant.

"He barely got out of there alive. The villagers are outraged and they're refusing to pay taxes. They're mad enough to go to war. So now what to do?" he asks rhetorically. "If I send another tax collector, I'll have to send an army with him."

The thoughts he has been wrestling with all morning come tumbling out. "That's a lot of money, a lot of men, a long way to go. Whatever I do, it has to be soon, right after the rains, because if I wait, they might make an alliance with Kosala, though I don't know if they're smart enough to do that—or maybe they are but wouldn't want to. They don't particularly want us either though. They just want to be left alone.

"They're sitting on some rich territory between us and Kosala, and I can't afford to lose that. But war? I don't want to go to war." Udena personally has little liking for the hardships of battle, which he hasn't experienced first-hand and has no intention of doing so. "My father had a hell of a time subjugating them—I remember those days..." His voice trails off.

Samavati sits silently, waiting for him to resume. When he doesn't, she asks gently with her natural good sense, "Can't you send someone else, a different tax collector, someone to apologize? And maybe grant them a consolation like reducing their taxes? That way they'd know you're sincere."

"It's not so simple," he replies.

"Why not?"

"For one thing, sending someone else would insult Sutasoma. He can't go back, even with an army, they'd kill him, but he can't not go either—it would be an insult. His family is influential and proud. His father was an important advisor to my father. I don't want to anger them."

"And finding him another position?"

"Not easy, either. He's a wild one, terrible temper. He antagonizes wherever he goes." Udena snorts. Then with considerable force the realization dawns: The same can be said about him! And as though speaking to himself, he comments bitterly, "But he at least is tall."

"Tall? What's that got to do with it?" asks Samavati, not seeing a connection.

Udena is silent for a moment then turning his face toward her, he says, "He's tall, so that means he's a good official."

"My king…" Samavati begins in wonderment, but he interrupts her, now sitting up.

"My father always said that height is an important quality in a ruler. It means he's born to rule, if he's a noble, that is. One can't be a great ruler if he isn't tall…and I'm not," he adds in almost a whisper.

"Ohhhh," she says as new understanding suddenly fills her. "Oh, my husband, you *are* a great king. The qualities of kingship don't depend on height; they're inside. One can be tall and be a bad ruler, and be short and be a great one. You're not tall but you *are* a great king."

Now it is his turn. He looks at her, his eyes large with surprise. "Is that so?"

"It is!" she says emphatically. "And all your people know it. Why, you're keeping us safe from Kosala, which is annexing everything in sight. But we're still independent, the whole doab is independent, and that's because of you. And you care for your people—you set up a public almshouse to feed refugees fleeing from the pestilence. Not all kings do that," thinking of his hard-hearted father. "Surely you recognize all the good you are doing. Your people love you."

He is silent, taking in the truth of her words, sifting through a lifetime of belief about the limitations imposed by his stature.

For the first time, Samavati sees into the heart of this man, her husband. She sees the little boy who was inadequately loved, a brooding child who was hungry for more of what was only stingily given, the ache of it marking all his youth. And it still does. She has heard enough about his father, whom she was grateful to have never met, and his timid mother to now see truly what their parenting produced. And her own large heart opens to him. From that moment, Samavati's relationship with Udena changes. While still playing the role of wife, she becomes mother as well, loving him as his own didn't have the courage to do. She doesn't fool herself. He is a boy inside, yes, but that makes the man more dangerous. Henceforth, she walks a fine line—Samavati is good at that—and in her dual roles she pleases him greatly.

CHAPTER 13.

ARITTHA'S ADVENTURES IN BHAGGULAND

*J*uly 24. Arittha is back! Finally. The monastery is abuzz because he hasn't arrived alone. He brought Nakula's wife and brother with him. The monks are scandalized. Even Sati, himself so recently censured, is concerned. Arittha knows the rules. Traveling in a party with a woman is forbidden. What was Arittha thinking?

The Venerable Harika puts it more strongly. "That bhikkhu received special permission to travel, and what does he do? He flaunts the Vinaya, he flaunts the Blessed One, he flaunts all of us! It's a disgrace! Monks have been suspended for less," referring longingly to Candana's still unresolved plight. To himself he says, Things are moving along splendidly!

He continues his judgment, "Bhagava was much too liberal. *I* knew he shouldn't have allowed him to go. What can you expect from a vulture killer?" Harika can't resist the delicious slur. He is talking to the Venerable Uttara, a brahmin by birth, whose views on social status are similar to his own. It is gratifying to speak openly knowing he'll be supported.

Here it is again—social hierarchy, the silent issue in the sangha. All bhikkhus know the Buddha's radical teaching that everyone has the ability to awaken, but some who haven't yet experienced the inner truth of the Dhamma tenaciously cling to bias. Some bhikkhus born to the brahmin class, even some who are noble-born, feel little incentive to question the cultural beliefs that so agreeably elevate their own status. Skeptical of the ability of bhikkhus from lower classes—much less, heaven forbid, those who are outcastes—to progress significantly, they glibly dismiss those who do as exceptions. The connection that exists among these class-bound bhikkhus is expressed in whispered remarks and pious smirks, such as Harika and Uttara are exchanging now.

Ever since he made the decision to take Sona and her brother, Arittha knew that once back at the monastery, there would be legal charges and foul remarks. He would have much to face, and he braced himself. He is convinced of the rightness of the decision, he can explain, but why should he have to? Accustomed to making his own decisions, he recoils at the need to defend his actions like a child. Why should he be subject to disciplinary rules wielded by vindictive bhikkhus who hold his outcaste origin against him? Wouldn't it be easier to be rid of the bother and return to his old independent life? The questions assailed him during the return journey, and now on his first day back in the monastery, his stomach is clenched.

His doubts aren't new. During the 16 months he has been a monk, Arittha has often questioned his monastic vocation. The Venerable Candana advised patience. "Being a bhikkhu isn't easy. Everyone who enters the order feels the rub—there's much to deal with. Give yourself time, friend, before you make a decision."

At ordination, bhikkhus vow to live the holy life, but they are always free to change their mind and disrobe. Candana doesn't want Arittha to jump to that option too soon. It is easy to throw off the robes, but it wouldn't solve the real issue, the reason why Arittha ordained in the first place, which is to find deep and abiding peace. Candana knows that to grow spiritually, Arittha needs to move past his rigid insistence on personal independence and to open to the messy, interconnected nature of life. But he can't explain this—not yet—because he senses an explanation would arouse greater resistance in the man. So he couches his counsel in generalities and waits for, hopes for, time and experience to do their work. The sangha is the perfect place for that to happen.

June 13. Six weeks earlier, when Arittha left Ghosita's Park, he walked quickly along the riverbank and through the narrow suburban lanes,

which, in this first downpour of the season, were already turning to mud. All kinds of filth from the crowded quarter were beginning to float in the streets, a rising tide of rubbish. Despite the countless times he'd seen it, Arittha was still repulsed. He picked up his pace and walked as fast as he could out of the district, away from people. Soon he connected with the road leading northwest, and was heading off into the forest, his beloved forest. Despite the horror of the preceding day, a sense of peace arose in him and he began to relax.

The Buddha had recommended that Arittha take shoes for the journey because there would be rough terrain. Arittha selected hemp-soled sandals from the meager supply in community storage, but they didn't fit well. His feet were long and narrow, and his toes hung over the edge and bits of detritus collected on the shelf of sole along the sides. Once out of the muck of the streets, Arittha removed the shoes. He wiped his feet clean in the wet grasses beyond the suburbs, then wiped the shoes and put them in the sack slung over his shoulder. He hated shoes. He had grown up shoeless, and on this point at least his views were consistent with monastic protocol: Whether on the monastery grounds, on almsrounds or traveling, bhikkhus usually walked barefoot. It was a sign of simplicity.

Barefoot, Arittha moved easily and happily. His destination was Crocodile Mountain, which wasn't a mountain at all but a large low hill that had achieved the designation "mountain" by contrast, because it was located in the otherwise low-lying alluvial plain of the Yamuna River.

The swampy area along the riverbank was a crocodile habitat; so Arittha took a more northern route, which being at a marginally higher altitude and further from the river, was outside crocodile territory. He nonetheless traveled carefully, because the forest held many dangers for the heedless.

For five days, Arittha didn't think. The anguish of recent experiences had been so intense and his joy at returning to the forest so great that he happily released himself from the burden of thought. His body knew what to do—how could it be otherwise? He was home. He walked through the rain along deer paths and other tiny byways made over the centuries, where tamped down undergrowth provided some solidity of footing; he ducked low-hanging branches and negotiated masses of shrubbery and fallen trees; three times he stopped at hamlets to beg surprised farmers for almsfood, but all passed as if in a dream. Moving through timelessness, he was hardly aware of what he was doing, yet he did it unerringly. It was one of the most perfect experiences of his life.

As he drew near his destination however, thoughts arose again. He thought about Nakula, about what the Buddha had told him of Nakula's family and other clansfolk, and about the reception he might receive there. Mostly though, Arittha thought about his life. The monastery had never offered him the sense of freedom he was experiencing now. Why was he wearing robes and enduring the hardships, when freedom was so available and so simple? The question seemed to arise from a reconnection with himself, not from the alien, uneasy place he'd often experienced at Ghosita's Park. This new place—or old one—seemed itself the answer: He had abandoned himself when he became a bhikkhu, but now he was back.

June 20. On the morning of the seventh day, the terrain started to rise and Arittha knew he was on Crocodile Mountain. He broke through the forest into a clearing late in the morning, after eating the rest of the food a farmer had given him the day before. He had eaten sparingly along the way and had supplemented what he carried or begged with food found in the forest—roots, edible plants, a few berries; he was skilled at living from the wealth of the forest. Once he trapped a rabbit and apologized before killing it; he ate it raw because he had no way to make a fire. No one at the monastery need know.

An early morning rain had ended, and day was now bright and already hot. From where he stood in the clearing, Arittha saw terraced rice fields to his left descending the southern slope of the mountain toward the river. Several people, men, women and children, were working in the bunded fields, men driving oxen, and women and children, bent double, transplanting rice seedlings. Transplanting was a labor-intensive season when seedlings were moved from a tightly packed nursery to the flooded fields to mature. The nursery was out of range of Arittha's vision, but he knew it had to be near the bottom of the slope where it would be irrigated by redirected river water.

He hesitated. Should he go over and talk to the farmers or walk into the village? Several of them looked up, surprised to see an orange-clad monk. What was he doing here? They called and motioned to each other, and soon all were staring at him from under their wide straw hats. Several bowed, their palms joined. This was awkward. Since he had ordained, Arittha had had only limited contact with laypeople; he knew how to behave as a bhikkhu on almsrounds and at evening talks, but now he faced a whole range of uncharted situations, and this was the first.

Arittha knew enough of monkly behavior to not bow back. Bowing was a one-way activity—householders bowed to monks, and junior monks bowed to seniors, but not vice-versa, since the one who bowed was acknowledging the merit and seniority of the other. It wouldn't do for a monk to acknowledge the merit of a layperson—not this way at least. Nor could he just stare at them. So Arittha inclined his head with what he hoped was appropriate dignity and moved on.

He walked into a pasture, which was occupied by a herd of grazing deer. They looked up at him for a long moment. He was certainly receiving a silent welcome to Crocodile Mountain. Arittha gazed back, and the deer returned to their earnest business, clearly unafraid. He thought fleetingly of the absent village cattle, knowing the herdsman must have already moved them from the field to the relative coolness of the forest. Continuing, he entered a small, ancient grove of banyan trees just beyond the village outskirts. The Bhaggus, like all villagers in the Middle Country, believed benevolent spirits inhabited trees and, when clearing land for the village many years ago, they had left a stand of venerable primeval trees. This became their sacred grove where they performed religious rites.

Then into the village. Immediately Arittha knew something was wrong. Charred remains of three huts stood like skeletons, dismal sentinels announcing that tragedy had been a recent visitor. There was bad news here, and he was bringing more. He moved past quickly, his eyes downcast, not wanting to look at the awful remains.

In the village center, several elders, too old to work in the fields, squatted under a banyan. This was their gathering place as well as a schoolroom when the children weren't required in the fields. The elders stood up and greeted Arittha with surprised bows. Their memories of the Buddha's stay during Vassa last year were still fresh, and they were pleased to see this member of his order. But why, they asked him, had he traveled so far—wherever he'd come from was far since no bhikkhus lived in their immediate vicinity—and why had he traveled during the rainy season?

Arittha took a deep breath and explained that he brought news for the Venerable Nakula's family. The clansfolk looked at each other and were silent. Then one man spoke up, "Reverend sir, you saw the burnt houses as you entered our village. One of those belonged to Nakula's parents. His father was one who died in the fire. His mother, she's my cousin, was badly burnt; she won't live much longer."

Arittha's face contracted in horror as he listened; his hand involuntarily brushed across his brow. "I'm sorry to hear it," he said quietly.

The elder explained that the fire had occurred the day before the rains arrived, when everything was parched from the summer's long dryness. The young daughter of one of the families had been left to tend the oven while her parents were in the fields. She must have gotten too close, her clothing caught fire and in her agony she must have run through the hut, a living torch. The dwelling went up in flames and, because a steady wind was blowing that day, two neighboring houses caught fire as well. The girl, her baby brother, the elderly wife of one of the villagers and Nakula's father also died. Nakula's mother would die soon. It occurred to Arittha later that Nakula's father had died on the same day as his son, and both violently.

"I'll take you to Nakula's wife," the elder offered. "She's just come in from the fields. She's going to visit her mother-in-law. I think she's still at home."

Together they walked to a small thatched-roof hut, made of wattles mortared and plastered with mud adobe-style, much like all the others. The door was open, but the elder tapped anyway. A voice within told him to enter; he did so, motioning to Arittha with a downward wave of his hand to stay outside.

There was a low murmur; then a woman's voice shrieked, "Tell him to go away! Tell him I don't want to talk with him—or any of them, those vermin! Tell him, do you hear me, tell him!"

The Buddha had warned him, but still Arittha was unprepared. Such an outburst of anger! His jaw clenched involuntarily. He stood at the threshold, listening as the elder tried to reason with her, quietly insisting between her shouts, "He's come a long way, Sona, he has a message for you, you must hear it whatever it is." More shrieks.

Finally, the elder reappeared in the doorway. He had composed his face on his way to door, but the effects of the conversation showed in the slump of his shoulders. Still, he managed to say politely, "She says you may come in, Venerable."

Arittha stepped into the single-room cottage, the house where his friend had lived. It was clean and simple, with an earthen floor; at one end was a hearth and clay oven, and next to them, large earthenware storage vats for grains and other dry foods. Three beds lined the walls. Arittha's attention focused on the woman standing at the hearth.

Big-boned, tall and square, she reminded him of a hawk—the females are bigger and stronger than the males. She had towered over the frail Nakula. In anticipation of Arittha's entry, she had hastily put on an upper garment to cover her chest. That material was relatively clean, but her lower garment was stained with mud from the field as were her ankles and feet. She was wiping her arms and hands on a cloth near the hearth. Her daughter, also mud spattered, was a young teen who physically took after her father; she stood near one of the beds, eyeing him warily.

"What do you want?" the woman demanded, her eyes narrowed with suspicion; there was no pretense at hospitality.

Arittha responded simply, "I want to come in and talk with you for a minute."

"Well, so, you're in. What you have got to say? Sit!" she commanded, pointing to a mat near the hearth. Arittha sat. Then she sat too, and he felt a fleeting sense of relief. Never mind monastic protocol, he was relieved that her large form wouldn't be looming over him.

She waited. He quietly cleared his throat and began, "I've come to tell you...I have a message for you..." he stumbled over the words. He hadn't planned how to say this.

She stared hard at him.

He blurted it out. "Nakula is dead. He..."

"Dead!" she exploded, her features contorted and her body straining toward him. "Dead! What are you saying, you vile man? My beloved is dead? I don't believe you! You're lying!"

At the monastery, Arittha lit like tinder under a spark in response to criticism, even though he usually held it in. Now however he received her abuse calmly. He shook his head and said mournfully. "No, it's true." He paused for a moment, then softly dropped the other piece of news, "He was killed."

She shrieked and leapt up from her mat. She grabbed her hair and began pacing the room. Her daughter, already convulsed with sobs, turned away from them both. The elder who had escorted Arittha, moved to the girl and put an arm around her shoulder.

"Liar! Liar!" Sona wailed over and over.

While she paced, Arittha retreated into his own anguish, which intensified because he knew it was just a fraction of hers. He wanted to comfort her but could only sit miserably. And compassion flowed from him. Compassion, tender regard for one who is suffering, which the Buddha taught was one of the heavenly mind states—Arittha was experiencing it for the first time in his life.

As Sona gradually accepted the truth of his statements, the force drained from her wild accusations. She became quieter, then moved to the mat and sat again. Now, softly Arittha began to explain what had happened, stopping several times to allow for her periodic protests and screams. Eventually, by the time he spoke of the cremation, she was sitting with her head in her hands, sobbing.

"I was his friend," he confessed, "I blame myself for his death. I want to tell you this. I blame myself because I could have prevented it, I'm sure of it. If I had fought differently, I could have saved him."

She heard but was so overwhelmed by her own grief that she didn't respond. Instead she said brokenly, "That recluse Gotama has made me a widow twice." "Widow-maker" was the epithet a growing number of women who had lost their husbands to monastic life were using to describe the Buddha. "First I became a widow to a monastery, and now, to death! I knew no good could come from this! No good. My beloved, my beloved," she moaned. Her daughter moved over to her, and she rose and they wept in each other's arms while Arittha sat.

Then Sona looked down at him and said in sudden realization, "My mother-in-law, she mustn't be told. She's very sick—she won't live much longer..."

"Yes, I know."

"This mustn't be the last thing she hears. Her husband died; she's dying—that's enough for anyone. She mustn't know that Nakula's dead, too. Still," she paused, an idea forming in her mind, "you can go see her; see her and if she wakes up, talk to her, tell her you're Nakula's friend. She's so confused she won't wonder why you're here. You can say you've come from Nakula. That will comfort her. Yes, yes, you must!"

Overtaken by this idea and without waiting for Arittha's response, Sona turned to her daughter, "Sukka, take this bhikkhu— what's your name?"

"Arittha."

"Take the Venerable Arati to Nana and see if she's awake. Tell her he's your father's friend. And don't cry! Do you hear me, don't cry!"

Arittha rose and let himself be led out the door by the girl and the elder. The news was out. Several elders and a clutch of children too young to be in the fields were standing near the doorway when Arittha emerged. As he passed, the listeners moaned and consoled each other. They had heard it all. The women daubed their eyes with the end of their garments; the children raced off to announce the news.

Arittha stopped before the elders, "I'm so sorry to bring this bad news." He didn't know what else to say.

The trio, followed by some of the elders, moved in a little parade down the lane toward the house where Nakula's mother was being cared for. Before they reached it however, a woman emerged from the house and hastened up the lane toward him. One of the children had already told her. "Venerable, Venerable, I'm Nakula's sister. Is it true?"

"Yes, it is. I'm sorry."

She wailed, a wordless shriek, an animal sound. Her husband, who had followed her, put his arms around her and they stood in the lane; she leaned against him and sobbed on his shoulder. Arittha stood in front of her, his long arms dangling helplessly at his side. Then she lifted her head and turned to Arittha and said, "You won't tell my mother, will you? You mustn't tell her!"

Arittha reassured her, and he was relieved when she stepped back, allowing him to pass. When they arrived at the cottage, they didn't need to go inside. Nakula's mother was lying outside on a cot in the shade of a tree. The reason was immediately clear, for the smell of her putrefying flesh was intense. She had been badly burned. In an effort to keep the wounds moist, a damp sheet had been placed over her torso and wet dressings covered her arms. A woman was coming from the cottage with more wet cloths to renew the dressings on her face and head. The medicinal remedy used to prevent infection (Arittha later learned it was neem oil) hadn't worked. She was conscious and in great pain. As a falconer and hunter, Arittha had specialized in death; yet this sight made his knees go weak.

A middle-aged woman stepped forward to greet them. She was a cousin or something—Arittha didn't catch her name or relation to the dying woman. He nodded to her and walked past to the frail form in the bed. Sukka, who preceded him, whispered to her grandmother, "Nana, this venerable is here to see you."

Her eyes were dark holes in the raw and savage landscape of her face; yet as she gazed at him, they held a look of great kindness.

"Venerable," she whispered hoarsely in welcome and stretched out a thin, cloth-covered arm.

Arittha knelt at her bedside and said, "Old mother, Nakula asked me to bring you blessings." It was an outright lie but he didn't care.

"Nakula?" she asked.

He nodded. "Yes. I was, am…" correcting himself, "I am a good friend of his. I am Arittha, and he told me to say that he loves you and he sends his blessings. The Blessed One too, he asked me to bring you his greetings and good wishes." This part was true.

She closed her eyes. "Ahhhh," she sighed and was still for a moment. When her eyes opened, they were filled with tears. She whispered, "My husband, Nakula's father, is dead. He can't receive their blessings," her voice broke.

Such tenderness and grief! Arittha had never witnessed its like before. If only he could reach out and comfort her somehow, but he knew his touch would be intolerable. He hoped she sensed the emotion flowing from his heart. He had no name for it.

"I know, old mother, I know. But you can receive them for him. You will do that, won't you?" His voice threatened to break and his vision blurred; he bowed his head.

She nodded slightly and her lips moved into a grimace that was a smile.

"Thank you, Venerable. Thank you. I can die more easily now." She closed her eyes again.

The others were crying. Sukka didn't try to control her tears, despite her mother's instructions. In wordless gratitude all bowed to Arittha, murmuring, "Venerable." He was crying too.

CHAPTER 14.
FACING THE
CONSEQUENCES

Initially Arittha planned to stay with the Bhaggus for three or four days. That seemed a respectful interval—it would honor their grief and give him a chance to rest and obtain provisions for the return journey. He was eager to get back to the solitude of the forest. That he was expected at the monastery lent support to his decision to leave as soon as was seemly.

The villagers offered him shelter in a lean-to outside the village that served as a hayshed. It was a meager shelter, wooden poles and a leafy roof, but Arittha was satisfied —he would have been happy under a tree. The cattle had eaten most of the hay during the dry season; so there was plenty of room, and he liked the sweet smell of the remnants. It made good bedding and was much more comfortable than the wet forest floor had been.

As he settled in on the first evening, making a bed for himself in a back corner behind piles of the remaining hay, Arittha noticed that his every movement was an effort. The trek to Crocodile Mountain had seemed effortless, but now his entire body felt leaden. Was he getting sick? He should be tired, but not like this, he thought. Emotional exhaustion was new to Arittha and he only barely recognized it for what it was. Unable to meditate, he lay back on his bed and reviewed all that had happened. His world had changed, this he knew. His mind started to drift: The power of Nakula's wife— the Blessed One had warned him, but he hadn't been prepared... Nakula's mother, he couldn't let his thoughts linger on her yet...the mystery of the peaceable Nakula and his father dying violently on the same day...How can human beings understand such things? Soon his speculations faded and, amid the growing intensity of lightning and thunder and the pummeling of the rain on the roof, which somehow stayed waterproof—another mystery—he drifted into sleep.

That night Gutta, Nakula's mother, died. Several villagers came to Arittha in the morning to offer food and tell him the news. They begged him to oversee the cremation and conduct the funeral ceremony. Arittha agreed. He hadn't done this before, but his memory of Nakula's funeral was all too fresh, and he knew that they wouldn't care if the details weren't properly observed. They won't know the difference, he thought, then added ruefully, Neither do I.

In the afternoon, after the rain had ceased, villagers built the pyre in the cremation grounds near the sacred grove. The village always kept a supply of dry wood for such occasions. A sturdy young clansman, one of Gutta's nephews, carried her frail body through the puddled village lanes. Wrapped in a white cloth, she was hardly bigger than a lamb and just as light. Arittha led the procession, walking next to Gutta's body. As he walked, he experienced an extraordinary connection with her; threads of energy felt to be running between her body and his. It was still another mystery—he'd have to think about it later. The entire community followed, for all were related in one way or another. They walked in muddy silence. They'd seen so much death in the past week and a half.

They processed first to the village shrine in the sacred grove. The shrine consisted of the central trunk and prop roots of an ancient banyan tree, augmented in places with wooden construction. Arittha asked the village shaman to join him in the ritual. This was partly a matter of intuitive diplomacy, for the shaman was the only one in the village who wasn't entirely pleased with Arittha's presence among them. But it was also a practical matter: Arittha didn't know the rituals. He had never been interested in such things, and besides, details varied from village to village. Happy that someone could ease the people's spirits by performing their ancient rituals, Arittha stood aside benignly as the shaman sprinkled flowers and holy water on the crudely carved deities on the shrine. The nephew easily held the body during the brief ceremony.

Afterwards, they proceeded to the cremation ground, which was a muddy slough. Cala, Gutta's daughter and Nakula's sister, as well as Sona stood next to the nephew as he placed the body on the pyre. Arittha recited prayers. Then without having rehearsed it, he spoke from his heart about this kindly, loving woman, a follower of the Buddha's way, a devoted wife and mother, whose son resembled her in so many respects. He spoke of Nakula's death as well, and tears poured from his eyes for the second time in two days, and he didn't care. Amidst his own tears, the father of the children who had died in the fire asked Arittha to say prayers for the newly dead, and he did. Then Arittha lit the pyre. All were silent, each person saying his or her own farewells and prayers to the much loved woman and to other dear ones recently lost.

Arittha decided to stay with the Bhaggus longer than he had planned. The clansfolk were so kind, living such simple, peaceful lives; he was comfortable with them. Arittha hadn't known community until he arrived at Ghosita's Park, and there acrimony gave the concept of community a bad name. But Bhaggu village was a revelation—here was how life should be. He relaxed, he was needed, he could breathe. They almost felt like his own.

And he, theirs. After the funeral, Arittha came to be regarded as more than an esteemed bhikkhu; he was linked to them as though he were a relative, he was their own very special blessing, and they were proud to have him in their midst.

A monk on almsround is supposed to maintain custody of his eyes, but when he went into the village to beg each morning, Arittha had to remind himself of that practice many times. It was hard because he had discovered children. He was entranced by the children who, even this early in the day, were chasing after each other and laughing in the lanes.

Had he ever laughed as a child? Arittha couldn't remember—it was such a long time ago—but he was sure he hadn't laughed much.

Nor had he played. Arittha's mother had died giving birth to him, the second of her two sons. His father never got over the loss. Always a quiet undemonstrative man, he became dour, and the boys grew up in a grim and silent household. While they were still very young, a woman in their hamlet of falconers looked after them during the day when their father was hunting, but having a large family of her own, she had little time or affection to spare for them. As soon as the boys were old enough, their father moved the family to a more isolated spot, one more suited to his inarticulate nature. Arittha's brother, who was two years older and was learning his father's habit of sternness, was often charged with watching young Arittha. No, laughter and play weren't part of Arittha's youth.

Almsrounds were a simple matter, for the trip to the lanes was short. He was there early, before the farmers went to the fields, and he didn't have to beg long before his bowl was brimming with plain but nourishing food. Often a child or young man would rush up to him with offerings. He could put on a lot of weight this way!

Because he finished his meal quite early, Arittha had time on his hands. Rather than returning to the hayshed, he often ate in the village on a stool provided by one of the families, and he stayed there for a while watching the children play. They were outside in all weather, naked or wearing scant clothing, reveling in the rain and the mud. Nothing stopped them, least of all their parents. What was this good earth for if not to live, work and play in it?

Although he hadn't intended it, when a group of children ran to him one morning, laughing and asking him to throw a stick for them, well, of course he did, and one thing led to another. Quite naturally, Arittha began to join in their games. The children loved it and so did the adults—a bhikkhu who played! Arittha loved it too, and he laughed.

Later, in the afternoons, he meditated in the sacred grove, sitting even in the rain, which he welcomed as a friend. And in the evenings, he went to the village center to sit under the banyan tree with the villagers. Quite naturally they asked him questions; they knew what it was to have a bhikkhu in their midst. At first, Arittha demurred, reluctant to speak the Dhamma. It hadn't occurred to him he'd be asked to teach. But they persisted and, hesitantly, he complied.

He quickly warmed to the task, speaking simply after his own fashion rather than reciting the Buddha's word verbatim, which he didn't remember. Many bhikkhus would have been horrified had they known. He spoke accurately however, and he was amazed. Unaccustomed to talking and never having taught before, he found that the teachings somehow flowed from him. He had learned more than he'd realized. How had that happened? The Bhaggus, being simple people, understood Arittha even better than they had understood the Buddha the year before: The Buddha had to make an effort to speak in ways they could connect with; Arittha did it naturally.

One evening two and a half weeks after his arrival, just after sunset when the bellies of the tattered clouds glowed soft pink, the village headman approached Arittha in the village square. "Venerable Arittha," he said quietly, his hands in anjali, as he sat down before him. "We in Bhaggu village have been blessed to have you live among us. You've become part of us. The village council wants to invite you to stay here with us, to make our village your home. Would you honor us?"

Arittha was dumbfounded. He looked at the man, his mouth open, but no words came out. Bhaddaji repeated the invitation. When Arittha still didn't reply, he assumed Arittha had reservations about the proposed arrangements; so he explained, "We'd build you a real refuge—you wouldn't have to live in the hayshed. And of course we know that you'd want leave and travel sometimes. We understand that. But whenever you're with us, we would be honored to provide you with all your requisites—food, material for robes, medicine—all of them." Bhaddaji was well versed in the needs of bhikkhus, having organized support for Vassa the preceding year.

Arittha didn't have the presence of mind to say "let me think about it, I'll tell you later." Instead he mumbled something; afterwards he couldn't remember what, except it was neither yes nor no.

Undeterred, Bhaddaji said it for him: "Venerable, please think about this. If you can't answer now, you can let me know later. Even if you decide to leave soon, we'll welcome you if you decide to come back. Please think about it."

Arittha smiled—his smile, rare as it was, illuminated his whole face. Regaining his composure, he said, "I'm very honored, friend, to you and everybody. Yes, I'll think about it. I'll let you know."

Arittha thought about little else during the next few days. Here it was, he couldn't put it off any longer: What to do? Stay? Return? Disrobe? Go and come back later, as a bhikkhu, as a layman? The more he thought, the clearer it became that he knew only one thing for sure: He needed to go back to the monastery for now. He was obligated to Bhagava, to Candana, to those who supported him; he couldn't just disappear. He could think about the other options later. Or maybe—wisdom visited his mind—he won't have to figure anything out; maybe the answer would become clear by itself.

And so Arittha spoke with Bhaddaji, again expressing his gratitude, and made plans to leave in two days.

July 11. She confronted him. "I'm going with you."

Arittha was flabbergasted. "Going with me?" he repeated dumbly. "You want to go with me? You can't do that!" Life on Crocodile Mountain was one staggering experience after another.

"Yes, I can and I will. And my brother is coming too. We've talked about it. It's settled."

Oh, shit! He paused to collect his thoughts and then said, "Madam," in a grave tone, trying to impress her with the weight of his expertise, "the trip is long and hard under any circumstances, and in the rainy season, it's, it's..." he groped for a word to adequately describe the horror of the journey but was unable to find one since in fact he loved it. So he continued, "Even for a person like myself, who is used to such travel, it's very, very hard. I assume you don't usually do this kind of thing?" knowing she didn't.

Sona was silent.

"It takes at least seven days, probably more, walking over rough terrain for more than two watches a day," he said, a watch being the equivalent of three hours. "Much of it will be in the rain, sleeping on the wet ground at night. There's no comfort in it." Then he added, "It's no place for a woman."

That did it. "Who are you to say what a woman's place is?" she lashed back. "Are you a woman? No! So how do you know? How do you know what a woman can do? I'm going and that's final!" she declared.

No woman had ever spoken to him like this, but he was getting used to Sona's ways. Ummpff! I probably shouldn't have said that, he thought, recognizing he could have been more discreet. The concept of discretion was another new thing.

His gaffe notwithstanding, the force of Sona's determination convinced him that she could make the journey. But he stalled; he wasn't ready to concede. "Why do you want to do this?"

Another mistake. Her fury burst out like a flame. "To talk to the Recluse, that's why! He's ruined my life twice. First he took my husband, now he's killed him. He's a murderer; nobody else did it, him, him alone…" Her voice trailed as desolation rose within her like a blank wall, pitiless, offering no exit. "I've got to talk with him," she declared more quietly but grimly, and she turned away for a moment to hide the grief that had replaced her anger.

Arittha was relieved he wouldn't be part of *that* conversation! Then he noticed with a start that he was assuming the conversation was going happen. Which meant he would agree to take her to Kosambi. Well, won't I? he asked himself. Isn't that what I'm going to do? It's what I *should* do. If she's determined to do it, why should I stop her? Maybe Bhagava can help her.

Still he was reluctant: There were rules. He knew traveling with a woman violated monastic rules. He assumed the Bhaggu didn't know though, and he didn't want to make the topic part of this dialogue. It had to be his own decision, whether to violate the Vinaya or not—it wasn't open for discussion.

He began calculating options. What if I found a way to take her and her brother and not commit an offense? I could leave some kind of marker on the trail and they could follow a day behind. But for eight or nine days? No, that wouldn't work: If they overlooked even one marker, they'd be lost. Well, what if I walked far enough ahead so I won't be walking with her but still able to check on them? He almost smiled at the ridiculousness of the notion. The forest was so dense in places and visibility so limited they could get lost in a couple hundred yards. Then he thought, She has suffered the kind of shock that can break a person and I'm quibbling about a minor rule. I'm worrying about what some might think! Who's going to think about it anyway? The crocodiles?

But he knew: He was worried about the crocodiles at the monastery. He was willing to do it; he wanted to. He could admit the offense later and take the punishment. He felt sure Bhagava would understand; so would Candana and his friends. Well, he thought, correcting himself, "friend" in the singular. Now that Nakula is dead, I have only Sati. But he recoiled at the idea of being the center of controversy in the poisonous atmosphere at Ghosita's Park. It wasn't his style; he was always outside, able to walk away when he wished. Then Arittha made his decision: Of course, I'll take them! And I'll accept the consequences, whatever they are.

Arittha postponed his departure in order to accommodate Sona and Jambuka, who had to make preparations. They planned to leave in four days.

July 12. It wasn't settled as far as Jambuka's wife was concerned however. Jambuka had agreed to accompany his sister, but Ubbiri hadn't agreed to the plan. She was present when they'd discussed it but had kept quiet. She wasn't stupid. She knew she'd have a better chance changing her husband's mind if she spoke with him alone. She couldn't remember a time when she'd persuaded Sona to give up something she was set on. Trying to dissuade them both together would be impossible. She would wait until she was alone with him,

without the children. And here it was—the next morning, as they were finishing breakfast. Their oldest child was on his way to the fields, the two middle children were outside playing and the youngest, an infant, was already fed and asleep in the baby sling next to their bed.

"Husband, don't go! It's long and hard and dangerous."

He was silent. He expected this.

"If you care for your family, you won't do this! You wouldn't leave us for months. We need you here, you know that! Besides it's planting season."

He extended his hand toward her to placate her, but she brushed it aside. "Promise me you won't become a bhikkhu, promise me that!" voicing her main fear, unaware she had conceded the initial point.

"Believe me," he responded, "I'm not going to become a recluse. It's not the life I'm called to. You don't have to worry," trying to soothe her. "As for the transplanting, most of it's done now. They can easily finish without me," which Ubbiri already knew.

"Let someone else go instead," she whined.

He looked at her squarely. "Who?"

A close male relative needed to accompany Sona. Their older brother suffered from chronic illness and had trouble even walking around his house, while Sona's son, who was sixteen, was frail like his father; he could never manage the journey. One of Sona's great griefs was that neither of her children had inherited her robust constitution. Though her son was as tall as she, he had no aptitude for things physical, a good boy, but no aptitude at all.

"No. There's no one else; I need to go," Jambuka said flatly. In order not to arouse more anxiety, he was letting duty carry the responsibility for his decision. Actually, however, he was eager to make the trip. The Buddha's visit last year had awakened in him a yearning, and the several recent deaths in the village created a sense of urgency. He didn't want to ordain, but he deeply wanted to hear the Dhamma; it was the medicine he needed.

"Remember your family, Jambuka! Don't be like Nakula. Don't make me a widow before my time!"

"Wife," he growled growing impatient, "enough! I said I'll return. In two-and-a-half months, I'll be back. And that's what's going to happen. Now leave it!" And he rose and walked out. Ubbiri looked after him reproachfully, still unconvinced.

She squatted down on the earthen floor by the hearth, her special thinking place. As she pondered the hideous possibility, her fear grew. It grew so big it propelled her up off the floor and through the door. She had to talk with Sona! Calling to her two children to go inside and watch the baby, she raced to Sona's house.

By the time she found her sister-in-law, walking with two women to the fields, Ubbiri was frantic. She snatched Sona's arm and pulled her away. The two other women exchanged glances— they knew what this was about. Without preliminaries, Ubbiri said, "Sister, don't let him ordain! He wouldn't be going except for you. He's doing it for you. I'm counting on you—don't let it happen!"

"Don't worry, don't worry, Ubbiri —it won't. There's not a chance! He'd have to answer to me first." They both knew what that meant. Jambuka, like everybody else in Sona's world—everybody except Nakula, that is—yielded to her will. No one ventured to stand against her.

Ubbiri gazed at her doubtfully. How was it that Nakula, the quiet one, managed to evade her? And if he did it, why not Jambuka? She wanted to say more, but there are no words for anguish; so she walked off, her jaws clenched, shaking her head.

Sona understood her anguish well, and thinking of Nakula again, she cried inside. Why did he do it? Usually he listened to me— usually he was sensible—but here on this, on the most important point of all, he wouldn't budge, he was completely selfish. Why did he do it? She remembered how she had tried to reason with him, then she had raged and finally pleaded. Oh yes, she understood Ubbiri's fear, all right. How he had made her suffer! And in that moment she hated Nakula again. She hated him as much as she loved him, hated him almost as much as she hated the Buddha.

July 15. On the morning they left, Ubbiri walked with them, the baby in her arms, in the rain to the edge of the sacred grove. She smiled bravely, trying to hide the fear in her heart but unable to do anything about her eyes, which were brimming with tears. Would he come back? They bowed goodbyes to each other; then Arittha and his companions walked into the grove, toward the pasture and the forest beyond. Ubbiri stood staring at the empty air, tears flowing down her cheeks. The farmers, already in the fields, waved goodbye from a distance.

The journey back to Kosambi wasn't what Arittha had expected. Instead of flowing into every moment of precious solitude, he was saddled with two villagers who found the going hard. Yet despite their presence and despite the ugliness that awaited him at Ghosita's Park, it wasn't so bad. Sometimes he walked with them, and sometimes slightly ahead in the silence that was natural to him. Sona and Jambuka likewise spoke little, each yielding to their own thoughts and to the rigors of the trek.

Their pace was slower than Arittha's had been alone, but he was grateful for it: It gave him more time to think about what had happened on Crocodile Mountain. He was flooded with thoughts.

Nakula's mother was a big part of them—the way she extended her arm to him in welcome. When he had addressed her as "old mother," he wasn't simply being respectful. It was as though his own mother were welcoming him at the end of her life, telling him at last that she loved him and saying goodbye. A life-long yearning, which he hadn't realized was there, cracked open like a chasm within. As these feelings washed over him, and they did repeatedly, he would move ahead of his companions and let the tears fall freely.

Arittha understood too that his desire to return to the forest had something in it of his great hidden longing for his mother. With his real one gone, the forest had been his mother. And now there was another, Nakula's, who in a way, had become his own.

Gratitude welled up for being able to minister at her burial. He had buried her for Nakula, her family and the whole village, and now he knew that he had buried her for himself as well. He felt certain that his mother had loved him, and he loved her too—oh yes, how he loved her!

July 24. At noon on the ninth day, they emerged from the gloom of the forest to heavy skies and a fine rain and stood at the head of what had been the road to Kosambi. A watery landscape stretched before them, flat and gray; the suburbs and city ramparts in the distance added texture, wrinkles in the monochromatic vista. Sona walked over to Arittha and said quietly, "Thank you, Venerable Arittha. I know you broke your rules to do this. I'm very, very grateful." And she smiled.

Arittha was surprised—and a little ashamed. She knew all along that he was breaking the rules. But she didn't know the extent of his indecision. He had decided to accompany them on the journey, that's true, but up until a few days ago, he'd been debating leaving them at the road head and going on alone, putting on a burst of speed at the end and distancing himself from them. That way, he would have done the needful—they wouldn't have gotten lost—and he still could have entered the city alone; no one need know they had traveled together. But that would have been deceitful. A coward's way out. And then on the fourth day he remembered, too, that the land would be flooded almost to the suburbs. What had he been thinking? Even if he wanted to, nobody would be leaving anybody. They'd all have to swim like fish once they left the forest.

The trio surveyed the flood silently for a few moments; then, following Aritthha's instruction, they moved forward single file into the hardest part of their journey. They waded through the ankle-deep muddy water along the shoulder of the submerged road, their feet making squooshing sounds as they moved. With Arittha in the lead, they tried to find vegetation for more solid footing, and they watched for snakes and other water creatures. Arittha put on his sandals for this part of the journey; Sona and Jambuka were already wearing sturdy shoes, which seemed to grow heavier with each water-logged step. Finally in the late afternoon, muddy, soaked and tired, they arrived together at the west gate of Kosambi. Sona was more tired than she'd ever been in her life, more tired than she'd thought possible, but she most certainly wasn't going to admit it to Arittha or her brother. Then they parted, Sona and Jambuka walking into town to a relative's house, and Arittha to Ghosita's Park.

CHAPTER 15.
THE DEEPENING SCHISM

July 26. The Venerable Harika wants action quick, but he wants it in a special way. He wants a say in Arittha's case. The town is talking about it; it's just the kind of issue he's looking for. So it won't do to wait until Uposatha, which is a week away, because then the bhikkhus meet as two communities. Schism has its drawbacks.

The day after Arittha arrived, Harika went to the Buddha directly, dispensing with the charade of working through Uttara. Harika has lost patience with the mealy-mouthed monk. "Bhagava," Harika said quite reasonably and very clearly, "we need to deal with Arittha's offense soon. The whole town knows he traveled with a woman and it's in an uproar. We've had enough problems already; we don't need townspeople to think even worse of us."

The Buddha was always sensitive to the townspeople's opinions—a fact of which Harika was appreciative, and he listened sympathetically. And he quite reasonably agreed. "You're right, friend Harika. We do need to act soon and with one voice. It's important to send a clear message to the townspeople."

So what's he waiting for? Harika wonders now. That meeting was two days ago and he *still* hasn't called the monks together! Harika chafes, but he hasn't been wasting time. He has been fanning the bhikkhus' discontent into contentiousness. Several in his faction are now angered at the delay and are grumbling openly.

Although the Buddha agrees with Harika, he has his own plan, one which he sees no reason to explain to the venerable: They will consider Arittha's case after Sona and Jambuka visit—as he knows they will soon. It will be a challenging encounter, but Sona's comments will do much to clarify the situation: They will shape the monks' deliberations and either put the suspicion of impropriety to rest or create a greater uproar in town. The Buddha is willing to take the chance. He is confident he can trust Arittha, and he knows Sona.

Sexual impropriety between the two is as improbable as ghee mixing with water. Moreover, he appreciates the difficulty of denying Sona once she makes up her mind. Recalling the power of her opposition last year when Nakula ordained, he smiles for a moment, empathizing with what must have been Arittha's predicament when she insisted on traveling with him. He's glad he wasn't in Arittha's place!

They appear at the monastery this evening, the third evening after their arrival. Word spreads among the gathering monks that Nakula's widow is present, and they look for her, discreetly of course, among the seated assembly. She isn't hard to spot. Sona's head and shoulders loom above the others; she is taller than the women and even many of the men. The monks are awed. They didn't know women grew that big. Moreover her trip through the forest—nine days during the rains without roads to guide them—is an astounding feat. Most of them couldn't have accomplished it themselves. Feeling vaguely threatened, more than one monk thinks ungenerously, Poor Nakula—no wonder he went forth! Who would want to live with a woman like that?

The Buddha, too, is informed of Sona's arrival. Entering the lecture hall, he observes to himself, with a small intake of breath, Here it is. The Buddha takes his seat on the dais at the front of the hall. Upavana sits on his left as usual and Candana, in his special, ambiguous position up front near the wall. The monks are seated more or less according to seniority—though they're never too precise on that score—and the townspeople, the bulk of the audience, are behind and along the sides. The rain has just stopped and it's too wet to sit outside; so everyone is jammed inside. The screens have been raised for ventilation, but inside or out, the humidity is total and everyone is perspiring heavily.

"Welcome, friends," the Buddha addresses the assembly once he is seated. He looks at Sona and Jambuka and greets them specially. "You've traveled a long way. I hope you're rested from your journey." He might as well face this right away.

Sona's face is like the monsoon itself. She sits in stormy silence. Her brother bows in anjali, murmuring docilely, "Yes, Bhagava."

The Buddha says, "Sona, we know you are carrying deep grief. The clansman Nakula was a fine man and…"

"Grief!" she erupts. "What do you know about my grief? Did you understand my grief when you stole him from me? Who are you to talk about my grief? I don't give you permission!"

A gasp escapes the audience. What low rudeness! How delicious! This is going to be interesting! How will the Blessed One handle this one? Many lean forward to hear better.

The Buddha regards her for a few moments in silence. Tension rises in the hall. Then he says quietly, "Nakula's time to go forth had come. His life as a householder was done. He thirsted for liberation as a man in a desert thirsts for water. He left his good family with great sadness, but leave he had to. He said as much, and he told you, too."

Sona is silent.

"Nakula was a fine man, a fine husband and father, and a fine bhikkhu. Like all beings however, he was subject to the consequences of his karma, which extend not only over this life but back through past lifetimes." The Buddha lives in a culture that doesn't question the notion of rebirth; his statement is not controversial.

"So now, because of his karma," and he repeats the phrase to make sure Sona understands, "due to his own karma, the bhikkhu Nakula died at a relatively young age. He died in a violent way, which none of us wish for ourselves or for those we love. But the laws of karma work impersonally and they work exactly, based on our thoughts, words and actions in this and previous lifetimes. We inherit the consequences of everything we do, whether good or evil."

Sona listens intently, her eyes fixed on the Buddha's face.

Then he shifts tack: "Nakula was a stream-enterer," referring to the first level of enlightenment. The Buddha often announces a disciple's level of spiritual attainment after his death. And he now asserts, "For one who has broken through to stream entry, the journey yet to be traveled on the path of purification is next to nothing in comparison with the mass suffering already extinguished. He crossed the ocean, now there are only two or three drops remaining.

"Sona, there are three kinds of sons: the superior kind, the similar kind, and the inferior kind. The first kind is the son who goes forth and ordains, even though his parents engage in bad conduct and have not taken refuge in the *Tathagata*, Dhamma and Sangha." When referring to himself, the Buddha often uses the word "Tathagata." A term he coined, "Tathagata" means "Thus gone one" or "enlightened one" and it points to the fact that, having attained liberation, he is one who is no longer bound by a notion of a self.

He continues, "A similar son is one who goes forth and whose parents also take refuge and engage in virtuous conduct. The third kind of son, the inferior son, is one whose parents take refuge and engage in virtuous conduct but he himself doesn't do so. The bhikkhu Nakula was a similar son—his late parents, Nakulamata and Nakulapita, were the most trusting of my lay followers; gentle, virtuous people, they also were stream-enterers. Their son followed them in every way.

"In a future life, he will travel beyond and they will follow him. They, all three, have entered the ranks of the noble ones." He uses the word "ariya" which literally refers to the Aryan race, the people who migrated to the Indian subcontinent in prehistory, but the Buddha uses it to denote nobility by virtue of spiritual development.

Again he is silent for a moment, then dropping his voice—many strain to hear him better—he says, "And there are three kinds of daughters. You, Sona," the Buddha states, "are the first kind. Your parents did not take refuge in the Tathagata, Dharma and Sangha, but you will do so. I said that Nakula's time to go forth had come. Yours has not yet come, but it will. When conditions are ripe, you too will ordain and follow the path of purification."

There he is, doing it again, bringing women into this! Most of the bhikkhus and laymen recoil at the mention of the nuns' order. They pretend it doesn't exist. Women leaving home and family! As capable of attaining enlightenment as men? Acknowledging the Blessed One as the tamer of gods and humans, yes, they are prepared to do that—that's one thing. But this notion of his that women should leave their families and can become enlightened, well, that's... that's preposterous!

Harika is interested, though. Why not? he thinks. His mother was strong-willed and intelligent, far stronger than his father. He knows women have all the capabilities that men do, except maybe driving oxen before a plow or engaging in combat, though this woman here could probably do both those jobs admirably. His own father, on the other hand, never managed anything more effortful than lifting a vessel of sacred water. Furthermore, the bhikkhuni order, the order of nuns, holds intriguing legal prospects. He hasn't had time to think about that subject yet, but he will, he will.

Sona is stunned. She has always been in command—even when situations fly out of control, she usually manages to regain command. But now she sits frozen, flummoxed, moving not a muscle— this is entirely beyond her scope.

As if picking up on her thoughts, the Buddha observes, "There's a deeper kind of command, Sona. It is the command of letting go, of relinquishing, and someday you will know it."

Ever since he arrived on Crocodile Mountain for Vassa last year, when her heart told her that Nakula would follow him, Sona has devoted herself to hating the Buddha and all he stands for. But now amidst the wild waves of her grief and fury, his words evoke a vision of an isle serene in the distant sunshine—and she hates him all the more. For she knows intuitively that the image invalidates everything she understands herself to be, everything she holds important. Where is solid ground? This is terrifying! Still, she can't ignore the vision…

Riveted by the Buddha's words, Sona and the rest of the audience are carried along as he segues into a sermon on relinquishment.

The Buddha often uses the same images and topics in different ways. He has talked about two kinds of searches before; tonight he talks about three kinds: the searches for sensual pleasure, for being and for the holy life. The last search he explains is vitiated by holding on to wrong views. Unconsciously most in the audience relax as they listen. Ahhh, this is more like it! This is the sort of sermon they expect—words that shake things up a bit and take them to the limits of their understanding without galvanizing them to serious action.

All three searches need to be relinquished, the Buddha declares. No problem, think many. The search for the holy life has never been a first priority anyway, and most don't understand what the search for being is—what in the world is that? Why bother about it? As for the search for sensual pleasure—now, that's the tough one— many resolve to reduce their own activities in that area a bit. When he finishes, the assembly is content and pleased. They happily forget the unsettling reference to the nuns' order. It is easier to consider relinquishing their search for sensual pleasure than revise their ideas about women.

As the listeners acknowledge their appreciation with "excellent, excellent, excellent," Sona knows it is time to raise another subject. By guiding her to Kosambi, Arittha violated the Discipline—this she knew from the outset, but during the past two and a half days in town, she has learned just how controversial his action is. Delighted speculation is flying about—did he do it with her? How could he have managed with the brother around? How would it affect the or-der of monks who are having enough trouble already, as everybody knows? Sona is outraged. By agreeing to guide them, Arittha simply and bravely did the compassionate thing and, in whatever way she can, she is going to make sure everyone understands this. She isn't a mother for nothing. She knows how to defend her own.

Sona is about to speak up uninvited, when the Blessed One gives her the chance—as if he were reading her mind again. "Sona," the Buddha says, "how long will you stay in Kosambi?" He already knows the answer: They won't travel until the rains are over.

"Until after the rains are over, Bhagava," she replies sweetly. "It's too hard to travel before that." Her shift in tone is striking.

Then she says it: "My good brother and I want to express our gratitude to the Venerable Arittha for guiding us on the journey here. It was a very hard trip, but I had to come. I couldn't stay at home when my husband..." she doesn't finish the sentence. "I had to come, and the venerable responded to my request with great compassion— just like the fine, worthy bhikkhu that he is." She looks at Arittha who is sitting among the monks, and bows deeply from the waist in his direction, her palms joined in anjali. She prolongs the bow in order to give everyone a good chance to see it.

Request! It was an order, thinks Arittha, but he is amazed and grateful for her comments. Unpracticed at receiving praise, he grows more embarrassed with every word. His usual solemn expression is replaced by as red a scowl as his dark complexion will permit, emotions contending uncontrollably within.

"He brings great credit to the order of bhikkhus. We could never have made it without him," she adds when once again upright.

Damn! thinks Harika, that weakens the case. *But* it doesn't invalidate it, he counters silently, calculating that while speculation about sexual impropriety will be dampened, the fact still remains that Arittha violated the Vinaya; he traveled in a party with a woman, and that can't be ignored. Rules are rules.

As long as they remain in Kosambi, Sona and Jambuka regularly attend the Dhamma talks. And she is true to her promise to her sister-in-law: Two and a half months later she returns with her brother to Crocodile Mountain. And as the Buddha foretold, six years later, Sona leaves Crocodile Mountain and goes forth, joining the nuns' order, at the age of forty-one. After seven years as a nun she becomes an arahant, reaching the highest level of spiritual attainment.

July 28. The afternoon after his encounter with Sona, the Buddha calls all the bhikkhus together, including the visiting seniors. Aside from talks he has given, public and monastic, which they all attend, this is the first time all the resident bhikkhus have met together since the schism in March. Entering the lecture pavilion, monks from opposing factions eye each other uncomfortably. Arittha is most uncomfortable of all.

So what's changed since I've been gone? Not a damn thing, Arittha fumes. They're still at each other's throats, and today they're at mine.

Candana knows Arittha is on the edge; he's ready to throw off the robes. Before the meeting, Candana spoke with him, choosing his words carefully. "Friend Arittha, I appreciate what you did. It took courage—courage and maybe" he said with a suggestion of a smile, "a bowing to necessity. I understand and so does Bhagava. You were in a difficult spot and you made a good choice. Overall, this is a minor matter. I hope you can keep it in perspective—even though some of our brothers don't."

Arittha grimaced.

"It's true," Candana sighed, "We haven't made much progress toward harmony, but please be patient. The holy life in the Dhamma is important, the most important thing anyone can do. It's worth working for, even fighting for. We need your help, though, Arittha. If you get angry at today's meeting, you won't help your situation and you'll undermine our cause. We don't need more of that. But if you can keep your temper, I think the issue can be resolved simply."

Arittha reluctantly agreed and now, as he walks into the lecture hall and feels the tension, he knows that watching his tongue is going to be hard.

The Buddha, sitting at the front of the hall, welcomes the bhikkhus, saying, "I called you all together this afternoon because I have some things to say to you. But first, we need to address the issue raised by the Venerable Arittha's action. You know that he traveled with Nakula's wife and brother, at her request. The situation is unprecedented; she wanted to be here following Nakula's death, but by escorting her and her brother, friend Arittha has violated the rule that prohibits bhikkhus from traveling with a woman."

The Buddha comes straight to the point. Looking at Arittha he asks, "Was there sexual impropriety between you and Sona?"

"No," Arittha answers simply, and not a monk among them disbelieves him.

Fearing the case is about to slip away, Harika speaks up. "Bhagava, if I may interject," and taking the Buddha's silence for consent, he declares, "I think we all believe the venerable, but the point remains that he broke the law, and at a time when regaining the trust of the lay community is critical…" and he continues with his lapses-in-discipline doctrine.

Sati rolls his eyes. Arittha's body tightens and he digs his fingernails into his palms, but he holds his temper.

Good man, thinks Candana, appreciating Arittha's effort.

The Buddha responds quietly, "What you say, Venerable Harika, contains much merit. You're right: It is important that we maintain the lay community's trust, and it is true that the monastic sangha can only thrive when the Discipline is observed. In addition to the Discipline, however—*in addition*" he repeats the phrase for emphasis, "the Dhamma must be practiced. The Discipline *and* the Dhamma—they are as much a part of each other as day and night. That's the first harmony: The Dhamma-Vinaya in thought, word and deed." Referring to them as though they were one term, hyphenating them if you will, the Buddha hopes to transcend divisiveness, hoping the monks will have the good sense to do so themselves. "When we practice both the Dhamma and the Discipline, we find harmony in our hearts and minds and the sangha is naturally harmonious.

"The Venerable Arittha violated the Discipline—this is clear. And too it is clear that he acted out of compassion for Nakula's distraught widow. We must always allow for compassion—it is one of the heavenly mind states." Then he turns his head slowly, looking at each bhikkhu as he says, "The Venerable Arittha should be penalized, but the penalty should accord with the offense and must take into consideration the element of compassion."

There goes expulsion, thinks Harika, who hadn't really thought it a realistic possibility anyway. He bows to the Buddha in acknowledgment, but another layer of animosity settles in his heart: The sooner Bhagava is out of here the better. Minister Bharadvaja has been saying this for weeks, and Harika has brushed the comment aside, but now it resonates. Maybe the minister is right. We're not going to make much progress as long as he's around.

Argumentative by nature, Harika usually finds himself in a state of resistance. Whatever the circumstances, he finds reason to criticize. He is comfortable with contention, looking for what's wrong rather than what's right. Yet, even as he wishes the Buddha were gone, he is bothered by his own deepening opposition. A tiny sense of uncertainty creeps cat-like into his mind. Bhagava is his teacher after all. He left his brahmin roots to go forth in the Buddha's order, but lately he finds himself in opposition at every turn. Could I be wrong? he wonders. Surprised at the thought, he glances down momentarily. Then he tosses the cat out, and, looking at the Buddha again, his copper eyes blaze with righteousness.

The Buddha continues, "It would be appropriate to lay two days of penance on the Venerable Arittha, after which he is to be rehabilitated." He doesn't ask for the community's assent, and he dispenses with the protocol of requiring Arittha to come up front and confess.

Having concluded the matter, the Buddha turns directly to the topic of discord in the sangha. This isn't the first time he has addressed the issue. He has raised it in several public talks as well as in talks to the bhikkhus individually. Just last week in a Dhamma talk, he pointed out that disunity in the sangha harms everyone, everyone suffers as a result. "When the sangha is divided, there are quarrels, recriminations, denigrations, and expulsions. Laypeople who are unsympathetic are not converted and some who are sympathetic change their minds." Every bhikkhu present knows the truth of these words from the inside. The Buddha also declared that one who divides the sangha lives in a state of misery. At this, Harika snorts and thinks, He's not talking about me! My cause is good. But that's the moment when the little cat-doubt first made its way on silent paws into his mind.

So far the Buddha's exhortations have had no appreciable effect. That's why he's trying a different tack now. He hopes to jolt the monks to their senses. With the matter about Arittha out of the way, he begins: "Wake up, bhikkhus! You're asleep. You're wasting your time with quarrels and recriminations. Wake up and see what's really happening. Aging and death are rolling in on you. Just like great mountains of solid rock reaching to the sky might draw together from all sides and crush beings the world over, so aging and death roll over all beings. Nobody is spared. Regardless of class, you can't defeat them—not by war or subterfuge or by buying them off with wealth. Nor by arguing and fighting among each other. See this clearly! There's no hope for victory.

"A person of wisdom, a real bhikkhu, settles faith in the Tathagata, Dhamma and Sangha. He conducts himself by Dhamma with body, speech and mind. So now I ask you, each one of you: What are you doing to prepare? Wake up!"

The bhikkhus are shaken. Their teacher has never been so blunt. Many feel they've been physically yanked out of their ordinary reality and thrust into a bigger dimension. From there, their quarrel looks small and silly.

The Buddha continues. He points out that aging, sickness and death aren't the burdens people usually think they are. "They are divine messengers. They appear among human beings and carry the message of mortality. A negligent person ignores their message. But one who heeds it and directly sees that he is subject to these forces—he is filled with a sense of urgency. He undertakes noble thoughts, speech and actions, and he acts in harmony with others. So what about you, bhikkhus—are you listening to the divine messengers? Or are you negligent?"

Harika looks around uneasily. How are his followers reacting? The Buddha's words are powerful, there's no denying it. Harika reviews his own position and, because he's urgently looking for it, he finds reassurance: My strategy will provide a context from which we can heed the divine messengers more effectively. That's the point. I just need a little more time, that's all. Once Bhagava leaves, the secular and the religious forces will align with each other, and order will prevail. *Then* the bhikkhus can work together in harmony and cultivate nobility of mind; we'll be a real community then. More comfortable now, the tension in his shoulders dissipating, Harika listens to the rest of the Buddha's talk with some equanimity. But watchful, always watchful.

At the end of the meeting as the gathering begins to disperse, Harika observes the Venerable Vappa approaching the Buddha. Vappa salutes his teacher and kneels at his feet. Harika has a good idea what he's saying: Vappa is going over to the enemy. Traitor! His shoulders tense up again.

As Candana leaves the meeting, Sati approaches him. "Sir," he says, "I want to remind you that I promised Sagata I would talk with Nakula's family."

"Yes?" Candana replies noncommittally. He hasn't forgotten. He's been waiting to see what Sati would do.

"Well, she's here, and I think I should talk with her. Will you arrange a meeting?"

"I think you're right, Sati. Yes, I'll arrange it and will let you know." To himself he observes, He's maturing, he's taking responsibility. Candana finds Sati's initiative especially laudable because Sona is so intimidating. Many monks a good deal older than Sati would hesitate to talk with her. Candana leaves the meeting mightily proud of both Arittha and Sati.

July 29. Two days of penance! Arittha is seething. He has to appear in the lecture hall on two afternoons and confess his offense. It's intolerable! This is the gist of Arittha's diatribe as he and Sati walk together on almsround two mornings after the meeting. Arittha is too impassioned to abide by the protocol of silence. Flashing through his mind are images of two hawks, one soaring in a cloudless sky and another, himself, tethered to the post of sangha. He's worse than tethered: He has to squat in humble posture and confess an idiotic transgression.

"Dung, Arittha, That's a load of cow dung!" declares Sati. Sati isn't abiding by silence either.

Arittha stops and looks at his companion, amazed. The boy is growing up, he thinks approvingly, as though cursing were a sign of maturity, which is what Arittha has always considered it to be.

"There's only this afternoon left, for heaven's sake. It's not the end of the world. There have to be rules if you're a bhikkhu, you know that. It's part of the price of living the holy life."

Is this Sati? Sati the rule-hater? Arittha wonders at the changes that have taken place in his friend in his absence.

Sati continues, "It was the best Bhagava could do. He's on your side, Arittha. So just accept it and move on."

But Arittha isn't willing to let go so easily. The memory of Migajala smirking at him in the lecture hall yesterday afternoon when he did penance still rankles. He knows that toady! Migajala is one of the arrogant ones who enjoy taunting him about his outcaste origin. Thoughts about this afternoon's impending ordeal assail him. Maybe today Harika or Uttara will be there, too, the bastards!

"Oh right!" Arittha exclaims. "Move on, with that miserable Migajala sneering at me when I confess, like he did yesterday. I know what's in his tiny mind—bigotry, that's what!"

The mention of Migajala touches a raw spot in Sati. He's silent.

Arittha continues, "You don't understand. You were a fisherman but you were born noble."

Sati knows there's no point explaining how often he felt the sting of ridicule; he didn't belong to any class and was criticized by all. Instead, he quotes the Buddha, "Whosoever has severed all bonds, who trembles no more, who is done with all ties—him I call a brahmin."

"Oh fuck off!" Arittha replies. He starts to turn away, but Sati stops him.

"Arittha! You're as stuck as the bigots who criticize you. Don't you see that? You're no different from them. Your anger is your prison and you're locking yourself in. They're not doing it to you. You're doing it to yourself." Sati has had many occasions to ponder this truth for himself, but he has refrained from sharing it with Arittha because it wasn't hard to anticipate his reaction. Now, however, it erupts from him.

Arittha looks at him for a long moment without commenting, then he stalks off. He'll do almsround alone today. Afterwards, though, he thinks about Sati's words, and he realizes with a jolt, He's right!

Arittha remembers a story the Buddha told about a conversation with a brahmin who cursed him. Bhagava asked the man if visitors to his home ever refused the food he had offered them. The brahmin, puzzled, admitted it had occasionally happened. "And did you consider that the food still belonged to you?" The brahmin said yes, of course. "And so brahmin, we who don't abuse anyone, refuse to accept the abuse and tirade you have let loose on us. It still belongs to you." Arittha has heard the story before, but he never connected it with his own life. Now he sees: He's been accepting other people's anger and bias and letting it inflame his own. In fact, he is no different than they are. Oh!

And there's something else: Reviewing the curse he flung at Sati in parting, he notices it didn't feel right on his tongue. The violent language he's accustomed to, it's... well, too violent. Something shifted on Crocodile Mountain. His usual way of talking isn't exactly right any more. He senses there are other things too. This is a surprise! He hasn't planned it, but the old Arittha is changing. He wonders what the new one will be like.

CHAPTER 16.
INTRANSIGENCE

July 29. "I'm very sorry, Bhagava, he's changed his mind."

This is bad news! The Buddha has been hoping to talk with the king. He has been waiting for the right time. Udena's refusal to see him after the killing was a blow. Then Sagata's unfolding drama meant he had to postpone any further initiative for a few weeks. In mid-July, however, he asked Minister Ghosita to find an appropriate time to broach the subject with Udena. For days, the king's ill humor kept it from happening. Then at a state dinner five days ago the king's mood was dramatically changed; he was actually smiling, comparatively relaxed and only a little drunk. The entire company was relieved. Ghosita spoke to him then.

"Why not?" Udena replied handsomely, spreading his arms in a gesture of largesse. "He's been waiting a long time." A meeting with the recluse would please Samavati greatly, and he would like to please her. An image of their new-found intimacy arose before him and made him smile. "Yes indeed, why not?"

Ghosita was elated. The date was set—they'd meet the next week. Finally! But then, just yesterday, the king changed his mind again with no explanation. The king has never been known for his consistency.

Ghosita is relating the news to the Buddha and a small group of seniors with whom he has been consulting, the Venerables Sariputta, Ananda, Upavana and Candana. They sit crowded on his porch—Candana and Ananda are squatting on the ground, which is too wet to sit on—and an air of despondency settles over them all. They all know how important a meeting would be. It's no longer a question of winning Udena's adherence; they recognize that hope for the chimera it is. Now they would settle for quelling his active opposition, and for a few days it seemed like it might be possible. But now this! It's a major setback.

The Buddha listens in silence, shaking his head, then he says, "You did your very best, Ghosita, as always. We're grateful to you. This is unpleasant news, but there is no forcing him." He pauses and gazes into the distance for a moment. Then he observes quietly, "The time will come, though. It will come." The others look at him, wanting to know more, but they don't ask.

With everyone feeling distressed, the Buddha concludes the meeting.

There's nothing else to discuss now. All rise. Ananda and Candana rise a bit stiffly, the result of the awkward squatting position too long held. All salute their teacher and prepare to go to the lecture hall for the evening's talk. The Buddha remains seated though. Tonight's talk can wait a bit.

The news has brought matters to a head. This Vassa is indeed exceptional, as Candana observed the day he arrived. Aside from instructing the Kosambi followers, which he has done assiduously, the Buddha has been thwarted in his two other purposes—to resolve the differences in the monastic sangha and to win the king's support. The second isn't going to happen now. And the first hasn't happened yet. He'll make one more effort, and if that doesn't work...

He thinks about the bhikkhus at Ghosita's Park: Candana—he'll have to stay a while longer and remain the guardian of the Dhamma here. Musila, Udayi, promising young Sati, Arittha and others. For the sake of the bhikkhus as well as the laypeople, it's important to keep the precious flame of the Dhamma burning brightly in Kosambi, to guide them on the path of liberation, even if the king opposes it.

Then he turns his attention to Harika—ah, Harika, that thorn. Though Harika has given cause for censure many times over, the Buddha is convinced he has proceeded wisely by not pressing—and not speaking to directly to Harika about the matter. The direct approach won't work: Harika is a horse with the bit between his teeth; he'll let loose, but at the right time, when he's ready, when he sees his error himself. Any effort to force the issue would entrench him in his resistance. What a huge ego! What a closed mind! Made all the more intractable by his brilliance. Yet under it all, under Harika's inveterate righteousness, the Buddha senses a troubled heart, a man who doesn't believe anybody could care for him, a man who, despite his brilliance, has very little insight into his own true nature. This is where his real training in the Dhamma must start.

The Buddha knows Harika's genius could serve a powerfully constructive purpose in the order if Harika were properly motivated. And he has an inkling that that just may happen, in time.

Meanwhile, the issue is taking a tremendous toll on the community. The Buddha has repeatedly weighed that damage against the probability that censuring Harika wouldn't solve the problem. Even if he were expelled—and there's no legal grounds for doing that; Harika has done a lot of mischief but he hasn't violated any precept that requires expulsion. But even if he were expelled—pushing that option a little further, the Buddha muses that the king wouldn't stop opposing them and Bharadvaja, another misguided man, would continue to interfere. Without Harika, they'd just find another pawn, like Uttara.

The Buddha's thoughts are complicated by the fact that he agrees with Harika about protecting local authority. The issue is new, and Harika is ahead of him in considering it. His relationship with the budding monastic communities needs careful consideration. The Buddha recognizes this. He has never been interested in power in a conventional sense—if he had been, he would have stayed in Kapilavatthu and become ruler of the Sakiyas. No, he wishes only to spread the Dhamma. Unfortunately, like everything else in life, it's not so simple. The tensions between the religious and the political spheres, like those between the Dhamma and Vinaya, can't really be blurred away by hyphenating them and invoking an ideal of unity. But there's no need to delve into that thicket now. Nor does he have to be in Kosambi when he takes stock—in fact it's better to be somewhere else, away from the thorns.

August 1. The Buddha waits until Uposatha when each faction is meeting in its own place. Unannounced, he walks into the dining hall where Harika's group is gathered. They are now one member short, since Vappa is observing Uposatha with Candana's group in the lecture hall.

"Venerables, may I join you?" Of course no one objects. The residents look covertly at Harika and wonder what is going to happen next—Bhagava has never met with them before. Then they look at the Venerables Sariputta, Ananda and Narada, the three visiting seniors who are present. Surely they know what this is about.

The Buddha has brought his meditation mat. He sets it down at the front of the group next to Harika and Uttara. Then surveying them all, he declares bluntly. "Enough, bhikkhus. No more altercations, no more contentions, disunion and quarrels!"

His directness is breathtaking, but Harika has been preparing for something like this—it was inevitable. He has developed a carefully balanced response. One deep inhale, then he starts. First, a flattering request: "Bhagava, may the Blessed One, the King of Truth, be patient!" Then he says, "May the Blessed One quietly enjoy the bliss he has obtained already in this life!" This might be understood as a respectful expression of goodwill, except for his next point, which is *the* point: "But Bhagava, Reverend Teacher, it is self-evident that responsibility for these altercations and contentions, for this disunion and quarrel, rests with us and us alone."

The bhikkhus gasp. Harika has just dismissed the Buddha! Harika has claimed that affairs at Ghosita's Park are the business of the resident bhikkhus, and he has told the Buddha to stay out of it. Even though they are Harika's supporters, they are astounded by his insolence. No one speaks to Bhagava like this! They are not at all happy to be associated with Harika right now.

The Buddha ignores the remark; instead he repeats his warning. Harika repeats his response. It's a face off. According to custom, a denial uttered three times is considered final; so before the Buddha makes his statement for the third time, he delivers a discourse about a wise king in ancient times. It's his final effort. He hopes to give Harika time to reconsider; maybe the story will change his mind, since his teachings and exhortations have failed to do it. At the end of story, the Buddha draws the moral, saying, "Now, bhikkhus, if kings who wield the scepter and bear the sword can be so mild and forbearing, so much more must you who have embraced the religious life let your light shine before the world and be mild and forbearing."

Then, he says it, for the third time: "Enough, bhikkhus. No more altercations, no more contentions, disunion and quarrels!"

And for the third time, Harika replies, "May the Blessed One, the King of Truth, be patient! May the Blessed One quietly enjoy the bliss he has obtained already in this life! The responsibility for these altercations and contentions, for this disunion and quarrel rests with us alone."

Failure. Obstinate fool! the Buddha thinks. He's not receptive to the Dhamma, and these sheep are mindlessly following him. There's no more trying here. Disgusted and sad, the Buddha rises from his seat and walks out of the hall without further comment.

The Buddha's talk that evening has a different tone. No longer is he seeking to persuade or reason the bhikkhus into reconciliation; instead he comments on their folly.

"Loud is the noise that ordinary men make. Nobody thinks himself a fool when divisions arise in the sangha. Nor do they consider another person's views higher than their own. They think they are the sole possessors of truth. They like to open their mouth wide, but all that comes out are bewildered words. They may be clever words and the one speaking them maybe be eloquent, but the result is insidious, in fact dangerous delusion. And those swayed by such words are likewise deluded; they don't truly see the nature of the one who leads them or the folly of where they are being led." It's a direct condemnation of Harika, and all the bhikkhus know it. Harika squirms uncomfortably.

The Buddha continues, "'He has reviled me, he has beaten me, he has oppressed me, he has robbed me'—in those who nurse such thoughts, hatred will never cease. Know for sure, bhikkhus, hatred isn't appeased by hatred, but by non-hatred alone. This is the law, ancient and inexhaustible. In our monastic life, we must keep ourselves under restraint. Only those who do so settle their quarrels."

In conclusion, the Buddha offers a hint about his imminent actions, but few pick up on it. "If a man finds a wise friend, a constant one, he can walk with him, overcoming all dangers, being happy and mindful. But if he finds no wise friend, let him walk alone, like a king who leaves his conquered realm behind, like an elephant in the elephant forest. It's better to walk alone, because there is no companionship with a fool."

CHAPTER 17

THE BUDDHA'S ABRUPT DEPARTURE; HARIKA'S LOSS

August 4. He's gone. At first the bhikkhus don't realize it because the Buddha often meditates in his hut in the mornings, and Upavana or one of the other visiting seniors brings him almsfood. But the door to his hut has been closed all morning. Curious.

His need to know gets the better of him and the Venerable Uttara goes to the hut in the early afternoon. Standing at the door, he knocks tentatively. When no one answers, he quickly checks over his shoulders, both of them, to make sure no one is looking, then opens the door and peeks inside. Empty. The Buddha's robes, bowl and sitting mat are gone. Where can he be? He didn't say goodbye to the sangha—you'd expect him to do that—and it's Vassa, when travel is prohibited; so it's strange he's not here. Strange too is the fact that the Venerable Upavana is still here—Uttara saw him after the noon meal. As his attendant, Upavana always accompanies his master.

Uttara seeks out Upavana and asks. "Yes, friend," responds Upavana, "Bhagava left, and I don't know if he's coming back. Whenever he sets out like this, he wishes to be alone. On such an occasion he shouldn't be followed." Not a problem. Uttara doesn't want to follow, but he does very much want to tell Harika. Right away.

Seeking him out—Harika is sitting on the porch of his hut—Uttara breaks the news. They exchange meaningful glances. They both know this is the Blessed One's response to Harika. Uttara isn't sure how to feel about it—is it a victory or a condemnation?

Harika knows though. It's both, and he's conflicted, as he has been rather often lately. On the one hand, he's delighted. It's even better than he'd hoped, since he had assumed they'd have to wait until the end of the rains, over a month from now, for the Buddha to leave. Now he and Bharadvaja can stop their fiddling and get moving. At the same time, he's uneasy. All the bhikkhus will know he's the cause of Bhagava's early departure. It's hard to hold the moral high ground when everybody is blaming you. A horrible suspicion strikes: Maybe they won't follow me! And a sickening feeling begins to churn in his stomach.

Later that afternoon, Uttara provides Harika with another juicy piece of information. Ananda has told him that the Buddha has gone to Parileyyaka and he plans to remain there indefinitely. The hamlet is eighteen miles from Kosambi. Ordinarily it's a two-day walk, but in the rains, it will probably take three because he has to walk through the forest, the roads being impassable. For this reason, Arittha went with him. He knows the route; in fact, Parileyyaka is one of the places he stopped on the way to and from Bhaggu village. The plan is for Arittha to stay in Parileyyaka a day or so to rest and then return to the monastery.

Arittha, if no one else, is completely satisfied with the arrangement. He gets to be in the forest again, quite unexpectedly, and he can spend time alone with the Buddha. Until very recently, the prospect of being alone with the Blessed One would have created considerable anxiety; now though he's eager for it. He suspects he's going to learn some things about himself, about the new Arittha whom he's just beginning to notice.

As the day wears on, Harika's nausea increases. The other monks, including those in his own faction, look at him accusingly. Even the strongest supporter didn't want the Bhagava to leave like this. Harika sees anger in their eyes, and one or two make unpleasant comments to him. Even worse are those who don't speak. He knows they're talking behind his back. The implications are horrible. And the disgrace—he's just beginning to know the taste of disgrace.

Which is part of the Buddha's plan. The day after Uposatha, the Buddha met with his senior advisors and Minister Ghosita. They gathered on his porch again—and again Ananda and Candana crouched on the ground. Ghosita thought, I've got to build something for small meetings like this, a private place where others won't be coming in and out—for next time.

The Buddha interrupted Ghosita's thoughts, declaring bluntly, "Friends, I'm doing more harm than good here. I've been unable to resolve the schism and the king still refuses to see me. "Ghosita," nodding at the minister, "tells us that Udena is gloating and talking about us like we're failed petitioners, like the tradesmen who come requesting boons and are rejected. I don't mind personally, but by staying, I'm just subjecting this center, in fact the whole order, to ridicule. It's not a wholesome environment for teaching. My presence is weakening our position more every day. The townspeople are talking, and talk spreads—like a plague," he added gloomily. "This mustn't continue." He paused, shaking his head. "The most useful thing I can do is leave."

No one spoke. The Buddha wasn't asking their opinion. Like most other religious and secular leaders of the time, his was the final authority. The bhikkhus knew that their teacher saw more clearly and wisely than they did, and by and large they accepted his decisions without question. Moreover, since his failed effort with Harika at Uposatha, most of his listeners had independently reached the same conclusion: Bhagava needed to leave. They nodded in sad agreement.

His presence hasn't healed differences, but the Buddha hopes his absence will. At the meeting, he outlined a plan, observing, "It will take a good deal of organizing, but, Ghosita, you're good at that." The Buddha smiled appreciatively at the minister. Ghosita has a large network of contacts and he doesn't need a hundred percent support. Yes, it could work!

The Buddha also declared, "It's time to confront Venerable Harika." Everybody brightened. Finally! They all understood why Harika hadn't been penalized, but they had yearned for action, some way to assert that the sourness that so marred daily life at Ghosita's Park was unacceptable. Now they made no pretense at equanimity. Ananda permitted himself a small smile and exchanged glances with Candana. All relished the prospect of Harika being brought to account. And despite their personal preference for earlier action, they also appreciated Bhagava's restraint and subtlety. That is his way, subtle but effective, *very* effective. They all broadly smiled their approval when the Buddha advised Candana to speak with Sati about having a long-postponed talk with Migajala. The Venerable Upavana even laughed.

August 5. Harika has never felt so vulnerable. His status in the community has plummeted, the bhikkhus have turned against him and his carefully wrought plans are on the line. As he arrives at Phagguna's for a meeting with Bharadvaja, he feels naked.

He doesn't intend to mention this to the minister. In fact, he's been desperately trying to devise a scheme whereby Bharadvaja could help him regain his status. Which adds to his uncertainty now, because he hasn't found one. Even his mind, usually so ingenious, has deserted him. He waits for the minister as usual, in one of Phagguna's parlors, his thoughts scattering like leaves before a monsoon wind. Setting aside his bowl, which is filled with almsfood, he fidgets.

The minister arrives, rather late and in an expansive mood. Bharadvaja didn't have to hear it from Harika to know that the Buddha has left. Victory! The recluse is gone, the monks are divided and the king is delighted. A splendid turn of events!

"Greetings, Mr. Minister," Harika offers in a morose voice. Bharadvaja, whose ears are fine tuned to nuanced expressions of power and lack of it, looks at him sharply. "What's the matter, Venerable?" he asks. "Aren't you happy? You got what you've worked for—what *we've* worked for."

"Yes, of course," Harika replies unconvincingly.

"And so?"

For once Harika has no response. He sits mutely and drops his gaze.

"Listen, Venerable, I don't know what your problem is, but we should be celebrating. We've achieved success. Our work is done."

Done? This is a surprise! "Our work is done?" repeats Harika, not sure he heard it right. He thought they were moving into the next phase now, the one where he would become the senior (or at least Uttara would, which is almost the same thing), the phase where monastic rules are strictly enforced and soft-minded monks either fall in line or find other lodging. And where he works closely with the king to ensure order in both secular and religious realms. "Done?" he repeats.

"Yes, done."

"But I thought…"

"Oh, come now," Bharadvaja interrupts superciliously, "you're an intelligent man. You know that in the government sphere, plans are always changing. And now they have," he concludes, as if it were as simple as that.

"But the things we discussed…"

"Our work is done," Bharadvaja asserts with finality. He doesn't feel obliged to discuss with this monk the king's inconsistencies . Or to explain that Udena suspected the Buddha of being an agent of the great kings to his north and now that he has left in delicious haste, Udena is content to drop the matter.

"The king is pleased with your efforts, Venerable. He commends you." Which is a lie, but Bharadvaja wants to end this meeting soon and on a pleasant note if possible.

"But we…"

Tiresome man! "Venerable," he says impatiently, "King Udena is in full control of matters concerning his kingdom. He doesn't need your help. So go back to your monastery and meditate or whatever it is you do there. We're finished." And without further comment, he stands up and leaves.

Harika sits, staring after him and then at the door that he closed behind him as he strode out of the room. The lavishly appointed room might as well be a desert.

Phagguna enters shortly afterwards. He is surprised to see Harika still there, staring into space. He asks politely, "Venerable? Are you all right? Can I assist you?"

Harika mumbles something, picks up his bowl without looking at Phagguna and makes his exit.

Harika has lost. It's a whole new world, and he *is* lost.

That afternoon, Sati walks in the simsapa grove with Migajala. Migajala accepted Sati's invitation reluctantly. Almsrounds with Sati was onerous enough. His duty is done; the less contact he has with this dumb monk, the happier he'll be. "Dumb" is a feeble word to bear the load of grudge Migajala carries against Sati. Harika has been doing a good job priming him, but the two younger monks had little natural sympathy for each other even before. Nonetheless, some tone in Sati's voice when inviting him signaled that he had better accept. What's this about? Migajala wonders uneasily.

As they walk in the suffocating heat, Sati appreciates the irony here—not too long ago it was the other way round: Migajala issued an invitation to him on Harika's instructions.

Sati comments casually on the size of the tree trunks. "They're so wide a person could stand behind one and not be seen at all from the front, don't you agree?"

Migajala glances at him and wonders if the heat has softened his mind.

Sati doesn't wait for an answer. "It's true. I remember an afternoon last February in fact when I was walking to the latrine, and I saw you and the Venerable Harika in the porch area. I was on the path but you didn't see me. I didn't want to disturb your conversation—you both were so *very* interested in one of the waterjars; so I slipped behind a tree. Maybe you remember the conversation?"

Migajala's mouth drops open and he stares at Sati. He can be referring to only one thing!

Forget compassion. Sati is taking malicious pleasure in this conversation. He smiles sweetly, thinking, I could get good at this.

Their conversation falters and Migajala suddenly remembers he has something else to do.

"Oh that's too bad," Sati says. His smile turns wicked as he comments honestly, "I'm enjoying it."

Harika learns about the conversation within minutes. So Candana knew all along! Then why the hell did he admit to forgetting to empty the jar? Harika has never figured that out. He eventually dismissed it with the thought that Candana isn't too bright, though he knows that's not true. And if Candana knows about the waterjar, then the Blessed One knows too. That thought jolts him. And who else?

Harika reddens. He's embarrassed—no, not just embarrassed, he's ashamed. Now that he has been unburdened of the delusions that blinded him, he recognizes he has committed offenses—several of them actually, and they're far more serious than the waterjar lapse he accused Candana of perpetrating. Immersed in his own plans, Harika hasn't viewed himself as subject to the very rules he has been bent on enforcing. If someone else had committed them, he'd be in the forefront of those calling for expulsion. He, the law-and-order man, would demand his own expulsion! But Bhagava didn't penalize him—he didn't even say anything! Why not? Why did Bhagava let him continue with his accusations? Why did he continue letting him look like a fool? Harika writhes under the transformation in perspective—from standard-bearer of moral integrity to blackguard!

He needs to get away. Now. In this day so seriously out of joint, Harika walks out into the heat and humidity, past the city gate and through the suburbs that line the city's southern belly, and then westward into the more sparsely populated area along the river. Heavy rain clouds are beginning to amass, but he walks on anyway, deeper into marshy territory he hasn't traveled before, hardly noticing.

August 6. Another shock. On the second morning after the Buddha's departure, townspeople refuse to provide almsfood to the bhikkhus. This has never happened—individual households have refused, yes, that's to be expected, but not most of them, not all at the same time! Yet, at house after house, the bhikkhus are met with closed doors. At some, masters or servants come to the door and declare that they have no almsfood for bhikkhus who are divided. "You're supposed to live according to the Dhamma, but you're as ill-tempered as householders. Your quarrels have forced the Blessed One to leave. He doesn't support you and neither do we. There will be no more almsfood from this house, not until you settle your quarrels." The message is clear.

The morning's almsrounds are long and unproductive. Many bhikkhus return to the monastery with empty bowls. Those who do receive food share it with their brothers, giving preference to bhikkhus in their own faction, but they all finish the noon meal hungry.

That afternoon all the bhikkhus, in both factions, meet in one group to discuss the almsfood dilemma. There's a certain urgency to their meeting. "Brothers," the Venerable Sariputta declares, "the townspeople are tired of your quarrels. They're saying so in a way you can't ignore. Our survival depends on their goodwill and you have worn it out. You *must* resolve your differences."

Several bhikkhus speak up, but members of Harika's faction, being unaccustomed to thinking for themselves, are hesitant, and Harika isn't there to take the lead. "Where is he anyway?" one of the bhikkhus in his faction asks. "Has anyone seen him?" No one has.

Differences between the two groups are deeply entrenched. The waterjar issue has long since been overtaken by recriminations and counter-recriminations, which have washed over each other like waves breaking against the shore. Most of the bhikkhus have become enormously attached to their views. The emotional effort required to maintain their position is even more compelling than their belief in its rightness. Yielding now would be like abandoning a daughter. You don't just turn your back and walk away if there's a family emergency; you see how you can keep her close even in the face of the difficulties. Hungry as they are, the bhikkhus are unable to reach consensus. Uneasily they leave the meeting, stomachs rumbling, hoping tomorrow will be different.

As they disperse, Candana suggests that Uttara check on Harika to make sure he's all right.

Uttara's knock on the door of Harika's hut is met with silence. He knocks again, harder this time, and hears a series of deep coughs. He opens the door and is assaulted by a stink. Harika is lying on his cot in his under-robe; he is doubled up with a coughing spell, and his under-robe is damp with sweat and soiled with urine and feces.

"Venerable, you're sick!" Uttara says with concern, and he strides over to the cot.

It takes Harika a few moments to stop coughing. He spits out the sputum, using his outer robe, which is crumpled beside him on the bed like a handkerchief. Then he looks up at Uttara helplessly and nods. He tries to speak but his voice is a raspy whisper. Harika's chest has always been weak, and, with the tensions of recent months, his overall health has suffered. He has lost a lot of weight. Yesterday's traumas and the long walk in the rain were more than his body could withstand. He felt it coming on last night and since the morning, Harika has been unable to get out of bed.

Uttara puts a hand on his wet, hot forehead. Shocked, Harika involuntarily winces and pulls back. No one has touched him in years. But Uttara patiently extends his arm and maintains contact. "Ummm, a fever," he murmurs. "Have you had anything to eat today?"

Harika shakes his head.

"We need to get you some food. And juice. I'll see what food stores we have." Uttara isn't sure any are left. What with today's scant alms meal, the bhikkhus have probably demolished the modest supply, but there's no point mentioning this to Harika. Surely there's juice at least. "I'll talk with Udayi and get you some honey. It'll help with the cough. But it sounds like you've got a deep respiratory ailment—it needs to be treated. We'll get physician Sirivaddha to take a look at you tomorrow. And now let's clean you up."

Even in his sickness, Harika is surprised. Here's an Uttara he never suspected. Gone is the vacillating bhikkhu; here is a compassionate man, a bhikkhu who knows what he is doing and who cares.

It is indeed a different side of Uttara. Before he went forth, Uttara was a teacher in the humble village of Prayaga (modern day Allahabad), thirty-five miles east of Kosambi. A timid man relatively learned in the Vedas, he was hard to dislike, but he received little respect from his young brahmin students. They made fun of him behind his back and forgot about him once they left class in the afternoon. He yearned for a more prestigious post, one that would take him out of the shabby village, bring a larger income and, not incidentally, command greater respect. It didn't occur to him that real respect is elicited by one's nature and actions. Uttara's relatives in Kosambi promised to secure him a better position in the capital city, but his wife didn't want to leave her family. Uttara's one excess, aside from envy, was his love for his wife and daughter. He adored them and was prepared to sacrifice whatever was necessary to make them happy. He yielded, accepting a paltry future in Prayaga for their sakes. But he was never able to overcome his disappointment. He felt doomed to a second-rate existence.

When the monsoon failed in 454, the region was devastated by drought. Udena's father, King Parantapa, who was not a philanthropist, refused to establish an almshouse in Kosambi. Many suffered from famine and disease; among them were Uttara's wife and daughter. Uttara nursed them tenderly and frantically, scraping together every bit of food he could find, even denying himself food, but it was no use. They sickened and died in his arms. Uttara never recovered. His life became as desolate as the surrounding countryside. When he heard the Buddha speak at a public gathering in Prayaga the following year, it was easy to leave lay life and follow him.

He didn't leave his grief behind, however. As a bhikkhu, Uttara lives only a short distance from his grief. Unwilling to confront it and unable to get past, he keeps it caged like a wild animal, and he fears it. In the same way, he maintains a distance from monastic life. He hasn't yet discovered his place at the monastery, and even though he's a senior, a sense of belonging eludes him. Having learned the Buddha's basic teaching, he is able to recite it by rote when required, but hasn't made it his own. He finds the Vinaya easier to relate to because he has only to memorize rules, and what's so hard about that? He memorized the Vedas even as a boy.

Now though, as he tends Harika, life catches Uttara unaware and forces him into the present moment. A natural authority flows from him, and he's at ease in a way he hasn't known in a long time. It won't last though, because this latest encounter with nursing, coming in the context of months of tensions in the monastery and now the food emergency, is about to reawaken his grief—there are so many features resonant of the old anguish. The animal has broken out of its cage.

August 7. The alms story is the same the next day. The bhikkhus visit houses where they haven't been before, hoping to find a more welcoming attitude, counting on people's natural generosity. Amazingly however, most refuse. How do so many people know about their schism and Bhagava's departure? And how is it that they've all decided to demonstrate their disapproval in the same way at the same time? The lucky bhikkhus who do receive food steal a few bites on the way home before they're obliged to share.

Nothing else has worked, but finally hunger forces the bhikkhus to recognize that schism isn't a viable long-term prospect. They *must* stop quarrelling now, with or without Harika's consent.

Harika's pneumonia worsens. He is delirious, ravaged by high fever, shaking chills and coughing spasms. Sirivaddha prescribes treatment, but shakes his head gravely. It's uncertain whether the venerable will survive. "Stronger men than he have succumbed," he warns, trying to prepare the bhikkhus for the worst. And he cautions that the condition is contagious.

Undeterred by the danger to himself, Uttara becomes Harika's primary caregiver. During the nightmare in Prayaga, when the town's few doctors were overwhelmed, many families called on Uttara because he has a natural ability with the sick. They died of many things—hunger was the first, but diseases, including pneumonia, preyed on their weakened systems and killed them by the dozens. Uttara gave freely and never realized that the respect he so deeply craved was offered in abundance by grateful, grief-stricken families; the fog of his own grief was too dense for him to notice. Now he brings meals to Harika at all times of day (sick bhikkhus aren't restricted by the noonday rule). And he makes sure he is comfortable, washing Harika's robes, giving him sponge baths, and, along with two other monks, manning the bed pan and the sputum bowl.

Even in his delirium, Harika sometimes regains enough clarity to notice Uttara's ministrations. And Uttara's tears. Uttara, who never seemed to muster enough energy for any emotion beyond puzzlement and envy, is unashamedly crying. Whether he's bringing food or sponging Harika's body, tears run down his face like the rain outside. Neither of them mentions it.

CHAPTER 18.
PEACE IN A NEW KEY

September. Harika survives. Sirivaddha is delighted and relieved because he thought Harika's case was hopeless, and he takes losses as an indictment of his professional skill—not the first or last physician to do so. He has enough experience to know however, that his doctoring isn't the only factor in a patient's recovery; the patient's temperament also plays a role. At some deep level Harika's combative nature joined the battle against the force of death and bested it.

His convalescence is long. Sirivaddha returns several times to check up on his patient, advising rest and warning that resuming the normal pace of life too soon could cause a relapse. Since it will be weeks before Harika can walk on almsrounds, several monks take turns bringing him food, relieving Uttara of that task; they also bring food to Uttara so that he can have respite amidst his arduous duties.

The Buddha would be pleased, for he has periodically chided negligent bhikkhus: "If you don't tend to one another, who will tend to you?" and, "Whoever wishes to tend to me should tend to the sick," implying they are one and the same thing. The monks of Ghosita's Park, so recently at loggerheads, are doing a superb job of tending.

Compassion isn't their only motive however. Some of the monks, especially younger ones, attribute Harika's illness to the Buddha's magical powers, his *siddhis*. They assume the Buddha is punishing Harika, and they're scared. They examine their own roles in perpetuating the schism, and they are suddenly very keen to make amends. Ideological differences carry little weight against their fear.

The Venerable Vappa is especially accommodating. Relieved that he switched to the right side while the Buddha was still here, he hopes he has avoided the Blessed One's rage, but you never know; so he's making doubly sure. He offers to be of service however he can. Suspecting that the Buddha's mild exterior hides a wrathful deity, he watches other members of Harika's former faction for signs of illness or misfortune.

As Harika recovers, bhikkhus from both factions drop by to visit and offer kind words. Even Candana comes. Harika is surprised, in fact staggered, by the attention. How can this be? The bhikkhus are caring for him! It doesn't feel like Ghosita's Park. He likes it, but he doesn't know how to say so.

In fact, much *has* changed. The bhikkhus are learning to be a community again, and Harika is unaware how much his illness has contributed to the shift. Moreover, they are alone again, just the regular monastic residents, because with the ending of Vassa, the seniors who accompanied the Buddha left Ghosita's Park to begin their own wanderings. Arittha looked after them longingly, and Candana, standing at his side as the monks departed, promised Arittha that he would have a chance to be itinerant soon. Sati was especially sorry to see Ananda depart, but he sensed they would meet again. He was also sorry to say goodbye to Sona. Telling her about Sagata's regrets was hard, but her response was far mellower than hers to Arittha on Crocodile Mountain. And there was something else: Sati is young enough to be her son, and they immediately felt a strong bond. When Sona left, they both had tears in their eyes.

For his part, Harika has a lot of time to think. The problem is there isn't a single comfortable thing to think about. The Vinaya, his mind's usual habitat, certainly isn't one—thinking about the Vinaya is like walking barefoot on sun-scorched stone. The failure of his late utopian plans is even more painful. What else is there? His thoughts, always active, now race helter-skelter trying to find a pain-free topic. It is a futile effort. He is restless and sleep, elusive. Sirivaddha prescribes rest, but Harika knows that "rest" means more than confining his body to bed.

Harika's thoughts pull him into an ever darker place: Reality has turned out to be far different from his dream. He has been disgraced; he's a fool and a bad bhikkhu on top of it. What's left for him? How does he invent a new role for himself? Does he want to? He wonders if he should disrobe and return to Varanasi to follow his father as a priest, but the notion is so unappealing that he drops it immediately. The more Harika thinks, the sorrier he is to be alive.

Suicide however doesn't feel like an option. For one thing, he's barely strong enough to get up out of bed.

Still looking for external answers, for a new set of plans, Harika still doesn't realize that the rest he really seeks can only be found inside, in his heart and mind. Always absorbed in using his mind, Harika has never gotten to know it. Instead of frantically searching for a new plan, he need only stop, turn his gaze inward and open the door to the alien territory from which he has barred himself all of his life. He doesn't yet understand that just this inner journey is the Buddha's Way. Instead, isolated, he feels like he is facing a wall, one that stretches out in all directions, even above and below, an unending vista of hopelessness. He slips into depression. Harika begins to sleep a lot; it's a response that at least has the benefit of helping him regain physical strength.

September 25. Udena is in a good mood. There have been several favorable developments recently—since the ascetic left town, in fact. To Udena's way of thinking, the Buddha's departure confirmed his own stature as a world-turning monarch. It also demonstrated the efficacy of the Vedic rituals. For all the ascetic's sanctimonious claims to being the tamer of gods and humans, a fully enlightened one and a—what's that ridiculous word?— "Tathagata," he slunk out of town like a whipped dog when things got tough, when in fact the many ceremonies that he, Udena, had paid Bharadvaja handsomely to perform succeeded in enlisting the gods' aid against the ascetic's pernicious influence, succeeded in making his continued stay in Kosambi untenable.

And now he's gone, and the proof is in the harvest. The rains were good, so the harvest will be bountiful and the people, happy. Moreover, Ghosita has just reported that the national coffers are fuller than ever. What else could these things mean except that his kingly role as mediator between heaven and earth has been blessed by the gods and his policy toward the ascetic Gotama and his crew has been just? Yes! His success as weather-maker and securer of justice and prosperity for his people is confirmed.

Even his tiresome problem with Kora looks like it is resolved. Udena has taken Samavati's suggestion and has appointed another tax collector, a young man from a family he wants to reward. The new appointee was instructed to be conciliatory and to inform the villagers that their taxes are forgiven for the year. The man traveled cheaply, without an army behind him—it took some courage to do that; Udena must remember to commend him, maybe give him a little monetary bonus. Most importantly, the man was successful. Kora is back under the king's control and apparently happy to be there—it's the best possible outcome. Udena has also found a position for Sutasoma, the young rogue, a position with suitable prestige but where he can't do much damage; both the man and his family are satisfied.

To celebrate, Udena is spending a day with his family, his three wives and nine concubines and their children, on an excursion to his royal pleasure park, Udakavana, just north of Kosambi. Udena decided to make it a bit of a state occasion as well, to give his people something to celebrate too.

It has been a major logistical effort, something akin to mounting a battle. Last night, the elephants were brought from the royal park where they are stabled; their trumpeting was heard throughout the palace grounds as they were crowded into the stable area and tethered at the ankle to iron stakes. Their smell grew stronger as the night wore on, and the distressed horses didn't cease neighing in their stalls. No one got much sleep. The wives and concubines had to have their toilette completed at an unseemly hour, and being sleep-deprived, most are short of temper, as are their body servants.

Today, the weather is perfect, though, cool and cloudless—another sign of the gods' favor. Quite early, servants went on ahead in carriages with the food and supplies, as did the orchestra and dancers. Then after the morning meal, amid much flurry, the women and children were mounted in gaily colored canopied seats on the elephants' backs, while a mahout rode astride the neck of each, holding the jeweled reins of the bridle and a goad. Once all were safely mounted, Udena ascended the royal tusker using a golden ladder. The animal remained kneeling until the king was seated astride the neck and had taken control of the reins. After he had mounted, a specially chosen mahout scaled the rump. He sat toward the rear of the brightly colored carpet covering the animal's back, grasping cords attached to a girth around the belly to keep him from slipping. In this position the mahout acted as a rear guard in the entirely unlikely event that the king needed help controlling the animal.

The state elephant is an enormous bull, light gray in color, which everyone is pleased to refer to as white. On this occasion, as on other state occasions, he is adorned with jewels befitting a royal one—a golden tiara on his head, his bridle set with jewels and gold, a necklace of precious stones and a constellation of jewels dangling from each ear. On his legs are gold and silver bangles, and above his ankles, ropes of bells that sound as he walks. Udena is inordinately proud of the beast.

The king is something of an expert on the subject of elephants. He not only maintains a stable of them in his royal park, but also maintains a wild herd deep in the doab around Kora, which is another reason he didn't want to lose the village. One of the Princess Vasuladatta's attractions when Udena was courting her was the elephants of Avanti. They are larger than most; his own splendid beast is an example. During their courtship—which was resolutely opposed by her father the king— Udena managed to escape from Avanti with Vasuladatta and several sacks of gold; they did so aboard a fine she-elephant. This is the animal, named Bhaddavati, that Vasuladatta is riding today. It didn't take her father long to see the advantages of the liaison between his daughter and the wealthy king to his north, and over the years King Candopajjota has sent three more elephants and other tokens of goodwill to Udena. Everything considered, Udena thinks it is a fine match. He has been trying for several months to induce Candopajjota to give him another bull elephant, and now that his world-turning stature is manifest, maybe he'll succeed.

Relaxing near a lotus pond in the shade of the expansive crowns of seven *kadamba* trees in the perfectly groomed landscape of the royal pleasure park, the party is finishing a sumptuous picnic. Female servants have been solicitously tending their needs, while the female orchestra that plays in the harem serenades them with soft melodies. Udena enjoys looking at the musicians more than listening to their music. After the meal and serenade finish, five female dancers gracefully perform their art, their lithe bodies scantily attired and glistening with oil. Yes, thinks Udena as he watches them appreciatively, it's good to be a world-turning monarch.

The dancers finish, and conversations start again among the ladies. Three little girls—Vasuladatta's daughter, the young princess, who is eight, and two daughters of the harem—are sitting in the grass laughing and happily making chains from wild flowers and clover. They are the most carefree members of the company. Not present are two of Udena's other children, both infants, who remained behind in the nursery.

The family is comfortably reclining on carpets strewn with cushions. A couple of the concubines are dozing. Udena closes his eyes for a moment and sighs contentedly. Scenes of this morning's grand procession through the streets flash agreeably through his mind: The royal equerry preceding the procession and the phalanx of mounted horsemen behind; the townspeople lining the streets, crowding to get a closer view of the magnificence. He recalls their shouts as they showered the procession with flower petals; musicians played, and he, Udena, gazed down benevolently from the lofty back of his beast. Yes, he thinks, Samavati was right—my people do love me. It occurs to him now that not even the great northern kings, Bimbisara and Pasenadi, could have failed to be impressed.

Turning from these satisfying thoughts, he gazes at his adoring wives and concubines. Every one of them a beauty—well, almost every one of them. He doesn't notice that one of the concubines keeps glancing at the encampment of noble horsemen who accompanied the procession and who are now sitting and laughing a short distance from the royal family.

Udena banters with Magandiya and two concubines, who are reclining on a carpet near him, but as he talks his eye falls on the group farthest from him, on Vasuladatta and her six-year old son, Prince Kumara. The prince is lying with his head in his mother's lap. Udena's mood collapses. The boy should be running around, shouting and getting into mischief, but all he ever does is lie about like this and complain. A really unpleasant child. Like his mother.

To change the subject, Udena abruptly looks toward Samavati, who is sitting in the group with Vasuladatta. He'll walk with her and tell her about Kora, that's what he'll do. It will please her.

"Samavati, come, let's stroll together," he calls loudly, interrupting Magandiya, who thought she had fully engaged her lord's attention.

Magandiya feels slapped. The other women pause in their conversations. Vasuladatta, who has been stroking her son's brow, stops in mid-stroke. As Samavati rises from the carpet, every one of them—except perhaps the one of the straying glances—looks at her enviously, evaluating her movements and appearance, and any good points they themselves possess suddenly seem inadequate in comparison.

Samavati is keenly aware of their reactions—she knows them too well to doubt how each is responding—and she feels the heaviness in the air. It robs the moment of any enjoyment. But she needs to focus on the task at hand, for she has something to tell her husband. It has been two months now, and she's sure of what she has to say. She has been waiting for the right moment. This is it.

As they walk away from the group into a grove of *asoka* trees, the king chats casually. When they achieve privacy, he stops under one, whose profusion of orange-yellow blossoms in springtime later turning bright red have made it a symbol of love.

"Touch it with your foot, Samavati," the king teases. "Let's see if your rare beauty will make it bloom." He is referring to the myth that says when a beautiful maiden touches the roots of the tree with her right foot, it will immediately burst into blossom.

Laughingly she does so while Udena looks up, solemnly expect-
ant. Nothing happens. Samavati smiles and says, "But my king, I'm
not a maiden."

"No, but you're my queen and that's more important than being a maiden."

His words remind him of his own importance, and he remembers what he wants to tell her. He explains about the developments in
Kora and, although he doesn't actually thank Samavati for her suggestion, he smiles on her kindly. She responds with her sweet smile
and says, "That is indeed good news, Great King."

Then she continues, "Husband, I too have good news." She
pauses for effect. Samavati is not above being a little dramatic when
appropriate. He looks at her intently—there's only one thing he
wants to hear.

"I'm pregnant."

"Pregnant!" he shouts. "You're pregnant!" Forgetting his kingly
bearing, Udena grabs and hugs her like any happy father-to-be.
"Pregnant," he whispers again, letting the joy sink in.

Now he holds her at arms length and looks lovingly into her
face, "Samavati, my darling, you make me very, very happy. My dearest Samavati. The boy will be as beautiful as you and as strong as me."
He pauses, then adds, "And taller than both of us." They laugh.

But a pang of foreboding strikes Samavati—and if it's a girl?
She'll be happy whether a boy or girl, but her husband won't. She
sighs. Life is not in anyone's control, not even a king's, and nobody,
nobody can do anything about it. But Udena doesn't agree. He is a
world-turning monarch, isn't he? He won't consider the possibility of
a girl!

"You've given me a better gift than the blossoming of ten thousand asoka trees!" he declares. "Let's go back and tell everybody the
good news," he says enthusiastically, giving her a quick kiss. With his
hand on her elbow, he turns her around; then carefully, so carefully,
as though cupping a delicate asoka blossom, he guides her back.

Returning to the group, Samavati experiences another pang,
quailing at the reactions that will greet their news. She doesn't want

to face them. Should I have waited and told him another time? she wonders. But no, she realizes, they'll have to know sooner or later; it may as well be now. She takes a deep breath.

Samavati is right. The women's jealousy when she left to walk with the king can't compare with their horror when they learn she's carrying his child. Some can't bring themselves to smile. Magandiya suffers one of the worst moments of her life.

September 30. Candana listens to the sound of the breeze gently rustling the leaves. It's a last moment of freedom before he steps into the confines of Harika's hut. He is aware that he is holding his breath.

The important thing is still unsaid between them, and he is nervous because he has a proposal to make, something that could affect the future of the entire order. It involves Harika, and, excited as he is about the idea, Candana wonders if they can or should skip over the lie, cover it with grass, and move on. Although he is pretty sure he has worked through his own anger, he knows that unless it is addressed between them, it will fester. Moreover, even if they can put the waterjar and its consequences behind them—Candana doesn't hold much hope for that—isn't it too ambitious to try to raise a new proposal now?

I've got to start with the proposal at any rate, Cananda thinks. He knows it is pointless to raise the waterjar issue; it would heighten Harika's resistance and cause more bitter words. There have been too many of those already. No, Harika has to come to it when he's ready, and who knows if that will ever happen. An apology might be too much to hope for. But no point speculating; presenting his proposal skillfully is going to be challenge enough.

Sighing again, he pauses for a moment on the path and shifts his attention from the breeze to the silence that is always present within him. Touching into it with a deep breath, Candana exhales and proceeds more lightly.

The door to Harika's hut is open. Candana sees him on his cot, evidently sleeping, as he has much of the time lately. Candana understands this reaction all too well, recognizing in Harika's listlessness the place he himself occupied not too many months ago. Life is full of paradoxes! He knocks on the door and Harika awakens.

"May I come in, Venerable?"

Blinking, Harika nods unenthusiastically and sits up.

Candana enters and take a seat on the mat near the bed. He asks after Harika's health, and they exchange a few polite comments. Then Candana begins, "Venerable, I have an idea I think might interest you." Bad start—too quick, too blunt, too possessive, he criticizes himself. Maybe he's broken the egg even before he has started.

Harika is silent.

"As you know the disciplinary rules are still in the making; no doubt they'll continue to evolve for years. But it's not too early to start to codify them, to provide a clear framework that everyone in the order can understand and live by. It would make life much simpler."

Harika looks at him sharply to see if there's innuendo in the statement, perhaps an oblique reference to past problems? But he doesn't detect any.

"This is something that you can do," Candana declares nervously. "Better than anyone else in fact. You could classify offenses and associated penalties for each of the Patimokkha rules. It would be a great gift to us all."

Harika still doesn't comment, but Candana thinks he detects a glint of interest in his copper eyes.

"Of course, you'd have to take your work to Bhagava and consult with him. That would mean meeting with him, probably for an extended period, like during the next Vassa, so you can review things with him."

Harika is indeed interested, but the idea of consulting the Buddha is off-putting. He has never willingly consulted anybody on anything. He has never needed to. Being thoroughly self-centered and brighter than most—his mind is usually several steps ahead. Harika usually hands down pronouncements. Consulting is a waste of time. His work with Bharadvaja of course was an exception, and the disastrous outcome of that endeavor has reinforced his go-it-alone inclinations. Besides, conferring with his teacher would mean conceding the latter's authority, which Harika is loathe to do. He has been vaguely aware of some contradictions in his reactions, but has never examined them. Instead he rationalized, saying in the past that the Buddha was too far away to consult, and when, to the contrary, the Buddha was right there at Ghosita's Park, Harika was too involved in his strategy, too entrenched in opposition, to consider it.

Now though, he's been thoroughly routed, and unfamiliar assumptions have seized dominion over his thoughts and actions: He's a fool, his plans are a shambles. Where's his brilliance now? What is there to rely on if not his brilliant mind? Desolate, confidence shattered, Harika thinks himself an idiot and a hopelessly unworthy bhikkhu. The Buddha would never want to see him! So although Harika has leaned forward to listen, when Candana finishes, he draws back and shakes his head. "No, I don't know..."

Candana jumps in. He supposes Harika is wondering if the Buddha would agree to see him, much less work with him after the mess he's caused here, but he pretends to misunderstand.

"Well, he didn't ask me to raise this with you, if that's what you're getting at. I'm not acting on his behalf; so there's no guarantee he'd accept your suggestions. That would have to be between you and him." Candana wants to make this point, knowing it will allay any suspicion that he is acting as the Buddha's mouthpiece. He wants Harika to understand that the proposal is an independent initiative, and it would become solely Harika's project.

"But would he see me?" Harika asks plaintively.

"Why not?"

Harika has no response. They both know why not. Harika is silent, looking down at his feet, and Candana is unable to gauge his reaction. He waits.

When Harika looks up, it's with a hard gaze. "What's the catch?"

"What?"

"The catch. You know—what's in it for you? You, the virtuous one! The Venerable Candana, all wisdom and virtue! What have you got to gain from this great idea of yours? And why are you telling me about it—after what I've done to you!"

So! Here it is! The façade has dropped, and Harika's inner turmoil is spilling out like blood from a grievous wound. He wouldn't argue a case in the Vinaya with such illogic, but as far as Candana is concerned, he's making perfect sense.

The abuse continues, "Why didn't you ever say anything? You let me look like a fool! And why aren't you saying anything now? You supercilious hypocritical brahmin bastard!" He spits out the string of words.

Candana narrows his eyes and gives him a long, hard look, but says nothing. He knows that silence will inflame Harika more than anything he can say, and he finds a sweet pleasure in it. Also he knows that refusing to get involved in Harika's confusion will leave him thrashing air and hopefully force him to examine himself more closely. It's not often that your pleasure is reinforced by wisdom.

Finally, quietly, Candana says, "You're the one who needs to say something to me, Venerable. Not the other way around."

They stare at each other, the silence stretching out between them. Then, amazingly, tears come to Harika's eyes. His body, which was rigid with anger, sags and his shoulders droop.

"I thought it was for a good reason, but I was wrong. It wasn't good enough," he chokes out the words.

Harika hasn't yet examined his assumption that ends justify means. Another one. His subtle mind, so busily engaged with external matters, hasn't looked at itself. He's hasn't understood that such looking is the heart of the Buddha's way.

He whispers, "I'm sorry," and drops his gaze.

There! He said it, he finally said it. Candana knows he can't hope for more. This apology must satisfy because prolonging the old antagonism harms everyone. "Venerable, this situation has caused me pain. A *lot* of pain," Candana emphasizes. He has carefully rehearsed his response, just in case there was an apology, but his voice quivers

in spite of himself. "And others too. You already know that. I appreciate your apology, and it's over now, finished." He hopes so anyway.

He takes a deep breath, reaching for energy to start afresh.
"Now we need to move on. There is something important that needs
doing, and you're the one to do it."

Harika doesn't respond.

Candana ventures into the next part of the proposal; there's
nothing to lose. "The proposal has another aspect," he says carefully,
"something that would make it even more significant: You could write
it down. The minor rules too, classifying and writing down rules and
protocols that govern community life."

Harika looks at him sharply. Candana has added what he hopes
will be the irresistible lure: the minor rules and protocols, and their
implications for local autonomy among the monastic communities.

"You could copy your version on birch bark and take those to
Bhagava. Then you could revise it with him and make an official
written document. It would be the framework of the Vinaya as it de-
velops over the years, as it must do. Bhikkhus would still memorize
the Patimokkha of course, but they'd have the written document
for verification. There would be fewer mistakes that way. And no
one would have to try to memorize the minor ones—those are going to multiply and get more complex as we go along and become
more experienced in community life. So it will be important to have a
written compendium."

Excitement edges Candana's voice. He's been excited about
the idea ever since Khujjuttara spoke with him one evening after
a Dhamma talk. She shared her and Samavati's secret, and he was
stunned. Candana always considered himself quite open-minded
about the capabilities of women, but their project made him seriously
expand his views, and, yes too, it exploded his notions, which he had
hardly noticed, about the limited capabilities of slaves. Their project
is brilliant, and Candana quickly saw its application elsewhere in the
service of the Dhamma. The Vinaya is a natural starting place. Who
knows where it could go from there!

By the time he's finished making his proposal, the force of the
idea has filled him, and Candana feels like an eager boy. He wants

to shout, "Isn't it terrific?" but he contains himself and waits for Harika's response.

The minor rules, too! Harika lights up. To articulate the day-to-day rules and protocols facilitating community life, the ones developing right here at Ghosita's Park! They would become the standard as bhikkhus settle into community life, and *he* would have identified them. Then maybe Bhagava would let him continue to formulate them as well as codify the Patimokkha—a lifetime activity, his legacy to future bhikkhus! The prospect is stunning.

Harika isn't ready to let his interest show though. His mind swings into its usual opposition mode, looking for reservations: Writing is fine for practical matters like business contracts, but sacred scriptures are far too important to put onto birch bark. Harika concurs with the general cultural opinion here. Still, the idea *is* brilliant, he admits to himself grudgingly. Leave it to Candana to come up with something like this, on top of all his other sickening virtues!

Weighing the proposal, Harika has a premonition that sooner or later the Vinaya is bound to be written down, whether he's part of the process or not; there are just too many practical advantages. But (slipping into his old social views) it would mean non-brahmins would have ready access to sacred knowledge, and he's inherently opposed to that. Knowledge is power, and power belongs in the hands of the brahmin class. The fact that he himself is following a teacher who isn't a brahmin is one of those inconsistencies that Harika has never been able to reconcile. Still, he has long dreamt of systematizing the Vinaya—maybe he could do it *without* writing it down. Now there's an option!

Then, with the mercilessness of a starving tiger, self-doubt strikes. Why am I thinking about the Vinaya? he asks himself angrily. I'm not worthy! Someone who lives the rules, not just knows them, needs to take this on, not a failure like me.

The reputation of one who *is* worthy instantly fogs his mind: the Venerable Upali. Harika has never met the venerable but he has heard much about him. Upali is one of the Buddha's most senior monks—a former *barber* for heaven's sake!—but he's a man with a mind for the rules. Already he is Bhagava's foremost advisor on the Vinaya. Upali's reputation is prodigious, while mine is—what? he asks himself—a lying troublemaker! The hopelessness of his existence overwhelms him, like the cesspool he saw in Varanasi when he was six and has never forgotten. It horrified him.

Dimly Harika hears Candana's voice, coming from far away. Oh, yes, Candana, he forgot he is here. "What was that?" he asks.

"I was remembering Bhagava's words. 'You can search all over the world and find no one more worthy of love than you yourself.'" Some irresistible impulse draws the words to Candana's lips; he is surprised to hear himself say them.

Harika is surprised too. "Oh, spare me your piety and learning!" he retorts, and he thinks, Those words sure as hell don't apply to me! Though Harika usually tries to maintain a certain level of civility with others—with a few lapses admittedly—his inner discourse has degenerated along with his self-esteem. And now he has reached his limit. Besides, he has to urinate. Waving his hand, Harika says abruptly, "This has been a tiring meeting, Venerable. Excuse me; I need to rest. I'll think about your idea later."

Broken eggs.

In the weeks following Samavati's news, Udena can't do enough to please her. For starters, he orders that the bricked-up windows be unbricked. Then he thinks better of her whole roof-top situation. Climbing the outdoor stairway is dangerous. Even though the rains have ended, she could easily slip; he doesn't want her to fall and risk hurting herself or the baby. So he orders Magandiya to switch quarters with her. Both women protest vehemently, but he is firm; this is too important to be swayed by women's whims.

Samavati is so distressed that, to placate her, Udena promises to have the covered stairway to the rooftop built soon and to allow her to return with the baby after he is born. Not that she'll be carrying him. That's what maids are for. Udena will graciously allow Samavati to nurse the infant for three days; after that, a milk nurse will take over. He doesn't want breast-feeding to drain her strength and make her breasts sag. Nor will the child live in Samavati's quarters, for the king will want access to her when he wishes; he can't have a bawling infant, even his own son, disturb his pleasure. Of course the nurse will be allowed to bring the prince up to his mother as frequently as she wishes. There is nothing personal in these restrictions. It is simply part of the code that governs harem life, the standard practice of kings.

Samavati has to satisfy herself with these terms, all of them. She makes plans to hide the transcripts in Khujjuttara's apartment on the third floor of the building.

In the end, moving isn't so bad. Increasingly Samavati's days become focused on the life growing within her; so living in Magandiya's apartment, which is lavishly and comfortably furnished, becomes less offensive. Happily, Magandiya took her pet mynah with her, along with its ornately jeweled cage and other paraphernalia. Magandiya has devoted many hours to teaching the bird to talk and boasts that it has the biggest vocabulary of all the birds of the kingdom.

Although Samavati and Khujjuttara have temporarily suspended their transcriptions, they continue their morning meditations. Many times, Samavati offers lovingkindness to the regular occupants of the apartment, Magandiya and the mynah, and even to the space itself. And she wonders if the merit of their meditation here will have a positive effect on Magandiya's temperament. She hopes so. She also fervently prays it will have a salutary effect on her baby. What Samavati refrains from praying for, however, is a boy. Such a prayer would be a capitulation to the kind of insecurities and fears that grip almost everyone in this unhappy place. The more she witnesses their suffering, the more she is determined not to be like them.

To fulfill his promise, Udena does have the indoor stairway built. Workmen convert one of the storage rooms on the third floor of the servants' quarters into a stairwell to the roof and they build a covered walkway to her apartment. As a surprise, he also has ornamental potted trees moved to the rooftop as well as potted flowers. After the baby is born, Samavati will have her own garden.

During the last weeks of construction, the noise and disruption become intolerable, and Magandiya persuades Udena to let her move back to her own quarters. Because Samavati can't be allowed to climb the steps, she is moved to the apartment of one of the concubines, who is sent to live with relatives. The woman leaves feeling unwanted. Why do these things always happen to me? she wonders, and she doubts she'll be allowed to return. He'll find someone more desirable for sure. Her life is ruined. If Samavati hadn't gotten herself pregnant, this would never have happened!

Magandiya doesn't appreciate the king's gesture of letting her move back to her quarters early. Indeed, she has grown more hateful. She detested Samavati's suite and cursed the extra two flights of stairs every time she had to climb them. She'll never forgive Samavati for dislodging her, nor for having a baby. She considers ways to poison the child if it's a boy.

CHAPTER 19.

THE TURNING WHEEL OF SAMSARA

April 18, 445. "Venerable Candana Bharadvaja!" The voice, calling from outside, startles Candana, who is resting after the noon meal.

When he was a layman, Candana was proud to be a member of the prominent Bharadvaja clan. Later, as a monk who had severed worldly ties, he was glad to forget the connection. More recently, during the tensions at Ghosita's Park, Candana found himself recoiling at his own clan name and at the association it might imply, to someone who didn't know better, with the Royal Chaplain. Now, as the sound of his name splits the air assertively, announcing itself to all in earshot, Candana notices that his relationship with it has changed again. It's just a name, nothing more, neither desirable nor undesirable. He is quite pleased as he rises from his cot. A polite knock. Walking to the door, Candana wonders what this call is about. He opens to see a man in his sixties, who is dressed simply in white garments and the red, yellow and black turban that indicates he is in the king's service.

The king's servant! Candana couldn't be more surprised if he beheld his late wife standing before him. As a sign of respect, the man removes the turban. It unwinds as he does so.

"Venerable Candana Bharadvaja," the servant repeats the name more quietly now that they have eye contact, and he holds the hand without the turban in a half-anjali. "I have a message from Great King Udena. He wishes to speak with you and he invites you to a meeting at the palace the day after tomorrow at this time."

Nodding assent, Candana collects himself enough to ask, "Did he say what he wants to talk about?"

"He said it's a matter of mutual concern."

That much he guesses. Candana nods again.

The man hesitates, wanting to say something else but uncertain whether to risk it. He decides to go ahead. Heedless of his spotless garments, Tuttha sinks to his knees, setting the muddle of turban cloth next to him in the dust. He bows three times, his forehead touching the ground. Then kneeling and joining palms, he says in a tremulous voice, "Venerable, I have gone to the Blessed One for refuge. I am a lifelong follower, and I come here occasionally to listen to the evening talks. Would you please give me a teaching, something I can take with me, something to illuminate my days?"

One unexpected development after another! Now Candana recognizes him. He doesn't come often to Ghosita's Park and when he does, he isn't wearing the king's livery. In fact, Tuttha has been hesitant to come, fearing he would be recognized and word carried back to his master. The king might be furious—who knows what his fate might be then? But oh, how he longs to be here! And this is his chance, maybe his only chance, to speak privately with a senior bhikkhu.

Candana is silent for a moment, letting the appropriate teaching arise within; then slowly he recites the Buddha' words, "Wakefulness is the way to life. Awake, reflect, watch. Work with care and attention. Live in the Way and the light will grow in you. By watching and working, the master makes for himself an island which floods cannot overwhelm."

Tears fill the man's eyes. In an age of scant opportunity to see beyond the harsh routines of life, for those who yearn, words of wisdom are precious nourishment. They are to be held to the heart and treasured like gold.

Candana says the words again a few times, asking the man to repeat after him so that he can memorize them. Much experienced in committing messages to memory, Tuttha learns easily.

"I am very grateful to you, Venerable," he says after he has mastered the words, his voice quavering with gratitude. Bowing again three times, he picks up the turban cloth, rises and slowly backs away, for the moment oblivious to his dusty appearance so ill-befitting a king's messenger.

Candana smiles and hopes his meeting with the king will be as gratifying.

April 20. The Venerable Candana is shown into the audience chamber. He has seen magnificent rooms before—he has even owned a few himself—but he has never seen one like this. It is enormous. A long, high-ceilinged hall located in the front building of the palace, it is supported by two colonnades of intricately carved, brightly painted wooden pillars. They divide the chamber into three sections, the narrower outer two aisles, and a broad inner way which all tread in order to approach the throne at the opposite end. The floor is inlaid with patterned brick and stone, and a wool carpet woven in the king's colors of red, yellow and black runs up the center. White muslin cloths festoon the ceiling; the cloths above the carpet in the center section are gold-threaded. The plastered walls are ornately painted with flowers, vines and an image of the benevolent king himself. Originally the image was that of his father, but early in his reign Udena had the face repainted to portray the current occupant of the throne.

Facing Candana at the opposite end of the room, atop a six-step dais is a dazzling throne, where the king is now sitting. It is made of elaborately wrought gold and is covered with more precious jewels than Candana has seen in one place before. The legs of the throne, which are vase-shaped, seem to be of ivory, though it's hard to tell because they are so encrusted with gems, and the seat, which is upholstered in Udena's colors, is capacious enough to enable him to sit cross-legged with room to spare. And so he sits now. The vertical rise of each step of the dais is also inlaid with jewels, and the third step is wide enough for chairs, clearly a space that officials occupy on appropriate occasions.

This not one of them. Aside from the king on his throne, the only other officials present are a scribe, who is sitting at a small table at floor level near the throne, and Royal Chaplain Bharadvaja, who is fidgeting as he stands on the floor near the scribe, his head reaching only to the seat of the throne. I'm not even standing on the first step of the dais, he fumes.

Two comely female attendants hover about the king on the dais wielding royal flywhisks. Two others are stationed behind, each holding a long pole that rests on the ground with a stiff woven fan attached like a flag at the top; they slowly rotate their wrists to fan him. They are wearing only diaphanous white skirts held at the waist by a twisted belt in the king's colors and a few bangles and anklets. One who is fortunate enough to have won the king's favor also wears an ornate gold bracelet. While tending to their official duties of making the royal body comfortable, they assume pretty poses that show their breasts and other parts of their bodies to advantage.

Candana is not indifferent to female beauty, but he's well-trained in the monastic practice of retaining custody of the eyes. If there were ever an occasion where custody is called for, this is it. Besides, the meeting is too important to allow his eyes to stray, and he doesn't want to give the king or that insidious Bharadvaja a chance to smirk.

Having been escorted by a servant down the long carpet-way, Candana is now standing before the throne and, resolutely fixing his eyes on the royal personage, he says, "Great King."

"Venerable."

What happens next? Candana wonders. Udena waves a hand indicating a chair on the floor near the dais, opposite Bharadvaja. Aside from the scribe's small table, it is the only other piece of furniture in the hall at floor level. Nor are other people present. In an unusual move, Udena has forbidden his courtiers from attending the audience, and they are intensely curious about what is going on. Some have stationed themselves outside the hall and, having seen Candana enter, have quickly spread the word so that his presence is widely known among them even as he sits down on the chair and prepares to listen.

"Queen Samavati gave birth to a prince on the fifteenth," the king announces proudly. "Perhaps you've heard?"

How could he not? The city has been in a happy uproar since the baby was born in the pre-dawn hours. Within minutes of the event, drummers began marching through the streets to proclaim the good news, and few in the city have slept well since. But no one minds. The birth is an excuse to take off from work; public festivities began right away. Walking almsrounds these past three mornings has been challenging. The bhikkhus have tried hard to maintain a monkly demeanor as they solemnly wove their way through the increasingly drunk but happy throngs.

Looking up at the king, Candana nods and says, "Yes, Great King, there is much joy over the news."

"The queen would like you—*we* would like you," Udena corrects himself, "to perform a blessing ceremony for the prince. The child is very dear to us. Prince Kumara, is ailing. He always has been—from the day he was born," he adds sourly. In his heart Udena blames the prince's sickliness on his mother. Skinny as a peasant, cold-blooded as a lizard—how could you really expect her child to be healthy?

"It may be that our new son will become king someday."

Candana nods.

"The child's name is Bodhi, Prince Bodhi," the king declares. "Bodhi" means "Enlightened One." Udena thinks it's a silly name for a prince and possible future king. What does enlightenment have to do with kingship? Still, Samavati has the right to name her child, and Udena is happy enough with whatever it is. The name doesn't matter as long as the boy is strong and lusty.

Candana starts. He hasn't heard that. Bodhi! How did the queen get her husband to agree to that?

"I'll be honored to conduct the ceremony," Candana replies agreeably. There is no such ceremony in the Buddha's tradition, but that's a small matter. He is willing to be creative. Later on, when he has time to think about it, Candana decides that a ceremony marking birth is a good idea. Why shouldn't it be as standard as funerals? Birth and death are both part of the wheel of life, and from a practical point of view, it's another way to bring the Dhamma to laypeople, touching the family at a particularly meaningful moment.

The king explains, "We want you to bless him that he may live a long and healthy life, be a fine prince and, if it comes to it, a great, strong and wise king."

Candana nods again.

"And," adds Udena, holding Candana's gaze, "that he be tall."

Tall? There's no telling what idiocy a king will come up with! He doesn't question it though. Candana isn't the first to observe that power and wisdom seldom coexist in the same person. Candana nods gravely.

They set the date. The ceremony will be a week from today— it's an auspicious date according to Udena's astrologers.

"Of course I will wish to make an offering to your, ah, monastery. He stumbles on the word "monastery" but recovers, asserting, "a *generous* offering for your services."

Candana notices that Bharadvaja is sneering but doesn't catch the implication. Udena doesn't explain that the Royal Chaplain will perform a major sacrifice to bless the prince two days earlier, and Udena will give him a significantly larger donation. Of course that's as it should be—brahmin priests expect handsome recompense and besides, the king and the chaplain have a long working relationship.

"We are grateful, Great King," Candana replies.

Udena nods graciously. Bharadvaja continues to sneer.

Assuming the meeting is concluded, Candana starts to rise. As he does, Udena asks casually as though it were an after-thought, "By the way, is Master Gotama planning to visit our capital anytime soon?"

"Not that I know of."

"I see," the king replies noncommittally, but he smiles broadly and glances meaningfully at Bharadvaja.

"We must arrange for you to teach the ladies sometime soon, Venerable. Some of them have been asking for teaching, and I'm sure you'll do a fine job."

It's a good thing Candana has had so much training guarding his senses because his mouth wants to drop open with astonishment. Teaching the women of the palace! In addition to blessing the prince and meeting with the king! Just a year ago, his monastic career, even his life, felt like they had ended. How has all this happened? Bhagava himself didn't succeed in seeing the king. Satisfaction and pride combine and fill his chest. Candana smiles inwardly, relishing the moment; then he shifts his attention away. He's not going to get tricked by those sly foxes of emotion. It's just the wheel of *samsara* turning, turning.

Udena dismisses him with a wave of his hand, and nodding once again, Candana leaves.

April 25. "You've never traveled out of Kosambi, have you, Sati?" Candana puts the question as they are walking in the simsapa grove.

"No, sir. My father traveled on government business when I was very young, but I never went." Sati notes that he is able to talk about his father without a hitch in his voice or in his heart. Candana notes it, too.

"Well, I want to send you on a trip. To Savatthi, Rajagaha, Kapilavatthu, Vesali, rural areas, everywhere. I want you go to these places and stay a while. You'll meet other brothers and show them that we at Ghosita's Park aren't all disputatious and contentious. We've got quite a reputation, you know. And it's not over yet." Maybe it never will be, Candana adds to himself. "But I think we're through the worst of it, and we need to heal the distress that our disputes have created elsewhere in the order. I want you to play a part in that healing. Are you willing?" He stops and, turning, looks into the young monk's eyes.

Sati's eyebrows soar and his head juts forward. He wants to shout, "Willing? I'd love to!" But training prevails and he says quietly though emphatically, "Yes, yes sir, I *am*."

He doesn't fool Candana. With eyes twinkling, he says, "Good. I'm glad. I'm sending Arittha, too. I've already spoken with him. You'll be good company for each other."

Arittha's long experience will be invaluable when they meet difficulties on the road. Although bhikkhus usually travel alone, when there's danger, the Buddha prefers they go in pairs. Because Sati is young and inexperienced, Candana thinks he'll be safer traveling with someone, and Arittha is the perfect choice. Arittha has made much progress in his own training, and Candana greatly respects his efforts. He knows how hard community life is for Arittha; he's like a caged bird who longs to fly. Now he'll have the chance.

Candana resumes walking and Sati follows his lead. Sati would like to jump ahead with exuberance, but it would be unseemly to move in front of his mentor. "Just don't let him prove me wrong about the contentiousness part. Don't let his tongue get the better of him." Candana says. Arittha is working hard on gentle speech, he's come a long way, but, well, nobody is perfect.

"Oh, I won't, sir. I'll watch him very carefully," Sati replies earnestly. Then it occurs to him, and he looks sideways: "And, uh, how long do you think these travels will be? I mean, how long will I— we—be gone from…here?" As thrilling as the prospect is, it means he won't be with Candana, and that recognition is jolting. Not that I can't be on my own, of course, Sati reminds himself sternly. I'm eighteen; I'm a man, it's time to get away. But still…

"I don't know—months, maybe even a few years. You'll return when it's time." Candana swallows and inwardly amends his statement, If it's time. Candana is letting go of Sati and Arittha, but especially of Sati. He's made the decision; it's the best for all of them. Sati is not his son and he mustn't try to hold onto him. But sending Sati on his way is just a first step; letting go in his heart is going to be a lot harder. Still, he is trying. Candana is opening his hand and letting both birds fly; they must decide for themselves where to roost. His heart will have to take care of itself.

Candana continues, "You'll be doing important work, and you'll receive training in other centers that will deepen what you've learned here. And meeting people on the way, that's training too, being with it all as you live the holy life. Then, when you return," he pauses, "well, we'll be glad to see you."

They both feel into the meaning behind these words and into the unknowns that stretch out into the future...

They walk in silence for a few moments, then Candana says, "There is one favor I ask."

Sati's eyebrows, which have returned to their customary location, soar again. He's asking me a favor? Anything, gladly!

"I want you to go to Savatthi first. If you and Arittha leave next week, you'll be there easily by Vassa. You can spend the rains at Anathapindika's Park with Bhagava."

Sati is thrilled. He's always wanted to see Savatthi, and he'll have a chance to be with Bhagava under much different circumstances this time. "Yes, of course!" he says enthusiastically.

Again with a twinkle in his eyes, Candana adds, "The Venerable Harika will be traveling with you. He's going to spend Vassa at Anathapindika's Park, too."

ABOUT GRATITUDE—
THOSE WHO HAVE
HELPED

Writing this book was not a solo effort. I continue to bow in wonder to the Mystery that animated it from start to finish. How did this happen?

There are several people to whom I am deeply grateful. I thank especially Stephen Batchelor who so unexpectedly offered abundant support, patiently responding to my questions about historical topics, commenting on a draft and providing connections with others who might be helpful as this book makes its way in the world.

Leigh Brasington supplied (unbeknownst to him) the circumstances in which the inspiration for the story arose. He took time, in the midst of an extended retreat to read a draft and provide helpful feedback. And I am especially grateful to him for his enthusiastic support of the book now that it has been published.

Sara Jenkins, whom I consulted frequently throughout this process, gave me her time, sound advice and enduring support, as she has so kindly done with other writing projects and with plain everyday living over the years. Sara, my dear, you are a jewel!

For their helpful comments on the draft, I thank Bruce Toien, and Kathleen Kistler. My sincere thanks also go to Gerry Gold, Jane Gold, Pushkar, Jason Siff, Susan Greene, Gail Toien, Heather Karp, Sharon Beckman-Brindley, Ayya Sobhana, Bhante Sona, and Ajahn Amaro, who variously responded to questions, provided resources and support or offered wise counsel. Denise Gibson, with whom I am happy to have worked again, designed the beautiful cover and interior.

Helping me find my way amid the daunting complexities of self-publishing were Matthew Flickstein, who stepped in at the last minute to guide me through the epublishing process; Cheryl Wilfong, who shared her perspective on the publishing industry, enabling me to better see this effort in context; and Toinette Lippe, who, drawing on her generous spirit and her long experience in publishing, went out of her way to research and reply to my many questions. Thank you, my friends. I am so deeply grateful.

My gratitude goes to Jackie Erskine, Poppy Furrow and Deborah Qele Smith. My dears, your caring support makes a bigger difference than you know! And I thank many friends at the Insight Meditation Community of Charlottesville who have offered good wishes.

ABOUT TIME— NOTES ON FICTIONALIZING BUDDHIST HISTORY

The Pali Canon, which contains the most accurate information extant about the Buddha and his world, consists of over four thousand pages of text. Chronologically speaking, these are organized like scrambled eggs. The scriptures' main focus is on the Buddha's teachings, not on culture, historical events or personalities. While countless followers have benefited from this didactic perspective, many contemporary readers would like to make historical sense of the era and to understand the people who lived then. What were their lives really like? What did they feel and think about? That includes the Buddha himself, who, by his own admission, was a human being, although an awakened one, not a god. *The Kosambi Intrigue* tries to answer some of these questions.

The central theme of the story is the schism that occurred in 446 BCE at the monastic center known as Ghosita's Park in the bustling city of Kosambi in the Ganges River basin. The schism was the first major crisis in the Buddha's order. A short historical narrative of these events appears in the *Vinaya*, that part of the canon that deals with monastic disciplinary rules. (The word "vinaya" means disciplinary rules. While these rules were formulated during the Buddha's life, they were written only after his death. Following convention, when referring to the written text, I have consistently italicized the word; in the text of the novel where the unwritten rules are frequently referenced, I italicized it only the first time.) The narrative in the *Vinaya* provides the story's framework. Scattered references elsewhere in the Pali Canon have also been helpful. Work of scholars over the past century who have sorted through the complexities of canonical and other sources has been an invaluable source of information for this novel as well. So too, have some works on contemporary India.

The schism at Kosambi, which occurred during the ninth year of the Buddha's mission, is presented in the *Vinaya* as a purely monastic matter. I have imagined a larger significance by setting the monastic events in the midst of a political intrigue initiated by the suspicions of a king. There is no historical evidence to indicate secular political involvement, but King Udena's irascible personality and his hostility to the Buddha and his order make it is easy to read between the lines and find intrigue.

An underlying theme of the story is the division that existed among the monks between those who gave priority to the Teaching (Dhamma) and those who favored the Discipline (Vinaya). Using a trumped-up dispute over a waterjar, certain monks and individuals in Udena's government exploited this division, I believe, for their own ends.

The texts don't identify by name the key monks involved in the schism. We know, however, that a character like Candana (learned and noble-hearted) and one like Harika (contentious, devoted to the Discipline) existed and were central to the quarrel.

Other historical figures are the Buddha; the Venerables Ananda, Upavana and Sariputta; King Udena; Queens Samavati, Magandiya and Vasuladatta; the wise and loyal Khujjuttara; Royal Treasurer Ghosita and the court brahmin Bharadvaja, whom I have designated as Royal Chaplain. According to scripture and commentary, Samavati was indeed the daughter of a rich merchant and, later, became Ghosita's adopted daughter; Ghosita did donate his park to the Buddha. Prince Bodhi was likewise a historical figure. Though the texts indicate he was Vasuladatta's son, not Samavati's, I have opted to make the change in the interest of the narrative. This decision is nicely supported by the fact that Vasuladatta, who was not a follower of the Buddha, is unlikely to have named her son "Bodhi" ("Awakened One"). The dissolute monk Sagata existed and was reportedly dead drunk at the city gate when the Buddha and his monks arrived in Kosambi for the rains retreat in 446 BCE, but there is no textual indication that he killed anyone or that he was executed.

The canon extols Nakula's wonderful parents—his mother, Nakulamata, and father, Nakulapita—but there is no mention of Nakula himself. Why not? This is strange. Could it be that Nakula existed but scriptural reference to him was deleted because some unseemliness was associated with his name? That is what I think. I envision Nakula as a monk who was killed by Sagata. Nakula's wife Sona and her family in Bhaggu village are likewise fictional, but since Nakula's parents are recorded to have lived there and presumably Nakula himself had at one time, it is likely that other members of Nakula's family did, too.

Also fictional are Migajala, Uttara, and other monks whom I have described as living at Ghosita's Park. In all cases (except Candana and Harika), I have chosen names of monks who lived during the Buddha's era. Two characters deserve special mention: Sati and Arittha. They were the inspiration for the novel. Each is mentioned in the scriptures, though not in connection with each other, nor in connection with Kosambi, and I'm not convinced they were historical figures. Let me explain.

The idea for the story ambushed me while I was on a meditation retreat. You never know what is going to arise on a retreat! During that retreat, the teacher, Leigh Brasington, mentioned the scripture that refers to the monk named Sati (Number 38, *The Middle Length Discourses of the Buddha*). I was familiar with it. While the scripture centers on the Buddha's teaching, what had always caught my attention when reading it were the several references to Sati's social origins: He was a fisherman, which means he was an outcaste. These repeated references to his profession seemed disparaging; they were sly slurs, and they irritated me.

Sati is characterized as a monk who misunderstood the Buddha's teachings and was called before the Buddha to explain his misconceptions. When he did so, the Buddha criticized him as a misguided man who didn't have a spark of wisdom. Poor Sati! Reportedly, his shoulders and head drooped and he sat glumly and silently while the Buddha used the occasion as a platform to expound the Dhamma to the assembled monks.

Though we will never know for sure, I think that Sati was created as a heuristic device by monastic editors. I think he was fictitious. The Buddha believed all people regardless of social background could attain enlightenment, but his followers didn't necessarily agree. It is possible that later editors of the scriptures were among those who didn't. This is all the more plausible because class structure and prejudice hardened in the centuries following the Buddha's death. Holding the social biases of their culture, these editors assumed, I believe, that listeners and readers of this scripture would be similarly biased and that Sati's social position would heighten their determination to understand the Buddha's teaching correctly. They wouldn't want to be like Sati—not in any way! As I envision it, the editors added the references to his fisherman profession for good measure. They didn't count on a Western reader a couple of thousand years later who would have an opposite reaction, who would sympathize with Sati.

And Sati wasn't the only one. There was also Arittha (Number 22, *The Middle Length Discourses*), who likewise was used as a foil for the explication of the teaching. His delusion was even more fundamental than Sati's and his profession, by society's standards, was perhaps more odious—he was a "vulture killer," which is to say a hunter. As in Sati's scripture, this one referred frequently to Arittha's repugnant social origin. Repeatedly addressing Arittha as a former vulture killer, the Buddha criticized him, too, as a misguided man without a spark of wisdom. As the Buddha castigated him, Arittha likewise "sat silent, dismayed, with shoulders drooping and head down, glum and without response." To our modern sensibilities, this is cruel treatment. I wonder if it actually happened this way—I prefer to think not. I wonder if Arittha even existed. In any case, it is stated elsewhere in the canon that Arittha was eventually suspended from the order for his pernicious views.

So, returning to the retreat: While Leigh discussed the Buddhadhamma, I was lost in indignation. And just then, in the middle of the meditation hall, this story began to germinate. To offer a counterpoint to a couple of millennia of bigotry, that's what I was called to do! (The exclamation point at the end of the preceding sentence only hints at the force with which this thought struck me.) I needed to make Sati and Arittha into full human beings, not to focus on their "wrong" views, but rather to show that, social outcastes or not, they were essentially like anyone else in the Buddha's order. And they were essentially like us—we can relate to them, despite our radical historical, geographic and cultural differences. They had their strengths and weaknesses as we do, and, like us, they could grow into more clear-sighted, bigger human beings. Isn't that finally the most important item on the human agenda: to consciously try to move past fears and unhealthy habitual reactions in order to inhabit a bigger, kinder place, a place of greater awareness? This is what the Dhamma is about. It is a scaffold that supports us as we grow, regardless of timeframe, culture, gender or challenges of the moment. Growth is ultimately what this story is about.

I have allowed individuals who populate the story to be full human beings; in fact, I have insisted on it. Biographical details in the scriptures and commentaries are scant to say the least, and they are typically didactic, aimed at portraying an individual's spiritual attainment or lack of it. Though such flatness is understandable, it doesn't serve the purposes here.

Portraying the Buddha presented a challenge. How do you describe the personality of a fully enlightened being? Traditional believers considered him a god, a viewpoint that rendered the question of a human personality moot. Others, while recognizing that the Buddha was human, assert that he transcended personality. My response is offered with humility. I have portrayed a human being who laughs, sweats, engages in black humor and is irritated on occasion; yet overall he is kindly, wise, and serene. It is my effort to depict one who reached spiritual heights that most of us hardly dream of.

I have adopted certain conventions to make the story accessible to modern Western readers, even though these compromise historicity. For one thing, I have written the story in idiomatic, contemporary American English. I have assumed that speech that is natural to our ears will more powerfully evoke the informal ways people of the time

must have communicated than would the more literal, but often awkward, rhetoric found in some translations.

And there were other decisions: To spare the reader confusion,
I have largely stuck to Western terms when referring to units of time
and measure. The traditional Indian calendar was fairly cumbersome
and inaccurate regarding specific dates. Since a chronological framework is important in the tale, I have used the Gregorian, rather than
Indian, calendar. Moreover, the Indians didn't divide the day into
hourly units. While none of the characters use the term "hour" in
their speech and I have tried to avoid it in the general narrative,
where imagination failed to find a suitable alternative, I have used
the word.

The bimonthly observance of Uposatha, which is frequently
mentioned in this story, occurs on new, full and half moon days. It
must be possible to figure out these dates in 446 BCE and cast them
in terms of the Gregorian calendar, but I don't see a reason to do
it. For ease of understanding, I have simply assumed that Uposatha
occurred on the first and fifteenth of each month. Harika's role in
developing the Uposatha observance and the reference to Candana's
contribution are pure imagination.

We know that the Buddha formulated the rule prohibiting
drinking in the monastic order in response to Sagata's excesses at
Kosambi, but don't know how many disciplinary rules existed at the
time of the Kosambi schism.

The scriptures and commentaries recount many miraculous
happenings connected with the Buddha. I don't reject the possibility
of such events, but they aren't part of this story. It is miracle enough
that a being such as Sidhattha Gotama, later known as the Buddha,
existed and that many courageous people followed him, intent on
achieving liberation from the prison of their minds. This is a miracle
that never fails to inspire me. Some readers may consider fairly miraculous the Buddha's ability to read minds, which I have presented in
the story. I disagree. Many people have experienced moments when
they know what another person is thinking. It seems reasonable to
assume that a supremely enlightened figure like Buddha was able to
do this much of the time.

Westerners who have had exposure to Eastern thought tend to be more familiar with Sanskrit terms than Pali. Sanskrit developed after the Buddha's era and was a literary language, while Pali, which I have largely chosen to use, was close to the spoken language of the Buddha's day and later became the language of the Buddhist scriptures. Hence, I have used the terms "Nibbana" (not the Sanskrit "Nirvana") and "Dhamma" (not "Dharma"). I have kept the use of Pali words to a minimum, however, employing only words that occur frequently and seem to add to the authenticity of tone, as well as words for which there is no English equivalent, such as "Tathagata," a word the Buddha coined and which he used to refer to himself. These are explained in the glossary.

The role of writing during the Buddha's era needs comment. His was an oral culture. The Buddha's teachings were preserved by word of mouth and they weren't written down until the first century after his death. Script, however, had existed in the Indian subcontinent since about the seventh century BCE. In the Buddha's time, its use was limited mainly to business, legal documents and short personal letters. As noted in the story, there was a general sense that the mind was a more appropriate receptacle for sacred teachings than birch bark. Birch bark, being the main material on which records were kept in the Buddha's time, was quite fragile; anything written on it might easily be lost. Still, it is possible that even as early as the Buddha's era, some creative individuals, unnoticed by history, began writing down the sacred teachings. The tools were there and somebody had to be first. Why not Samavati, as imagined by the story? This would provide a solution to a small historical mystery: The *Itivuttaka* is a record of the Buddha's teachings in Kosambi; it has survived to become part of the Pali Canon, and Khujjuttara is cited as its chronicler. How did that happen? Since we can assume that Khujjuttara died along with other women of the harem in the palace fire (which is a historical event), it is plausible that her recitations from memory were transcribed by her mistress, Queen Samavati. The queen was the daughter of a wealthy merchant, who might well have been literate, for many merchants at the time were. And her father might have taught Samavati to read and write. Moreover, common-sense suggests that, if she had transcribed the Buddha's talks, she would have given the precious document (or a copy) to her stepfather, Ghosita, for safekeeping. How else did it escape the palace fire? At any rate, this is the solution I propose. Additionally, I have imagined that Sati's father was a court noble in Kosambi, and that he too was literate.

The Buddha's teachings cited in the novel are mainly derived from the *Itivuttaka*, hence they are things he actually said while in Kosambi.

ABOUT TERMS

Ananda, Bhikkhu—A senior monk in the Buddha's order, Ananda historically was one of the Buddha's closest advisors and his cousin. A man with a great heart and a prodigious memory, he is said to have remembered every teaching he heard. Sixteen years after our story ends, Ananda became the Buddha's attendant and thus heard almost everything the Buddha taught. After the Buddha's death, Ananda recited the teachings to a gathering of senior monks, some of whom likewise memorized them. These became the foundation of the Pali scriptures. Initially passed on orally, they were later written and were thereby preserved for future generations.

Anjali—A gesture of respect in which hands are lifted to the chest or head with palms joined.

Arahat—One who has reached highest level of spiritual attainment short of Buddhahood. An *arahat* possesses perfect understanding unblemished by impurities of mind.

Arittha, Bhikkhu—Despite the fact that Bhikkhu Arittha is mentioned in the Pali Canon, I think he may have been fictitious. (See my comment in the Preface.) Arittha was a hunter, or vulgarly a "vulture killer," by trade and thus would have been a social outcaste by society's standards—but not by the Buddha's standards.

Ariya—The Aryans were a group of related tribes who entered Northwest India in the 2nd millennium BCE and spread across the subcontinent. While discussion of the relations between the Indo-Aryans and the indigenous Dravidian races remains controversial up to this day, even during the Buddha's time, the word "*Ariya*," which referred to the Aryan race, carried connotations of superiority. The Buddha, however, radically shifted its meaning by using it in a spiritual context to designate followers who had achieved certain levels of spiritual attainment. As used by the Buddha, *ariya* meant nobility by virtue of spiritual development.

Bhaddaji—A fictional character. Headman of Bhaggu village.

Bhadrakka, townsman—A fictional character. A wealthy and unscrupulous banker who came to Ghosita's Park to complain about Bhikkhu Sagata's behavior.

Bhagava—A title of reverence by which religious leaders, regardless of tradition, were commonly addressed. A title the Buddha's followers used when addressing him.

Bharadvaja, Pindola—A historical figure. I have made him the son of the court brahmin who plays a large role in our story, though I haven't found historical confirmation of that connection. At the time of our story, Pindola was a young boy. According to the texts, however, he later left the ranks of the Bharadvaja clan and joined the Buddha's order. He was highly intelligent and arrogant.

Bharadvaja, Nadi—A fictional character. I invented him as the tutor to the young Prince Udena and imagined that, when the prince became king, Nadi Bharadvaja assumed the prestigious position of royal chaplain, which is the traditional progression for tutors to a crown prince. Upon his death from a fictional snake bite, Nadi was, according to our story, succeeded in his post by his nephew, Unnabha Bharadvaja.

Bharadvaja, Unnabha—A historical figure. I found no reference to his first name, so I selected one from the literature of the day. He is characterized in the texts as a proud brahmin and member of the great Bharadvaja clan who was an influential member of King Udena's court. I've imagined him in the prestigious position of royal chaplain, which means he was first among the powerful men surrounding the king.

Bhaggu—The historical name of tribal territory in the kingdom of Vamsa. I have located it in the wilderness 40 miles northwest of Kosambi. Also the name of the clan that occupied Bhaggu territory.

Bhikkhu—"Monk," the term the Buddha and others regularly used to refer to a man who had left family and "gone forth" into the holy life in the Buddha's order. The term is still used today. During the Buddha's time, bhikkhus were mainly wanderers, only settling for the three-month rains retreat, but even during his life, some were beginning to be more sedentary, becoming closely identified with specific monastic centers like Ghosita's Park. This more sedentary life-style became characteristic of the order as a whole in later times.

Bhikkhuni—Pali word for "nun." A woman who has left family and "gone forth" into the holy life in the Buddha's order. The order of bhikkunis was established during the early years of the Buddha's mission but after the establishment of the order of monks. In that patriarchal society, the order of nuns was controversial from its outset. It died out in the 12th century but is being revived at present.

Bimbisara, King Seniya—A historical figure. He ruled the great northern kingdom of Magadha. He was a wise and ardent follower of the
Buddha.

Bodhi, Prince—A historical figure. While texts indicate that Prince
Bodhi's mother was Queen Vasuladatta, it suits our story to make
him the son of Samavati. Adding to the credibility of this choice
is the fact that Vasuladatta, who was no follower of the Buddha,
would not likely have named her son "Bodhi," "Awakened one."
Historically, Prince Bodhi inherited the kingdom from his father.

Brahmin—a member of the priestly class, the highest class in the Indian
social order. The Buddha frequently extracted the word "brahmin"
from its social context and used it to refer one who understands
the real nature of things. He referred to himself on the night of his
awakening as a "brahmana."

Buddha—Buddha literally means "the awakened one." Siddhattha
Gotama was born in the leading noble family in Sakyia, a republic
in the foothills of the Himalayas. He left a life of luxury at 29 and,
after six years of strenuous spiritual practice, attained full enlightenment. The dates of the Buddha's birth and death are traditionally
given as 563 to 483 BCE. More recently however, scholars have
determined that he lived at a later time. Knowing that his life span
was eighty years, they have arbitrary set his dates at 490 to 410 BCE.
Our story uses the more recent dates.

Cala—A fictional character. Nakula's sister.

Candana, Bhikkhu—A central figure in the Kosambi intrigue, he is described in the *Vinaya* as "erudite; he had studied the Agamas; he
knew the Dhamma, the Vinaya, the Matika; he was wise, learned,
intelligent, modest conscientious, anxious for training." How much
more praiseworthy can one be? The name of this bhikkhu, however, isn't mentioned in the text—perhaps for the same reason that
Harika's name is omitted (see "Harika" in this glossary). I selected
the name "Candana" because it is euphonious and refers to a deva
(minor god) in the Pali canon. This seemed appropriate. While
most references to Candana in the *Vinaya* studiously avoid mentioning his name, I did come across one obscure passage concerning
a monk who may have been our Candana, and the name as cited
there was remarkably similar to the one I chose.

Candopajjota, King—A historical figure. Father of Queen Vasuladatta
and ruler of Avanti, the kingdom to the south of Vamsa.

Class—Indian society was divided into four classes even as early as the Buddha's day: the priestly class (brahmins), nobles or warriors (khattiyas), peasants (vessas) and dependent workers and servants (suddas). There were also the classless or outcastes, who did not have the dignity of class identification. During the Buddha's era, these classifications weren't held with the rigidity that developed in later centuries.

Cunda, Bhikkhu—A fictional character. Member of Harika's faction.

Dhamma—Teaching. In India of the Buddha's day, "Dhamma" (or "Dharma" in Sanskrit) referred to the teaching of every sect. Followers of the Buddha commonly used the word "Dhamma" to refer specifically to the Buddha's teaching. These days it is often referred to as the "Buddhadhamma" (or in Sanskrit, as the "Buddhadharma").

Ghosita, Anupama—Ghosita was a historical figure; however, I couldn't find references to his first name, so I assigned him one. Ghosita was a banker, the wealthiest man in Vamsa and royal treasurer in King Udena's government. He was a devout follower of the Buddha and contributed his beautiful pleasure park for the use of the Buddha and his monks, as indicated in the story. According to the texts, Ghosita was the beloved stepfather of Samavati.

Ghosita's Park or Ghositarama—The name of the park that Ghosita donated to the Buddha's order. The description in the story is based in historical evidence.

Gutta—The name is fictional, but the character it refers to is not. She was Nakula's mother. In the texts, she is referenced not by name, but in terms of her relationship to her son, Nakulamata.

Harika, Bhikkhu—The character was historical, being the central figure in the schism that developed at Ghosita's Park. Some of Harika's comments in the story and some of the Buddha's to him are found in the *Vinaya*. That the texts don't mention his name is, I suspect, an example of discretion, an effort by editors with a long-range historical vision not to blacken the name of one of their brothers. I selected the name "Harika," which I found in an index to canonical texts. It sounded right, as it referred to a man who had been an executioner. Both the occupation and the sound of the name seemed suitably drastic to use for this character.

Itivuttaka—The word "itivuttaka" translates as, "Thus it was said." According to the scholarly commentary, the name refers to the manner in which Khujjuttara began all the passages when reciting the Buddha's talks to Samavati and other women in Udena's palace. The *Itivuttaka* became part of the collection of the Buddha's teachings known as the Pali canon. (Please see the Preface for further comments about the *Itivuttaka*.)

Jambuka—A fictional character. Sona's brother.

Karma—The Pali term is *kamma*, but since the Sanskrit term is commonly used in the West, I've used it. Strictly, "karma" refers to volitional action and carries the understanding that all actions have consequences. Often it is more broadly understood to mean both actions *and* their consequences.

Karuna—Compassion, one of the heavenly mind states taught by the Buddha. The other three heavenly mind states are lovingkindness, sympathetic joy and equanimity.

Kasina—A simple mental object like a disk upon which monastics focused in order to train their mind in concentration. *Kasinas* are still used as aids to deep concentration.

Kosala—One of the great kingdoms in the Ganges Basin at the time of the Buddha. Northeast of Vamsa, it was ruled by King Agnidatta Pasenadi.

Kosambi—A major port and rich commercial center on the banks of the Yamuna River not far from that river's confluence with the Ganges. It also held a strategic position on a major north-south overland trade route. The city became the capital of the kingdom of Vamsa during the reign of Udena's father, King Parantapa.

Kukkuta, Bhadda—A historical figure. A wealthy banker in Kosambi, Kukkuta was Ghosita's associate and a follower of the Buddha. He too donated his pleasure park, which was outside Kosambi, for the use of the Buddha and his monks.

Kukkuta, Vijaya—A fictional character, Bhadda Kukkuta's wife. Though Kukkuta no doubt had a wife, there's no way to know her name.

Kumara, Prince—A fictional figure. Since it isn't likely that Udena wouldn't have had a son before Prince Bodhi, I've imagined Prince Kumara to be the sickly son of Queen Vasuladatta. He would have inherited the throne had he lived. But, moving beyond the framework of the story, I imagine him to have died at age twelve, after our story ends.

Magadha—Located northeast of Vamsa, Magadha was one of the two great kingdoms in the Ganges basin during the Buddha's era. Magadha was ruled by King Seniya Bimbisara.

Magandiya, Queen—While historically, Magandiya was the third consort to King Udena, it worked better in our story to elevate her to
the second spot. She wouldn't have quibbled. She was a beautiful,
spiteful, small-minded woman who considered Queen Samavati to
be her rival. She eventually had the women's quarters in the palace
set on fire. The conflagration killed Samavati and the other women
of the harem. This event occurred after our story ends. When King
Udena discovered her role with regard to the fire, he had her put to
death.

Metta—Lovingkindness. One of the central teachings of the Buddha,
followers are instructed to practice lovingkindness for all beings.
(Please see "karuna" in this glossary.)

Migajala, Bhikkhu—A fictional character, a member of Harika's faction.

Musila, Bhikkhu—An imaginary character, a monk in the Buddha's order at Kosambi. A supporter of Candana.

Nakula— I couldn't find any reference to Nakula, but his father and
mother are mentioned in the Pali texts; therefore Nakula must have
existed. (Please see the comment in the Preface about the puzzling
fact that reference to Nakula is omitted in the texts.)

Nakulamata and Nakulapita—Nakula's mother and father ("mata" means
"mother"; "pita" means "father"). Identified only in terms of their
relation to Nakula, not by their own names, they lived in Bhaggu
land. The Buddha said they were his most trusting lay followers.

Parileyyaka—The village the Buddha went to when he left Kosambi
in disgust and sadness in 446, having been unable to resolve the
schism in Ghosita's Park.

Parantapa, King— A historical figure, creator of the kingdom of Vamsa
and father of Udena.

Pasenadi, King Agnidatta—Historically, Pasenadi was king of Kosala
during the Buddha's era. With little interest in spiritual matters and
possibly of limited intelligence, he nonetheless was politically astute,
if not ruthless. He was a strong supporter of the Buddha.

Patimokkha—Literally "unburdening" or "freeing" oneself, the term refers to primary rules or precepts that govern monastic living. The
practice of reciting the Patimokkha at Uposatha began during the
Buddha's lifetime, and it continues today. I imagined that Harika
initiated the practice of reciting the rules and following the recitation with confession and that Candana coined the term "patimokkha" to refer to the rules. There's no way to know how many

major monastic precepts existed at the time of the schism or exactly how or when the practices associated with Uposatha developed.

Phagguna, Gopaka—A fictional character. A wealthy townsperson who happily allowed his home to be a meeting place for Minister Bharadvaja and the Venerable Harika.

Rajagaha—The capital of the great kingdom of Magadha.

Sagata, Bhikkhu—A historical figure, though I've only come across a brief reference to him. He reportedly was drunk on the streets of Kosambi the day the Buddha arrived for *vassa*, the rains retreat, in 446 BCE. Everything else about Sagata in this tale is fictional.

Sakiya—The name of the clan and the land in the foothills of the Himalayas from which the Buddha came. Today the region is in southern Nepal. During the Buddha's era, Sakiya was a republic governed by the noble Sakiyan clan. It was not however independent; it was a vassal state of Kosala to its south.

Samsara—The cycle of existence characterized by birth, maintaining and dissolution without knowable beginning or end. Humans were believed to perpetually wander in the cycle of *samsara* until they attained liberation.

Samvati, Queen—Historically she was Udena's second queen, but it worked better in the story to make her his third queen. Samavati was a follower of the Buddha. He commented that she was his lay follower who was foremost in the practice of lovingkindness. She was the stepdaughter of royal treasurer Ghosita and the daughter of a wealthy merchant who, along with Samavati's mother, died in an epidemic.

Sangha—Community. In the Buddhist tradition, the word refers to the community of monastic followers but was enlarged to refer to lay followers as well.

Sankhara—Karmic knot, an inborn or conditioned pattern of behavior. *Sankharas* are understood as areas in which one reacts automatically, unmindfully, and thus they function as obstacles on the path of awareness and freedom.

Sati, Bhikkhu—The central character and the inspiration for this novel. I have portrayed Sati as a young monk in the Buddha's order, intelligent, kind and a disciple of the Venerable Candana. The kind of young man everyone naturally loves, except for a few characters in this novel. We watch him grow as the story progresses. Although Sati is mentioned in one of the Pali texts, I question his historicity. (Please see my comment in the Preface.) The only things we know about him from the scripture is that he misunderstood the Buddha's teaching and he was the son of a fisherman, which means he was an outcaste. I however have imagined that he was born of the noble class but slid into classlessness as a result of a political intrigue involving his father.

Sona—A fictional character. Since Nakula must have existed because his parents did, so too Nakula's wife must have existed. I've created a wife to reckon with.

Sutasoma, Vasula—Fictional character. An official in Udena's government who causes a near uprising by raping a tribal girl.

Savatthi—Capital of the kingdom of Kosala during the Buddha's era.

Siddhi—A Sanskrit term meaning a great yogi's spiritual powers. Although the term became developed in the Mahayana tradition of Buddhism and especially in the Tibetan tradition, there are many references in the Pali texts to the Buddha's extraordinary powers. It is not unrealistic to imagine that the Buddha's reputation engendered fear in the hearts of monks who crossed him, as did some of the monks in Harika's faction in Kosambi.

Simsapa—Rosewood tree, a kind of magnolia. Simsapas were known to grow in Ghosita's Park during the Buddha's era. In one of his well-known teachings, said to have occurred in Kosambi, the Buddha was walking in a simsapa grove. He picked up a handful of leaves and likened them to what he taught (suffering and its end) and then compared them to the leaves overhead, saying they represented all that he did not teach (i.e., the many things unrelated to the holy life).

Sirivaddha—A fictional figure, the physician who attended monks at Ghosita's Park.

Sudda— Dependent workers and servants, the lowest of the four classes that characterized the traditional Indian social structure. The classless were outside this structure.

Sukka— A fictional character. The daughter of Sona and Nakula.

Tuttha—A fictional character. Servant to King Udena and a follower of the Buddha.

Ubbiri—A fictional character. Jambuka's wife in Bhaggu village.

Upali, Bhikkhu—A historical figure, a barber by profession before he ordained. Upali had been barber to Ananda and other aristocrats from Sakiya. When these young men decided to join the Buddha's order, Upali, who was a sudda by birth, decided to do the same. His noble associates insisted that Upali be ordained before them, which meant he would always be senior to them. In a society where class considerations were predominant, this was an extraordinary decision, testifying to the sincerity of these young men. Upali's capabilities went far beyond barbering. He became the foremost authority on the Vinaya, a fact that aroused enormous jealousy in Harika.

Uposatha—A traditional observance in the Middle Land on new, full and half moon days, characterized by fasting. At the suggestion of King Bimbisara, the Buddha introduced the observance in his order, and it became an occasion for avowal of disciplinary transgressions and purification. Harika's role in fashioning the observance, as told in this story is imaginary. Uposatha continues to be observed today by some monastics.

Uttara, Bhikkhu—A fictional character. A member of Harika's faction.

Vamsa—The kingdom ruled by Udena in the southern Ganges basin.

Vassa—A three-month retreat, which became customary during the Buddha's day. Held during the rainy season, from mid-June to mid-September, it was a time when the monks gathered together to hear the teaching and to get out of the mud and floods that inundated the Indian countryside.

Vasuladatta, Queen—A historical figure, Vasuladatta was the first wife of King Udena and daughter of the king of Avanti, the kingdom to the south of Vamsa. A colorful story is told in the texts of how Udena wooed her in Avanti and, in the face of opposition from her father, fled with her aboard an elephant to Vamsa. Little else is said about her, however, once she became queen, which leads to my characterizing her as a cold and reserved woman.

Vinaya—The body rules of conduct governing monastic life. The *Vinaya* or the *Discipline* is one of the three categories or baskets into which the Pali canon is divided. The *Vinaya* was recited orally during the Buddha's lifetime.

Watch—Indians traditionally divided the day into watches (or *yamas*). A watch was generally understood to be the equivalent of three hours, though inconsistently, sometimes it referred to a shorter period.

ABOUT THE AUTHOR

With *The Kosambi Intrigue*, Susan Carol Stone discovered her inner novelist. She is also author of *At the Eleventh Hour* (Present Perfect Books 2001), a memoir about caregiving and mindfulness, and co-author of *The American Mosaic* (McGraw-Hill 1995), about workforce diversity. Long engaged in meditative spiritual practices, Susan ordained as a lay priest in the Zen tradition and has lived in Zen and Theravadin Buddhist monasteries. She teaches Mindfulness-Based Stress Reduction at the University of Virginia, is co-leader of the Insight Meditation Community of Charlottesville, and has taught mindfulness in prisons and at middle school. Susan also has a Ph.D., which has no bearing at all on this novel. She is attempting to encounter her senior years with grace.

Made in the USA
Lexington, KY
24 November 2013